LUNA TANGO

ALLI SINCLAIR

Originally published by HarperCollins (ANZ) 2014

ALSO BY ALLI SINCLAIR

A Woman's Voice

The Codebreakers

The Cinema at Starlight Creek

Burning Fields

Beneath the Parisian Skies

Under the Spanish Stars

For Pa - a true gentleman, adored and
loved by many. I'll forever miss your cheeky smile and the twinkle in your eye.

CHAPTER 1

Present Day - Dani

Dani McKenna stood on the stone steps of *Escuela de Danza Vida*, still unsure which was the lesser of two evils: ditching her first assignment and killing her career as a features writer, or diving into the world of tango and dredging up torturous memories. Glancing at the gray sky, Dani willed a beam of light and a choir of angels to sing and deliver an answer in a silver box with a blue bow. She got nothing other than a pigeon flying past and pooping next to her new red heels.

'Fine.' She huffed and yanked open the heavy wooden door, ready to be rid of the diesel fumes spilling from buses, the headache-inducing horns, and suffocating midday heat. After two days in Buenos Aires, she'd yet to discover why this city was known as the Paris of the Americas.

Dani took tentative steps into the expansive foyer, where pristine marble covered the floor and a wrought-iron balustrade snaked up the wide staircase. Cool air soothed her hot skin and she relaxed her shoulders, happy to be free from the craziness outside, including wayward pigeons.

She balanced on her gorgeous, but incredibly uncomfortable,

heels as she adjusted her white silk shirt and tucked her newly high-lighted blonde curls behind her ears. She'd much prefer faded jeans, ballet flats, and a retro T-shirt but this assignment required her to dress like a professional, despite feeling like a phony. Dani squeezed her eyelids tight, remembering how much money she'd just spent on a new wardrobe. But if all went to plan, her new garb would convince the world, and herself, that she was more than capable of doing this job. Or so she hoped.

A gust of wind rattled the door leading to the street. She could still chicken out. After all, if her colleagues at the magazine were right, her mission was doomed anyway. But she chose to ignore their warnings, even though her interview subject, Carlos Escudero, hated the media with more passion than he'd ever danced tango. His refusal to publicly talk about the motorbike accident that destroyed his dancing career and ruined the relationship with his dance partner only motivated journalists to dig deeper. They were determined to unearth the story that lay beneath the well-rehearsed statements from the estranged couple. So far, though, the journalists' efforts had smashed into a wall of anger and silence.

Pushing out a long sigh, she adjusted the shoulder strap of her handbag. As much as she wanted to be the one to finally discover what happened on that fateful day, Dani wasn't so naïve she thought she could succeed where so many seasoned journalists had failed. Besides, his personal life wasn't why she was here. Her job was to get Carlos Escudero on board with her history of tango articles and nothing else.

She lowered her head and shook it. *Seriously? She'd taken to lying to herself now?*

The tango history stories were important, her career depended on them, and uncovering the mystery behind the motorbike acci-dent appealed, but they were nothing compared to the opportunity to learn about Carlos Escudero's mentor, Iris Kennedy. He'd been privy to a side of Iris the rest of the world hadn't seen, a side Dani desperately needed to discover. If she could get some understanding about the passion that drove Iris to abandon her husband and five-year-old daughter in favor of becoming a tango diva on the world stage, then Dani might finally exorcise the demons that had chased her since childhood. Although she had no intention of finding and meeting the elusive Iris because, even after two decades, the pain remained raw. Through Carlos, however, Dani might finally comprehend her mother's actions.

She narrowed her eyes at the ancient elevator. No matter how many times she chastised herself, Dani found it impossible to enter one of these boxes without being slammed by the memory of the last fiery argument between her parents. No child wants to witness such venom, especially from her own flesh and blood. She planted her foot on the marble steps, even though her mind tried to convince her that dashing out the door, sight unseen, was the best option. Perhaps it would be better if she knew nothing about Iris, as the truth had the potential to rip Dani's heart out. As much as she tried to deny it, though, the stars had aligned and Dani's arrival in Argentina offered the perfect chance to build her career and heal old wounds or make them deeper.

'Ah, to hell with it.'

Dani powered up the stairs and arrived on the eighth floor. Puffing, she wiped the back of her hand across her wet brow then on her navy linen pants. She didn't look down for fear she'd just put a streak of makeup across the expensive material. Dani placed her hand on the ornate brass knob but froze when the slow whine of the *bandoneón* slipped through the gaps around the doors. The accordion-like instrument had thousands, possibly millions, of fans all over the world, but for Dani, the music of the *bandoneón* was akin to fingernails scraping across a blackboard.

She grimaced then turned and scooted to the edge of the staircase, overwhelmed by the emotions crashing in on her. The fear of failing, decades of hurt, anger, sadness, confusion . . .

Needing some air, polluted or otherwise, Dani moved to step down but the heel of her new shoes caught in a small hole of the old floorboards. Grabbing the balustrade she kept balance but her handbag clattered to the floor, the contents spilling across the landing. She got on her hands and knees and gathered the lipgloss, half-eaten chocolate bars, and a stash of colorful gel pens and sticky notes she'd bought at the stationery store down the road.

The thick wooden door swung open.

'¡*Hola!*' a deep, cheery voice echoed in the stairwell.

She looked up and found Carlos Escudero in the doorway, leaning slightly to the left as he rested his hand casually on a wooden cane. His shoulders were broad, hair perfectly styled, and he had gorgeous olive skin.

God, he's more beautiful in the flesh.

'Beautiful' wasn't a word she normally used to describe men, but he qualified. His dark eyes hinted at the untold stories she so desperately wanted to discover and she bit her lip in an effort to contain the thousands of questions that threatened to break free.

Stuffing the remaining contents in her bag she got on one knee as he moved forward and held out a hand. Letting his warm fingers wrap around hers, Dani stood and adjusted the bag on her shoulder, heat rushing up her neck and across her face. 'Thank you.'

'You are not hurt?' Concern clouded his handsome features.

'I'm fine, really.' Dani smoothed down her hair and wished she'd worn her flats instead of the stupid high-rise heels. But man, they did look good.

Carlos glanced at her shoes. 'They are a work of art.'

'Thank you.' For a woman of words she was doing a cruddy job.

'Please, come inside.' Smile lines crinkled around his eyes and he gestured for her to follow as he limped through the doorway. Taking a deep breath, she followed him across the landing into the studio then she halted. Bright daylight streamed through arched windows on the southern side of the room and the scarred floorboards suggested a long history of passionate stories that had unfurled across them. Tango music played through tinny speakers as a young couple floated across the floor and memories of her mother and father in happier days rose to the surface. A ball of sadness formed in her belly.

Carlos motioned toward a comfy couch and she sat as he stood next to a set of speakers in the corner of the room. Dani opened her mouth but he held up his hand in a gentle manner then pointed to the dancers, their feet and legs moving with perfect precision. The track finished a moment later and the couple split apart, wiped themselves with towels and took long gulps from drink bottles.

Picking up his, Carlos Escudero flicked through the screens, then his gaze fell upon her. Dani adjusted her position on the sofa and gripped her handbag with sweaty fingers.

'Please excuse me but this class is running late. I hope you do not mind waiting. Are you sure you are not harmed?'

'I'm fine, I promise.'

'I just need to find this one song . . .' His concentration returned to the phone.

She wondered how people could speak so badly of this man when he showed no signs of the surliness or uncooperative behavior she'd been warned about. 'You are Carlos Escudero, right?'

'But of course! And you wish to learn tango, *sí*? We will talk about the lesson plan and cost when I am finished with these students, yes?'

'Actually, I'm not looking for tango lessons.' She stood and gave her friendliest smile, hoping he didn't notice the slight waver in her voice.

Carlos stopped fiddling with the phone and put it down. He returned the smile but it had left his eyes. Dani's heart raced, aware this moment could change everything. *Think fast, McKenna.*

'Then why are you here?' He crossed his arms, the curve of his biceps showing through the black shirt.

'I believe you worked on the UNESCO application to get the tango listed as an Intangible Cultural Heritage of Humanity.' That was a mouthful.

'*Sí.*'

'My name is Dani McKenna. I'm here as a guest of Tourism Argentina and I'm writing articles—'

'I cannot help.'

'But you don't know what I want to ask.'

'I am done with the journalists. They are nothing but parasites.' He spat out the words and elements of the Carlos Escudero she'd heard about surfaced.

5

Bubbles of indignation rose in her belly. 'Just so you know, I'm not—'

'No.'

Who did he think he was? If it had been anyone other than him, she'd have stormed out and found someone else to interview. But no one else had the tango experience and knowledge he possessed and no one else knew Iris like he did. She had no choice other than to stay and suffer his rudeness.

Carlos angled a finger at her. 'You dance.'

'What? Oh no.' She shook her head and backed away. 'I have two left feet and—'

'Nonsense!' He pointed to the young man who stared at her with wide eyes.

'The heart,' Carlos said.

'What?'

'The heart. This.' He thumped his closed fist over his chest. 'Dancers must have their hearts facing each other.' He motioned for her to stand chest to chest with his student. 'Jorge will assist.'

Was this some sadistic torture he lumped on every journalist who dared cross his path? She shuffled into position, annoyed with this Argentine's arrogance. Although for as long as she stood on his dance floor, she had a chance of getting what she wanted.

'It does not matter what the feet are doing,' he said. 'It is unimportant. You are not two dancers. You are one heart.' His flowery words were a stark contrast to his gruff demeanor.

'But I don't know how—'

'*¡Basta!* You will learn. Allow the music to flow into your soul. Let the melody, not the rhythm, dictate your dancing. This is what makes the tango unique. You dance now.'

Carlos pressed play, faced the hesitant couple, and raised his eyebrows. Dani let go of Jorge, shoved her hands on her hips, and raised her eyebrows back at Carlos.

'You choose not to dance?'

She pursed her lips.

'Okay. Goodbye.' He gave a dismissive wave and turned to the stereo again.

The obscenities wanted to burst out but she willed them to remain within. 'Fine. I'll do it. Just don't expect Ginger Rogers.'

The music started and the melancholic notes floated through the studio, goose bumps sprouting all over her body.

Jorge offered a gentle smile. 'Do not worry, I will help you.'

'I hope you can work magic,' she said.

He held out his hand and Dani took it, their fingers entwining in a clammy mess. As much as she wanted to escape this humiliation, Jorge's friendly eyes reassured her.

'Dance!' Carlos yelled.

Dani flinched then squared her shoulders. Jorge placed a hand on her waist and with a small movement, guided her in the direction he chose. The haunting combination of violins and piano washed over her and she basked in the beauty. Then the *bandoneón* started and her jaw tightened. Dani closed her eyes and tried to concentrate on the soulful notes of the other instruments and the singer's passionate voice. She felt Jorge move slightly to the left and Dani followed, placing her foot with care. As much as she wanted to hate the tango she—

'*¡Mierda!*'

Her eyes flew open at Jorge's expletive. 'I'm sorry!'

Carlos banged his cane on the floorboards. 'Continue!'

Jorge let go, rubbed his foot then held her again, determination renewed. They moved to the right and this time Dani kept her eyes open. She took a hesitant step, pulled back, leaned forward, and smashed her head.

'Argh!' Jorge rubbed his brow.

'Oh God, I'm sorry!' She turned to Carlos. 'I can't do this. He's going to end up in hospital before the end of the song. Listen, I'm not here for a lesson. All I want is to ask a few questions—'

A smile raced across Carlos's lips and his eyes sparkled. A belly laugh followed.

'What?'

'I never thought I would see the day,' Carlos spoke between bursts of laughter, 'when there would be evidence of a person with two left feet.'

'You are hilarious.' She didn't bother concealing her sarcasm. 'I tried to tell you I couldn't dance but you wouldn't listen.'

'My listening skills are very good but I chose not to believe you, yes? I find you amusing. Tell me your name.'

'Dani McKenna.' *Like I said before, if you'd paid attention.*

'Dani is short for Daniela, *sí?*' He stroked his chin with his thumb and forefinger.

She nodded.

'Daniela is a perfectly good name. This is what you were born with, this is what I will call you.'

She wanted to argue but had no desire to explain why she detested her full name. Sorrow wrapped around Dani as the last words her mother said echoed in her heart. *I'll love you forever, Daniela.*

'Have you learned the martial arts?' Carlos asked, saving her from jumping into the all too familiar well of grief.

'No. What does that have to do with tango?'

'In martial arts you must be completely focused on the other person at all times. You have to adapt and pay attention to what the opponent is doing. A slip of focus means defeat and inevitable pain. It is the same for tango.'

'But you said tango is a meeting of two hearts. What's this opponent business?'

'Tango, like love, is complicated. Tell me, Daniela McKenna, why should I talk with you?'

'I work for a magazine and Tourism Argentina has sponsored me to write about the evolution of the tango lifestyle over the past hundred years.'

'Not interested.'

'Why not?'

'I am not interested.'

'That's it?' Panic grew within at the possibility that her chance for career success and personal healing had just started a slithery descent into the Valley of Failure.

'I will tell you this. The foreign journalists think tango is about sex, sex, sex.' He pounded his fist against the wall and Dani flinched inside, unnerved by his anger. Or was it passion? 'It is not about the sex. It is about a meeting of the souls. It has nothing to do with the physical and everything to do with the spiritual but none of you people understand.'

'I'm not like other journalists.' Of course she wasn't. Other journalists wouldn't endure this humiliation. Perhaps he was testing her resolve. 'I want to immerse myself in the tango culture and appreciate why people the world over are enchanted by this dance and music. My articles will depict what it's truly like to live and breathe and love tango.' *Then I might finally understand why my mother did what she did.*

'No.'

'Are you always this difficult or is it only when you speak to journalists?' she asked and he gave a half shrug. Surely misunderstanding the meaning of tango was not enough to hate journalists with such fervor. 'If you had no intention of helping me then why did you make me dance?'

His lips twisted into a smirk and Dani grabbed her bag and marched to the exit.

'I'll be back,' she said over her shoulder.

'I'll be locking the doors.'

Dani sat in her hotel room and stared at the laptop, willing her inbox to ping with incoming mail. She'd sent a message to Adam only minutes ago and even though she didn't expect an instant reply, she wanted one.

She leaned against the pillows and studied the flocked red flowers pressed onto the pale gold wallpaper. Somehow, the retro room comforted her.

The bell sounded on her laptop and her heart tripped and banged against her chest when she read his name in bold. The bastard still had an impact on her life.

She clicked on the email and sucked air between her teeth.

Dani,

I hope you're feeling better since the last time we spoke. I don't know how many times I can tell you I'm sorry. I wish there was a way I could help you see why this is right for everyone and I hope one day you'll understand my actions.

How are the stories? No doubt Tourism Argentina is treating you like a queen. Use your fluency in Spanish to woo the locals, get the scoop, and write me some killer feature articles. I like your idea of digging deeper with Escudero. As we discussed, though, he's going to be a hard sell and I'm not sure you have the chops for it. Though I wouldn't mind you proving me wrong.

You've nagged me for so long about giving you this break into features, so don't mess it up. We both know making coffee is not one of your strong points. Take advantage of your time there and make sure it's the best damn writing you've ever done. Make Escudero talk. You're a smart girl. Figure it out.

Cheers,

Adam

She stared at his sign-off. *Cheers.* Her jaw tightened and tears burned her eyes. *Cheers? Cheers?* Where did he get off saying cheers? Cheers you say to friends. Cheers you say to work colleagues. Cheers you say to . . . Oh. Well, technically she was his employee and nothing else now. Life had gotten complicated way too quickly, although she should thank her lucky stars for her timely escape.

Dani ran her fingers over the bare skin that once proudly displayed an engagement ring. Throwing it at Adam's head had given her little satisfaction and she still couldn't get used to seeing her naked finger.

Even though she'd witnessed her parents' relationship fall apart and her own attempts at love had been rather pathetic, she'd given in to Adam's charms and allowed him to enter her life with an estranged wife and son in tow. A tinge of guilt raced through her for being part of the reason Adam hadn't reconciled with his wife earlier. After all, she knew what it was like for a parent to take off and leave a kid wondering what they'd done wrong. She didn't even begrudge Adam returning to his family, but it was the way he did it that hurt most. Really, who visits their ex to tell them they're getting married and—*whoops!*—accidentally sleeps with said ex and decides the relationship is back on?

The only reason Adam let her branch into features was because he felt guilty for dumping her and going back to his wife. He probably thought that once Dani had established herself she'd leave the magazine anyway. That would be easier than him inventing a reason to fire her. The three weeks he'd given Dani to research and write the articles were longer than most journalists at the magazine received, but she suspected it had nothing to do with this being her first gig and needing extra time to perfect her stories. More than likely Adam had negotiated the assignment to run longer so he wouldn't have to face her in the office every day. The way Dani felt right now, she was more than happy with this arrangement.

Clicking onto her bank account, Dani checked the balance then read Adam's email again. Reaching out to her ex had been a mistake.

She logged off and slammed the laptop lid shut. Carlos Escudero didn't know it yet, but he'd just met his match.

CHAPTER 2

Present Day - Dani

Dani sat on a faded emerald green brocade sofa and willed her foot not to tap. Her eyes traveled from the arched windows to the myriad photos hanging on the walls of the dance studio. Many of the images featured Carlos with various dance partners but there were none of him with the infamous Cecilia Ortiz, his ex-fiancée. Dani trained her eyes to look everywhere but directly at the man himself. Skilled in reading people, she knew better than to hassle someone like him into talking before he'd processed his thoughts. The fact he'd left the door unlocked when she'd returned gave her a glimmer of hope.

'It is an interesting offer.' He leaned back against the chair and clasped his hands behind his neck.

'Is that a yes?'

'No.'

God, she hated that word. She wanted to shake his shoulders and scream, *what will it take to get a yes?* But instead she clasped her hands on her lap and wore a pleasant expression.

'Are you telling me the money I've offered isn't enough?' she asked, unable to believe his greed.

'It's not the money, but if you would like to offer more . . .'

'No.' *Oh, that felt good.* 'I can't.'

Of course she couldn't. If she miraculously did get him on board, her bank account would have a nasty dent in it. Checkbook journalism didn't sit well but she viewed it as an investment in her future, because if he cooperated, she could get her stories and all her problems would disappear into the ether. Well, not entirely, but at least she could forge a new career in feature writing and prove to her grandma that the jump from teaching English to journalism wasn't an entirely insane career move. And if she just happened to find information about Iris . . .

'All right,' he said. So he *could* say something other than no.

'But what?' she asked, sensing his agreement had a catch.

'The amount is all right. Good, in fact.'

Crap. She should have started lower.

'I want more.'

'You said the amount was good. You said—'

'If I help with these articles, you do it on my terms. I am tired of the journalists writing what they like. It is my legacy to protect the reputations of generations of tango dancers before me. You and me, we work together and tell the real story of tango.'

She detested someone else having an influence over her writing but she could circumvent that later if she needed to. Journalistic integrity was more than a catchphrase for Dani but now wasn't the time to debate the state of modern journalism.

'Maybe,' she said. Ha! And her friends gave her grief for playing chess so badly in college.

'There's one more thing.'

Uh-oh. She nodded for him to continue.

'We go to the dancing tonight.'

'But—'

'You cannot write about tango if you cannot dance it. For every step you learn, I will answer a question.'

'Don't you recall my efforts yesterday?' She cringed inwardly and wondered if poor Jorge now walked with a limp like his teacher.

'I do, yes.'

'What makes you think you can teach me? Your deal is one-sided. You want money, control over my articles, *and* I have to dance for answers.' Sadist. He played this game beautifully and it crossed her mind that Carlos Escudero's experience with journalists meant he could see she was as green as a four-leaf clover.

'You take it or leave it, yes?' he said.

Oh, she should so leave it. She *desperately* wanted to leave it. But she couldn't. Never in her life had she needed someone's help so badly. It sucked on many levels to be in this position, although she'd be worse off back in New York. Images rushed in of Dani moping at her desk in the editorial department of the magazine and an apartment devoid of Adam's presence. She gave an involuntary shudder.

'You are cold?' Carlos reached for his jacket and offered it to her.

'I'm fine, thanks.' Huh. So he could be chivalrous. 'I don't see how I can say yes to your proposal. If you want me to learn steps as part of the deal then I'm going to have to decline.' God, how she wished she'd inherited her mother's talent for tango.

'I did not travel the world as a professional tango dancer because I am bad at it. I do not have my own dance studio because I am bad at it. When I teach you to dance, you will not be bad at it.'

She wondered what it was like living in Carlos Escudero's bubble. She doubted there'd be much elbow room between him and his inflated ego. Although, his self-assurance almost led her to believe he could teach her at least a couple of steps. Then reality hit and she shook her head.

'I can do this, you must have the trust in me.' Carlos dipped his chin and locked eyes with her. 'Trust in yourself.'

She did admire his attempts and thanked the Powers That Be that Carlos had no idea who her mother was. If he did, she'd have to suffer the embarrassment of explaining why the dancing gene hadn't just skipped Dani, it had fled. Also, she didn't want to deal with the inevitable questions that would accompany her revelation about Iris. No one outside the family knew who her mother was and she had no intention of revealing that to anyone. Somehow, Dani needed to find a way to understand Iris's idiosyncrasies and passion through Carlos. Learning tango could be the easy part.

'I still don't think it's a fair deal.'

'No student of mine has walked out this door unable to dance the basic steps of tango.'

'You've never had me as a student.'

'I do now.'

'What makes you think I'll say yes?'

'You have no choice.'

Her mouth fell open and she willed her brain to connect but to no avail.

'We make the deal, yes?'

She nodded, wishing she could disagree.

'You wait here. I will refresh myself then we go to the *práctica*, the dance hall, where the dress and attitude is casual. Here they practice tango before progressing to a *milonga* that is more serious and formal and full of rules. But at both these tango halls you will witness what it is to live and breathe tango.' He stood and limped to the office, shutting the door behind him with a click. Moments later the sound of gushing water filled the silence.

She leaned against the sofa, exhausted. It still felt like she was bribing rather than paying him a consulting fee, but she'd run with whatever worked. Normally, she could win people over but Señor Escudero appeared immune to her charms. Paying her first interview subject for his cooperation made her doubt her professional abilities and if she had to do this with every interview, she'd be broke before the year ended. That's if she got more articles after these ones. Everything depended on Carlos's help.

Needing a distraction, Dani's gaze fell to the files strewn across the coffee table. Averting her eyes, she studied the faded blue cornices, the perfect symmetry of the arched windows, the chandelier with missing crystals. The building held a rustic charm, not unlike Carlos. Somewhere, beneath his gruff exterior, lay hundreds of stories that would remain buried forever. Perhaps she and Carlos were more alike than she thought.

Dani stared at the files again, their magnetic pull impossible to resist. With the toe of her red shoe, she nudged the folder and a handful of black-and-white photos slid across the table and on to the floor.

'Oh dear, we can't have these lying around. They could get damaged or lost.' She leaned forward, opened the file, and dropped in the photos. Stealing a glance at the closed office door and hearing the water splashing, Dani quickly flicked through the pile. They were only historical images, not top-secret plans to take over the world, after all. What harm could she do?

Photographs from last century flashed before her. Mustached men in suits and women in low-cut dresses with full skirts clung to each other in seductive poses. Her ears hummed with tango music and muffled conversations from long ago. She gently thumbed through the matte photos with yellowed and tattered edges, conscious of the history that lay in her hands. These original images were no doubt invaluable, so why would Carlos be so careless as to leave them lying about?

Her mind drifted to her own stack of photos back at the hotel room. For years, Dani had collected images of her mother and hidden them from her grandma because mentioning tango in their house had been banned the day Iris deserted the family. Pretending tango didn't exist had been an easy task as no one wanted a reminder of the dance that stole her mother, but as Dani grew, so did the desire to understand her mother's actions. The breakup with Adam had been the catalyst that propelled Dani to gain answers about Iris; how could Dani have a relationship with a partner if she didn't understand herself or her own family? So when Adam suggested she go to Argentina out of guilt for his idiotic actions, there was no way she was going to say no.

Refusing to drag herself across the hot coals of personal pain again, Dani flipped through a few more photos until a couple that looked like a father and daughter caught her attention. The dark-eyed man sat on a chair, his expression serious and stern. Behind him stood a young woman with hands draped casually across his shoulders. Her light curly hair was pulled back in a loose bun and ample cleavage spilled from the neckline of the dress that hugged her curves. The woman's upturned nose and sparkling eyes hinted at her free spirit. She seemed familiar, but then again, Dani got this feeling with many people. She wondered if this would be a blessing or a curse with feature writing.

The door clicked open and a hollow feeling exploded in her chest. Looking up, she found Carlos leaning against the doorway, eyebrows knit and arms crossed tightly. Despite his angry pose and scowl, an air of sexiness hung around him, accentuated by his dark, slicked back hair.

'What are you doing?' he growled and limped to the sofa.

'These were just lying here and—'

He snatched the photo and busied himself stacking the files. 'You journalists are all the same. Why can you not leave things alone?'

'Carlos, I'm sorry. I—'

'No excuses! If you do not respect my privacy we cannot work together.'

Guilt swirled in her belly. 'I apologize. I shouldn't have touched the photos. They're just so lovely and . . . I'm really sorry. It was a rookie mistake.' She had nothing to lose by admitting her journalistic virginity, as she'd most likely blown her chances anyway.

His eyes narrowed and he tilted his head to the side. 'This is your first assignment?'

'Yes.'

'I could not tell. You are stubborn, like the journalists with many years' experience. Perhaps you will do well at this profession.'

She drew her lips into a tight line while Carlos stared at her long enough to make her uncomfortable. Dani's fingers found the edge of her shirt and she started fiddling with the hem.

'No.' His eyes bore into hers.

'No what?' This was exasperating.

'No, I am not helping you. Your chance is gone. Even if you are a new journalist, you should know that looking at the things of people is not polite.'

'I'm sorry, Carlos. Really, I am. But if I don't write these stories my career will be over before it's started. No one thinks I'm cut out for this job and—'

'You are desperate.'

'I am.' Groveling had never appealed but given the circumstances . . .

'Maybe I will forgive you. Just this once.'

'Thank you.' Dani let out a long breath, unaware until now she'd been holding it in. She sensed his forgiveness was because he saw an opportunity to mold a rookie journalist to his way of thinking. *I'd like to see him try.*

'Can I ask a question?'

He tucked the file under his arm. 'You have not learned dance steps so you do not get to ask questions.'

'You're right but how about you give me a question in advance and I'll do two new dance steps before I ask another one?' It was a cheeky proposal and she had no idea if he'd go for it.

'Like a loan?'

'Something like that.'

'I will charge interest.'

'Uh . . .' She nodded, unsure as to whether agreeing would be a smart move.

'Know this: I do not trust you.'

'Fair enough. You have reason to doubt me but I promise, I meant no harm and I am truly sorry.'

He gave one sharp nod. 'One question only. Then you and me, we go to the dancing. I will work out your interest later.'

She was out on a limb, feet dangling high above ground, waiting for the branch to snap. The only way to fix her faux pas was to agree to his terms, whatever they ended up being.

'Okay.' Pointing at the photo on the top of his pile, she asked, 'Who are the young woman and old man?'

He glanced at the image and froze. His eyes didn't meet hers. 'Why do you want to know?'

'She intrigues me.'

'Ask another question.'

'This is the only question I have.' She contemplated batting her eyelashes but refused to resort to such tactics.

'I will answer, but we speak of this only once.'

'Deal.' She waited but he didn't open his mouth. 'And?'

'He is Eduardo Canziani, Argentina's greatest tango composer and singer. She is Louisa Gilchrist, his muse. She killed him because she loved another man. Louisa and her lover escaped the country and were never found. End of story.'

CHAPTER 3

1953 - Louisa

Standing in the empty, high-ceilinged hallway, Louisa Gilchrist pressed her ear against the wooden door of the music room. The silver tray laden with delicate china and a steaming teapot balanced precariously in her hands but she couldn't pull away from the crisp notes of the *bandoneón* flying through the cracks of the door. Louisa closed her eyes and pictured Roberto Vega's fingers running across the seventy buttons of the concertina-like instrument, his passion pouring into every note.

Using her elbow to push the brass handle down and nudge open the door, Louisa entered the room quietly. Roberto's eyes were closed, lost in the moment, his lean body swaying gently with the cadence. His mentor, Eduardo Canziani, sat on a velvet chair with a high back and wings, his fingers forming a pyramid as he studied his protégé's performance.

No one paid attention when she placed the tray on the oak desk, ensuring she didn't rattle the china. Louisa took time to pour the tea into the cup, soaking in every note and enjoying the caress of Roberto's music.

'Eduardo, your tea,' she whispered.

'Shh.' He waved his hand and she placed the cup on the table beside him. Tears dropped from his cheeks and on to his starched collar but he didn't notice. It never failed to surprise Louisa how Roberto's music had such an effect on people, including his tough mentor. Offering Eduardo a napkin, she gestured for him to wipe away the tears but instead he turned and glared at her with steely eyes.

Louisa bit her lip, waiting for the onslaught.

'What is this?' he growled, grabbing the napkin and throwing it on the floor.

'I thought—'

The music halted the second she spoke. Roberto gripped the *bandoneón* on his knees, and studied her with dark, worried eyes.

'That does not mean you can stop!' Eduardo angled a stubby finger at Roberto. 'Go to the beginning!' He thumped the table with his fist and made the crockery on the tray rattle. 'Louisa! Pass me the'—Eduardo flicked his wrist at a pile of papers on the desk—'the . . . the . . .' He kept waving as a bright red rash rushed across his face. 'Pass me that!'

'The sheet music?' she asked and handed it to him, her hand shaking.

'Yes! Of course!' He snatched it and sifted through the papers.

She took this as her cue to leave and scurried through the door, not daring to look at Roberto. Rushing down the hall, she stopped to straighten the jasmine that had fallen to the side of a vase. A warm hand grabbed hers and she looked up to find Eduardo, his eyes downcast.

'I am sorry, Louisa.' His voice held genuine remorse.

'Thank you, but apologies aren't going to fix this. It's getting worse, isn't it? This forgetting names of simple things?'

'Yes.' He withdrew his hand and leaned heavily on the table. 'I don't know what to do.'

'Go see a doctor,' she said quietly then instantly regretted her words, worried they would only fuel his anger.

'No.' He shook his head vehemently.

'Eduardo,' she gently rubbed his back, 'you need to see a professional. I can only help you so much. People are going to notice soon enough.'

'No, they won't.'

'They will, and you know it. It's not a failing. It's life. It's horrible and cruel and unfair that dementia has hit you but we have to come to terms with this. You need professionals to help you.' Whenever they had this conversation she never knew which way Eduardo would turn. Although, despite the possibility of anger or tears, she persisted, hoping one day he would finally listen and get the help he badly required.

'I will not do it. You're all I need.'

'I'll assist as much as possible, but I can't do it alone. Maybe if Roberto knew—'

'No!' He hit the wall with his fist, causing Louisa to flinch even though she'd half expected him to react this way.

'But—'

'No! No one but you will ever know.' Taking a deep breath, he said, 'I'm aware this is a burden and it's unfair of me to expect you to take this on but I trust you more than anyone.' He lowered his voice and drew his bushy eyebrows together. 'Maybe you should leave. It's not like we're in love, is it? I'm asking you to do wifely duties yet we're not . . .'

Louisa shook her head. 'I won't go. I'll never forgive my grandmother for what she did to my grandfather. The nursing home killed him, not the dementia. He should have been with family, we could have given him a much better life.'

'You were only a child. You couldn't have done a thing.'

'I can help you, although I can't do it alone. Please, Eduardo, at least go and see a doctor. Maybe there's a treatment—'

'We will see, all right?' He mustered a warm smile, the dark anger in his eyes disappearing.

She nodded, aware he had no intention of doing as she suggested. Eduardo squeezed her hand and ambled to the music room, slamming the door behind him. She hovered in the hall, waiting to hear him take his frustration out on Roberto but nothing happened. Thankful Eduardo had his emotions under control again, she padded down the passage, glancing at the gilded frames that contained photos of her and Eduardo with Argentina's elite: film director Lucas Demare, tango musician Astor Piazzolla, and myriad football legends. Each and every one of those people adored Eduardo and he and Louisa were always the first to be invited to social functions and intimate dinner parties. People reveled in his jovial public persona, oblivious to his private world crashing in on him. He couldn't pretend forever, but for as long as he wanted to try, she'd support him. She owed him that much.

Louisa entered the kitchen and set about preparing Eduardo's supper. How different her life was from when she was in Britain, but World War II had changed many lives, including hers. She could never have imagined that her parents would need to send her to a home for children in Wales to escape the London Blitz, and she certainly never thought her parents would die in those bombings, leaving her an orphan at age thirteen. As soon as the war finished four years later, she'd taken her inheritance and fled to Argentina, determined to find her only living relatives, rumored to be in Gaiman, on the Atlantic coast. After months of searching, she'd returned to Buenos Aires, destitute, lonely, and with an uncertain future. Louisa could never have predicted meeting Eduardo in a bar or that the moment would alter her life forever. She'd welcomed his friendship and had made it clear that was all he'd ever have. He appeared happy with this arrangement, yet she still couldn't understand why he'd chosen to pluck her from the slums of La Boca when other women in the bar had been prettier, funnier, or more intelligent. Maybe Eduardo had focused on Louisa because she was so young and innocent, a lost lamb who could barely speak Spanish. It didn't take long for him to become her family and since then, she'd never forgotten his kindness.

Breaking the crusty bread and arranging it on a wooden platter, she sliced a lemon and dropped it into a jug of iced water. Her mind whirred from past to present, still in awe of Eduardo and his ability to hide his illness. Everyone thought his forgetfulness was due to his creative genius and they had been right, until recently. So far Eduardo had been able to mask the symptoms with Louisa's help. It broke her heart that this disease had hit him early and, instead of looking forward to twenty or thirty years of more creative brilliance, his life would diminish and the world would lose the greatest tango composer in history.

Tears fell in glossy drops onto the kitchen counter and she wiped them away with a cloth.

'You and me, we put up with a lot.' Roberto's silky voice made her stop and turn around. He leaned against the doorframe, a lazy smile gracing his lips.

'We each have our reasons.'

He stepped forward and took the cloth from her. His fingers grazed hers and Louisa had to steady herself as her pulse raced and goose bumps broke out on her fair skin.

'Let me help.' His deep voice reverberated through her body.

'I'm fine, really, I am.' She took the cloth and scrubbed at an invisible spot.

'You are a strong woman. More capable than most people I know.'

'No, I'm not.' She didn't look at him, scared the dam of tears would explode. They fell into silence, the air thick with unspoken affection and shared secrets.

Roberto spoke first. 'Why don't you deliver his supper and we'll go for a walk?' He ran a finger under her chin. 'Fresh air clears the mind.'

She should have balked at his touch, but instead she enjoyed every delicious second. His warm fingers exuded a deep caring on a level Louisa never thought she'd experience.

'I'll meet you in fifteen minutes but I can't stay long,' she said and loaded the tray.

'It's never long enough.' He reached into a jar on the counter then pulled out his hand. 'Where are the cashew nuts?'

'Eduardo finished them this afternoon.'

'He always gets what he wants,' Roberto mumbled as he left the kitchen, picked up his *bandoneón* case and slipped out the back door. Louisa stood for a moment, basking in his sandalwood cologne. She understood his agitation with his mentor and she hated being caught in the middle. Her loyalty between both men was tested regularly and she'd yet to find a way to make it all work. A small sigh escaped her lips.

When she returned to the music room, Eduardo glanced at her over his glasses then returned to studying the mountain of paperwork.

'Please, eat.' She placed the tray on his papers but he shook his head and pushed it aside. 'Eduardo, don't make me supervise you like a naughty two-year-old.'

'Fine.' He threw the pencil down then slapped meat on the bread, and took a large bite. Half the sandwich hung out one side of his mouth. 'I am eating, all right?'

She nodded and quickly departed, his erratic changes in mood weighing heavy on her shoulders. He needed help and it was up to her to make sure he got it.

Wrapping the navy blue coat around her shivering body, Louisa dashed down the marble steps of the mansion and onto the street. The lamps barely lit the wide paths as she hurried along in the darkness, pulling the fur collar around her ears. She rounded the corner and Roberto stepped out from the shadows, *bandoneón* case tucked under his arm. Louisa broke into a wide smile and slipped her arm through his as they headed straight for the local park.

Stones crunched underfoot as they strolled over to their favorite bench, overlooking the bandstand. They sat and she nestled into him.

'I hate having to sneak around,' she said.

'There are other choices, Louisa.'

'No. We can't.' Her voice relayed the sadness that plagued her every waking moment.

'Don't worry, we'll find a way. We always do.' He draped an arm casually over her shoulders and she snuggled closer, inhaling the eucalyptus from the branches rustling overhead. 'His temper is getting worse. I am concerned for you, Louisa.'

'I'm all right, I can look after myself.' It hurt not sharing the reasons for Eduardo's outbursts, but she could never go back on her word or betray someone's confidence.

Roberto shifted to face her, the light of the full moon glinting in his eyes. 'I know I'm there most times, but I fret when I'm not. You two are alone in the house at night and I grow more afraid for your safety every day.'

'He's not well at the moment, soon he'll be fine.'

'But will you be fine? Please, Louisa, let me help you.'

'You can't.' She shifted on the bench. 'Let it be. Please.'

'You are stubborn. I like this.' His smile reached his eyes and she relaxed again. A moment later she felt his body tense. 'He refused me again today when I asked to perform at his next concert. I don't understand. Why take me on as his protégé but not let me play in public?'

'I don't know.' And she truly didn't. Eduardo had never been one for logic, even before his affliction had surfaced.

'He missed a couple of notes at the concert last week. The audience didn't notice, but I saw the look on the musicians' faces. They're too afraid and loyal to say anything but one day, someone's going to mention his slips to the wrong person. Or the audience will notice he's losing his edge, then what will happen? Although, they'd just about forgive him anything, including the way he treats you and me.'

'You haven't told anyone how he's behaving, have you?' she asked.

'Only Héctor.'

'But he hates Eduardo. Who's to say he wouldn't tell someone? It would be to his advantage, you know.'

'Yes, it would, but Héctor isn't the type to go behind people's backs.'

'True. It's not like he's afraid of face-to-face confrontation.' The last time Héctor and Eduardo had seen each other it had ended in a punch-up that was splashed across the front page of every newspaper in South America. Neither man had explained the reason for their fight. Not even Louisa knew why.

Roberto fixed a steady gaze on her. 'Why do you always defend Eduardo?'

'I don't.'

Entwining his cold fingers with hers, he said, 'One day, I'll have enough money to whisk you far away from here. From him. I'll treat you like a princess and you'll never want for a thing.'

'Your sentiment is lovely, but I don't want to be a princess. Fairy tales are for children. All I want is for us to be together, but we need to wait some more.' She breathed deeply and exhaled, the air fogging in front of her. 'Neither of us has money and living in the slums is the fastest way for a romance to die, no matter how strong the bond. Only rats and parasites survive in those hellholes.'

'If I could make a name for myself, earn a reputation and money, we could get a small apartment in Palermo and be rid of Eduardo forever.'

'It's not that easy.'

'Why not? You love me, yes?' His wide, expectant eyes begged for her answer.

'Of course I do. I love you with my entire being.'

'Then come away with me. We'll make it work.' He squeezed her hand tight, like he was afraid to let go and lose her forever.

'I want to . . . I . . .' She pulled away and held her head in her hands. Roberto rubbed her back as she fought to get the words right. 'More than anything I want to be with you but I can't turn my back on the man who saved me from poverty.'

'He relies on you too much.' He removed his hand from her back and she sat up. Roberto stared into the darkness, his jaw set hard. 'I hate it when people think you're his lover.'

'I'm not.' Her words came out fast.

'Everyone else thinks he has sex with you to keep his creative juices flowing. It disgusts me to think he could touch you . . .' He let the sentence fall away and shook his head, as though trying to dispel a repugnant image.

'The only man I have ever wanted is you. One day we'll have the chance to be together the way we want.' She closed her mouth before her internal sob became audible. Through blurry eyes, she checked her watch. 'It's nearly twelve o'clock, I have to go.'

'One of these days I will serenade you from midnight until the sun peeks over the horizon.'

Louisa leant in and kissed him on the cheek. 'I would love nothing more.'

'Then why don't we do it? Stay out with me while the clock strikes twelve. Enjoy the crispy cool evening as the dew forms on the garden. Let me play you songs that will capture your heart.'

'Roberto'—her tone held much sadness—'let's talk about this later. I really have to go. I'm sorry.'

'Nothing ever happens between us that he should be worried about.'

'He wouldn't see it this way. Eduardo would feel betrayed by the two people he trusts most. He'd think you were trying to take me away from him.'

'I am.' Roberto flashed a grin before his expression turned serious once more. 'He's not rational.'

'What artist is?' She squeezed his hand, hoping to defuse Roberto's rising anger.

'We should leave. We could live on a beach surrounded by jungles. Or go inland where we could own a cashew plantation.'

She allowed a small smile. Although she didn't encourage his jealousy, every so often she didn't mind. 'Where are you talking about? Belize? Guatemala? Colombia?'

'Brazil,' he said with confidence, as if he'd given this great thought.

'Brazil.' She let the word hang in the air, surrounded by hope. Shame quickly fell upon her. She shouldn't entertain such ideas, no matter how unrealistic.

'Yes. That way I wouldn't have to worry about running out of cashew nuts ever again.'

Despite her serious mood, a small laugh left her lips. Roberto held her tight as she closed her eyes briefly, allowing his love to caress her. If only she could tell him his chance to continue Eduardo's legacy would come sooner than expected.

'I would be fine without him,' Roberto said with cockiness. 'Well, maybe not. He is an excellent teacher and at times quite engaging in conversation.' Kicking out his legs and resting his feet on the gravel, he said, 'I know when he finally lets me play in public the doors will be thrown wide open.'

'Patience is all we need.' The skin on her face felt cooler, as if the temperature had dropped a few degrees. She leaned over and rested her cold lips against his warm cheek. 'I love you, Roberto Vega.'

'And I you.'

The words floated across the night chill and wrapped warmly around her heart. Reluctantly, she stood then hurried through the darkness, refusing to look at the man who was the one bright light in her life. If her eyes met his, she'd run into his arms and never let go.

CHAPTER 4

Present Day - Dani

The city lights cut through the dark night, casting a Vegas glow on the bricked pavement as Carlos ushered Dani down the pedestrian mall, *Calle Florida*. Abandoned flyers littered the ground and made the going slippery as they wove between young families heading out to dine, even though it was close to midnight. Dani's stomach growled and she hugged her torso.

Visions of the woman in the photo played in her head. She desperately wanted to ask more questions but Carlos had spent the last half-hour scowling, muttering, and refusing to make eye contact. She'd apologized so much she'd started to sound insincere. So she'd given up, figuring he couldn't be that peeved if he was still taking her to a *práctica*. Although, she did wonder if he was planning to humiliate her in a public dance hall. *Good luck, sunshine.*

Even though he used a cane, Carlos set a quick pace. She took two steps to his one but her mind traveled faster than her legs.

'You are slow. Hurry.'

'I'm doing my best.' She switched gears and lengthened her stride.

They arrived at Avenida 9 de Julio, the world's widest avenue where cars sped along with no regard for anyone's safety, including their own. Pollution pooled in Dani's lungs and she broke into a coughing fit and grabbed Carlos's shoulder to steady herself. The moment her fingers touched him, his body stiffened. After catching breath, she straightened and took away her hand while his dark eyes studied hers and his expression softened. Caught in the moment, Dani smiled.

He drew his brows together, the spell now broken.

'We take a taxi.' Carlos stepped off the gutter and entered the mayhem. Lifting his hand, he whistled loudly and a black-and-yellow cab slammed on its brakes. This New York–style action stirred nostalgia within, and homesickness for the city she'd adopted three years ago overwhelmed her. Carlos opened the door and she climbed in, settling on a cracked vinyl seat. A halo of cigarette smoke hung above them as Carlos slammed the door and barked an address at the driver, who sped off so fast she slid along the seat and crashed into her companion.

'Sorry,' she mumbled, shuffling back to the far side of the car.

Carlos gripped the handle on the door so hard his knuckles turned white and he concentrated on the blurry street outside, not paying Dani any heed. Normally, she'd be annoyed with someone behaving like this but instead, she found his shifting demeanor intriguing. Life had taught her everyone has a story and their behavior was a result of underlying events—past and present. Carlos didn't appear to be naturally cantankerous and his current state may be a result of the dodgy leg from the motorbike accident. With the furor he was subjected to after the event, no wonder he was cranky.

They wound through narrow streets and zipped between blocks of ramshackle houses into suburbs with natural arches of trees over wide streets and row upon row of ostentatious mansions decorated with elaborate stone carvings.

In all the surprise and haste of this unplanned trip to the *práctica*, Dani had forgotten about being scared of running into her mother.

Now fear crashed into her like a rogue wave. Thankfully, Dani's chances of bumping into Iris were slim, as she'd recently escaped the tango world and become a recluse, rumored to be living in a remote region of Argentina. If the story was true, and she hoped it was, then Dani would be fine.

Carlos continued to stare out the window, showing no sign of wanting to engage in conversation. Guilt pricked her conscience at the thought of having wangled her way into his trust by convincing him all she wanted was his help in writing the articles. Sure, she needed his assistance, but the hidden motive of surreptitiously gaining information on Iris made her uneasy. Especially since he'd already given her an extra chance after he'd caught her snooping. And even if she did explain her situation, she doubted Carlos, or anyone for that matter, could fully understand her desire to learn about Iris but not want to see her. Dani was petrified that, should Iris discover her daughter was in Argentina, she would be coerced into playing happy family. That was the last thing she wanted. So whether she felt guilty or not, she had to keep this secret to herself and find a way to get the information she wanted without upsetting anyone. *Good luck, McKenna.*

The taxi halted, then they exited and stood on the footpath. Tango music and murmuring voices drifted through the open doors of La Gardenia and once again, the *bandoneón* had the same effect on her as fingernails down a blackboard. How could she cope with being in a dance hall with *bandoneóns* killing her ears for the next few hours?

Carlos cocked his head in the direction of the doors and she tentatively climbed the marble staircase. Images of her mother's slender figure draped in silk and sequins flashed before her. Dani had no idea how many pictures she'd collected over the years but all showed Iris's long, dark hair framing a natural face that appeared younger than her real age. Along with the photos, she'd read hundreds of superficial articles about Iris, who was always referred to as *La Gringa Magnifica*, the Magnificent Foreigner. In Dani's mind, though, she was still Iris Kennedy, the woman who forced a little girl to grow up faster than she should have.

Dani reached the top of the stairs and her feet stopped. Carlos turned around, frowned, and held out his hand.

'Come.'

'I . . .' How could she explain the emotions zapping through her?

'You are all right?'

'Yes, fine.' She hoped her forced smile would do the trick. Carlos gave no reaction, as if he'd been subjected to female vagaries his entire life. She followed him into the hall and her eyes strained to adjust to the dimness. Fairy lights hung haphazardly from the ceiling as Carlos and Dani moved through wide hallways to a large court-yard where lush vegetation wrapped around the columns of the historic building.

Carlos gestured with his cane to a small table in the corner. She wove between the clusters of chairs where women sat and stretched their long, tanned legs and stiletto-clad feet. Everywhere Dani looked people laughed, flirted, and whispered in secluded corners. The place was reminiscent of a pick-up joint but the atmosphere felt distinctly different; it was more like a group of friends gathering for some saucy, yet harmless, dancing.

A waiter brought over two glasses and a bottle of water. Carlos poured the drinks as Dani sat and tried to ignore the screeching notes of the *bandoneón* accompanying the other instruments. Instead, she concentrated on an older couple on the dance floor: The woman was as voluptuous as her partner was rail thin. Her generous frame followed the man with ease as he twisted and turned, guiding her gently, then they burst into a succession of staccato movements, making it look oh so easy.

Hoping to break the uncomfortable silence, Dani nodded in the couple's direction. 'They've been dancing together for years, I take it?'

'I doubt it.'

'But it's like they can read each other's minds.'

'That is the point.'

'Huh?'

'This is a question?' The corners of his mouth twitched.

'Truly, it wasn't.' Why did she feel like she'd just walked into a trap?

'It sounded like an inflection at the end of your 'huh', yes?'

'You're an English teacher now?'

'I believe this is another question. You dance.' He stood, held out his hand and helped her up.

Carlos's cane hung off the back of the metal chair. She opened her mouth to ask about it but closed it again, thinking it best to leave the subject alone. He motioned for her to take a place on the dance floor and as she stepped forward, a lump lodged in her throat. Every molecule of her being told her to bolt but pride and ego wouldn't allow it. Anyway, she couldn't pass up an opportunity to see how Carlos danced without a cane, considering his noticeable limp.

'¡Carlitos!, ¿cómo andas?'

Dani turned to see a short, round man with a wide grin and bright blue eyes. He ran his hand through graying hair, then slapped Carlos on the back like an old friend. Carlos grimaced.

'Gualberto, I am fine. This is Daniela.'

'Hi, I'm Dani McKenna.' She refused to look at Carlos but hoped he got the message she wasn't impressed about him using her full name. Dani held out her hand and Gualberto wrapped his fingers around hers, giving them a tight squeeze. 'You're Gualberto Ghilardi, the *bandoneón* player, right?'

'*Sí*. The one and the same.' The light caught his gold eyetooth and he gently relaxed his clasp around her hand. Even though he was renowned for his *bandoneón* skills, his long fingers looked like an average person's. 'You have heard of me?'

'Yes, of course! I've read articles about your career and I've also watched your performances on YouTube.' She didn't dare tell him that listening to him play had been torture. The man had talent, no denying it, she just wished he played an instrument that didn't cause her to cringe every time she heard it.

'I am flattered, I think.' He narrowed his eyes then said, 'I hope you are not doing the stalking thing.'

She laughed. 'No stalking, I promise. I'm just studying the tango.'

'Good. It is a lovely thing to learn. I hope my cousin is treating you nice.' He glanced at Carlos.

'You're Carlos's cousin?' She couldn't keep incredulity out of her voice.

'Yes, although we do not advertise this fact. We like to keep family connections away from our professional lives.'

'I understand.' *On many levels.*

'May I ask you to dance?' Gualberto cocked an eyebrow at Carlos and said, 'I am stealing this beautiful specimen.'

Carlos shrugged nonchalantly and Gualberto held out his hand. She placed hers in his and they plunged into the crowd, dodging stationary couples. Although she'd been nervous a moment before, Gualberto's affable manner relaxed her.

'There's music playing, why isn't anyone dancing?' Dani asked, happy Gualberto wouldn't make her stick to silly rules about dancing for answers to questions.

'Ah, this is the *cortina*, the curtain. It is like intermission music between groupings of songs.'

'Oh,' she said, not convinced she'd ever get her head around this tango business. Not that she really wanted to. Well, she did, but only enough to get her stories done and gain some understanding about what drives a person to ditch her family, fly to the other side of the world, and become a tango legend.

Gualberto gently shuffled her into place, maneuvering her arms into the correct position, ensuring their hearts were aligned. The haze from the lights hindered her ability to peer into the darkness easily but she spotted Carlos sitting at their table, looking down and massaging his injured leg. He didn't seem perturbed about not dancing with her.

'How does Carlos dance with a damaged leg?' Although they'd just met, Dani sensed Gualberto would be more open to her prodding than Carlos.

'He doesn't.'

'But he was about to get on the dance floor.' A slight breeze shook the gardenias hanging in pots above their heads, sending a sweet floral scent drifting through the air.

'He only ever comes to watch his students dance in the real world. He does not do this dancing. Never. Not since . . .' He swept a hand over his leg.

'Well, why would he—' The music drowned her sentence. The melody of the violins, cello, and flute filled the air, then the *bandoneón* took center stage. She wanted to cover her ears but it would be a tad difficult explaining to the world's *bandoneón* expert that his instrument repulsed her.

Leaning forward, Gualberto said, 'Follow me.'

He gently nudged her to the left, his light touch guiding her with ease. Dani locked onto his moves and the music swept through her body. She closed her eyes, took a step forward, two back, then one to the side and connected with something bony.

'*¡Mierda!, Mi pierna!*'

Oh shit. Her eyes flew open and she dropped her hands to her side. Gualberto rubbed his leg and shook his head.

'I'm so, so sorry, Gualberto.' Carlos was right, tango and martial arts had a lot in common.

'You should ask for your money back.' He straightened and gave her a lopsided grin. 'My cousin, he has taught you nothing.'

'He's not my dance teacher. Officially, anyway.'

He shot her a questioning look then cocked his head towards their table. Carlos and his cane had disappeared but his jacket hung on the chair. 'My leg hurts. Let us sit, yes?'

Gualberto led the way to the table and Dani followed, pushing through the crowd like a salmon swimming upstream.

He pulled out a chair and motioned for her to sit, then he signaled a waiter to bring drinks. Dani concentrated on the dancers, admiring how they moved as one, as if they had telepathy and could anticipate each other's moves. The waiter returned with a carafe of red wine and three glasses. Gualberto filled hers to the brim. She leaned forward, took a tentative sip, and let the liquid slide down her throat, warming her insides.

'I am not shy and I will ask this. Are you and my cousin . . .?' He arched an eyebrow.

She stopped mid-sip and squeezed her eyes shut as red wine burned her throat and nostrils. 'God no!'

'Yes, it would have surprised me.'

'What's that supposed to mean?' She doubted she'd be Carlos's type. He wasn't hers even if he did look like a Ralph Lauren model.

Gualberto leaned forward. 'How well do you know Carlos?'

'Not very well. I'm working on stories for a magazine—'

Gualberto slapped his thighs and let out a belly laugh. 'Oh, ho, ho! What is my cousin doing with a journalist?'

'He doesn't like them much, does he?'

'I believe he would like to stick the hot pokers in his eyes rather than be near people from your profession.'

'I gathered as much. May I ask why?'

Gualberto cast his eyes around the room and leaned his elbows on the table. 'You do not know his history?'

'Only from what I've read and heard from other journalists. Is that why he has a problem with them?'

'I am not sure if this is right for me to tell. Perhaps you should be asking him.' He studied the couples on the dance floor then returned his attention to her.

Leaning forward, she said, 'I can't speak for my colleagues, but I promise you I would not betray anyone's confidence and I don't plan on telling Carlos's story unless he wants me to. I may mention him briefly in my article but I'm focusing on the dance, not the man. And I had planned on contacting you so I can write an article about your musicianship.'

'From a well-balanced angle.'

'Is there any other way to tell a story?' Then she remembered Carlos had experienced many pointy angles. 'Scrap that. Just know these articles will do tango proud.'

'Is this how you get information from people? You charm them with sweetness, yes?'

Dani gave a small laugh. 'I bet you woo people with your charisma.'

'Maybe I do.' His lips kicked up at the corners. 'I will tell you, but it is only for the benefit of my cousin. If you understand his history you may find a way to work with him. It is important for him to have hope and if he can trust a journalist, maybe he can trust in other aspects of his life, yes?' He nodded, as if agreeing with himself. 'The most important trait a tango dancer has is trust.'

'Okay,' she said, not entirely sure where he was going. Guilt tugged at her sleeve again. Maybe she should tell Carlos who her mother was. 'Is that why he can't dance the tango anymore? Because he doesn't trust his dance partners?'

'Ah, it is not that simple, but yes, there is truth in this. But please, do not do the Google on my cousin. You will find many stories but none are one hundred percent true. I am one of the few who know what happened the night of his accident.' He fixed his eyes on hers and she willed her expression to remain nonchalant. 'You have done the Google. I can tell.'

'How?'

'Your eyelid. It is moving funny.' He pointed and she rubbed her eye with her finger.

'Gualberto, first, remind me never to play poker with you, and second, I don't fully believe what's on the internet unless I've written it. I prefer to talk directly to the source. However, if you are willing to give me a heads-up, I'm all for it.' She placed her hands on her lap.

'Hmm.' His brows furrowed and he paused so long Dani thought he'd given up on the subject. Taking a sip of wine, he put the glass down and said, 'Carlos, he has toured the world, performed for dignitaries, including presidents, but it was a woman who was his undoing.' He let out a low whistle. 'This Cecilia Ortiz, she captured the hearts of thousands. Her beauty and talent was only second to *La Gringa Magnifica*.'

She sucked in air so fast a sharp pain caught in her throat. *Oh god. Change the subject. Change the subject!*

'You are all right, Dani?' He placed the back of his hand against her forehead. 'Do you not feel well?'

'I'm fine.' She breathed out and forced her voice to steady. 'This Cecilia Ortiz was Carlos's fiancée, right?' She already knew the answer but had to steer away from her mother becoming a topic of conversation.

'Yes.'

'And?'

Gualberto cast his eyes around the room, no doubt searching for his cousin. 'They were not perfect away from their adoring fans.' He sighed. 'Such tragedy.'

'So it wasn't an easy relationship?'

'You are correct. Carlos, he is a private man and I do not blame him. I am still surprised he is talking to you. The journalists blamed him for many things. This killed the relationship he had with Cecilia. *Kaput!* With his hands he mimed a bomb exploding. 'She left him and now he teaches the dance that broke his heart.'

'Why does he teach if it gives him so much grief? He doesn't give the impression of hating it.'

'He knows nothing else. Would you ask Sir Paul McCartney to plumb a sink? No, you would not. Plus he needs the money.'

'How badly does he need it?'

'It is not my place to say.'

'Sure, I understand,' she said. 'He's got to live, right?'

'Ah, but it's not for living, it's—' Wariness flashed across Gualberto's face. 'You are very good at making people talk. Do not worry what the money is for. My cousin only knows tango.'

Up until now she'd been focused on the tango stories but this conversation with Gaulberto piqued her interest. She'd figured Carlos was a complicated soul but hearing his cousin talk about him made her question exactly what had gone on with that accident. What Gualberto *hadn't* said came through loud and clear for Dani. She tapped her finger on the table and casually said, 'Let's suppose Carlos didn't cause the accident. Why would he let the public think he did?' she asked. 'Was it Cecilia's fault?'

He mimed zipping his lip then gave a small shrug.

'If it was Cecilia who did wrong and he loved her deeply, he'd take the flak, wouldn't he? And with the public and media constantly blaming him, she probably started to believe them if she's a gullible person.' She studied Gualberto's noncommittal expression but his eyes told her what she needed to know. 'Why *wouldn't* he hate the media?'

Gualberto raised his eyebrows but his lips remained closed.

'How did the accident happen?'

Exhaling Gualberto said, 'You have to ask Carlos this. I was not there.'

'But you're willing to believe your cousin. Because families stick together.' *If they're not mine, that is.*

CHAPTER 5

Present Day - Dani

A man coughed behind Dani and she turned around. Bright lights shone in her eyes and it was impossible to read Carlos's expression but she figured he wasn't impressed. It might have had something to do with his hand on hip and his tapping foot.

'I see you have given up on this dancing business.' Carlos sat on the opposite side of the table.

'I don't think your cousin wants broken feet and split shins.' She turned to Gualberto. 'Sorry again.'

'No offense, but you all lack the soul required for this dance.' He laughed and raised a glass in the air. 'To foreigners and their inability to dance like an Argentine.'

'Aside from *La Gringa Magnifica*.' Carlos leaned back and put his hands behind his head. 'She is a foreigner with an Argentine soul. If you have done your research on my dance you would know of *La Gringa Magnifica*, yes?'

Dani stared at her wine glass, wishing she could dive in and disappear into the rich red liquid. She hoped they didn't notice the goose bumps on her arms, her taut shoulder muscles and throbbing temples. She also prayed they couldn't sense her mentally super-gluing her butt to the chair so she didn't dash out the door.

'Daniela?'

She looked up to find Carlos arching an eyebrow. His use of her full name grated on her but she was willing to let it slide . . .for now.

'Sorry,' she said. 'I didn't hear you.' Like hell, she didn't.

'Do you know of *La Gringa Magnifica*?' Carlos asked again.

'Yes.' She drew the *S* out longer than needed.

'An amazing performer. My country is obsessed with youth and we are also great patriots which is why it was a surprise when my countrymen fell in love with a thirty-five-year old foreign tango dancer all those years ago.' Carlos took a sip of wine and placed the glass carefully on the table. 'But when she danced . . . ah, her strength and beauty inspired many young Argentine women. She was an Australian, like you, *sí*? I still find it difficult to believe a country with the kangaroos and the bear things—'

'They're not bears, they're koalas.' Her words sounded snappier than she'd intended. 'Sorry, I'm a tad tired. I'm not used to starting my evening at midnight.'

Gualberto smiled like he'd already shoved a plan up his sleeve. 'Ah, then we must train you if we are to take you to more dance halls during your stay, won't we Carlos?'

'She needs to learn to dance to write her articles. This is the agreement.' He concentrated on his full wine glass.

'Maybe she could be the next *Gringa Magnifica*.' Gualberto patted his cousin on the arm. 'But I fear you have work cut out for you.' He winked at Dani.

She forced a smile but felt like a phony. How could she have ever thought the constant references about her mother wouldn't affect her? *You're an idiot in denial, Dani McKenna.*

'Have you done the Google thing again?' Gaulberto filled Dani's glass.

'About the Australian tango dancer?' She took another sip, keen for the alcohol to do its job. Within moments the pain in her temples had eased. 'I know a little about her.' Dani shifted in her chair. 'So, Gualberto, what made you want to start playing the *bandoneón*?'

A *tsk* came from Carlos. He shook his head, full lips twitching at the corners. 'This is a nice diversion but I am aware of these tactics. Cousin'—he turned to Gualberto—'do not answer unless she learns a new step.'

'Oh no.' Gualberto shook his head vehemently. 'If I dance with this lovely lady I will need to use your cane.'

The cousins laughed and Dani crossed her arms and narrowed her eyes into a faux glare. A flash of electric blue sequins drew her attention to the far corner of the courtyard. A tall, thin woman in a fitted dress danced with natural grace, her long arms and legs forming beautiful arcs. Dani's stomach lurched and she gripped the sides of the chair so hard she split a nail.

'Excuse me.' The men stood as she got up and she smiled a thank you for their chivalry. They took a seat and carried on talking as she hurried away.

A sea of bodies twirled and turned as Dani wove between half-empty tables and apologized profusely when she stepped on toes. The odds of this woman being Iris were about the same as Dani reuniting with Adam . . . i.e. zilch . . . but she couldn't resist the urge to get a closer look. Not that Dani had any idea what she would do or say if the woman was her mother. What does one say after twenty years of silence? *Hi Mum, nice to see you. Love the dress.* Yeah, right. Her heart told her to stop and turn around but her feet forced her to the edge of the dance floor, where she halted and searched the crowd.

Blue sequins flashed again and Dani stepped forward, trying to avoid being swept away by the dancers. The woman's pale skin caught the lights and her dark hair swung across her face to reveal heavily painted, serious lips. Her long lashes closed for a moment, lost in the music, passion oozing from each graceful step.

Dani let out a long sigh.

It wasn't Iris.

The woman disappeared into the crowd with her partner and Dani chewed her lower lip. Buenos Aires was a city of ghosts.

'There you are.'

Warm breath grazed her ear as the deep voice jolted her into the present.

'I thought we had scared you away.' Carlos jutted his chin in the direction of the dance floor. 'Are you ready for more?'

She shook her head. 'Sorry, but I'm done for tonight.'

'Your stories will be short.'

'I know we have a deal but I'm tired.' She made a show of rubbing her ankles where the buckles dug in. They hurt, but not as much as her brain.

'We go now but we return tomorrow. And you will get real shoes.' He nodded at her feet. 'Beautiful but not practical. You need the right tools, yes?'

As soon as Dani slipped on the violet shoes, she fell in love. The soft leather straps caressed her feet and even though the heels were high, the cushioned soles gave the impression of walking on clouds. They were *almost* as comfy as her runners.

'Wow,' she said, looking up and smiling at Carlos, who had crossed arms.

'I tell you they are no more practical than those things you had on last night.' He gestured toward the red shoes abandoned on the floor of the tango shoe shop.

'But these ones are comfortable, I promise!'

He grabbed a pair of closed-in, low-heeled, poop-brown shoes. She screwed up her nose then stopped, worried he'd think her ungrateful.

'This is what you should wear, Daniela. They are not pretty but they work. They have more structure. Those purple ones are for professionals. These'—he thrust the ugly shoes at her—'are perfect for beginners. Unfortunately, they only come in left and right.'

Dani laughed even though she didn't agree with Carlos's philosophy. Dressing like a professional, whether it was for journalism or dance, definitely made a difference. If she looked the part, she had a better chance of succeeding. Alas, Carlos had other ideas.

She moved her feet from side to side, admiring the violet contrast against her pale skin. She stifled a sigh.

'Fine. I'll take the brown ones, but mark my words, one day I'm going to return to this shop and buy these shoes.' She punctuated this with a firm nod. 'And I'll be a good enough dancer to do them justice.'

Dani caught Carlos's lips twitching, laughter shining in his eyes. She squeezed her own lips together, trying to suppress the belly laugh threatening to tumble onto the shop floor.

Straightening his back, Carlos said, 'I hope the store does not go out of business before then.'

CHAPTER 6

1953 - Louisa

From the mansion's third floor, Louisa peered at the masses swarming along the tree-lined avenue. People bashed metal ladles and wooden spoons against pots while traffic came to a standstill. The protestors raised their voices in disapproval of Juan Perón for allowing the Eva Perón Foundation for the poor to crumble after the passing of his wife. Burning piles of rubbish cast an eerie orange glow along the sidewalk as acrid smoke curled above people's heads. A shot rang in the distance, causing Louisa to jump.

'Stay away from the windows, you'll get hurt.'

She spun around to find Eduardo in the living room doorway, his sturdy build taking up most of the doorframe.

'The people are growing more restless. They only want to be heard by the government.' Her gaze returned to the crowd below, their chants growing louder as more people joined the throng.

'Those people you feel sorry for are the ones who attacked and burned the Jockey Club and the National Democratic Party head-quarters.'

'It was their way of protesting against Perón's violent response to the explosion in Plaza de Mayo.' Louisa detested political discussions with Eduardo because of their opposing views, but he insisted on dragging her into them, perhaps in the hope that she would one day agree with him.

'Those people you support are thugs. What is this country coming to when police and firemen refuse to attend calls of help from the affluent?' Eduardo adjusted the glasses on his nose.

'It's a strong way of showing the rich they will not be bullied any more. I'm not saying it was right—'

'It couldn't have been more wrong,' Eduardo said.

'The people are tired. They're hungry. You were poor and struggling once. And me.'

'We have a different life now, Louisa. I didn't spend all this time earning money to give it away to commoners.' He strode over to the leather armchair and sat.

'But—'

'It is time.' He gave a curt nod.

'For what?' A hollow feeling grew in her stomach.

'We go to America next week.'

Her wobbly legs threatened to buckle and she sat heavily on the sofa. Eduardo had mentioned it many times before but she'd put it down to rambling. This time, though, his stony expression and the conviction in his voice told her he was serious.

'Shouldn't we wait to see what happens here?'

He swept his hand in the direction of the street. 'You've seen the people. The future is already decided. If we don't leave now we could lose everything.'

'America is not a good idea. You know Buenos Aires. You're familiar with the cafés, bars, and concert halls. America is a new country, a place where you'll have to speak English all the time. I don't think it is in your best interests to go.'

'I will not let this disease rule me.' He straightened his back.

'Perhaps the doctors could slow it down—'

'Enough!' He glowered at her. 'We are going. The decision has been made.'

She willed her voice to remain calm and soft, the perfect way to temper his mood. 'Is it because of your promise to Carlos Gardel?'

'Of course it is. It has taken nearly twenty years to honor my promise and I am not giving up my chance to follow in his footsteps. The world must know that tango is not how that absurd Rudolph Valentino has led them to believe.'

'I admire your loyalty, Eduardo, but America isn't the same as when you made the promise to Gardel and—'

'I am not a man who goes back on his word. We go next week.'

A lump formed at the back of her throat and she swallowed hard. 'So it's the three of us traveling?'

Eduardo shook his head, a stray lock falling across his forehead. He ignored it. 'Are you talking about Roberto? No. He will stay here.'

'Why?' Panic rose within and she forced herself to remain calm, at least on the outside.

'Because it is time he made his own career.'

'But he's never performed live since you started mentoring him.' If she could make Eduardo doubt his decision then it would buy her time to change his mind.

'He will perform after we leave. He is ready. I also need him to manage my affairs here.'

First Eduardo wouldn't let Roberto play in public, now he was being handed the concert circuit on a plate, minus his mentor's presence. Perhaps the disease had taken a bigger toll on Eduardo than she'd thought. His logic didn't make sense and the angry determination in his eyes told her to leave the subject alone until he calmed.

Eduardo turned, strode up the hallway, and slammed the door to the music room. Louisa went to the other side of the room, pulled back the drapes, and pushed up the window. A cool breeze danced across her skin as she stared at the crowd below. These people wanted a better life for themselves. She'd experienced hunger and the daily struggle to remain healthy despite fatal diseases regularly sweeping through the slums. She understood the protestors' desire to have a soft, warm bed, fresh food, and a pair of shoes that didn't leak. Louisa closed the window again as thick smoke wafted up from the bonfires on the street. Tears cascaded down her cheeks. She needed to talk Eduardo out of this plan but with him dangling a carrot in front of his protégé, it would be hard for Roberto to refuse, no matter how much he and Louisa longed to be together.

'Louisa!' Eduardo boomed from two rooms away.

'Yes?' She tried to sound cheerful but her voice cracked.

'My sheet music! Where is it?' He appeared in the doorway, his body shaking and eyes bulging as looked up and down the hallway. 'I can't find it. Someone's stolen it! Who would dare steal my work?'

'No one's stolen it, Eduardo,' she said calmly, placing her hand on his arm. 'We'll find it. Take a deep breath.' She breathed in and looked deeply into his eyes. 'Breathe in, two, three, four. Out, two, three, four.' Louisa repeated this a few times and within moments, his ragged breathing settled. She studied his salt-and-pepper hair and the lifelines etched on his face. Eduardo looked like a younger version of her grandfather, just before he was diagnosed with dementia. Nostalgia washed over her, and she wished for another chance to see her grandfather alive when he was lucid. She'd tell him how much she loved him and how she'd never wanted him locked away.

Bringing herself into the present, she went to the music room and walked over to the window seat. 'Last time I saw it was . . .' Lifting a pile of English-language magazines, she grabbed the sheet music and triumphantly handed over the pages. 'Here.'

'Thank you, Louisa.' He hung his head and a succession of sobs echoed through the room. Wrapping her arm around him, she made hushing noises, her heart breaking as she witnessed this talented man losing confidence.

'What would I do without you?' He looked up, his eyes full of tears. 'You know me better than anyone. I saved you from poverty but you've saved my reputation and sanity many times over. I'm aware my behavior makes your life difficult but the anger's like a speeding train and it's impossible to stop at times. Please.' He grabbed her hand so hard she stifled a small cry. Fear etched in the deep creases on his face. 'Don't ever leave me. Promise you'll never go. I'd never survive without you.'

As much as she wanted to promise she'd stay, she couldn't offer her word. Confusion reigned and she closed her eyes, wishing for an easy solution. Whichever way she turned, either Roberto or Eduardo would be deeply hurt.

She leaned over and gave him a kiss on the cheek and headed for the door.

'Louisa?'

'Yes?' She turned to face him.

'I know you can never love me in the way I want, and I appreciate you sticking by this crusty old fool and feeding the muse. You are an angel walking among us.'

She gave a small smile and went upstairs to her room, closing the door behind her. Flopping on the bed, she took a deep breath and stared at the ceiling. The fading daylight caught the crystals on the chandelier, casting a kaleidoscope of colors on the wall. A wave of pity for Eduardo swept over her. All he ever wanted was time to create the music that brought joy to many and a chance to honor a promise he'd made to his own mentor. Eduardo needed her help to get him through the rough stages of the disease, to guide him to peace when he was paralyzed by fear, and to support him when he felt all was lost. After everything he'd done for her, she couldn't deprive him of his wishes. She didn't want another man to suffer like her grandfather because someone couldn't be bothered to help. Eduardo was right. The decision had been made.

The door clicked quietly behind Louisa as she stepped into the cool evening. Hurrying down the dark street, she crossed the deserted road and ducked into the shadows of the park. She didn't need light to guide her through the twists and turns to arrive at their bench seat.

She sat and waited. The cold metal bit through her winter jacket and froze the backs of her legs and buttocks. It hardly mattered. Since Eduardo had delivered the news of their imminent departure, a deep chill had settled on her soul. Pulling the jacket closer to her body, she stared into the darkness as the minutes dragged on.

Stones crunching beneath solid boots drew her attention to the park's entrance where Roberto stood for a moment. He walked toward her, his slow, deliberate steps leaving her desperate with anticipation for his strong arms to wrap around and cocoon her from the world once again.

He drew close then held out his hand. She let his warm fingers entwine with hers as she stood and looked into his eyes before dissolving into tears, burying her head in his wool jacket. Roberto gently stroked her hair, his fingers occasionally catching a curl.

'My love, we will find a way.'

She pulled back, her vision blurry. 'How? He's already made up his mind.'

'I know.' Roberto gestured toward the bench. They sat and she snuggled into him, breathing in his sandalwood scent.

'What do you want to happen?' The words came out before she'd realized the implications of hearing an answer she didn't want.

'What do you mean?'

'Eduardo's told you about looking after his affairs, right? And how he'll let you perform once he leaves?'

'Yes. He says my performing is like a legacy he is leaving for the Argentines while he is away.' Roberto puffed out his chest.

'So you're his replacement.'

'No one could ever replace Eduardo. This is a time for me to be my own person—with Eduardo's blessing.' His tone held excitement.

'You'll get to live your dream and make a name for yourself.' Louisa looked into his eyes. 'You deserve this.'

'I've worked hard, yes, but it means nothing if I cannot share it with you.'

'But he needs me and I have to help.' She desperately wanted to elaborate but couldn't.

'I need you, too, but . . .' Roberto paused as if searching for the right words.

'It's your dream.'

'It's our future.' He trailed his fingers down her face and around to the nape of her neck.

She stared at her turquoise heels. 'I have no idea how I'll get through my days without you.'

'So stay with me.'

'I can't.'

'You're not his possession, Louisa.' Roberto shifted away and a shot of cold air slapped her side.

'I'm his muse,' she said, scrambling. 'He can't perform without me.'

'He's using guilt to make you stay with him.'

She'd spent many nights contemplating that thought but she always came to the same conclusion: Eduardo had never used guilt to get what he wanted.

'Roberto, I love this country. Argentina adopted me when I had no home and no family and she took me in her arms and embraced me like I was her own child. By being Eduardo's muse and him producing more tango, I can return some of what I owe the Argentine people. *Our* people.'

Roberto frowned then scratched his head. 'You are too loyal. I've seen the way he treats you.'

'He has his reasons.'

'No reason is good enough to behave the way he does with you.' His tone turned steely and his body tensed. 'Call me selfish, but I want you with me. Let's forget about Eduardo and leave for Brazil like we've talked about. Let's do it.'

'Roberto, I want to. Believe me, I want to with my whole heart, but it's not possible.'

'Maybe you don't want me and you're using him as an excuse.' He crossed his arms and stared into the dark corner of the park.

'Roberto.' Louisa placed her hand on his knee. 'This is not true.'

'Leave him.'

'I can't.'

'Something's wrong with him,' Roberto blurted.

She sucked in the cold air and it pained the back of her throat. 'What do you mean?'

'His temper is getting worse and he's more forgetful. The other day he gave me some music and told me I was ready for it, yet he'd given me the same piece two weeks before.'

'Eduardo's been under stress lately—'

'There you go defending him again.' He pulled farther away, the gap between them now a wide valley.

'He's the closest to family I've got. I'm like his daughter.'

'He only treats you like a daughter because you won't return his romantic overtures.' Roberto drew his lips into a taut line. She didn't take offense at his words as they'd been spoken in anger. 'I can't compete with him, can I?'

'This is not a competition. I love Eduardo like a father, but I love you, like this.' She leaned forward and placed a finger under his chin, guiding his lips toward hers. Pure love danced in his dark eyes. Her body ached for his touch, for his hands to caress, stroke, and love her. A hunger grew inside and she kissed him harder, her eagerness quashing any fears of being caught.

Their bodies entwined with desire, their lips explored new territory. Until now, they'd held back, determined to do the right thing by Eduardo. But with their future as a couple in doubt, it was easy to give in to the feelings they'd ignored for so long, knowing this moment could pass and could never be relived.

'Come to my apartment.' His breath came out in short, shallow bursts.

'I can't—'

'Please.'

The significance of what they were doing weighed heavily on her shoulders. All she wanted was a few stolen moments with the man she loved, then she'd follow through with her commitment to Eduardo.

Roberto kissed her one more time and she arrived at her answer. 'Yes.'

CHAPTER 7

Present Day - Dani

Dani climbed the steps to the dance hall, grateful she'd shaken the paranoia from her last visit. Well, almost. Time and common sense had quelled her anxiety about Iris miraculously appearing in a *práctica* or *milonga* in Buenos Aires. Truly, it was as likely as Dani joining *Riverdance*. A small laugh slipped from her mouth.

Carlos stopped and turned. 'You are all right?'

'Yes, yes, all good. Don't worry about me.' She made a shooing gesture and they continued to the entrance of La Gardenia. The moment they arrived at the giant wooden doors, a familiar figure stepped from the shadows.

'Nice shoes.' Gualberto eyed off her latest purchase.

'Thanks.' Yes, they were poop brown. Yes, they were ugly, but man, were they comfortable. No need to tell Carlos, though.

The trio entered the large courtyard and sat at the same table as the previous night. The sweet aroma of gardenias floated across the warm evening as the music started, beckoning the dancers to take to the floor and twist and turn in ways that didn't seem humanly possible. The *bandoneón* made Dani clench her fists.

Dani's gaze traveled the room, seeking gray-haired patrons—

ones old enough to have frequented dance halls in the early fifties. Every spare second she'd had, and she'd had plenty due to insomnia, Dani had read up on Louisa Gilchrist and Eduardo Canziani, using actual books, not Google. What fascinated her most, however, were the mentions of Roberto Vega, Eduardo's protégé. The history books weren't entirely clear on the dynamics between the trio as there was no firsthand information, so Dani's reading had created more questions than answers.

Their story had latched on to her like a tick. Tonight she planned to ask patrons from that era about life back then and if someone opened up about the Canziani murder then who was she to stop them? It did fall into the history of tango. *Kind of.* Also cracking a cold case would send her career skyrocketing. She could ditch her job at the magazine as well as Adam and his ex-current-whatever wife and get on with a new career and new life.

But Dani knew she wasn't fooling anybody, especially herself. The death of Argentina's greatest composer remained a scar on the patriotic pride of the Argentines, so if a foreigner uncovered evidence that had been misconstrued . . .

Don't be ridiculous, McKenna, professional investigators have worked on this case for years. Why would you be the one to solve it?

She had enough going on with her Tourism Argentina pieces and her personal project. Not that she'd asked Carlos questions about Iris's private life, because every time someone mentioned her name, Dani's brain froze. Maybe she should leave well enough alone and just do her history of tango articles. That way, her life would be less complicated and she didn't have to worry about betraying Carlos's trust. Then there was the potential story behind the motorbike accident but with Carlos's tight lips, she had more chance of cracking the Canziani case.

Dani turned her attention to Carlos, who rubbed his knee. He caught her looking and removed his hand, leaned forward, and grabbed a glass of water, taking a long drink.

Gualberto stood. 'Please excuse me, I spy a friend I have not seen in a long time.' He dived into the crowd and disappeared.

Gualberto's vanishing left Dani squirming in Carlos's solemn presence but she remembered he could enjoy himself—he'd proven it at the shoe shop. It was nice, but also sad, to glimpse fun Carlos. She'd liked what she'd seen, but looking at him now, with rigid posture and intense eyes, Carlos laughing again could be way off in the future.

'Your lesson begins now.'

Anxiety flipped her stomach. 'Okay.'

Carlos cleared his throat. 'The woman is the most important person of the couple. The woman should only move if the man creates a desire in her to do so. She must trust the leader at all times and the leader must deal with her reality and he should adjust his movements for her.'

'I thought it was a macho dance.'

'No. This is why you have much to learn.'

'Fabulous.' She'd spent the day alternating between false bravado and pure panic about dancing tango again.

'You will learn.' His smile gave her a smidgen of confidence. 'The follower must surrender one's need for self-preservation and allow the leader to take control.'

'So it is a macho dance! And that contradicts what you said before.'

'Tango, like love—'

'Is complicated. Got it, but know this: I will only follow the male because it is a dance, not real life. I have not, nor will I ever, let a man tell me what to do. Women have their own brains and we can survive quite well without men if we choose.' She wanted to add a childish 'so there,' but resisted.

'You have finished with your ladies' freedom speech, yes? Or shall I wait for you to get it out of your system? Remember, we have not got all the night.'

'I'm done.' *For now.*

'Venting is cathartic, no? But please refrain from doing so when I am teaching.' He cleared his throat. 'It is important for the leader to make sure the follower feels safe because if she does not, she will not reach a state of meditation and this would be of great tragedy.'

'Are you talking about a Tango Nirvana?'

'Yes. It is called *entrega* and is the Holy Grail of tango. Holy Trinity, in fact. It is when two dancers meld perfectly into one and their moves and souls are entwined with the music. Magic is created in this moment. Of course, it cannot last forever, but once it is glimpsed, the dancers search for it with desperation. Unfortunately, most never find it again.'

'It sounds like you're talking about love.'

'Love?' His eyebrows shot so high they nearly collided with his hairline. 'Pfft. Daniela, please do not get us distracted. The next rule of tango is about discretion. Yes, there is passion but it is a conversation between the man and woman. It is not an open discussion for the world to see.'

'No groping on the dance floor, eh?'

'What is this 'groping'?'

'When someone feels . . . Oh, never mind. Okay, closed conversation. Got it.'

He rubbed his thumb and forefinger against his chin. 'We move on to the next aspect. Your expression. You must be serious and your face should convey the power of the emotions of the dance. No smiling.'

'I need to know all this before we get on the dance floor?'

'There is more—'

'I am sorry for my absence,' said Gualberto, his face flushed. 'It is good to meet with old friends, *no?*'

'Yes, it is,' she said.

'Enough chitchatting. You cannot be a wallflower,' said Carlos, nudging her leg with his cane. 'You have questions you want to ask, *sí?* Time to get busy.'

'Has the theory part finished? Are you going to teach me some real moves?' She asked.

'My leg, it hurts tonight. Gualberto will show you. I have taught him everything he knows.'

His cousin grinned and shrugged his shoulders. A small wave of relief rippled through Dani. Even though she hadn't yet danced with Carlos, she got the distinct impression it would not be a walk in the park. More than likely it'd be a crawl across broken glass.

'Rightio.' She stood and held out her hand to Gualberto, who remained seated. 'What? You've changed your mind?'

'Sit.' Carlos grumbled.

'Why?' She placed fists on her hips.

'Sit down,' he said with more force.

'Don't use that tone with me. I don't care who you are.'

'Do as he says, Dani.' Gualberto motioned toward the chair.

She sat heavily and crossed her arms. 'Fine.'

'We are at the next rule. The lady must wait to be asked to dance. ¿*Entiendes*?' Carlos clasped his hands around his cane and rested his chin on top.

'Yes, I understand.' She hadn't made it to the dance floor and already she'd messed up.

'It is not polite for a man to go up to a woman and ask her to dance. It puts pressure on her to say yes and makes him embarrassed if she says no. Argentines do not like to lose the face. Instead, we have *el cabeceo*. It is all about the eyes and is fair for both parties. If someone wants to dance they do the eye contact and nod. If the other person agrees, they do the same. The contract is made but it is always the leader who goes to the follower. Then you dance for three songs. It is called a *tanda*.'

'Why three?'

'It is just so. Sometimes it is four or five, but mostly three. Do not say thank you before you have finished the *tanda* with your partner.'

'Why not?' Learning Mandarin would be easier.

'These are questions.'

'But you're going to shove me on the floor in public where I might get arrested for assault. I need to understand what I'm letting myself in for.' *What on earth did Iris see in this stupid dance? It's full of rules, rules, rules. Where's the fun?*

'You *gringos* are fond of saying thank you but if you say this it means you are finished dancing with your partner. If it is said before the *tanda* is finished, you are considered rude.'

'That's it?'

'*Sí*. That is it.'

'Easy.' If only it was.

'Show me.' He leaned back and fixed a stare on Gualberto. Dani sipped her drink and wished for something stronger than half-melted ice cubes.

Gualberto caught her eye and gave a small nod. She returned the same, feeling like an amateur. He stood and took her hand, lead her to the dance floor while the *cortina*, the interval, played. Gualberto gently moved her body into position and he wrapped his fingers around hers and placed his other hand on the small of her back. At least Gualberto seemed a tad more sympathetic to her dancing incompetence.

'Ready? You follow me. We go slowly, slowly. But I ask a promise of you.'

'Yes?'

'Do not close your eyes like the other time. This is dangerous.'

'Yeah, sorry about that.' And she meant it. Poor Gualberto had been kind and she had repaid him by almost crippling him for life.

'Do not worry. We will change this. But you must listen to me.'

'Understood.'

'Stand with your feet together. Put the weight on your toes. Do not let the stomach protrude.'

Bummer. She thought she'd been holding it in. She shouldn't have had that hamburger for lunch. Or the fries. Or the milkshake.

'Open your chest.'

'Pardon?'

'The chest, open it. Like this.' He took a deep breath and puffed out his torso. 'You let the air in. You breathe better. You dance better.'

'I couldn't dance much worse.'

Gualberto joined her laughter, then his expression turned serious. 'Carlos is a tough teacher but he is the best.'

'But you're teaching me, not him.'

'He knows what he is doing. Do not worry, he will make sure you learn.'

She liked Gualberto's devotion to his cousin but so far Carlos had made Gualberto do all the dirty work. After all, sending the poor man for more punishment seemed pretty mean. But Gualberto didn't appear to care, and she enjoyed his company. Not in a romantic fashion, more like an older brother.

'So what shall I do?'

'You follow. I lead. We will do something to surprise Carlos. My cousin, he expects a lot from people. With good reason.'

'What does that mean?'

'Let us concentrate on this first. Worry about your questions later, *sí*? Chin up. The floor is Medusa. You look at it and you turn to stone. Feet together. Left forward. Draw in right to left.'

Her temples throbbed from concentrating but she allowed Gualberto's smooth voice to guide her.

'Right foot step to side. Draw in left to your right. Step back on left.' He paused and let her catch up. 'Let us continue. Step back on right. Cross left in front of right.'

She looked down to find her feet in what can only be classified as a dance position. Dani met Gualberto's eyes.

'You have completed some of *el basico*.'

'And I didn't hurt you! Yay!' She let go and clapped her hands together. 'More! More!'

'You are ready?'

'Yes!' Adrenalin pumped through her body, spurring her on. It briefly crossed her mind that her mother may have felt the same way when she first learnt tango, but rather than wallow in sadness, Dani chose enjoyment. Musings about her errant mother could be left until the wee hours of the morning when insomnia came to visit.

'You need to finish *el basico*.'

'But I thought I'd just learnt a step?'

'It is the first part. This is the next. Do it all together and you can ask Carlos a question.'

'Got it.' The way she was going, these articles would be complete by the end of the week.

'Back to the cross over. Step back on the right foot. Draw back the left next to right. Step with left to the side. Bring your right foot in. ¡*El fin*!'

'That's it?' He nodded and she let her excitement bubble over. 'Let's do it again!'

Gualberto counted and she followed diligently, reveling in learning the first ever dance step in her life. She counted her lucky stars that her grandma Stella couldn't see her now. Since Dani announced her business trip to Argentina, her grandmother had refused to speak to her. The hurt hadn't yet subsided. She closed her eyes briefly, remembering Stella's angry words: 'Do not expect me to support this. When your mother left, you and I made an agreement that we will not be involved with tango, *ever*. If you see Iris, you'll only end up more hurt than you already are.'

It didn't matter how much Dani had promised she wouldn't track down her mother, Stella wouldn't sway. So now Stella wasn't on speaking terms with her own daughter *or* granddaughter. Dani still couldn't comprehend how her grandmother could be so extreme, especially as Stella had brought her up when her father passed away a year after Iris had left. But Stella's rule over her prevailed, even though Dani was an adult and lived on the other side of the world. Sure, her grandma had given up a lot to raise Dani and whether it was from guilt or a sense of duty, Dani usually did as Stella wished, except for this trip to Argentina. It took a long time to learn, but some things took precedence over pleasing others and finding out about her mother was Dani's ticket to understanding herself. If Stella did miraculously show right now, Dani would be hauled off the dance floor and subjected to a lecture on why dabbling in the tango was like courting the devil. Until this moment, she would have agreed, but the thrill of learning a step, even if it was the most basic, almost outweighed Stella's potential wrath. *Almost.*

'Come. We show Carlos.'

They squeezed through the crowd until they reached the other side of the dance floor. Carlos was deep in conversation with a gentleman in his early sixties. His well-tailored suit and perfectly styled hair gave the impression he had money and taste.

'Excuse me, but you might want to see this,' Dani said. The men looked at her and Carlos folded his arms in an 'impress me' gesture.

She took her position with Gualberto and he guided her through the movements. Once they'd completed the steps, she looked over to find Carlos sporting a noncommittal expression.

'What do you think?' She wished his opinion didn't count, but it did.

'It is not bad. I owe you an answer, *sí*? Do you have a question?'

'I have lots. First though, I need a drink. I had no idea dancing could be so taxing.'

Carlos signaled to the waiter and she and Gualberto joined the men at the table.

'Daniela, this is Diego Alonso. Argentina's finest tango orchestra conductor.'

The gentleman took her hand and brushed his lips lightly against her skin. He gazed at her from under a veranda of dark lashes, offering a smile that could woo the hardest of female hearts.

'It is nice to meet you. Carlos, he tells me you are writing about the history of the tango.'

'Yes.' His intensity unnerved her. She subtly pulled her hand away and rested it on her lap. The quartet fell into the silence born of people struggling to find a common thread for conversation.

'Daniela, I am surprised by your progress. My cousin, he has done well,' Carlos eventually said and slapped Gualberto on the back. 'We can work with this. Maybe you will be the next *Gringa Magnifica*. What do you think, Alonso?'

'Do not ask such a question. Iris and I do not talk anymore.' He dropped his gaze and lowered his voice. 'Not since she left me.'

CHAPTER 8

Present Day - Dani

The moment the words hit Dani's ears, all the enthusiasm fueling the new dance moves dissipated. This man had dated Iris?

'Yes, I am sorry about your breakup,' Carlos said.

She took in Diego's long fingers—the fingers that had once caressed her mother. Anger ripped through her. Iris shouldn't have been with any man other than her father. If she'd just stayed put and worked things out like a normal person . . .

'Ah,' Diego shrugged. 'It is life, no? A woman loves a man, she changes the mind, she leaves.'

So Iris still had a penchant for leaving and disappointing people she loved. Painful memories surfaced as Dani recalled how Iris had constantly disappointed her by saying she'd do something and then cancel without a solid reason. Like the time she'd promised to go to the art exhibition at Dani's kindergarten but never showed. It didn't matter that she'd won first prize, the only prize she ever wanted was her mother's love and presence.

'Well, the male may be the leader in tango but it is the woman who is in charge of romance and hearts.' Carlos thanked the waiter and took the bottle of wine.

Normally, Dani would join the conversation with a pithy comment but she could barely breathe, being so close to her mother's ex-lover.

'I thought Iris Kennedy kept her life off-stage private,' she eventually said, surprised her voice held steady.

'*Sí*,' said Diego, 'but she left of her own choosing and I have no reason to keep the secret now. If she does not return my calls, I will contact the magazines of the gossip and sell my story.'

'Really?' Dani said. What was Iris thinking, shacking up with this jerk? Her father had been the sweetest, kindest, most loving man yet she chose someone like Diego Alonso over him? What kind of woman did that make Iris? She didn't make eye contact when she asked, 'How long were you together?'

'Not long enough.' Diego saluted her with his wine and took a long drink. He finished the glass and put it down on the table with a clank.

'Were you serious?' It seemed strange to meet her mother's ex in a dance hall in Buenos Aires, but then again, her life had never been run of the mill. Iris had made sure of that.

'Diego, you must excuse Daniela. She is one of those journalists.' Carlos shot her a warning look.

'A journalist?' Diego laughed. 'Perhaps you will write my story.'

'Thanks, but I'm busy enough as it is.' Her core temperature soared and she used her hand as a fan.

'But it would be an exclusive!' Diego appeared rather chipper for someone who had just had his heart broken.

'Thank you, but no.'

Carlos raised his eyebrows. 'Why not?'

'Because I'm not into gossip stories. I told you, I'm not like the others.' Of course it would be a massive step in her career to break this kind of story, but the subject was way too close to home. Talking with her mother's ex and discovering sordid details of their relationship would be unbearable. She needed to stick to her original plan of understanding how tango changed Iris and not get involved with her romantic interludes.

'Hmm,' said Carlos. 'I am impressed.'

'You are?' she asked. 'Why?'

'You do have integrity. My gut was right. I like this.' He gave a nod.

Dani inhaled and tried to act like a semi-normal person. 'Breaking up is always hard to deal with. I hope you feel better soon, Diego.'

'I am afraid I will not. The heart, it is broken forever. I will never love again.' Diego poured more red wine and downed it in seconds. His sigh came from deep within, his large, sad eyes studied Dani. 'We have met before, *sí*?'

'No. I've only been in Argentina a short while.'

Diego tilted his head to the side. 'I feel like I know you.'

A thin film of sweat broke out on her forehead and she silently prayed Diego didn't make the connection.

'It is your . . .' Diego squinted and studied her further. Gualberto and Carlos leaned forward, placing their heads at different angles while Dani sat frozen in her chair. Until now, she'd managed to get away with her relationship to Iris but sitting in front of the man who had spent countless hours gazing into Iris's almond-shaped eyes, well . . . she couldn't lie her way out of this one as the minute fiction fell from her mouth, her left eye twitched like she'd been electrocuted.

'It is your eyes and your nose. See?' Diego's finger imitated a ski jump. 'It has a little dip before the end, just like my Iris.'

'What?' She hoped they didn't hear the crack in her voice or notice her parched lips.

'Your eyes and nose, they look like those of *La Gringa*.' Diego gave an assertive nod.

'No, I do not see it,' said Gualberto.

'I do not, either. All *gringas* look the same, do they not?' Carlos winked then burst out laughing and the other men joined in.

'Not funny,' said Dani, trying to hold her body steady rather than let it slump with relief. Then she laughed to show she was a good sport.

'You are wrong, my friends,' said Diego. 'Your journalist, she looks like my Iris.'

Dani kept her mouth closed. The world wouldn't end if they found out who her mother was but life wouldn't be easy, either. Especially with Diego on the scene. She got the distinct impression that if he found out who she was, he'd hound her for information about Iris. It saddened her to know that Diego, a complete stranger to Dani, knew more about her mother.

'Daniela?' Carlos used his eyebrow as a question mark.

'What?' *God, please no. Don't ask.*

'Do you know *La Gringa*?'

'No. How could I?' She choked on the words and convinced herself it wasn't a lie. Well, not technically. Had Carlos asked her if she knew Iris Kennedy and she'd answered in the negative, then that would be a lie. But Dani didn't know Iris since she'd taken on the persona of *La Gringa Magnifica*, so theoretically she didn't know her. A spasm developed in her left eye and she casually rested her fingers on it.

'Your eye, it is sore?' Carlos leaned forward and placed his hand on her arm. A tingle shot up her spine.

'My eye goes weird when I'm tired.' The spasm intensified and she pressed her fingers harder against her eyelid.

'Then we go,' said Carlos.

Dani kicked off the hotel bed sheet, her body boiling. A moment later she pulled the covers up, her skin cold and clammy. She tossed. She turned. She wanted to punch something.

'Damn it!'

Dani flicked on the bedside lamp then wished she hadn't. She squinted and reached for the manila folder she'd lugged all over the world for years. Inside were magazine clippings about the woman they call *La Gringa Magnifica*. She thumbed through the photos and let her finger trace the sequined dresses in a rainbow of colors.

She'd managed to squirm away from revealing her relationship with Iris tonight but it wouldn't take long until someone figured it out. Dani had enough to deal with and she dreaded the possibility of Iris discovering her daughter was in Argentina. Not that it would make any difference. After all, Iris hadn't contacted her for twenty years, so why would she bother now? And anyway, her mother lived as a recluse, so the chances of her hearing anything were remote. Though not remote enough. Apparently Buenos Aires was smaller than she'd thought, at least in tango circles.

She got out of bed, went to the bathroom and poured a glass of water. As she sipped it slowly, her legs moved in the directions Gualberto had shown her. When she crossed her feet, Dani paused, horrified she'd voluntarily executed a tango move—and enjoyed it.

'Oh no, it's not going to happen to me.' She slammed the glass on the counter, dashed out of the bathroom, and threw herself on the bed.

Tonight's brief flirtation with the tango had opened a small window for her to peer into Iris's soul. Dani had often wondered if Iris had chosen dance or whether it had chosen her. Even as a young child, Dani knew Iris wasn't like other mothers as she'd constantly struggled to fit into the role. After all, how many other mothers spent forty hours a week practicing tango instead of reading with their kid? Especially when, at that time, Iris wasn't dancing professionally.

It was only in recent years Dani had brought herself to watch her mother's performances on DVD. Guilt swamped her every time she did and her grandma's disapproving voice nagged at her conscience. Iris's ability was evident and the world was a much better place for witnessing her amazing talent. If only it hadn't meant the destruction of the relationship between husband and wife, mother and daughter.

Tears stung her eyes as she remembered how her father had lost his appetite after Iris left. How his gait had changed to a shuffle. How he'd withdrawn from the world. No one could doubt her mother had played a significant role in her father's demise.

Her phone buzzed with the familiar sound of incoming mail. Annoyed, she grabbed the phone and pressed on her inbox.

. . .

Dani,

The big wigs are hassling me. I've not seen any drafts. What's going on? You'll not only get management offside but Tourism Argentina will start asking questions if you don't show some evidence of your articles. I'm starting to doubt whether letting you do this was a good idea. If you're still mad at me, I understand, but don't let our personal differences cost your career.

Cheers,

Adam

Tears welled up and the screen blurred. Blinking hard, she willed them away but it did no good. Until their breakup he'd supported her in every way. He'd pushed her to do better, to dig deeper, to go beyond the limits she'd set for herself. Those were qualities she loved Adam for yet they had disappeared, just like his love.

She clicked on Reply.

Dear Adam,

Thank you for your email. I'm sorry I haven't given you an update earlier but I have been busy compiling material. Don't worry your pretty head because the articles will blow your socks off. I just need a little more time. I doubt I'm missed in New York and honestly, I'm not crying about not being there. And no, I'm not punctuating this with a wink face.

Watch this space.

Cheers,

Dani

It was childish to sign off with 'cheers' but it did give her satisfaction. She read the email one more time and hit Send before she panicked and spent the next two hours agonizing over every word. She wanted to write more and ask so many personal questions but Adam had made it abundantly clear where he stood in their relationship, both personally and professionally.

Checking the clock, Dani did a quick calculation of the time difference between Argentina and Australia. A woman who loved routine, her grandma would have just finished eating dinner by now. Dani reached for the laptop and fiddled around with it, plugging in her headphones and clicking on Skype. The last time Stella had spoken with her was a couple of weeks before Dani left for Argentina. Stella didn't let things slide easily. Did Dani really want a lecture now?

She repositioned her butt on the bed and accidentally knocked a file off the table. The photocopies she'd taken earlier that day at the National Library flew onto the floor and she picked them up, placing them in a neat pile. Her gaze lingered on the photo she'd copied of Louisa and Eduardo—the same image Carlos had in his file. Narrowing her eyes, Dani studied Louisa Gilchrist again. No matter how much she tried to deny it, a sense of familiarity hit her every time. Dani concentrated on each part that made up Louisa with her light-colored hair and curls, her pointed chin, her almond-shaped eyes, her . . . nose.

A gasp caught in Dani's throat.

No.

Shaking her head, Dani laughed. It's not uncommon to have a doppelganger somewhere in the world, so why wouldn't her grandma have one? After all, how many times had people asked Dani if she had a twin? Anyway, Louisa had laughing eyes and a beautiful smile; Stella wore a permanent frown.

But . . . if by some weird twist of fate Stella and Louisa were the same person, Dani could understand why smiling wouldn't be Stella's thing—she'd been accused of murder, lost her lover, and had to flee her home and change her identity.

Laughing at the ridiculousness of her imagination, Dani said, 'I should write fiction.'

CHAPTER 9

1953 - Louisa

The bright morning light shone in Louisa's eyes as she pried them open, trying to get a bearing on where she lay. Turning on her side, she gazed at the lace curtains billowing in the warm breeze. Had last night really happened? Guilt pressed against her chest and gave her the answer. At the time it had felt right, but with the new day, Roberto's loving touch plagued her with shame, though not regret.

Checking the clock, she sat up with a start. Eduardo's luncheon with his mystery guest was due to start in half an hour. Reaching under her pillow, she pulled out the letter Roberto had given her last night. The paper crinkled as she unfolded it with great care, not wanting to make a noise, even though Eduardo would be down in the kitchen bossing the staff.

My dear Lunita,

Without you in my life, the moon would lose its luster. The stars would lose their shine. The sun would lose its warmth.

My heart aches for you, my little moon, to cast your glorious light across my dark, lonely nights.

xoxoxo

A tear fell onto the page and smudged the *xoxoxo*. She reread Roberto's letter half-a-dozen times before opening her underwear drawer and placing it with his other missives.

After padding to the bathroom, she turned on the tap. As water filled the basin, she put in a couple of drops of lavender oil, heaviness flooding her heart. Her tryst with Roberto would forever be etched in her memory and her love and desire would always form an unbreakable connection to her lover.

The lavender aroma lifted her spirits a notch and her skin tingled where the cloth trailed across her body. In a way, it would be easier to be heartless and love Roberto with abandon, not caring what Eduardo thought. But her parents hadn't brought her up that way and even though they weren't with her physically, their spirits were her one constant. She glanced at the framed photo beside the bed, the only surviving image of Louisa and her mother and father. She couldn't go back on her promise to Eduardo, the closest person to family she had. Although breaking promises hadn't been foremost in her mind last night. She'd made a gaffe . . . delicious, sensual, wonderful, earth-moving mistake. And now she had to deal with the consequences.

Louisa slid on silk stockings, a red pleated skirt and white shirt. She tied the shirt's bow at the neck and stepped into red shoes. After many years living in dismal conditions and wearing drab, filthy clothes in London, then Wales and Argentina, she still found it difficult to adjust to wearing bright, fresh, designer outfits. Eduardo always expected her to look her best, and if it meant having a seamstress on hand twenty-four hours a day, he'd do it. And he did.

Glancing at the clock, she hurried out of the bedroom and down the stairs. Low voices murmured behind the closed parlor doors, and Louisa paused, fingers on the handle. She'd much prefer to stay in her room and reflect on the passionate hours she'd shared with Roberto. Being in the presence of others would burst her blissful bubble, but she had no choice other than to steel herself and flash her brightest smile. As an old hand at faking emotions, this shouldn't be too hard.

She rapped lightly on the carved wooden door and pushed it open. Roberto sat on an embroidered chair with his back stiff, sunlight streaming behind his shoulders. He hadn't mentioned coming to the luncheon and his presence knocked her off-kilter. She lifted her chin and refused to meet his eyes, for if she did, she'd surely break down in tears, knowing this would be one of the last times she would see him.

The mystery guest rose and strode toward her like they'd met hundreds of times. He towered above, his broad physique sporting a perfectly tailored navy blue suit. Stretching a meaty hand toward her, he said, 'It is nice to meet you, Miss Gilchrist.'

'It's nice to meet you, too, Mister . . .'

'My name is Stanley Wyler. Texan by birth, now a permanent fixture in California.' He proffered a well-practiced smile and she returned the same.

'Well, I am very pleased to finally meet our mystery guest.' It felt strange to speak English again.

'Please, sit.' Eduardo said in broken English, gesturing for Wyler to sit on a high-backed chair. Louisa sat on the Edwardian settee so Roberto wouldn't be in her line of vision.

'I hear you have an important role in this household,' Wyler said, his voice booming. His wink told her he thought like everyone else did—that Louisa and Eduardo were lovers.

'Eduardo feels his muse benefits when he is in my presence.' She was glad she couldn't see Roberto's expression.

'And you're traveling to my country soon?'

'I believe so.' Ripples of anguish threatened to overwhelm her like they did every time she thought about the move.

'Well I, for one, am glad. We will be seeing a lot more of each other once you arrive in my town.'

'Pardon?' Louisa was accustomed to Eduardo bringing home guests from all over the world and with various occupations but this one, this Stanley Wyler, felt different. His confidence and familiarity unnerved her.

'Has Eduardo not told you?' He raised his eyebrows at Eduardo, who sat on the sofa with nonchalance, swirling ice cubes in his glass. 'We are meeting today to hash out the final details about your move to Hollywood. I own a studio, you see, and I have a great love for tango. The people are tiring of the same old musicals and our studio is determined to change this forever. We are going to intro- duce a new generation of moviegoers to tango and your beloved Eduardo is going to help me do this.'

Louisa froze. Why hadn't Eduardo mentioned this before? As far as she knew, he was going to find work when he got to America, yet somehow he'd kept this arrangement with Stanley Wyler a secret. Between Wyler's rudimentary Spanish and Eduardo's passable English, the men had brokered a deal that affected the lives of many, including her and Roberto. Unable to form words that wouldn't come out with anger, Louisa concentrated on the thick stitching on her red heels. What else had he done that she didn't know about?

'Do not be alarmed, Miss Gilchrist—'

'Louisa.' Perhaps she wasn't as good at hiding her emotions as she thought. If a complete stranger could pick up that she was worried, then how could she possibly conceal her feelings for Roberto, especially now they had consummated their love?

'Louisa. Please, do not despair. My studio will ensure you and Eduardo will be well cared for.' His tone sounded genuine and she wanted to trust this bear of a man, but, like everyone else she met, he had to earn it. Wyler pulled an envelope from inside his jacket and handed it to Eduardo. 'Your passage to a new world. Louisa, I hope you will enjoy life in my country. For years, I've waited for Argentina to open her doors and encourage us to conduct business. I am grateful Perón is now forging economic roads with the presi- dent's brother, Milton Eisenhower,' Wyler said.

'Not everyone agrees with what Perón is doing,' she said. 'He won the support of the workers by promoting equality and promised he'd find a way for the bosses and employees to work together to build a strong Argentina. Yet now he's going against his nationalistic and anti-imperialistic stance by allowing corporations from around the world to enter and take over.'

'Enough, Louisa,' Eduardo said, his tone stern. 'Mister Wyler is a guest in our house. Let us not fill his ears with nonsense.'

'Ha!' Wyler slapped his thigh and loosened his collar. 'I like a good old discussion. Tell me, Miss Gilchrist, were you once a supporter of Perón?'

'I am a supporter of whoever makes Argentina a better place for all citizens,' she said.

A wry smile crossed his lips. 'As long as the foreigners don't barge in and buy up state-owned businesses?' Wyler leaned toward her, his eyes daring her to answer.

'Do you want my honest answer, or the one I should say because you're Eduardo's guest?' The words escaped before she could reel them in.

Wyler roared with laughter. 'You are a live one. I like you. I am happy for you to answer truthfully.'

Louisa's back stiffened, unsure whether to continue. Wyler appeared to have a thick skin so she wasn't concerned about upsetting him. What worried her was Eduardo's possible reaction if she spoke her mind.

As if sensing her dilemma, Eduardo cleared his throat and she didn't need to look at him to know he was scowling.

'I'm not sure if you know my background, Mister Wyler,' she said.

'No, I do not. Eduardo is a private man but we are better acquainted now, aren't we, Pas?'

Her eyes widened at Wyler shortening Eduardo's name. Rather than Eduardo correcting his guest, he nodded politely and cracked a thin-lipped smile that was more of a grimace.

'In a way, my history is like Eva Peron's,' she said, hoping Eduardo would let the Pas thing slide. 'Eva arrived penniless in Buenos Aires and had to work her way up in the world. She met the right person at the right time and was pulled out of poverty and entered a world of luxury.'

'Quite the fairy-tale,' said Wyler.

'I guess so.'

'Too bad Eva Perón's fairy tale didn't have a happy ending,' said Eduardo.

Louisa sensed Roberto shift in his chair and she glanced over. His eyes studied her with the same intensity as the night before.

'I would like to ask a question, if I may,' Roberto said.

Wyler leaned forward. 'Ah, yes, the protégé. Why haven't we heard you play?'

'I'll answer this,' said Eduardo. 'Young Roberto here has a talent that needs nurturing. He is excellent at the *bandoneón* but his playing is still immature. A player needs years behind him, not only for practice but to gain life experience. He needs to know the agony of a broken heart, to have a life in ruins, to understand misery, and lose oneself in melancholy. This is what should be in the soul of a *bandoneón* player.'

'I would like to hear you play, Roberto.' Wyler turned to Eduardo. 'If it would not be too much trouble. Perhaps we could take you to Hollywood and you could play in my orchestra?'

'He's not ready. Besides, he has to stay here and manage my affairs,' Eduardo said evenly.

'I am ready.' Roberto narrowed his eyes at his mentor. 'You want me to perform in front of audiences in Argentina, yet you won't let me play for one man? Especially the man who could employ me to play *your* music for his movies?' Roberto stood, glowering at Eduardo. 'You want everything for yourself and damn everybody else.' His gaze briefly traveled to Louisa. She shook her head, hoping he'd back off but it was like trying to stem the tide.

'I've had enough.' Roberto threw up his hands. 'I'm done. Done with it all.' Anger flashed in Roberto's eyes as he glanced at Louisa before he stormed out and slammed the door. Her body flinched on the outside but on the inside panic set in for Roberto's precarious position.

'Yes, he is done,' said Eduardo, pouring whiskey into his crystal glass.

'You're letting him go?' Louisa suppressed the desire to bolt after her lover.

Eduardo took a long swig and grunted. 'Ungrateful swine.'

The trio fell into an uncomfortable silence as Eduardo drank, Wyler drummed his fingers on the pile of *Time* magazines, and Louisa looked through teary eyes at the gilded portrait of herself hanging above the white marble mantelpiece. The artist's deft brushstrokes had painted an image that didn't represent the true Louisa. In the painting, the woman was genteel, sophisticated, and removed, but in reality, Louisa was heartbroken, confused, and devastated.

The luncheon dragged on with more talk of politics, Hollywood, and leaving Argentina. Her throat hurt from concealing emotions, and she studied the intricate swirls engraved in the fine crystal champagne glass. She took another sip and dizziness and nausea overcame her. 'Please excuse me. I need fresh air.'

The men stood and she left the room, urging herself to keep a slow pace.

Louisa moved through the dark hallways, trying not to brush against the china vases sitting on the solid wood stands. She could never understand why people would put precious objects in main thoroughfares. It was an accident waiting to happen. She slipped out the French doors, down the marble steps, and over to the gazebo hidden behind vines in the rear of the garden. Sitting on the striped cushions, she breathed in the jasmine and let her muscles relax. She closed her eyes and leaned against the trellis, enjoying the light breeze dancing across her skin.

'I thought I would find you here, *mi lunita*.'

Her eyelids opened and her heart raced. Roberto stood at the gazebo's open doorway, a cheeky grin matching the spark in his eyes.

'Thank goodness!' She sat up but was overcome with wooziness and slumped against the trellis again.

'Too much champagne at lunch, *lunita*?'

'Maybe.' She patted the seat beside her, confident they wouldn't be seen from the house. 'Why do you call me little moon?'

His private smile stirred desire in her once more. 'It is because . . .' He gestured to the half-moon birthmark on her lower back, hidden by clothing.

She frowned but secretly enjoyed his knowledge of such an intimate place. 'I was going to find you after Wyler left.'

'He's likely to stay for dinner and breakfast.' Roberto slipped his hand in hers, their fingers entwining. He stroked his thumb against her skin and love flowed through her body.

'Angering Eduardo wasn't a particularly bright move, you know.'

'You're right, but I've had enough. My heart aches just thinking about your departure.'

'But he's given you an opportunity to fulfil your dream. Now you can perform in front of thousands in concert halls across the country.'

He wrenched his hand from hers and stared at the jasmine twisting around the trellis. 'If you don't want to be with me, you need only say.'

'Roberto—'

'No, Louisa. If you loved me, you would let all this go.' He gestured toward the house and expansive gardens. 'Damn Eduardo and his wealth. Damn Eduardo and his contacts. Damn Eduardo and his hold over you.'

'Roberto—'

'You're used to the good life. You never look uncomfortable when he showers you with presents. You parade throughout the concert halls in designer gowns and precious jewels. I can't give you this. Not yet. I can give you my love but obviously that's not enough.' He crossed his arms and scowled.

Unfortunately, his words held truth. Most young women in her position would have done the same, especially when the benefactor didn't expect sexual payment in return. Material wealth wasn't everything, but if she were entirely honest, returning to an uncertain life and poverty would be torture.

She sighed and fixed her eyes on his. 'Roberto, I love you more than heaven and earth and as much as I want to be with you, we do have other factors to consider.'

'Tell me what they are.'

'I can't, I'—this was getting too hard, too complicated—'I can't.'

'Not good enough.'

She looked to the bright blue sky, focusing on a wispy cloud. Keeping her promise to her father and honoring her word would most likely result in losing the love of her life. Confusion reigned and she massaged her temples.

Jealousy flashed in Roberto's eyes. 'Are you sleeping with him?'

'No! I was a virgin until last night.' She bit her lip and studied her hands clasped in her lap.

'I'm sorry. I'm angry at Eduardo, not you.' He placed his hands on hers. The warmth from his fingers traveled through her body and melted the chill at the base of her spine. 'I want to understand and respect your wishes but this situation drives me crazy. And after today's effort, he's going to ditch me. So I've lost you and my career.'

'It might not work out like that. I'll talk to him and smooth things over. Just stay away until I tell you it's safe.'

'Maybe I don't want to perform and run his affairs.' He furrowed his brows. 'Who's to say I can't make my own way on the circuit? I'll play in seedy bars again if I have to and I'll save every cent so you can be with me.'

Roberto reached into his jacket pocket and pulled out a cigarette. Lighting it, he inhaled deeply and let the smoke swirl above them in acrid cloud.

'When did you start smoking again?' She reached for the offending cigarette but Roberto pulled it away.

'Since this stress has gotten to me.' He turned his head to the side and took a puff.

'It makes you smell like a chimney. Please put it out.'

He gave a nonchalant shrug and kept puffing on his act of rebellion. They sat in silence while Roberto smoked and Louisa worried. He leaned forward and flicked the butt into the empty garden bed.

She decided to try another tack. 'Tango runs through your

blood. You live and breathe it. Could you really turn your back on it all? Your passion for the music is one of the qualities I love about you.' She placed her finger under his chin and lifted his head to meet her eyes. 'This is your dream. Do you want to destroy it because of a spat with Eduardo? He'll leave soon, then you can take the reins with his blessing and let the world see what a talented musician you are.'

'But he's taking you.'

'I don't know how it will happen but I will return. You have my word, and that's the most precious thing I can give.'

'Apart from your heart.'

'You already have that.' She smiled and gently ran her fingers down the side of his face.

'I miss you already.'

'I miss you, too, even when I'm with you. It's hard being in the same room and knowing what we share . . . shared . . . we can't relive again. Let's enjoy the last moments we'll have together for a while.' She edged closer. Sandalwood mixed with cigarettes drifted across the late afternoon breeze.

With pounding temples and a racing heart, she angled her body forward, anticipating the moment when their lips would meet. A small sigh escaped her mouth before they connected. His arms enveloped her, their bodies pressed against each other. Losing herself in the intoxicating passion, desire set every molecule of her being on fire. Her skin craved his touch. She wanted him. Here. Now.

Someone loudly cleared their throat.

Roberto and Louisa sprang apart. She spun around to find Stanley Wyler standing on the bottom step of the gazebo, staring up at them with glazed eyes.

'Canziani had a visit from his accountant so he sent me out into the garden to find you,' said Wyler, his gaze traveling from Louisa to Roberto and back again.

'I—we—'

'You don't need to explain. I don't know whether the old boy can see it, but for me, the chemistry between you two is obvious.'

Wyler climbed the last steps and placed his large frame on the cushions opposite.

'Are you going to tell him?' Louisa's voice shook.

Wyler took off his hat and wiped the back of his neck with a handkerchief. 'What you two do doesn't concern me. I now understand your reaction before, Roberto.'

'Could you employ me to work with your orchestra?' Roberto's tone bordered on desperate.

Wyler pushed his palms down his thighs. 'Ah, that is not possible. Even if you are as good as everyone says, I cannot risk getting Pas angry.' As if sensing their fear, he said, 'Don't worry, your secret is safe with me.'

'Thank you,' Louisa and Roberto said simultaneously.

'Although, Louisa, I thought you were'—he coughed into his fist —'How shall I delicately put this? Romantically inclined with the Argentine royalty in there.' He cocked his head toward the house.

'Uh . . .' She sensed Roberto straightening his spine. 'Lots of people think—'

'I don't care what they think. Hell, I don't care what I think. It's your life.' He raised his eyebrows. 'Pas has no idea, eh? I see the way he looks at you, Louisa. He's like a puppy dog. A cantankerous mutt, but a puppy dog nonetheless. He says he can't write or play without you nearby.'

Louisa gave a small shrug. 'I haven't had a chance to see if it isn't so.'

'Would you be game to?' Wyler didn't pause long enough for her to answer. 'What if it was true and he couldn't perform if you left him? Argentina would suffer the loss of their greatest musician, and in these turbulent times, they need national icons to unite them. Believe me, I've seen what instability can do to unhappy people. And, of course, on a purely selfish note, I don't want him to fall apart before we get these tango movies underway. Imagine how proud the Argentines will be when Pas succeeds in getting the world to fall in love with tango once more.' Wyler slapped on his hat. 'I should keep my big mouth shut but I have to say, Argentina, and my studio, can't afford to have Pas fail, and I imagine if he knew about what you two have been up to, his fall would be hard and fast.'

'I know.' She lowered her eyes. 'We had no intentions of going this far.'

Roberto's eyes pleaded Louisa not to elaborate. 'You two should go to the house.'

Leaning toward Wyler, Louisa wrapped her hands around his, surprised at their smoothness. Looking at him earnestly, she said, 'I can't thank you enough for your judiciousness.'

'I heard enough of your conversation with Roberto to know this is not a fling. However, I do suggest you think about what you're doing. Whatever you do will not only affect the two of you but will have great repercussions on the future of your country's lifeblood—the tango.'

CHAPTER 10

Present Day - Dani

Dani dialed her grandma's phone number. As it rang, she hoped it didn't answer. This way, Dani could say she tried to contact Stella and not have to deal with the continuing fallout.

'Hello?'

Damn.

'Hi . . . Grandma?'

'Dani?' Stella's icy tone sent chills down Dani's spine.

'Yes.'

'Where are you?'

Squeezing her eyes shut, she said, 'Argentina.'

'You run in to that mother of yours?'

'No.'

'Good. You're not learning how to dance *it* are you?'

'Um . . .' She couldn't lie to her grandma no matter how cranky Stella got.

'You are playing with fire, girl. That dance is a curse on our family.'

'I don't believe in curses. And anyway, have you seen me dance?

The most musical I've ever gotten was trying to work out how to use my phone and remember how that turned out?' She pictured the mass of wires on her desk at home.

'Things change. When are you going back to New York?'

'Not for a while. I've got to get the stories done and—'

'Don't give excuses, Dani. We made a promise to each other years ago. No tango. No Argentina.' Her voice lowered an octave. 'No Iris.'

'I was five years old for god's sake!'

'Dani!'

'For goodness' sake.' She gritted her teeth. 'Life changes. People change. Grandma, I'm not ringing for a lecture, all I wanted was to tell you I'm okay.'

Stella breathed through her nostrils and Dani could sense a shift in her grandma's demeanor. Even though they were continents apart they could still read each other.

'Sweetheart, I'm not trying to make you feel bad. I understand that you needed to do something rebellious after your breakup but I just don't think you've seriously thought about the ramifications of this trip to Argentina.'

Dani bit her lip for a moment while she debated how best to reply. 'There are many good reasons why this trip makes sense.'

'But do they outweigh the negative?'

'Can we drop this for now? Please?'

'I know you're a big girl and can look after yourself but I'm your grandma, it's my job to worry.'

'You don't need to, I promise.' Dani let the smile reflect in her voice. 'But thank you for caring.'

'Why wouldn't I? You're a good egg, Dani. I just want you to be happy.'

'Thanks, grandma. I miss you.'

'And I, you. Will you be home for Christmas? I thought we might go stay at those cabins near the lake. Do you remember that place?'

'Of course I do!' Dani said. At the time they'd been almost

broke but Stella had scrimped and saved to surprise Dani with a two-week 'happy graduation' vacation. 'Lake Eildon, right?'

'Yes, yes, that's it! Next time we'll bring more books.'

'And more chocolate!'

'Dani, I . . .' A sigh traveled down the line. 'I'm sorry if you think I'm harsh about this Argentina business but it's just . . . just the way I feel.'

'I understand.' And she most certainly did but that didn't change her feelings about being in Buenos Aires. Dani had her own life and if she messed it up then she was the only one to blame. 'So, grandma, I do have a question I'm hoping you might answer.'

'Why do I get the feeling I won't like it?'

Squeezing her eyes shut, Dani braced herself for her grandma's possible reaction. 'I've been doing some research on the history of tango—'

'I don't want to know about it. This is your work, not mine.' Stella's voice held a steely edge again.

'Let me finish, please? I was just wondering if you've heard of the tango composer and singer Eduardo Canziani?' Dani grimaced the moment the words fell from her mouth and she felt ridiculous. The pause on the other end was long enough for Dani to feel uncomfortable.

'Why are you asking me this?' Agitation shot down the line and zapped Dani, who instantly felt guilty for riling her grandma up again. She should have known better.

'He was around your era and I thought you may know of him or maybe you heard Iris play his music?'

'Why is it important? If you have to cover the tango, why don't you find some young upstart who's about to become famous? Keep it edgy, as you like to say. Why didn't you stick with teaching English?' Bitterness punctuated Stella's sentences and the barbed remarks pierced Dani's self-esteem.

'It was just a question. Listen, I have to go. I'll call you later.'

'Call me when you're in New York and not before.'

'Bye, Grandma.'

'Text Ness once in a while to let her know you're okay.'

The phone clicked in Dani's ear. 'Well, that was about as successful as last month's diet.'

Dani closed the laptop, pushed it aside and stretched her legs. Despite being cranky with her granddaughter, Stella had asked that Ness, her young neighbor, be kept up to date about Dani's well-being which of course, would be passed on to Stella. Typical grandma. Everything needed to be on her terms.

Running the conversation through her head, she analyzed Stella's every word and reaction about tango. Nothing stood out other than her grandma's irritation, which was expected. It wasn't like she thought Stella would burst into tears and confess she was Louisa Gilchrist and had killed Eduardo Canziani. Didn't criminals usually confess during the third conversation?

'I watch too much *CSI*.' She rolled her eyes and shook her head.

This talking with oneself was disconcerting. Some real-life company was needed, otherwise she'd end up like the old lady she'd seen in the park yesterday, who'd flicked seeds at the pigeons and had a grand old conversation with herself. Actually, the old woman had seemed rather content.

She glanced at the clock: five-oh-seven a.m. Way too early for anyone she knew in Buenos Aires to be awake. And all her friends in New York would be snoozing. *Pfft.*

Pulling out her phone, she selected 'Contacts' and stared at Carlos's name. If she texted him now, he'd get her message when he woke later. Sure, she could text Gualberto, but she didn't think his wife would appreciate another woman contacting him in the early hours, no matter how innocent. Texting Carlos sat better, even though he insisted on this stupid dancing-for-answers caper. At the rate she was going, she'd be in Argentina until Christmas 2025.

Carlos, what are the chances of us meeting for lunch today? Dani

Placing the phone on the bedside table, she turned off the light and snuggled under the covers. She'd do well to get some shut-eye so she could have a clear head for today's research.

The phone vibrated and a green light pierced the dark room.

Let us meet in 30 minutes. La Biela, Recoleta. Chau, Carlos

Dani blinked rapidly, surprised he'd replied so fast. Dashing to the bathroom, she stripped off her nightie and flung open the door to the shower. Cold water tingled her skin as she soaped up, all the while wondering why Carlos would be awake in the wee hours of the morning. Probably talking to himself, just like her. She laughed and spat out the soap that landed on her tongue. Today could be an interesting one.

Scooting past two red phone boxes that would have been more at home in London, Dani made it to the rendezvous twenty-eight minutes after receiving Carlos's text. She entered the café, excited to see if it lived up to the hype she'd read on blogs. Dani expected it to be almost empty but it was chock-a-block with patrons who had finished clubbing or were about to start their workday. The aroma of fresh coffee wafted around her as waiters in black trousers, crisp white shirts, and pristine aprons hurried between tables, balancing trays loaded with drinks and pastries. She eyed the sweets, her taste buds doing a happy dance with the anticipation of crusty flakes melting in her mouth.

Weaving between tables, she tried to spot her target, although she didn't really expect Carlos to be on time. She'd yet to meet an Argentine who knew the meaning of punctuality. Making a beeline for a small table at the back corner, Dani sat and the moment she did so, a waiter approached and peered down his nose at her. He placed a glass of water and a menu on the table, then turned on his heels and headed to the bar, busying himself with glasses and serviettes.

Above the bar hung a series of dramatic black-and-white photos of parks in Buenos Aires. Scattered on other walls were images of the Ferrari and Lamborghini families, a variety of antique brass horns, and a collection of postage stamps depicting classic cars from the twenties and thirties. Photos of Juan Manuel Fangio next to his Formula One cars hung on the walls too, paying homage to the Argentine who was still considered one of the world's best race car drivers. With the amount of car memorabilia spread throughout, no wonder the café name had changed from Aero Bar to La Biela—the connecting rod. Starbucks had nothing on this place.

Dani settled in and kept an eye on the door. Every time it opened, more revelers floated through in an alcohol-induced haze, but no Carlos. Eventually, a figure dressed head to toe in black graced the threshold. He paused, his dark eyes methodically searching the room. Dani waved to get his attention and, with a nod and a small smile, he limped between the hodgepodge of tables, oblivious to the wide-eyed female patrons watching his every move. She was pretty sure the dagger looks thrown at her weren't imaginary. Dani stifled a smirk.

'You are not one for sleeping?' He slid onto the neighboring chair, his musky cologne overpowering the coffee aroma.

'Sleep never comes easy but tonight it was impossible.'

'Hmm . . . The brain of a writer can never rest.' Carlos motioned to the waiter, who rushed over, took his order, then returned balancing a tray with coffee and pastries. He placed them on the table and gave Carlos a small nod of recognition.

'Do you get noticed everywhere you go?' she asked.

'Is this a question?'

'No!' Regaining composure, she said, 'Well, it is but why don't we forget the business side of things and hang out for a while?'

'Why?' He seemed genuinely perplexed.

'Because if we're going to work together, then knowing each other on a personal level might be nice.'

'Again, I ask why?'

Dani tilted her head and widened her eyes. 'Really?'

He shuffled back on the chair. 'If you must know about my life, I teach tango, I go home, I read. This is all.'

'Come on, Carlos, what's your passion? What makes you get up in the morning?'

'Hope,' he said.

'About what?'

'Hope that I will someday have a family like the one I grew up in.'

'You like your family?' She did a cruddy job of hiding her surprise.

'*Sí*. Do you not like yours?'

'It's complicated.' Dani fiddled with the coffee cup.

'Ah,' he said. 'Tell me more.'

'Tell me about yours first.' While he talked she could decide if now was the time to open up about Iris.

'Okay, I do not mind the sharing. I have no brothers, no sisters. My mother made costumes for the Teatro Colón, and my father made the shoes. They are now deceased.'

'Oh, I'm sorry. It must be hard.'

'It is at times. I miss having family. Although we were only three, we were close. I wish . . .' A small sigh escaped his lips and he studied the photos on the closest wall. 'Never mind. I have no family and no wishing can change this. Family is very important.'

'Sometimes having a family can be detrimental.'

'No. A family is the one place we can feel safe to be who we are. To be loved. To be cared for.'

'Not everyone has caring families.' Maybe she should wait a fraction longer for the big reveal.

'Family is family, even if they are, how you say, dysfunctional.'

'Sorry, Carlos.' Dani straightened her back. 'But I don't agree. Families are a bunch of DNA thrown together in the hope they don't kill each other.'

'What about the families who have adopted children? Should they get along more because they have been chosen?'

'It doesn't matter if someone is adopted or not, no one knows how a family will behave as a unit until they're together. And if that fails, then the family members are better off without each other.'

'What has made you so cynical?' he asked.

'Experience.' She crossed her arms to signal she would not discuss this further.

Carlos rubbed his chin with his thumb and forefinger. 'Families should learn to get along. Without family, what do we have? This is why I live with the hope that I will one day create my own happy family.'

'Yes, it sounds nice.' It truly did—for Carlos. The concept still eluded her, though. Sure, she and Stella were a tight unit and were a family but what about having a mother and father? Surely being brought up by your own parents put a different slant on family.

'I will tell you this, Daniela McKenna. My first memory from childhood is crawling on the floor at the theater. I was only this high.' He held out his hand to indicate the height of a toddler. 'All my childhood, the dance was around me. Always, there would be sequins caught in my clothes, or my nose would be filled with the smell of shoe glue.'

'So tango keeps the memory of your parents alive.' She placed her hand on his arm. He tensed then relaxed. Physical attraction stirred in her belly and mixed with a new sensation—a very deep fondness for this man. *Oh god, no.*

'In a way, yes, tango keeps memories alive but it is also, how you say, a double-edged sword. I have fond recollections of tango and my childhood but as an adult, tango became very complicated. My career was destroyed as well as my relationship with—' His mouth closed quickly. Coughing, he said, 'It is not important. But *así es la vida*, no? Such is life?' He lowered his eyes and shook his head, then looked up with a smile. 'I should not complain. Many are worse off than me. I am grateful for all in my life.'

'Even the bad stuff?' She wondered why he didn't mention Cecilia when the whole world knew about it.

'Yes, but it does not mean I'm happy about the bad things.'

'It's weird how one day we can be cruising along and then . . . *bam!* We trip and fall face first into a puddle of torment.'

'Such a philosopher.' He winked and her face flushed with heat.

Reaching for the pastry, she broke off a piece and popped it into her mouth. Caramel and icing sugar mixed with butter tantalized her taste buds and she tried not to roll her eyes as the combination melted in her mouth.

'I had no idea this stuff was so good. I think I've found a new addiction. Thanks a lot, Carlos. Now I'm going to put on ten kilos.'

'My pleasure,' he said.

'Here.' She pushed the plate toward him. He shook his head and held up his hand.

'You don't want one?' she asked.

'No.'

'Why did you order two?'

'They are for you.' He moved the plate in her direction. 'Many girls in Argentina are too skinny. All the day they talk and dream about food that will not touch their lips. They go to the shops and try to fit into tiny jeans made for a six-year-old, and they are never far from a mirror. This is crazy, which is why people in my country have the most psychologists per capita in the world.'

'Yes, I had heard. How do you think this obsession started?' Finally, they had focused on something other than tango and family.

'I do not know. There are many questions in the world we cannot answer. For example, why are Australian journalists ask so inquisitive? Did you make your mother crazy with all your questioning when growing up?'

'My grandma raised me.' She lowered her eyes.

'I am sorry. Did you mother die?' He reached over and rubbed his hand against the exposed skin of her arm. Goose bumps sprouted at his touch.

'In my grandma's eyes she did.' This was getting too painful, too personal. No way was she ready to tell him about Iris.

As if he sensed her reluctance, Carlos tilted his head to the side and narrowed his eyes. 'Maybe Diego Alonso is right. In a different light, you remind me of *La Gringa Magnifica*.'

She'd been floating along nicely and enjoying Carlos's company. Now she plummeted to the ground like a shot duck in hunting season. Maybe she would have been better off staying in her room and wallowing.

'I wouldn't mind having a break from talking about tango.'

'If we talk about life then tango must be involved.'

'Not for those outside of Argentina.'

He shrugged. 'Maybe, but you are here now and you cannot deny tango is everywhere.'

'I guess so.' She tore off a small piece of pastry and tossed it in her mouth. Tango was most definitely outside of Argentina, in fact, it had slithered its sticky tentacles into her life, strangled her family, then ripped it apart.

'Melancholy,' Carlos said, pulling her back into the cafe.

'What?'

'Melancholy is essential to tango, just like life. How do we know how to recognize joy when it arrives? A great tango embraces a series of emotions—love, heartbreak, unhappiness, felicity. How are we to grow without experiencing this range of feelings? Imagine if we danced the same steps or felt the same emotions every day.'

'It would be boring and we'd be stunted.'

'Exactly. This is why tango and life are similar. The world would be a better place if everyone understood and appreciated tango.'

'You could be right,' she said, not convinced. Her own life was testament to why tango should be shoved in a corner and ignored.

Carlos wrapped his warm hand around hers. 'Do you miss your home?'

'No, not really. There's too much drama there so it's better I distance myself.'

'You miss one person in particular, *sí?*' He glanced at their entwined fingers and let go, as if he'd registered what he was doing.

'Nope. Well, yes, sort of. But it's the past, right? Such is life and all that?' Dani forced her mood out of the doldrums. Carlos caught her eye and, for a moment, the world stopped. *Adam used to give me that look.* Scared by the intensity, she looked away, breaking the spell.

Carlos pointed at the photos on the wall. 'These were taken by the writer Adolfo Bioy Casares. He was a good friend of Jorge Luis Borges. Both men are icons in our country's literature.'

'Ah yes, I've heard of them.' Her gaze didn't shift from the images. 'The photos are absolutely beautiful.'

'On the surface, *sí*. Although darkness hides behind the beauty.'

'Like what?'

'See this photo?' He tapped the image next to him.

Dani angled her body to get a better look. The picture was too far away, so she rose and stood next to Carlos. Gazing at the photo, she studied the strong branches supporting eucalyptus leaves that fanned out over the park bench. 'It looks like a cave, huh?'

'This is the tree in the park near where Eduardo Canziani lived. You remember the man in the photo you snooped on, yes?'

She winced inwardly. 'Yes.'

'It is also the same park where Louisa Gilchrist and Roberto Vega met in secret. That tree you call beautiful witnessed a plot to murder Eduardo Canziani.'

CHAPTER 11

Present Day - Dani

'Do you really think they did it?' Dani sat on the chair and downed the last of her lukewarm coffee. Out the window, snippets of sunlight cut through the gray sky.

'Louisa and Roberto? All the evidence points to this.' His tone held unwavering certainty. 'If they are alive, and if they are found, they should be going to the courts and thrown in the jail until their deaths. They killed Argentina's greatest musician and composer and deprived the world of a special gift.'

'But what if new evidence proves they didn't do it?' she asked.

'You think they are innocent?'

'I don't know. I haven't looked into it much yet—'

'Yet? You will? What about the articles we were working on for Tourism Argentina? You will throw this away to write about Argentina's biggest scandal and bring disgrace upon my country- men? Eduardo Canziani's death is Argentina's concern. It is not the business of the foreigners.' Carlos straightened his spine and a wall shot up between them.

'You don't have a problem if I write about the tango your way but you have an issue with me doing my own investigation about a cold case? Don't you want to know what happened? And if Louisa and Roberto are guilty, find them and bring them to justice?' His change in attitude meant the lovely time she'd just spent in his company disintegrated into a steaming pile of dog doo. No way was she telling him about Iris.

'It should only concern my people.'

'I get you're patriotic but I don't understand why outsiders discovering new information is a problem.'

'You would not understand.' His eyes lost their spark and his expression turned stony.

'Try me.'

'It is too complicated. I am asking you to leave this story alone. It is not for the *gringos* to stick their noses in.' In his mouth, the word *gringo* didn't sound like a term of endearment.

Dani forced herself to remain calm. *Play it right, Dani.* 'Okay, I hear what you're saying.'

'Good. Do not ask more questions about the Canziani case.' He crossed his arms, signaling the end of their conversation and, Dani suspected, their blossoming friendship if she didn't leave this subject alone.

They sat in silence while the clanking of utensils and crockery filled the air, accompanied by the low mumble of patrons. Unable to bear the tension, she said, 'I think I might go. I need to get more work done.'

'On the Canziani case?' He stared into the distance, not meeting her eyes.

'No. I'm concentrating on the Tourism Argentina pieces. The Canziani thing was a distraction. You know how journalists are, can't keep their noses out of stuff.' She kept her tone light.

'Right.'

She stood and waited but his eyes wouldn't meet hers.

'So I'll see you soon?' She leaned over and kissed him on the cheek, as was the Argentine custom.

Dani left the café, hurt by his stony reaction. Their time had gone beautifully until she'd spoiled it with her idiotic musings about a cold case. Maybe Carlos was right. Perhaps she should leave it to the Argentines. Flashes of Louisa's smiling face haunted Dani and she shook her head, unable to budge the image. How the hell could a photo of a woman from so many years ago have such an impact?

The early morning heat slapped against her skin and she scrounged in her handbag for sunglasses. Putting them on, she noticed the women's attire had changed from sequins and stilettos to business suits and stilettos. No matter what time of the day or night, Argentine women looked fabulous. Glancing down at her jeans and T-shirt, Dani shrugged then realized she'd donned her red heels instead of her faithful runners as she'd raced out the door this morning. Argentina had influenced her already. Just how much influence she would allow, Dani wasn't sure.

She turned and hustled through the streets of Recoleta, barely noticing the Baroque buildings streaked with smog. Dani kept up the pace, fueled by desire to get to her hotel, have a cold shower, and collapse onto fresh white bed sheets.

As she marched along, she tried to let go of the angst about pushing Carlos too far. Although what annoyed her more was allowing an attraction for Carlos to form, especially since she wasn't entirely over Adam. Perhaps Carlos as rebound man made total sense. After all, his occasional aloofness, and him living in another country meant Dani could have a fling, get over Adam, find a new job in New York, and get a new life. It all sounded so calculated and, really, executing that plan didn't appeal to her one bit because her intuition told her the attraction to Carlos was more than fleeting.

'Men. Pfft.'

A gaggle of young women in tight short skirts, holding sequined clutches stared at her. Dani gave a lopsided smile. They giggled and went on their merry way.

She powered along with the hope that moving forward physically would encourage her mind to do the same. Easier said than done. Iris, Stella, Adam, and the pressure to produce kick-ass stories . . . they melded into one heavy ball in her stomach. She stopped in the middle of the path, her energy drained.

'*Che boluda, ¿qué haces?*'

She turned and found an old man in an immaculately pressed

suit. His gnarled hands gripped a dog leash but no animal was present. Scowling, he directed more expletives at her.

'*Perdóname*,' she said. Forgive me, I'm sorry. Of course she was bloody sorry. Sorry for a helluva lot of things. Though blocking the path of an octogenarian was the least damaging on her sorry list.

He huffed past and she gazed at the wrought-iron balconies. Buenos Aires had many layers, some astoundingly beautiful, and one needed to stop and appreciate its grandeur. Her breath caught in her throat and she coughed, resigning herself to the fact the city might be gorgeous but it sure as hell stunk like the inside of an exhaust pipe.

A cool breeze skimmed across her skin and the scent of rain hung in the air as thunderclouds swirled above. Tango music drifted into her ears, so close it drowned out the serenade of car horns. Closing her eyes, she lost herself in the moment, a little peace washing through her mind and over her weary body. Then the *bandoneón* cut in and her jaw clenched.

Her phone beeped, signaling an incoming email. The way her cheeks heated, she had a fair idea who it was from.

Picking up pace, Dani crossed the street, artfully dodging the traffic that rarely stopped for anyone. Skipping onto the curb, she turned a corner just as lightning flashed across the sky. Half a second later a crack of thunder reverberated above and fat drops fell, splattering everyone in sight.

She dashed to the nearest canopy that happened to be part of a five-star hotel. Taking cover from the deluge, Dani looked around for a taxi, but because she needed one, of course none were available. The scent of coffee and chocolate flooded her nostrils and she peered through the hotel's entrance. A young barista stood behind a counter, polishing a coffee machine with care and although she'd already consumed half her body weight in caffeine over the last twenty-four hours, she felt the need for more. What harm could it do?

The barista gave her a welcoming smile as she entered the café and a waiter appeared and guided her to a table. She ordered a coffee and waited for the barista to work his magic. There weren't any newspapers lying around like in most cafés in the city, so Dani's mind turned to the message on the phone burning a hole in her pocket. She stared out the window, watching people jump swollen gutters and dashing for cover. Then she studied the brass fittings on the bar and the grains in the antique wood.

Unable to bear it any longer, she pulled out the phone and checked her inbox. Sure enough, an email from Adam.

Dani,

I'm watching this space like you asked and all I can see are blank pages in my magazine. Management is on my tail and I can't wait. You promised me something excellent. Something big. And I need you to deliver. You've got three weeks to inbox me with the stories. And, just to add sunshine to your day, I'm reminding you Tourism Argentina's generous offer to sponsor your accommodation finishes soon so you might need to pitch a tent in the park. Sorry I don't have better news but business is business.

Cheers,

Adam

Adam's missive had changed things dramatically. Her gut told her that even though Carlos and Gualberto had offered to help her put an original spin on the tango and the *bandoneón* stories, the Canziani case had a much wider scope for increasing circulation. The answer seemed obvious: Go big, or go home. But she needed new evidence, or to find Louisa and Roberto. The case had sat for decades, so how the hell could she find concrete leads in a couple of weeks? It was a massive risk but she was broken-hearted and desperate to make a name for herself, so going out on a limb seemed logical. She'd never been averse to putting herself out there, so why should now be different? It was probably guilt slapping her in the face because Tourism Argentina had funded her stay and flights in exchange for stories on tango as a lifestyle. There was no way she'd have time to do both well.

The waiter arrived with her coffee and a *medialuna*, a pastry in the shape of a half moon. She smiled her thanks, took a sip, and stared out at the sodden street, where cars zoomed through puddles and soaked passersby. An older gentleman entered the café and the scent of fresh rain reminded her of when she was a kid, squealing as she splashed in puddles with her grandma nearby, lost in a world only she could access.

Stella.

Although her grandma was cranky about this Argentina trip, Dani missed Stella immensely. Dani smiled, wondering how she could let her overactive imagination run so rampant with the idea that Stella and Louisa were possibly related—or the same person. It appealed to Dani's inquisitive nature, which was great for a career in journalism but not so wonderful for trying to calm turbulent waters with her grandma. Dani Photoshopped Stella in her head, erasing the wrinkles and coloring the gray hair to honey blonde. Stella's almond-shaped eyes, long black lashes that curled at the outer corners, and nose with the straight bridge and distinctive dip were identical to Louisa Gilchrist's. But maybe she was distorting the image to fit her imagination. Dani had no photos of a young Stella to compare as her grandma had lost them when she immigrated to Australia from England in the nineteen fifties. But what if . . . *no.* Ridiculous.

Then Stella's intense dislike of tango crashed in on Dani. Until now, she'd thought Stella's hostility toward the dance was to do with Iris nicking off to Argentina and building her career. But what if it wasn't just that? What if Stella *was* Louisa? Dani had always believed murder was black or white. Guilty or not guilty. But if it ever came to pass that Stella was Louisa, Dani's view would turn to gray, without a doubt. She shook her head, convinced the tiredness was making her crazy. No way in hell could she imagine her round-faced grandmother killing anyone, no matter what the provocation.

'So this is what it feels like, teetering on the edge of insanity,' she muttered to herself and sipped the strong liquid. She let the coffee slide down her throat, reveling in the delicious warmth.

Dani had to leave well enough alone. Pursuing the Canziani case was ridiculous. Even if she worked twenty-four hours a day and had an army of sleuths investigating, the chances of uncovering anything, or anyone, of value to the case were minimal. It bummed her to drop it but she'd have to pursue the tango and *bandoneón* stories as originally planned and if that was the case, Dani had better make peace with one very handsome tango instructor.

CHAPTER 12

1953 - Louisa

Louisa settled onto the only sofa in the room. Striped cotton sheets hung haphazardly in front of the windows, barely blocking out the daylight shining through the thin material. She shifted again, but the lumpy stuffing made it impossible to get comfortable. In the corner of the small room sat Roberto's *bandoneón*, a magnificent piece of craftsmanship. When she'd first arrived in Argentina she'd thought the instrument was an accordion, but the Argentines made sure she understood the *bandoneón* came from a different family and was the heart and soul of tango.

Getting up, Louisa walked over and crouched in front of Roberto's prized possession. She ran her fingers over the buttons on both sides, imagining his fingers doing the same. When he played, love and passion poured into this instrument and created musical magic others could never replicate. The world needed to experience his talent, get lost in his music, and be transported to another realm.

She spied some papers and an envelope lying on the small table. She could tell from the stamp that the envelope contained yet another missive from Roberto's only surviving relative, Great Aunt Elda in Milan. According to Roberto, she was a crotchety, God-fearing soul who despised his lifestyle as a musician. But they were family, and in Roberto's eyes, that meant the world.

Picking up the other papers, she took in the curved lines and squiggles drawn on a crinkled sheet. It took her a while to figure out it was a map of Brazil. In the middle of the drawing was the name Chapada do Russo and it was underlined three times. In the top right-hand corner he'd written 'Louisa' in a love heart. Smiling, she folded the paper and put it into her pocket. Later, she'd sketch their dream home beside the name of the village then sneak it back into Roberto's house. She looked forward to his reaction.

Someone cleared their throat behind her and she stood, smoothed down her dress and turned to face the doorway. Héctor Sosa's lanky body leaned against the wall, his dark hair pulled back in an unfashionable ponytail he wore with confidence. The smile lines on his face grew deeper the minute their eyes connected.

'Héctor!' Louisa rushed over and threw her arms around him. 'It's been so long!'

'Yes, yes, it has indeed. Come.' He took her hand and they sat on the sofa. 'You look more lovely every time I see you. What is your secret? Ah! Don't tell me. It is love, yes?'

She didn't need a mirror to know she was blushing. 'Héctor—'

'You should forget about that scoundrel Roberto and be with me. He's no use to you. He's young, no experience. Me, on the other hand . . .' He ran a finger along her arm and she playfully slapped it.

'Enough!' She laughed and inched away, unable to recall a time when he hadn't made advances in a joking manner. Although, at times, she wondered if there was a smidgen of sincerity in his overtures.

'You and me together, our love is as natural as the sun rising and setting. As the butterflies flapping their wings. As the—'

'Such a poet!' She laughed. 'I've missed you! How was Uruguay?'

A dark cloud drifted across his handsome face and he pushed the ponytail over his shoulder. 'Let us say, it did not turn out how I wished. But I am here, in the presence of beauty and grace. Where is that rogue of yours? He left the door unlocked and I waltzed in. Lucky I didn't take the priceless china.' He nodded at two chipped cups and saucers, their interiors stained by tea.

'It's not a palace, but it is home for our most favorite *bandoneón* player,' she said.

'Lucky you said this, *mi amor*, or else I would have to throw you onto the street.' Roberto strode over to Héctor, who stood and embraced him in a bear hug so strong Roberto's face flushed red.

'It is good to see you again, old friend. I would have called but . . .' Héctor held out his hands in a questioning manner. 'You live in the dark ages, Roberto. Get a telephone. It would make life much easier.'

They slapped each other on the back and laughed. Héctor took a seat on the faded chair and Roberto sat next to Louisa on the sofa, gently running his fingers along her arm, unaware Héctor had done the same only a few minutes before. Goosebumps pricked her flesh at Roberto's touch and shivers ran up her spine. Her heart ached that this was one of the last moments she could enjoy this simple pleasure.

'Are you moving to Uruguay?' Roberto asked with a perfect Uruguayan accent.

'Ha!' Héctor slapped the chair arm. 'Your talent for mimicking others is most impressive.'

'It's because he's so good at music,' said Louisa, pointing to her ears. 'Excellent listening skills.'

'Roberto should listen to me when I tell him to forget Eduardo.' Héctor tapped his pipe on the arm of the chair. 'So this meeting you told me about, how did it go?'

'I'm staying with my mentor,' Roberto said.

'You're a fool.' Héctor stuffed tobacco in the pipe and lit it. The small room filled with pungent smoke and Louisa went over and opened a window. A light breeze billowed the sheets and she sat next to Roberto again, placing her hand in his.

'I do not have a choice. He keeps me off the streets and I'm not going to throw away my dreams because I can't stand the man who holds the key to my future. As much as I want to go it alone, I haven't performed live for ages. I can guarantee if I left him my life would be a living nightmare. He practically runs the tango industry here. Hell, he *is* the tango industry and he'll still lord it over me when he's in North America.'

'Pah!' said Héctor, puffing heavily on the pipe.

'Look, he took me under his wing as his protégé. As angry as I am with him for taking away Louisa, he's given me a once-in-a-life-time opportunity.'

'I could have given you this had I met you first.'

'Yes, but—'

'But I'm not Eduardo Canziani. I've heard it all before. If that bastard hadn't ripped me off, I would be in his place, whooping it up with the elite, and he'd be in mine, playing second fiddle, or second *bandoneón* as is the case.'

'We could tell people what he did,' Roberto said.

'Pfft!' Héctor waved his hand in the air. 'No one would ever believe Eduardo Canziani would steal music. In their eyes, I'm a jilted business partner. Not one person believed me when it first happened, why would they change their minds now? I have to accept that my lot in life is to watch a miscreant like Canziani get all the fame while I wallow in oblivion.'

'I'm sorry it turned out this way,' Louisa said.

He took the pipe out of his mouth and levelled his gaze on her. 'What are you going to do about America? I don't see you changing Eduardo's mind.'

'It's complicated.' Louisa kept her voice even as Roberto sighed and slumped next to her.

'How so?' asked Héctor.

'She's going with him and I'll stay here. At least then I'll earn seventy-five percent from my performances and in three years I'll have saved enough money and we'll be able to reunite on our own terms.' Roberto's words sounded rehearsed, as if he was trying to convince himself as well as the others in the room.

Hearing the hope clinging to his words, guilt rushed through Louisa. As wonderful as Roberto's plan sounded, she had no idea how long Eduardo would last in Hollywood. If Eduardo's dementia kept progressing rapidly, they could be back in less than three years. This would be enough time to organize for Eduardo's care and for her to make plans to marry Roberto. Time was all they needed, but why did it feel like the clock had sped up?

'So it's love in the slums or loneliness in the lights, eh?' Héctor scratched his head. 'Sorry, I don't mean to be flip, but there must be another way.'

'I'm afraid not,' said Louisa. 'Roberto's spent his entire life pursuing this career and he's only known me a couple of years. This might be his only chance to let the world see what a wonderful player he is and I don't want to mess it up for him.'

'I always thought you had a martyr streak.' Héctor raised an eyebrow as turrets of smoke swirled above him. 'I get the feeling there's more going on than meets the eye.'

'She's not sleeping with him.' Roberto put his arm protectively around Louisa's shoulders. She edged in to show appreciation for his support.

'I didn't say she was.' Héctor frowned. 'Look, he's a lying bastard. He steals, he cheats. I don't care if the Argentine public adore him. He deserves a comeuppance.'

'Maybe,' she said, caught in the middle of this ongoing feud. Eduardo had no right to steal Héctor's music but Eduardo's current mental health pulled at her heartstrings.

'There's been another complication.' Roberto squeezed Louisa's hand.

'And that would be?' Héctor took the pipe out of his mouth and cocked an eyebrow.

Louisa's cheeks burned with the memory. 'The producer Stanley Wyler found us in Eduardo's garden. He saw and heard enough to work out what was going on between us.'

'Is he going to tell Canziani?'

'He said he wouldn't, but he did ask us to think about what we're doing. He thinks our affair is complicated because it could affect tango's future.'

'That's a tad melodramatic. But what does surprise me is you

and Roberto seem to have accepted Eduardo's demands too easily.'
Héctor's pipe had gone out so he struck a match and relit it.

'Somehow we will make this work and build our future
together.'

'You are as romantic as the lyrics you write, Roberto, but your
backbone is weak.'

'We've made our decision,' said Roberto, straightening. 'Say
what you like but I will prove you wrong. Louisa and I will have it all
—my career, fame, money, love—maybe not all at once, but it will
happen. Louisa's promised we will be together and this is enough to
spur me on to do what is needed.'

Héctor puffed on his pipe and looked from Roberto to Louisa
and back again. Nausea swelled in her belly as she realized the
mistake she'd made by promising Roberto they'd be together some-
time in the next three years. How could she say this when she had
no idea what the future held? Now she had two men expecting her
to live up to conflicting promises. The strain of being pulled in two
directions overwhelmed her. She massaged her temples and willed
the headache to disappear.

'He's starting to lose it,' said Héctor. 'I heard he made mistakes
the other week at the Teatro Colón.'

'You told him this?' Louisa turned to Roberto.

He shook his head. 'No.'

'Word gets around. You know how musicians talk,' said Héctor.

'I didn't think anyone would have noticed.' She tried to stifle her
rising panic. Oh, to have a world where mental disease was accepted
as an ailment and not a repulsive failing. No one could predict how
his fans would react, and if they chose the road of pity, it would
destroy Eduardo. He wanted to be remembered for his contribution
to tango, not for his illness. At least in America, where tango wasn't
known so widely, it would take longer for people to notice his errors.
It would buy him time. She wondered if he had already thought
about this.

'He hasn't written new music for months,' said Roberto. 'He
blames it on the political unrest, but I'm not so sure.'

'He hasn't blamed you, his precious muse?' Héctor raised his eyebrows at Louisa.

'No, not yet.'

'You need to watch out for yourself. We creative types can get cantankerous if our muse isn't inspiring us.'

'I can look after myself.' Louisa sounded more confident than she felt.

'Well if your plan works out, and it possibly could, you two will end up together in wedded bliss. I feel like Cupid. You'll invite me to the wedding, yes?' Héctor laughed and they joined in.

'But of course!' said Roberto. 'You will be my best man.'

'I like this idea. Although I much prefer you be the best man and me be the groom. But alas, the love of my life has chosen another. Maybe one day I will steal her out from under your nose.' Héctor smiled but it didn't reach his eyes. 'Well.' He slapped his knees and rose. 'My work here is done. I'll leave you two lovebirds to enjoy your last moments together. For now. Louisa, I'll see you before you leave, I promise.'

'How about we meet opposite Bar Cien in San Telmo, seven o'clock tomorrow night? Eduardo has a meeting so he'll be busy.' Standing and giving him a hug, she said, 'Thank you, Héctor.'

'What for?'

'For being so kind to Roberto and me.'

'Bah! Don't be silly!' Héctor shoved the pipe in his mouth, spun on his heels, and waved his hand behind his head before disappearing into the hallway. The front door clicked behind him and once again, Roberto and Louisa were alone. Peace settled around them and Louisa leaned against Roberto, enjoying the strength and love radiating from him. Wrapping his arm around her, he nuzzled behind her ears.

'Roberto . . .'

'Yes, *mi lunita?*' His warm breath caused her belly to flip.

'Do you think we can do this?'

'What?' His cheeky tone hinted as to what he had in mind.

'Not that. Well, yes, that, but our plan? When I go and you stay and we work toward our future together.'

'Yes.' His tongue slid down her neck and she felt an overpowering need to have him inside her.

Turning to him, she placed her hands on his face and stared deep into his eyes. 'If we commit to this plan, we cannot turn back.'

'We will do it. Love me now.' He lay her down on the sofa and slid his hand up her skirt, searching for her garter belt. He deftly undid the clasps then peeled away the silk stockings and the rest of her clothing then his own.

They lay naked on the sofa and she stroked his forehead. 'I will love you forever.'

'And I'll love you until the moon loses its shine.'

Roberto's forceful kiss relayed an outpouring of love. The heat of their bodies rose, their legs and arms entwined to become one. Ecstasy and passion coursed through her veins and she let out a small whimper.

Pulling back, Roberto asked, 'What's wrong?'

'Nothing at all, *mi amor.*' Her lips met his and as daylight slipped into darkness, they ensured that their last moments together as a couple counted.

Streets lights shone in the newly formed puddles on the cobblestoned streets as Louisa stuck to the shadows of San Telmo. Dark corners and alleys weren't safe but she feared recognition by Eduardo's avid fans. Tonight, more than any other, she needed to remain anonymous.

Her low-heeled shoes clicked quietly across the slippery roads until she found Bar Cien. For sentimental reasons she'd chosen the place where she'd met Eduardo, then later, first laid eyes on Roberto. When the young *bandoneón* musician had entered the bar with other band members, her soul had lifted and floated across the room, entwining indelibly with his. What would have happened had she met Roberto first?

Standing in the shadows, she studied the bar's wooden shutters. They once hung off their hinges but were now painted bright green and sat flush against the daisy yellow window frames. The door that was once beaten and gouged by drunks had been replaced by a fire-engine red door, complete with shiny brass handle. Then, like now, she'd stood on the opposite side of the street with a pounding heart and a constricted throat, unsure as to what her future held.

The doors opened and a pair of drunks stumbled out, tango music and smoke trailing behind them. When the door swung shut again, the street fell eerily silent once more. This part of Buenos Aires always had an active nightlife, but tonight, for reasons she couldn't fathom, San Telmo remained mostly quiet.

'*Psst!*'

Louisa jumped, even though she had expected a visitor in the shadows. From behind her, cool fingers slid around her neck and rested on her throat, slowly stroking her exposed skin. Warm breath tickled her ear and she leaned against Roberto's chest. Turning to face him, she could barely see his handsome face through teary eyes.

'Louisa, *mi lunita*—'

'Please, don't say anything.' She stood on tiptoes, closed her eyes, and joined her lips with his. The stubble on his chin scratched her face and she basked in his love and warmth. Roberto pulled back, rested his hands on her shoulders and gazed deeply into her eyes.

'I thought we would have forever,' he said.

'Forever is delayed but for only a moment.'

He reached for her hand and slowly kissed each finger. She took in his hair curling across his forehead, his strong jawline, his straight nose. She tried to commit to memory every detail so she could get through the long, lonely years without him. She drew in a long breath, letting his love envelop her. Tears welled up and flowed down her cheeks and she gently extracted her hand from his.

'I can't do this. It's too hard.' She stepped forward, her body heavy with grief. Another figure emerged from the shadows and she jumped again, freezing with panic.

'It's only me, Louisa.' Héctor moved into the light, the lines on his face deeper than usual.

'I thought you were arriving later.'

'I have special errands to run this evening, so I'll say my farewells now, if I may.'

Louisa fell into Héctor's strong arms. She placed her head on his chest, closed her eyes, and smiled. 'I can't wait to see you again, my dear friend.'

'Ah, I do hope this is soon, but we don't always know what our future holds. We can plan, we can dream, we can wish. This is all we can do and the rest.' He sighed. 'Well, the rest is left up to those who possess more power than us.'

She couldn't work out if he meant God or influential people but she let his comment slide, happy for the chance to say her farewells. They broke their embrace and Héctor kissed her on the forehead, his eyes glistening in the streetlight.

Roberto cleared his throat. 'Louisa, you need to know something.' He held her hand and steadied his gaze. 'Has Eduardo shown you the latest lyrics?'

'Yes. They're the best he's ever done. Looks like his hiatus from before has paid off.' She paused. 'Why?'

'They're mine.'

'He stole them?' She was concerned by her lack of surprise. If Eduardo had done it to Héctor before his dementia appeared, why wouldn't he do it to Roberto now that he was ailing?

'That slimy bastard!' shouted Héctor, pounding the wall with his fist. 'First me, now you. His head should roll.'

Roberto grabbed Héctor's jacket. 'Leave it alone. We cannot risk Louisa.'

'No, he got away with it before. He's not doing it again.' Héctor tried to wrench away from Roberto's vice-like grip.

'How did he find them?' she asked.

'He went through my *bandoneón* case earlier today. I saw him stuff the papers in his jacket pocket.'

'He will pay!' yelled Héctor, pulling his arm free.

'No, Héctor, don't,' Louisa pleaded. 'You blowing up at Eduardo won't do Roberto's career any favors. Think about it, please.'

'I'm only thinking about it for you.' Héctor jutted out his jaw.

'I appreciate your sentiment but please don't do anything,' she said.

Roberto rubbed her back and gave her a sad smile.

'There's something else you should know,' Roberto said in an ominous tone.

'What?' she asked.

'The lyrics were about you but they didn't mention your name.'

She inhaled sharply. 'What?'

'I called it 'Luna Tango'. After . . .'

'I get it,' she said, not wanting Héctor to know about her half-moon birthmark.

How did this farewell turn into such drama?

'It is time for me to go. You two need time alone,' said Héctor, his lips pulled into a tight smile. He held Louisa's hands and kissed her on each cheek. 'Next time we meet it will be under happier circumstances.'

She grabbed his arm. 'You won't do anything rash, will you?'

'Of course not.' Pecking her on the cheek, Héctor saluted, turned on his heels, and swiftly moved down the hill, disappearing into the blackness.

Apprehension snaked across her shoulders and pulled her muscles taut. 'Do you think he's gone to see Eduardo?'

'Most likely but Héctor showing up and getting into a screaming match isn't unusual. Eduardo's probably half-expecting him to appear to have a final argument before he leaves.'

'But Héctor gives earfuls with his fists.' Only six months ago Héctor had turned up drunk at the house and landed a punch on Eduardo's nose. She'd then spent half an hour trying to stop Eduardo from using a gun on his former business partner.

Roberto ran his hand along her arm. 'Now, while they're busy—'

'Aren't you angry? Don't you want to punch Eduardo yourself?'

'Of course I'm angry!' A raging fire shone in his eyes. 'But we have to stick to our plan and I have to pretend Eduardo never took the music. If I don't, it will be a disaster and we'll never be together.'

'You two should never have been together,' said a deep, angry voice. Louisa and Roberto turned to find Eduardo stepping out from the shadows, body rigid, jaw set hard, and eyes glaring as he stared them down.

CHAPTER 13

Present Day - Dani

Once again, Dani climbed the scuffed marble staircase to Carlos's dance studio. He hadn't answered her calls, so she had two options: camp out on the doorstep of his apartment or interrupt him teaching a class. Either way, she had no idea how he'd react upon seeing her.

Her fingers rested on the brass handle as she hesitated, hoping he wouldn't make her dance again. But if he did, she'd suck it up. She'd even worn her poop-brown dance shoes just in case. Adjusting the maroon bag on her shoulder she raised her hand, knuckles ready to rap, but the door jerked open and Jorge and his dance partner scurried past as Carlos's voice boomed after them. She couldn't make out what he'd said but the tone didn't sound like he'd just twirled through a field of daisies.

'Fabulous,' she said.

Jorge gave her a pitying smile and dashed down the stairs, sports bag and towel flying behind him. His petite dance partner teetered on the steps, her spindly legs not carrying her as fast as she probably wished. They rounded the corner and disappeared, their retreating footsteps echoing in the stairwell.

Drawing a deep breath and puffing out her chest, Dani stepped through the door. Carlos was crouched over his stereo, fiddling around with the buttons and muttering under his breath.

'Hi.'

He looked up and drew his brows together. A moment later he broke into a smile.

'Daniela, it is nice to see you again.'

'Uh . . . nice to see you, too.' Perhaps her ability to predict people's behavior had started to slip. This didn't bode well for her new career. 'Did you get my message?'

'Which one? There were, I believe, nineteen.'

'So . . .'

He looked at her blankly. 'So?'

'Had you planned to call me?'

'But of course! I was waiting to make the plans with Gualberto but now you are here I do not need to call. We go dancing tonight.' He eyed her dance shoes. 'I see you are ready.'

'Yeah, I guess.' She had to get to work on her stories. With Carlos and Gualberto in the same room, she might be able to kill two birds with the one stone.

'Do you have a question ready for me?'

'I have lots.'

'Tonight you will dance like *La Gringa Magnifica* and I will answer every question.'

Back to that again. Now would be the time to tell him. Though why was this so flaming hard? What's the worst he could do? Laugh at her lack of dancing genes? Get angry because she hadn't told him earlier? Or tell her everything she wanted to know? Of course, the latter was her deepest fear. In her head, she was brave and able to cope with whatever she learnt about Iris but with the real possibility of finding out the truth, Dani just couldn't open up that Pandora's Box. She was nothing but a chicken.

'Daniela?'

'Sorry.'

'Where were you?'

'Inside my head.'

'It is a fun place, yes?' He winked and butterflies flapped their wings inside her belly.

'Let's just say, I'm not lonely.'

'Hmm.'

'Every writer has voices in their head,' she said.

'I believe this is so.' He said it with such acceptance she wondered if dancers experienced the same phenomena. 'How is your research going?'

'It's going okay. I've been making lots of notes.' She shifted from foot to foot.

'Do you have them with you? May I look?'

'Yes, but they're only notes, okay?' It was impossible to quash the defensive tone.

He gave a lopsided smile. 'You are nervous? Why?'

'Because this is my first assignment. I know I have a lot to learn and they're only—'

'Notes. Yes, I understand. Please.' He waggled his fingers. 'Do not be afraid.'

Dani stuck her hand in the bag and fished for the notebook, relieved she had started a new one after ditching the Canziani research. She handed over the book and fear twisted in her belly. What if he read it and thought it was garbage? She closed her eyes and gave a slight shudder.

'Do not worry.' Carlos placed his hand on her arm and his warm touch relaxed her—just a little. He turned his attention to her notebook:

Tango is the third dance in history where a couple embraced. The first dance was the Viennese waltz, popular in the 1830s. Next came the polka, in the 1840s. These dances weren't without scandal, especially when, in 1850, the theater director of the Paris Opera staged the Viennese waltz to regain the falling numbers of audience. Many citizens objected strongly to the lewd dance hold and it took many years, almost to the end of the century, for the majority of people to accept this new dance position.

. . .

The scandal of the Viennese waltz hold paved the way for tango, as many European immigrants arrived in what then was the small town of Buenos Aires, between 1880 and 1910. The history of the tango becomes murky at this point as no one can agree on the true origins of the dance.

Theory one:

After the British built the railway across Argentina, it opened up regions rich in minerals and land perfect for farming, but the country lacked the workers necessary for landowners to reap their riches.

The Argentine government convinced Europeans to come and work in their country. Migrants were offered accommodation and rations for their first week and some had their passages subsidized. Different to migration in other countries, the new arrivals in Argentina were mostly men. They hoped to work for a few years and return to their homeland rich and ready to marry or, if they already had family, bring them out to live with them. Unfortunately, many remained in Argentina, close to destitute and missing family from their home country.

Due to the influx of men, Argentina lacked women. There were only two ways in which a man could get near a woman: visit a prostitute or through dance. If a man wanted to marry, the best way to catch ~~her~~ the attention of his potential wife was on the dance floor, as this was the socially acceptable meeting place for both sexes. He needed to woo his dance partner by making sure she enjoyed herself and wanted to spend more time dancing with him.

The only way to impress a young lady was to practice dancing. The shortage of women meant men needed to practice with each other, even if it meant dancing with their direct competition. Recorded music wasn't common back then so they needed venues with live music. Brothels often had music to entertain the men while they were waiting their turn, so many clients took the opportunity to practice dance steps with other men while the women were otherwise 'occupied.'

This theory became popular after Argentine writer Jorge Eduardo Borges wrote an article linking brothels and the tango. Due to his popularity, his fans agreed and his theory grew to the point that it transformed into an accepted truth. The problem is, many people who write about the tango today start with this belief, rather than investigate deeper into the history.

. . .

Theory two:

Tango was born in the neighborhoods where the poor lived. These communities had a melting pot of nationalities and young boys learned to dance with their male relatives. Once they achieved a level of competence, these young men were passed on to their female relatives, who would coach them further.

The dance and music brought communities together. Men would bring out a flute, guitar, and bandoneón, *and they would congregate in the courtyards. The few women would join the men and enjoy some moments of happiness in their difficult and lonely lives.*

The music united people from many cultures and became a common language. The contradanza *was popular among the Italian immigrants and blended dance styles from all over the world to create what later became known as the tango.*

Theory three:

In the 1880s, the only dance seen in public in Buenos Aires was at theaters or dance halls. The brothel theory may also have stemmed from some less-than-savory dance halls that doubled as brothels, or from dance halls that were frequented by men and women whose morals were frowned upon by their Christian counterparts.

Carlos raised his eyebrows and continued staring at the notebook. Dani chewed her lip, inhaling deeply then letting it out in one long breath.

'It is okay,' he said finally.

'You don't hate it?' She leaned forward, not worried about showing her eagerness.

'These are notes, yes? You have covered the basics. I am happy to see you have not written about the men being homosexual.'

'I know them dancing together meant it could be interpreted that way but it wasn't the case, right?'

'Is that a question?'

'No.'

'You answered very quickly. Do you have a real question?'

'Are you going to make me learn a dance step if I say yes?' *God, please no, I am so not in the mood.*

'What do you think?' His eyes held a cheeky glint.

'I think your answer is yes,' she said as he motioned for her to stand in the middle of the dance studio. She allowed a small pout. 'Any chance I could ask my question before you torture me?'

Carlos shrugged. 'I am a gentleman and I would say ladies first but we have a deal, yes? Dance then question.'

'Can't you bend it? Please?' Pleading didn't become her but it was worth a shot.

'Sorry, I cannot help. I bent the rules once, I cannot do it again.'

'Yes you can! You made up the rules of the deal! And anyway, don't Argentines pride themselves on bending rules?'

Carlos laughed. 'I see you understand some of our culture. Just do as I ask and you will get what you want.'

'Fine!' She smoothed down her ruffled shirt. Straightening her back, she held her chin in the air. 'Teach me, *profesor*.'

'Walk.'

'What? Walk to where?'

'If you cannot walk, you cannot tango.'

'I've been practicing walking since I was one.' She hoped he got the sarcasm.

'Then you should be good at this.' Carlos grinned. 'Today you will learn the rock step, *la cadencia*. This you need to know for when the dance floor is crowded and you do not have the space to execute a traditional tango walk.'

'Okay,' she said, wiggling her toes in her shoes. Even though she hated this situation, it could be a lot worse. Without Carlos's help she'd be drowning in murky waters, pushed under the waves of deadlines.

'Start with the *paso basico*, the basic eight steps. Go.'

Dani puffed out her cheeks and concentrated on executing a perfect eight. She finished, slightly concerned it had come so naturally.

'*Muy bien*, Daniela. Now, do it again, but on step five, transfer your weight from one leg to the other and keep doing so as you slowly turn in a circle. Keep on the balls of the feet.'

She gritted her teeth and started the *ocho* and on step five did exactly as he asked, rocking from one foot to the other.

'Traffic on the dance floor is now clear. Continue!' He waved her on and she completed the *ocho*. '¡*Fin*!'

She stopped, astounded she'd mastered the rock step first go.

'We will make a tango dancer out of you yet. This is why you should listen to me. Remember when I said no one leaves my tutelage without learning to dance?'

'Yes,' she said with a slight hiss. His smugness irritated her but he was right, damn it.

'I will admit the improvement in your dancing is not just from my teaching. You seem to possess something I do not normally see with the *gringos*. Your dancing, it is raw but . . .' He shrugged. 'You should stay in Argentina longer and learn tango. There is talent hidden under your reluctance.'

Dani froze. *Oh no, no, no. Not me.*

'Are you serious? I've nearly put two men in hospital!' She forced out a laugh. 'Doing the rocking walk thing right was a fluke.'

'Fluke?'

'Lucky chance. Don't worry, I'll return to squishing toes and cracking shins shortly.' Keen to get off that topic, she said, 'Now for my question.'

'You have earned it.'

'Where do *you* believe tango started?'

'Ah, Señorita McKenna, excellent question. I will tell you what I know. Tango started deep within, nowhere else.'

She nodded for him to continue.

'Tango is not a combination of pretty steps. It is not the music. Tango is the journey of the soul. In one song, the dancer or musician can experience joy, heartache, jealousy, love, grief, desire, lust.' He stepped toward her and lightly brushed his fingers against the side of her face. Dani closed her eyes, breathing in his masculinity. 'One touch can convey these emotions and engage the soul of your partner. One movement . . .' Carlos grabbed her leg and wrapped it around his upper thigh. His powerful arms held her against his body and a small gasp escaped her lips. '. . . tells a story hidden within. Man and woman listened to their true selves and allowed their inner emotions to speak. That is how the tango started.'

'Wow.' She breathed out. 'Just . . . wow.'

'That is all.' Carlos gently guided her leg to the floor and he backed away as if finishing a business transaction. 'I need to get something. I will be one moment.'

He turned on his heels and Dani didn't blink, her gaze following his muscular frame as he entered the office and shut the door.

Closing her eyes briefly, she tried to make sense of what had transpired. This man was hot, no denying this fact. Passion oozed out of his every pore, yet people said he'd lost his love for the dance. If this was Carlos being dispassionate about tango then she would give anything to have seen him when it was his first love.

Needing to cool down after Carlos's demonstration, Dani wandered over to the open window. Cars and buses whizzed by, zigzagging along the road. A breeze brushed her clammy skin as she checked out the bookshelf next to the window. The shelves contained a plethora of books on tango. It truly was a researcher's dream. She ran her fingers over the spines, reading the titles in Spanish, English, French, and languages she couldn't identify. No wonder he'd been part of the UNESCO team. When she spotted a photography book featuring her mother, Dani pulled her fingers away as if she'd touched fire. Small beads of sweat broke out on her forehead and she spun around, ready to dash to the other side of the room, but her hip collided with some books. A few crashed to the floor and she bent down, gathering them in her arms.

A slip of paper fell out and landed face up. As soon as she read *Querida Cecilia—Dear Cecilia*—Dani stuffed the letter between the covers and placed it on the shelf as quickly as she could. With a rapidly beating heart, she stood and turned.

She halted.

Carlos stood in the office doorway, arms folded, not moving a muscle. He stared at her for so long she considered freaking out.

'I wasn't snooping, honest. It fell out and I put it back. Promise.'

She didn't dare meet his eyes, scared his handsome face might be twisted into disdain or anger. God, after this dumb-ass incident, any chance of him trusting her had been shot to pieces. So much for catching a break.

She bit her lip and studied the indentations on the wooden floor. He remained quiet. Whatever the outcome, she was ready for it. Dani looked up to find a grinning Carlos, his dark eyes surrounded by smile lines.

'Once again, I can see you are not like the others.' He sauntered past and picked the book from the shelf. 'It was silly of me to leave it in there. I must have forgotten. I must . . .' He shook his head. 'Never mind.'

He went into his office, placed the book with the letter on his desk, turned off the light, then shut and locked the door. Cocking his head toward the studio entrance, he said, 'We go.'

They sat at the same table at the *práctica* and Dani suspected this space was permanently reserved for Carlos. Since leaving the dance studio, Dani and Carlos had been shrouded in silence. Did he feel the stirring of attraction before, like she did, or had he just been demonstrating how tango arouses passion?

Dani snuck a glance at his long lashes, slicked-back hair, and strong jaw. No matter which angle she looked at, Carlos Escudero was growing on her. *Oh no.* After Adam, she'd made a pact to bolt the minute she met a man with excess baggage. Given Carlos's history, he needed a few carts to wheel around the bags containing his woes. Then again, she couldn't get away with just one carry-on.

'Dani!' Gualberto rushed over, gave a bear hug and kissed her on each cheek. 'It is good to see you!'

'You too, Gualberto.' She looked up to find Diego Alonso hovering beside their table.

'Diego! Please!' Gualberto motioned for Diego to join them.

Crap.

A slow, sleazy smile crept across Diego's lips as soon as he spotted her.

'Señorita Dani.' He leaned in to kiss her on the cheeks. Her skin crawled at his touch but she remained composed on the outside, even though turmoil reigned within.

'¡Che Diego!' Carlos slapped the older man on the back and they took a seat.

'Your stories, how are they?' Diego asked, leaning in a fraction too close.

'Getting there,' she said, studying the couples milling on the dance floor, waiting for the music to start.

'If you want a spectacular story, you should find La Gringa,' Diego said with an innocent air, but she didn't buy it for a second.

'No one knows where she is, right?' Dani pulled in her stomach as if protecting it from being punched. Did he think she'd fall for his ruse? The only reason he wanted her to write the story was so she could find Iris for him to go and haunt. She hoped other people didn't think she was as naïve as he did.

'Why would you not write about the most famous female tango dancer in history? Imagine what your boss would say if you interviewed the reclusive Gringa.'

He was good, she had to give him that. It would indeed be a massive coup . . . for someone else.

'Carlos and Gualberto are helping me write my articles.'

'Ah,' said Diego, 'but to have an exclusive with the woman who changed the face of tango as we know it. Imagine . . .'

She could imagine many things but Diego being without motive was not one of them.

'I don't think so,' she said, praying this damn conversation would curl into a ball and die.

'I guess you are not the journalist I thought,' said Diego. The challenge landed with a thud in the middle of the table. 'Your friend Señor Escudero could help you find her and introduce you. La Gringa choreographed some shows you danced in, yes?' He turned to Carlos. A flicker of apprehension sparked in Carlos's eyes.

Dani's stomach dropped. 'Thank you for the idea but I need to concentrate on the stories I have underway. Perhaps another time.' She hadn't spotted any flying pigs lately.

'Maybe Diego is right, Daniela. It would help your articles to talk with one of Argentina's best dancers and choreographers. Yes.' Carlos's eyes lit up. 'We should do this.'

'I . . .' Her clammy hands gripped the edges of the table. If she was too scared to dig for information about Iris with Carlos, how the hell would she could cope with seeing her face-to-face?

'Daniela, are you all right?'

'Too hot. Need air.'

'Please excuse us, Diego.' Carlos placed a hand under her elbow and helped her stand. Her legs wobbled and she collapsed onto the chair again.

'Water,' Dani gasped.

The three men reached for the water jug, Carlos grabbing it first. He filled a glass and passed it to Dani, watching her intently as she gulped it down. The ice-cold liquid helped her gain control and she placed the empty glass on the table.

'Thanks.'

'It is no problem,' said Carlos. 'You are ready to dance now?'

She stared at him with incredulity. 'I don't feel much like dancing.'

'Sometimes when we force ourselves to do something we do not want, it can be a positive experience.' He punctuated his statement with a self-satisfied smile.

'And sometimes doing something we don't want causes more grief than if we'd left it alone in the first place,' said Dani.

Carlos tilted his head to the side.

Sighing, she said, 'Don't worry about me. I'm fine. Let's do it.'

She stood and waited for Carlos to join her. He didn't move a muscle.

'Are you not dancing with me or do I have to wait for *el cabeceo*?'

'My leg . . .' He rubbed it with the palm of his hand.

Who was she to argue? She'd been blessed with health and had no idea if Carlos's pain was real or imagined. If it was as bad as he said, she didn't want to call him out for being a wuss.

'Daniela, please sit. We will talk about some moves then you can try them with my cousin.'

'Looks like it is you and me again, *bonita*.' Gualberto grinned, chivalrous as always.

'You keep doing this and your wife will hunt me down and beat me up.' Dani laughed but was a tad concerned, as she'd heard about Argentine women's reputation for jealousy.

'Oh, do not worry. My wife, she does not know this green-eyed monster.'

'I'm glad.'

'Let us get to the business,' Carlos said. 'First, your posture, it is all wrong.'

'Well, gee, thanks.'

'Do you want to learn? Do you want help with these articles?' Surprisingly, his tone sounded light.

'Of course I do.'

He stood and leaned slightly to the side, favoring his damaged leg. 'You need to keep the weight on the toes. It gives you control for when you are dancing. Pull up from your lower abdomen and pretend your back is a stretching band that is being pulled up, up, up.' He demonstrated and Dani stood, imitating his every move. 'Remember, connect the hearts, and the energy of you and your dance partner will ignite.'

Carlos stepped forward, wrapped his arms around her and pulled Dani so close his warm breath grazed her collarbone. This time, when her knees went weak, it was from Carlos's nearness not from freaking out about Iris or Stella. Standing straight, with her chest close to his, Dani concentrated on being in the moment, something that came easily, especially after experiencing his nearness only an hour before. His intoxicating cologne floated through the air. She desperately wanted to lean in for a better whiff but wasn't game.

'Stand straight!' he said.

Without realizing, Dani had angled her body forward and her nose was dangerously close to his neck. Pulling away, she tried to hide her shock at being wrenched out of her momentary lapse of reason.

'Sorry,' she mumbled.

His body shook with laughter. 'It is all right.'

She hoped he hadn't figured out what she'd been doing but his reaction told her he probably had. How embarrassing. Gualberto and Diego looked on, amusement on their lips and in their eyes.

'This emotion . . .' he said.

She looked up to find his dark eyes fixed on her. Dani's body temperature soared.

'Yes?' she asked, not sure whether he was referring to the dance or the girly crush she'd developed. Man, she was like every other woman in Argentina.

'This emotion is the most important part of the dance. Remember what I said about where tango started? Without emotion there is no point. Much like everything in life that is worth the while. Ready?'

Before she had a chance to say a word, Carlos dipped her backward and curls spilled across her face. Blowing them away with a large puff, she looked up, their faces inches apart. He held her for what felt like an eternity, his strong arms firmly gripping her body, their gaze not breaking, electricity zapping between them. He guided her to the standing position and let go. Dani smoothed her skirt, looking everywhere but directly at Carlos.

'Now, you dance with Gualberto.' He sat and sipped his wine.

CHAPTER 14

Dani's head spun as Gualberto led her to the dance floor. Once again Carlos had awakened a yearning deep within then disconnected himself. Barely able to walk straight, she stopped when Gualberto did and took the position he'd shown her before. Extracting herself from Carlos's embrace hadn't cooled her any and she hoped it was the atmosphere of the *práctica* that made her hot and bothered, not him. She couldn't work out which would be worse: falling for tango like her mother, or falling for someone removed from his emotions like Carlos. Both spelled trouble.

The music started and Dani counted through the steps she'd learnt. Her movements were less jerky and she followed Gualberto with a little more grace than the last time she'd plodded across the boards.

'You are doing very good,' said Gualberto.

'Thanks.'

'I am not talking just about the dancing. I am speaking of my cousin. You keep him happy.'

She faltered, but stopped before she trod on his foot. 'Huh?'

'I have not seen Carlos like this in a long time.'

'Like what?'

'Interested in tango. Since the accident, his heart has not been in it. But with you,' He paused, narrowing his eyes, 'with you it is different. The spark he lost has appeared again. It is nice to see.'

'Really? But he's not danced with me. He's held me a couple of times but—'

'His leg, it gives him trouble.'

'Yes, I can see. But it's sore every time he plans to dance with me.'

'He has a long way to go. Some days his pain is intense and he cannot get out of bed but since you have arrived, he is at the studio every day. I hope you will stay here as long as possible.' Gualberto gave her a hand a small squeeze, indicating they needed to continue dancing. She did as he wished.

A dark cloud loomed above, spoiling her rhythm. She turned her concentration to the task at hand and managed to keep up with Gualberto by centering her weight on the balls of her feet and trying to skim across the floor. Dani felt like she could finally get through a song without inflicting grievous bodily harm on her partner. The music finished and she sighed.

'You are happy?'

'Yes! I didn't kick you!'

'Let us not push our luck. We shall take a seat now.'

'But isn't it rude if we don't finish the *tanda* together?' she asked, a little too keen to keep going.

'Not if we both agree to stop.' Gualberto grinned and gestured toward the table where Diego sat next to Carlos. Their mouths moved in conversation but their eyes were fixed on her and Gualberto.

Dani opted to sit opposite Carlos as she was uneasy about getting too close to him again. Although, looking at him from across the table, she didn't feel any more comfortable. It was nice to have butterflies in someone else's presence again but getting carried away with a useless crush on an interview subject went against her ethics. It wouldn't do to disregard them with her assignment. *Oh, lighten up. Since when did a harmless crush become a no-no?*

'Daniela, you have done well with the dancing tonight. I will say I am surprised. And instead of giving you a bonus question to ask, you will get something better. Diego and I have agreed it would be bad if I do not introduce you to *La Gringa Magnifica*. If you interview her, your articles will be like no other and we will both have achieved our goals.'

'I—'

Carlos held up his hand. 'Do not thank me now. Thank me when we find her. Tomorrow we start our detective work. It will be fun, yes?'

Sunlight streamed through the open window as the white organza curtains flapped in the cool morning breeze. Dani rubbed her itchy eyes and dreaded looking in the mirror. Rolling over on the soft bed, she checked the clock: eleven-oh-two a.m. She'd barely had three hours sleep. Fat lot of use she'd be today.

Turning on her back, Dani slung an arm over her forehead and stared at the ceiling fan whirring above. The dull hum soothed her, but only a fraction. Carlos wanting to go the extra mile for her articles was wonderful, except for the one teeny problem that popped up like a cactus in a bed of gerbera daisies: her mother. She had options, but none of them appealed. One, she could tell Carlos about her cruddy relationship with Iris and call off the hunt. Two, not tell Carlos, find Iris, and have Carlos peeved because she hadn't told him the truth. Three, disappear on a permanent trip to the Amazon and find a tribe who'd accept her, foibles and all. Not surprisingly, none of these options included a happy, tearful reunion with her mother. If nothing else, Dani was a pragmatist.

'Bloody families.'

A rap on the door jerked her from the moment. Reaching for the white hotel robe, she wrapped it around her flimsy nightie, padded over to the door and peered through the peephole.

'Shit,' she mumbled.

'I heard that, Daniela.' She spied a toothy grin on the other side of the door. 'You are late. Did you not remember our meeting?'

Oh crap! 'I'm sorry, Carlos! I'll meet you downstairs at the café in five minutes.' Really? How could she make herself presentable in public with her hair a knotted mess and bags under her eyes big enough to carry basketballs?

'I will order us coffee. You need some, yes?'

'Yes. Thanks. Be there soon.' She dashed to the bathroom, turned on the shower, shed her clothes and stepped in.

'Ow!' Hot water burned her skin and she backed against the tiles, reached for the taps, fiddling them until she got the right temperature. *This is what happens when things are done in a hurry.* She despised not having more time to mull over her options, which was probably why her subconscious had blanked out their meeting. If she didn't talk to Carlos, she didn't have to decide.

As Dani lathered her hair, it occurred to her one of the reasons she hadn't 'fessed up about her mother was because she feared Carlos would put her in a headlock and march her straight to Iris. Especially after his speech about how families should work things out, no matter how difficult the problem.

'Bloody brilliant.'

Turning off the taps, she dried herself then pulled a brush through her wet curls, taking a little more care than normal. Being surrounded by beautiful people made her want to make more of an effort. Sure, beauty should shine from within, blah, blah, blah, but it did feel good when she walked down the street and caught the attention of hot-blooded Latin men. She was in her twenties for god's sake, she wasn't ready to book into a nursing home just yet.

Dani donned the paisley halter neck dress she'd bought at the upmarket Galerías Pacifico shopping mall. Executing a quick spin, she marveled at how the skirt elegantly fell into place when she stopped moving. Even the Queen of Jeans could appreciate the design and care that went into constructing such a beautiful piece of clothing. She bent over and strapped on the plum sandals she'd bought at the same shop, then swore never to enter the doors of Galerías Pacifico again. Under the ornate plasterwork, frescos, and magnificent architecture lay shops that hypnotized one with gorgeous merchandise that maxed out the credit card.

Leaving her room, she made her way to the café and found Carlos reading a newspaper at a corner table. Two large windows gave the perfect view onto the street where people rushed along, risking life and limb as they dashed between cars. Carlos looked up and his eyes widened.

'*Hola* Señorita McKenna.' He stood and pulled out a seat for her. A pot of steaming coffee sat in the middle of the table and Carlos poured a cup and passed it to her. Leaning against the chair, he placed his hands behind his neck. 'You look different today.'

'I didn't get much sleep.'

'No, it is not that. It's . . .' He squinted and tilted his head to the side. 'There is something not the same but I do not know what it is.'

Could he sense she was growing more comfortable with wearing feminine clothes? He would be a rare man if he did.

'I guess sleep escapes you because of the excitement about this angle for your story, yes?' He twirled the spoon in the sugar bowl. 'Diego wants to meet with you again to discuss *La Gringa*.'

She had to find a way to use the Argentine's term of endearment for Iris. It sounded rude if she didn't, but she doubted she could say the name without stumbling over the syllables, bursting into tears, or wanting to punch something.

'Why does Diego want to see me? I'm not going to write an exposé on his relationship with . . . with . . . *La Gringa Magnifica*.' There, she said it and not a tear in sight. 'He understands that, right?' Hadn't he done enough damage?

'Yes, he is aware of your feelings on the matter.'

'And he knows if we do find her, I'm not going to tell him where she is.' *Which shouldn't be a problem, as I'm not going to look that hard, if at all.*

'Yes.'

'Good.' She nodded, happy to have gotten it off her chest.

'But he would like you to deliver a letter.'

'Oh no, I'm not his detective and mail-woman. Tell him the deal's off.' She knew he couldn't be trusted.

'You may tell him this in person when we meet in three hours.'

~

The walls of the hotel room crowded in on her. Carlos had done his disappearing act and left Dani to her own devices and now her mind vacillated between telling the truth about Iris and making things worse, and keeping her mouth shut in the hope the whole situation would go away like a skin blemish.

The retro wallpaper she'd loved only a few days ago grated on her now. The room grew stuffy and she had an overwhelming desire to escape, even if it meant sucking in the fumes of the city below. Grabbing her phone, sunglasses, and handbag, Dani dashed from the hotel and headed to the Plaza de Mayo, a place she'd read about but hadn't visited.

Weaving through the crowded streets and navigating across cracked and raised paths, Dani found the plaza. The magnificence stopped her in her tracks. Now one of the biggest draw cards in the country, Dani fully expected this plaza to be swarming with back-packers and five-star tourists. Instead, the square held an air of melancholy. In the middle stood the Pirámide de Mayo, the oldest national monument in Buenos Aires. Directly behind the symbol of liberty lay the government house, Casa Rosada, the Pink Palace. She still hadn't decided which explanation sounded most plausible for the rose-colored building. It grossed her out to think they'd mixed cow's blood into white paint to protect the walls from the humidity of the city. She much preferred the other theory, which said the president in the eighteen sixties, Domingo Faustino Sarmiento, mixed the white of the Liberal party and the red of the radicals to try to defuse political tensions and symbolize Argentina as one nation. Dani gazed at the balconies framed by arches and wondered which one Eva Perón had used when she addressed the Argentine people.

Shuffling feet drew her attention and she spun around to find a group of elderly women marching around the square. White headscarves shrouded their lowered heads as the women held hands in a strong sign of unity.

'The Mothers of Plaza de Mayo,' Dani said under her breath.

She'd read an article about these women, who were known the world over as human rights activists. For almost four decades they'd gathered every Thursday to march silently around the plaza with white scarves that bore the names of their missing children—offspring who were stolen by the government during the Dirty War back in the nineteen seventies.

Standing to the side, Dani watched them march, their unity and strength overwhelming. Tears formed in her eyes and she wiped them away. The dedication of these mothers humbled Dani and her thoughts turned to Iris. As far as she knew, Iris had never tried to get in contact, yet here were these mothers, clinging to the hope their child might turn up alive, or at least their body, so they could receive a proper burial. The chances of either, though, were next to impossible. The Argentine government back then ensured that those who disappeared remained that way.

No doubt her mother knew about these women and Dani wondered why their plight hadn't guilted Iris into contacting her. Drawing a deep breath, she contemplated her options again. She could remain angry at Iris for being selfish, especially as she had a living child, unlike most of these women, or she could swallow her resentment and try to reunite with her mother and start afresh. She still had no insight as to why Iris left her, and her fear of asking Carlos about Iris meant she'd never get answers. Through hot, blurry eyes, Dani watched the women of the *desaparecidos*—the disappeared—and made a decision.

The large door closed without a sound, blocking out the noise of the traffic puttering along Avenida 9 de Julio. Delicately carved woodwork painted in gold decorated the main hall, and elaborate balconies and columns towered above. Dani gazed at the dome overhead until her neck developed a painful crick.

'Beautiful, no?' Carlos whispered.

'Absolutely breathtaking,' she replied softly. These walls contained so much history, so many stories, so many emotions. She gently touched a balustrade. Had her mother run her fingers along this very surface?

'This is not the original theater. The first Teatro Colón overlooked the Plaza de Mayo until the opera became popular, then they had to build a bigger theater. The acoustics in this theater are considered among the best in the world. Personally, I think it *is* the best.'

She had to hand it to the Argentines, they knew how to believe in their countrymen and achievements, especially when it came to culture.

'Very impressive.' It was nice to have Carlos impart information without a single question or flubbed dance step in sight.

'We go here.' Carlos pointed to the plush red carpet leading up the wide marble steps. He took her hand and they climbed the stairs, goose bumps breaking out on her arms despite the day's warmth. When they reached the landing, she expected him to break his hold but he didn't and she prayed her hands wouldn't get clammy. His every movement vibrated through her hand and she loved his skin touching hers. *Oh, Dani McKenna, what are you doing?*

They crossed the landing and arrived at the doors leading to the theater proper. Carlos gently let go of her hand.

'Close your eyes, Daniela.'

She did so without question and the door creaked open. Although she didn't peek, she could sense the expanse before her.

'Take four steps forward. Do not worry, you will not step on anything.'

A nervous laugh escaped her dry lips. 'Not even your foot?'

'Not even my foot. Come.'

A strong arm wrapped around her shoulder and guided her forward. The scent of leather, musk, women's perfume, and candle wax filled her nostrils. Her skin tingled with the electricity of audiences past buzzing from anticipation prior to a performance. And ghosts. A shiver ran up her spine as she thought about all the people, alive and dead, who had performed and watched concerts in this theater. Even though she fought it, images of her mother twirling on the stage appeared before her. Tears burned her eyes and she willed them away.

'You can open your eyes.'

'I don't want to.'

'Why not?'

'I just—'

'You will miss seeing one of the most beautiful theaters in the world. I am what you might call . . .' He paused for so long she thought she could hear his brain ticking over. 'One-sided.'

'Biased.'

'Yes, true. I am biased on many things, including this theater. Please open your eyes and enjoy the beauty.' She sensed him step away.

Dani peeled one eye open, then the other. Ornate gold ceiling roses surrounded dim lights that shone on the beautifully restored red velvet seats and layers of exquisitely carved balconies formed a semicircle around the theater. Thick red velvet curtains hung across doors at the rear of the balconies and the soft light cast a haunting glow.

'It is wonderful, no?' He turned and frowned, using his thumb to gently wipe away her trickle of tears. 'It is nice to spend time with someone who can appreciate beauty and magic.'

Carlos moved his hand away and a lump caught in her throat. The poor guy thought the theater's beauty had affected her, yet she shed tears for an entirely different reason. As mad as she was at Iris, Dani couldn't ignore the pangs of loss she'd fought so hard to quash.

Sniffing, Dani smiled and said, 'It truly is a special place.'

Carlos nodded and crooked a finger, beckoning her to follow. They sat in the front row, gazing at the stage surrounded by gold carvings and heavy velvet curtains.

'You played here as a kid?' she asked.

'Yes.'

'Did you understand the magnificence of this place or was it lost on you?'

'Hmm . . . these appear to be questions.'

'Are you ever going to let up on this? I'm trying to learn how to dance, okay?'

'You are doing well for someone with two left feet.'

She punched him in the arm playfully and he feigned injury. His face contorted with agony and he collapsed on her lap, looking up at her with big, brown eyes. 'My arm, it is damaged. You are very cruel.'

Holy crap. She wanted to avert her eyes, scared they'd betray the coils of passion spreading throughout her body. Overwhelmed by the desire to kiss him, Dani forced herself to study the balcony off to the side but barely took in the details. She prayed the reaction to his nearness would dissipate magically.

It didn't.

Carlos reached behind her neck and his warm fingers gently stroked the nape. She turned and found his face inches from hers. They locked eyes and ghosts of past romantic performances surrounded them. Her short breaths drew out to match his smooth, rhythmic breathing and they leaned into each other, heat sandwiched between their bodies.

The moment their lips touched, Dani's brain short-circuited. Any promise to stick to ethics and not get involved with her interview subject vanished into thin air. They pressed against each other while her body grew lighter, as if all gravity had disappeared.

Carlos's hand ran through her hair and his sweet lips overpowered her. Giving into the ecstasy, Dani wrapped her arms around his neck, the intense kisses growing as each second passed.

A door slammed and a voice boomed out from the rear of the theater. 'Ah! You are here!'

CHAPTER 15

'Disgusting.' Eduardo glared at Louisa and Roberto for what felt like an eternity.

Louisa pulled away from her lover. 'How did you—'

'Find out about you two?' A laugh laced with sarcasm left Eduardo's lips and echoed down the empty street. 'My mind may not be as sharp as it once was but I am not stupid.'

The cold mist thickened and the flickering streetlights cast an eerie glow. A pack of drunkards wandered out from the bar and the heavy door slammed behind them. They stood on the curb, drinks in hand, amusement plastered on their dirty faces at the scene unfolding before them.

Denying romantic involvement with Roberto was futile.

Eduardo balled his hands on his hips. 'How long this has been going on and what are your plans?'

'I . . .' Louisa said. 'I . . . I mean, we . . . uh—'

'You two make me sick, going behind my back.' He spat out the words then dropped his hands by his sides, his fists clenched. Hurt welled in his glassy eyes.

'Eduardo . . .' She used the tone that had always soothed his temper when it flared.

'How could you do this to me? I am your lover, not him.' Eduardo's booming voice echoed off the buildings.

She gasped then looked to Roberto, who froze. 'What? It's not true!'

'Ah, dear Louisa, please do not lie. Tell him the truth. Tell him we are lovers.'

Anger mixed with threat shone in Eduardo's eyes and she hesitated. If she didn't go along with Eduardo, he'd cause a scene in public and destroy the hard work they'd done hiding his illness. But she couldn't let him say these things and lead Roberto to believe it was true.

'I—'

'How dare you say that about Louisa!' Roberto set his jaw hard. 'You don't know her like I do.'

'And the half-moon birthmark? How would I know this if I hadn't—' Eduardo didn't have time to finish the sentence before Roberto's fist connected with Eduardo's eye.

Louisa's stomach churned and she held onto the wall, feeling bile rise in her throat. The two men tussled, spinning in a circle with their arms wrapped around each other's heads.

'Stop it! Stop it!' she screamed. The drunkards on the corner cheered and clapped. 'Stop them!' she yelled at the men, who ignored her.

Roberto grunted as he tried to control Eduardo, who seemed to have gained the strength of six men. His recent claims of a frail body were tossed in the gutter, along with her dreams. She took a deep breath and jumped onto the men, her legs dangling as she hung off their backs and grabbed at their faces, digging in her nails. She hoped the pain might at least bring one—or both—of them to their senses.

'Argh!' Eduardo's hands flew to his face and Louisa held on for dear life as Roberto fell away. Eduardo's muscles tensed and she held on tightly while he spun around and backed into the wall. Cold bricks slammed against her spine. Air flew from her lungs and she slumped to the ground, trying to catch breath.

'Animal!' Roberto lunged forward and rammed his forearm against Eduardo's throat, pinning him against the wall. Through gritted teeth, Roberto said, 'Louisa's put up with enough. You deserve to rot in hell.'

Roberto kept Eduardo pinned while he used one hand to rummage through his mentor's pockets. A moment later he triumphantly pulled out the sheet music.

'Let him go, Roberto.' Louisa's breath came in shallow, painful bursts. 'Let him be.'

Roberto removed his arm and Eduardo stumbled forward but didn't lose balance. He rubbed his neck gingerly.

'You're smarter than I thought,' said Eduardo.

Bending down, Roberto opened the *bandoneón* case and deposited the pages.

'You do not get Louisa *and* the music,' said Eduardo. He leapt forward, lifted his arms high and crashed clenched fists down on Roberto, who fell to the ground with a sickening thud, his head smashing against the stone gutter. Papers flew through the air and Eduardo lunged for them, scooping them in his arms before grabbing the *bandoneón* case and taking off down the street. He disappeared into the mist, the hard soles of his shoes battering against the cobblestones.

Louisa fell to her knees, the cold ground biting into her skin. A small breeze lifted the remaining sheet of paper and blew it against her hand. Grabbing it without thinking, she shoved it in her pocket as she rested her cold fingers on the prone body beside her. 'Roberto . . .'

She rolled him to one side and tore pieces from her silk shirt, crumpling them into balls and pressing them against the blood flowing out of the wound in his head. Tears streamed down her face as she maneuvered him so his head rested in her lap.

'Wake up, please, wake up.'

A couple of the drunks staggered over to where she sat, the

pungent alcohol fumes mingled with the metallic scent of fresh blood.

'He needs a doctor!' she pleaded.

The short one looked at Roberto and said, 'He's a goner.'

The tall one scowled at his companion and issued Louisa a reassuring smile. 'Don't you worry, missus. We'll help ya. Claudio!' he yelled at the young boy hanging near the entrance to the bar. 'Get Doctor Alvarez!'

The boy took off at a dead run and Louisa turned her attention to Roberto, who moaned and lolled his head from side to side.

'Stay still, *mi amor*. We're getting help.' She put more pressure on the wounds and used her other hand to stroke his cheek.

'It will be fine. We'll all be fine.' Her words came easily but she didn't believe them for a second.

After Roberto had gained consciousness, he'd refused to go to the hospital, only allowing the retired doctor to bandage his head. Some of the drunks had helped load Roberto into a taxi and she and Roberto had gone to his apartment where she'd set him up with an ice pack and waited for him to fall asleep before sneaking out.

Guilt trailed her as she hurried along the street to the house she'd shared with Eduardo. It had been a few hours since the incident in San Telmo, and hopefully it was enough time for Eduardo to have calmed down so she could talk with him. As horrendous as his actions were, she understood his reasons, or in this case, his lack of reason.

She didn't hold out much hope for negotiating the return of the *bandoneón* and the music but she had to try. Roberto could rewrite the music, or at least try to, but to buy a new *bandoneón* would cost a fortune. She had to act fast as Eduardo was likely to destroy the instrument or give it away.

Even though she had accumulated many personal possessions during her time with Eduardo, the only ones she wanted to retrieve were the letters from Roberto and the tarnished silver frame that contained the photo of Louisa with her parents. The photographer had captured the trio laughing with light dancing in their eyes, arms wrapped around each other. Although the image was burned in her memory, she longed to hold on to it. Somehow, touching the picture brought her closer to the parents she missed every day.

She halted out the front of the house and took in the intricately carved stonework around the windows and veranda columns. A dim light shone through a crack between the velvet curtains in the music room, and her heart beat hard against her chest. Climbing the steps leading to the double front doors, she wrapped her fingers around the handle then hesitated. Despite his terrible outburst, she did worry for Eduardo. He wasn't well enough to go to America and cope in an unfamiliar setting with a language he barely knew. Eduardo needed a bilingual person by his side, and up until a short while ago, the only person he'd trusted was Louisa. She wanted to help him, but after tonight's events, her resolve to stand by him no matter what had wavered. Perhaps she'd been wrong; maybe situations changed in ways that made it impossible to keep one's word. She couldn't stay with Eduardo anymore. She would help him, yes, but now he knew her secret, he'd be prone to further outbursts, and after tonight's violence, she worried for her safety. However, she did owe him an explanation.

Tentatively, Louisa pushed the handle down, opened the door, and entered the foyer.

'Hello?'

Nothing.

'Eduardo?'

No answer.

She methodically went from room to room, flicking on lights, but Eduardo, the sheet music, and the *bandoneón* couldn't be found. Dashing up the stairs to her bedroom, she retrieved the framed photo and stuffed it in a large bag. Opening her underwear drawer, she grabbed the map of Chapada do Russo and Roberto's love letters. She unfolded one and smiled at his beautiful penmanship and the words '*Querida Lunita*'. Dear Little Moon. Shaking herself out of the happy haze, she shoved them into her handbag. If

Eduardo found these papers it would only add fuel to the fire; she didn't want to hurt him any more than she already had.

She cast her eyes around the room that had once been hers. The four-poster bed with purple silk draped over its mahogany pillars; the dark red reading chair where she'd spent countless hours; the wardrobe full of designer clothes and shoes. However, all of them only possessions and scattered memories.

A wave of déjà vu crashed over her. Once again she had to leave a familiar home and head into an uncertain future. At least this time, she had a man she loved by her side. It wasn't what they'd envisioned, but sometimes life steered people in directions they could never have imagined. With little money, no instrument, and no careers, they were destined to struggle in the slums of Buenos Aires and they were about to test their love in the way they'd been trying to avoid. She still worried it was not enough to nourish their souls.

Sticking her hand in her pocket, she pulled out the paper that had blown against her leg in the alley. Carefully unfolding the crumpled sheet music, she laid it out on the bed and smoothed it with her hands. The musical score was a tad worse for wear but she could still read Roberto's distinctive writing: *Luna Tango*. Not that she'd doubted Roberto, but the evidence was clear. Eduardo had most definitely stolen from her lover. Her vision clouded as determination took over. Roberto needed . . . no, *deserved* . . . his music back and somehow she would find a way.

A loud rap on the front door echoed in the empty house. The banging intensified and she hurried down the stairs, crossed the foyer and flung open the door to find two policemen standing on the veranda, their faces solemn.

'Miss Louisa Gilchrist?'

'Yes.' Her throat clamped around the word.

'We are sorry to inform you but Eduardo Canziani has been found dead,' the older policeman said, his tone grave.

'What?' She clung to the doorframe.

'Found in an alley in La Boca,' said the younger policeman, with too much enthusiasm. 'Beaten to a pulp and shot with his own gun.'

Her knees buckled and she landed heavily on the tiles. Bile rose in her throat and she swallowed, trying to keep it down. 'It can't be true.'

'I'm afraid it is, Miss.' The young policeman helped her up and led her to the hardwood seat in the hallway.

'Robbery?' she asked.

'This is what we're trying to establish. Did he have anything of value in his possession?'

'Just his fob watch. Some gold rings. Probably cash.' She paused, letting her thoughts settle. 'Was there a *bandoneón* case with him?'

'No. Should he have had one?'

'He . . .' Oh god. Could Roberto somehow . . .? She shook her head at the thought. 'No.'

Louisa had managed to get through the police interview without any trouble but it wouldn't take them long to piece the events together. Her relationship with Roberto still remained a secret and the lies she told the police had flowed like a swollen river after a storm. It concerned her that in an effort to protect Roberto from appearing guilty, she might inhibit the investigation and Eduardo's murderer would remain free.

A sob caught in her throat as she wandered through the dark rooms of the mansion. She longed to see her lover, to hold him and seek solace in his arms, but she had to stay away in case the police followed her. She had no doubt when Wyler heard about Eduardo's death he'd go to the police and inform them about her relationship with Roberto. She wished Roberto had a damn telephone so she could find out if he was all right.

Once the media learned about the romance between the muse and the protégé, Louisa and Roberto would be in the headlines. It wouldn't matter how much she protested, no one would believe she hadn't had a sexual relationship with Eduardo, and so her being with Roberto would be classed as an A-grade affair. The public had grown bored with the political arguments in the daily news, and

Eduardo's death and his involvement in a love triangle would be the perfect outlet to channel their anger and grief for their country.

Heaviness fell across her chest and guilt plagued Louisa over her selfishness; Eduardo had needed her and now he was dead.

Louisa wiped her nose on her sleeve and headed out the back door, down the steps and into the yard. She stood on the grass inhaling the scent of jasmine, and allowed the cool night to wrap around her. A powder spray of stars twinkled above, surrounding the half-moon hanging in the inky sky.

The only reason Eduardo knew about her half-moon birthmark was because he'd accidentally walked in on her getting dressed one day. His vicious slander about them sleeping together had come from a place of hurt and it would be easy to blame his anger from tonight on illness, but she sensed much of his rage was driven by jealousy and pent-up frustration. That was harder to forgive.

She placed her head in her hands and squeezed her eyes shut. If Roberto had known about Eduardo's illness, he would have understood and negotiated the situation with the sensitivity it deserved. In her efforts to keep her word to Eduardo, she'd caused a chain reaction that should never have happened.

Louisa headed toward the gazebo. Stones crunched beneath her shoes and sliced the eerie silence.

Who would want to kill Eduardo? He'd spent years cultivating his gentlemanly persona. The only people he'd upset were Héctor and R—

'No!' she yelled into the darkness.

'Do you always scream at yourself?'

Startled, she looked up to find Héctor standing at the base of the gazebo's stairs, his dark suit merging with the shadows. It looked different to the one he'd had on earlier.

'It doesn't look good for you to be at Eduardo's house. Have you heard what happened?'

'Yes. Tragic news.' His words almost sounded genuine.

'Why are you here?'

'You're going to need my help.'

'Shh . . .' She strained to hear a low mumble out on the street.

The noise grew louder and a chorus joined in perfect harmony, singing Eduardo's most popular tune, *'Angel Sin Alas,'* 'Angel Without Wings.' Louisa rushed along the garden path, raced into the house, down the hall and into the music room.

Sneaking a peek through the curtains, she spied a procession snaking up the street. The people slowly made their way to the front of the mansion where they formed a cluster, spilling from the sidewalk and onto the road. Well-dressed men and women, young children, old couples, people in rags. Each one stood with glistening eyes, clutching white candles. The occasional woman's wail pierced the song, which ran on an endless spool. The atmosphere was thick with grief.

'They really loved him,' she said, not taking her eyes off the scene.

'You should back away from the window, you don't want anyone to see you.'

'Why?'

'Because they'll want you to come out, say some words, tell them how sad you are about Canziani's death.'

'I'm devastated. I can't even begin to tell you how much I miss him.'

Héctor raised his eyebrows. 'No one will believe you after your public altercation with Canziani this evening.'

'How do you know?'

'Word travels fast. One of my band members heard about you, Roberto and Canziani fighting in the street.'

'Oh.' This did not bode well. 'The police don't know about this, do they?'

'Louisa.' Héctor placed his hand on her shoulder and the curtains shut as she turned to face him. 'The public are going to want answers and they won't care how they get them. You and Roberto are key suspects.'

'But—'

'You need to leave the country. People saw you. They heard you. You are guilty before you can prove innocence. And with you being a foreigner, and an English one at that, well . . .' He gave small shrug.

'No one had a problem with me being English before. I am . . . was his muse. As long as he created music, they couldn't have cared if I had two heads and came from Mars.'

'But you don't have protection any more. Canziani's dead and they're going to blame you and Roberto, even if neither of you pulled the trigger.'

'What do you mean *even if*? I left Roberto at his apartment, fast asleep on his sofa.'

'At what time?'

'It wasn't long before the police arrived to tell me about Eduardo.' The tears welled again, her throat constricting.

'I was at Roberto's place only an hour ago and he wasn't there.' Louisa stared at Héctor, processing his words.

'Why wouldn't he be at his apartment?' she asked, her mind going into overdrive with crazy thoughts about Roberto going after Eduardo.

'I don't know, but they found Canziani's body in La Boca, not far from where Roberto lives.' Héctor pursed his lips.

'He would never have done it!' Doubt curled around her so tightly she couldn't draw a deep breath. 'Where were you?'

'Louisa, this is not the time to get suspicious, especially with the people closest to you.'

'You just accused Roberto! I'm asking you again.' She narrowed her eyes. 'Where were you?'

'I was at Flavia's.'

'Doing what?'

'Blowing off steam.' At least he had the decency to look coy about being at his lover's house.

'But you were angry with Eduardo. You took off down the hill and—'

He stared at her with wide eyes. 'You're saying I did it?'

'I'm sorry.' She shook her head with confusion. 'Please forgive me, Héctor.'

'I've forgotten already.' He forced a smile. 'Listen, you need to leave now.'

'What about Roberto?'

'He needs to go, too.'

'But leaving Argentina makes us look guilty.'

'If you stay, you run the risk of the public's wrath. Everything will fall on you, Louisa. Think about it. You're Eduardo's muse, you fell in love with his protégé, and you were in the street fighting with him. Even if his death was from a robbery, you will be blamed.'

'They said he was badly beaten and shot.' Her voice was barely audible.

'Yes.'

The shaking started at her feet and raced up her legs. Her entire body trembled and her skin turned cold and clammy. 'We need to find Roberto.'

'I will find him. Right now, you need to pack a bag and go to the port. You can take the boat to Montevideo with Roberto. Where you go after there is not my business, but understand you can never return to Argentina.'

'Yes, I know.' She closed her eyes for a moment and hung her head. 'I can't believe I'm fleeing yet another country.'

'I understand it's hard, but you don't have another choice.' Héctor looked at his watch. 'You've got two hours until the first boat sails for the day.'

'What if you can't find him?'

'I will, don't worry.' He pulled out a wad of pesos from his pocket. Holding her hand, he placed the money in her palm. She tried to close her fingers around the bills but couldn't.

'It's too much. I can't take—'

'You can and you will. Let me help. Please.' He kissed her on the cheek, shoved his hands in his pockets and waved a hand in the air as he exited through the concealed gate at the rear of the garden.

CHAPTER 16

Present Day - Dani

Dani and Carlos broke their embrace and swung around to find Diego Alonso striding down the aisle, unperturbed about witnessing two people kissing in the front row of a deserted theater. Carlos moved away from her but surreptitiously slid his hand up her leg. When his fingers reached the top of her thigh he removed his hand and rested it on the armrest, leaning his arm casually against hers.

Oh my god. She should have been appalled at being caught in the midst of a hot kiss but Carlos shot her a cheeky smile and regret disappeared into the ether.

'I am sorry for my lateness but it appears you managed to occupy yourself.' Amusement tinged Diego's voice and he bent over and kissed Dani on each cheek. 'Here it is.' Diego pulled out an envelope from his pocket and handed it to her, even though she hadn't decided what to do with it. As she slipped it into her bag, Diego said, 'Just ask her to read it. She will understand why when she does.'

'Carlos told you the terms, right? Neither he nor I will disclose where she is if we find her,' she said.

'Yes, of course. I am doing this to help you.'

'Why?'

He raised his hands and shrugged. 'I like you. I feel you will do her story justice.'

'Thanks,' she said, trying to gauge what level he'd reached on the bullshit-o-meter, Dani figured he'd blown off the chart. 'Do you have ideas as to where she could be?'

'No. I have tried all her usual places. She always had an affinity with the beach but every time we went she was sad.'

Memories flooded back of jumping through waves with Iris, building sandcastles, and taking strolls along the shore. Since her mother had left, Dani hadn't set foot near a beach, which had been a difficult task, as she'd spent her teenage years living on the Australian coast. Could Dani's aversion to the sea be a result of memories she wanted to forget?

Diego said, 'Iris cried every time we went. I do not understand why she would torture herself like this but she is an artist, like me, and masochism is in our nature, no?'

'I guess.'

'I have looked for her everywhere.' Diego sighed. 'You would think a famous dancer would be easy to find. Maybe you might have more luck. After all, you have never met her, so you can think outside the box, as they say.' His smile was wide and eyes full of hope. 'I am going to La Pampa for a break from the show preparations. Maybe you will have news on my return. Thank you and I will be forever grateful for your help in ensuring Iris receives my letter.' He stood, bent over and kissed her on both cheeks, then squinted at her. 'I still think you look like her.'

Dani's eye widened as she shook her head. 'I don't think so.'

Diego shrugged and took off up the aisle, leaving Dani and Carlos alone again in the softly lit theater.

'Who does he think I am, his personal courier? I thought he was at least going to give us a hint as to where Iris is.'

'Yes, I thought the same but the moods of Diego are hard to understand. He is not called *El Gemelo* for nothing.'

'The twin?'

Carlos nodded. 'It is like he is two people. Every day his mood is different. Sometimes it changes from minute to minute. No one could understand why *La Gringa* stayed with him for so long. Always, they are doing the fighting.'

'Really?'

'The last time was here.' He pointed at the stage and shook his head. 'Horrible.'

'You saw it?'

'*Sí*. They were at a rehearsal, he yelled, she said nothing, he yelled more, she yelled and left. No one saw her in public after that.'

'What was it about?'

'I could not hear all but I did catch something about missing sheet music and Eduardo Canziani.'

'What?' Her voice came out shrill. Carlos cocked an eyebrow. 'Sorry, but you know this story intrigues me.'

'And I asked you to drop it.'

'And I asked you why.' She could play this game.

'I think my explanation was enough.'

'Well, I . . .' Oh, she could finish that sentence but it would not be in her best interests to do so.

'You?'

'Doesn't matter.' She shook her head, alarmed at her foolishness. One kiss from Carlos and she was about to spout crazy ideas about her grandma's history and Dani's relationship to Iris? *Get a grip, McKenna.*

'I think it does matter. Look at the way your eyelid is doing this strange movement.' He tilted his head. 'You are lying.'

'No, I'm not.' Twitch, twitch. 'Don't be ridiculous.'

'Aha!' He pointed his finger at her eye. 'Look! The lid of your eye moves funny when you tell untruths. You cannot lie, no?'

'I'm not . . .' Her left eyelid went into spasms and she pressed her fingers against it. 'Fine. I suck at lying, but it doesn't mean I have to tell you everything. You haven't told me much about you.'

'I discussed my childhood.'

'But did you truly? You glossed over it. What was life really like with your family? Did they fight? Did they work all the time? Come on, tell me juicy stuff.'

'It is more important to be in the present and not judge a person by their past,' he said.

'But the past makes the person who they are today.'

'The past includes family relationships and I did not think you cared much for yours.'

Shifting in her seat, she said, 'It's not that I don't love them. They're just . . .' How could she explain? She couldn't lie because bloody Carlos had figured out her affliction.

'Please, do not be afraid.' He placed his hand on her arm and the second they touched, electricity zapped through her again. If he kept this up her brain would fry.

'I'm not afraid, I . . .' The longer she left it, the worse it would be. Dani didn't move the arm resting under Carlos's hand. 'Okay, I am afraid to tell you, but I'll do it anyway. My family is far from loving. My mother left me when I was five—'

'I thought you said she died.'

'I said my mother is dead in my grandma's eyes.'

'Yes, I do remember. Tell me more, please.' Carlos stroked her arm and all she wanted to do was climb onto his lap and continue where they'd left off before Diego had barged in.

'I thought you said it's more important to be in the present and not judge a person by their past.'

'*Sí*,' he sighed, gently pushing stray curls behind her ears. 'I say many things. Sometimes actions speak louder than the words, no?' He leaned over and placed his lips on hers again. Once more her body flooded with heat and her heart lurched. The delicious moment lingered, and the longer they kissed, the heavier the guilt weighed on her shoulders. Reluctantly, she pulled away.

'You do not like this? Maybe if I—'

'Carlos, I like it very much, believe me, but I need to tell you something before this goes further.' He nodded and she took a deep breath. 'As much as I like the recent developments between us, and even though this is probably an innocent fling—'

'I do not do the flings.'

'So what's this then?'

'I do not know.' He shrugged and a wicked smile snuck across his lips. 'But I would like to find out.'

'Me too.' Not allowing herself to hesitate, she dived in. 'I'd like you to answer some questions first. I promise it will all make sense when we're done.'

Carlos stretched out his legs and crossed them at the ankles. 'You are interesting, Daniela McKenna. Not like other women. Why is it you have not found a man yet?'

'Carlos! Are you going to cooperate?' He nodded, which helped steady her nerves. 'Thank you. Your mentor was Iris Kennedy, right?'

'Yes, she helped choreograph several of my shows. Why?'

Dani narrowed her eyes.

'You can ask me another one,' he said. 'But remember, I answer these questions in advance of you mastering the basic tango steps.'

'I thought we'd gone past that.'

'I am helping you find Iris, yes, but if you want more information, you dance. Agreed?'

'Fine.'

He pointed at her left eye. 'I do not see a funny moving thing with your eyelid. I believe you are telling the truth.'

It seemed appropriate to reveal her connection to Iris in the theater where her mother had performed. Dani took a deep breath and exhaled slowly. 'Were you and Iris Kennedy good friends?'

'She was my mentor and we became friends but now we do not speak.'

'Why aren't you in contact anymore?'

'Things, they got complicated.' Carlos closed his mouth and stared at the stage, darkness clouding his handsome features. 'If you must know Iris and I do not talk because we do not agree about Cecilia.'

'Your fiancée?'

'Ex-fiancée,' he said with certainty. 'Iris is the reason Cecilia and I danced together. Iris was like a mother to us.'

It took a colossal effort not to flinch. She imagined him having coffee with Iris at a café, talking about life, love, the universe.

Apparently her mother had strong maternal instincts for her dance students but none for her own flesh and blood.

A lump lodged at the back of her throat and a thin film of sweat broke out on her forehead.

'You do not look healthy. I will get you water. Stay here.' Carlos rushed out of the theater and the door closed with a bang behind him.

Alone in the beauty of the Teatro Colón, Dani tried to compose herself, even though it felt like she'd gone six rounds in the emotional boxing ring. Staring at the stage, she pictured her mother performing the moves that had captivated audiences. Her long, dark hair would have swept across her delicate features and her graceful steps would have demonstrated the passion she held for tango. If Iris had made a different choice, Dani would have grown up watching her mother performing magic and capturing everyone's heart, including her daughter's.

Holding her head in her hands, the years of hurt finally overwhelmed her. Dani had every reason to hate her mother but the reality was she'd never stopped loving her.

'Take this.'

Smiling her thanks, Dani took the glass and let the icy water slide down her throat.

'Take this, too.' Carlos handed her his neatly folded handkerchief.

'Thanks.' Her voice was barely above a whisper. Dabbing her wet eyes, she let out a small, nervous laugh. 'I'm sorry. I must be overtired.'

'This excuse would work on lots of people but not me. I have seen your reactions when people speak of *La Gringa*.'

'What do you mean?'

'There.' He pointed at the side of her neck. 'Your vein pops out when people mention her name.'

'It does?' Self-consciously, she placed her fingers on her neck. A heavy throbbing lay underneath. He'd already figured out the eye twitch, so there was no point in denying the vein, even though she hadn't even known about it until now.

'All right, no more beating around the bush,' she said. Carlos raised a questioning eyebrow, so she clarified, 'I'll be straight with you. Iris Kennedy is my mother.' She waited for his face to relay an emotion.

Carlos chewed his lip, his eyes not moving from hers.

'Carlos?'

'Diego was right.'

'Huh?'

'He said you looked like her.' He squinted. 'Yes, I see it. You have her eyes. Her nose. Is this the real reason you are in Argentina?'

'I'm having issues with my boss in New York. We were engaged and he's now back with his ex-wife; I've upset my grandma; I want to ditch my job as an editorial assistant but needed a break to get into feature writing and I talked my boss into letting me come here and write for Tourism Argentina and—'

Carlos held up his hand. 'You upset your grandma? Why?'

'She's scared I'll find my mother and get hurt again.' Pausing, Dani collected her thoughts. 'After everything I've blurted out, that's what you focused on?'

'Work and romantic relationships come and go, yes? But family, ah, family is what makes us who we are.'

'You don't think this family stuff of mine is all a tad weird?'

He shook his head. 'I do not understand how *La Gringa* could leave a young girl like you on the other side of the world. She has always been caring . . .' He stopped and searched her face, no doubt sensing her pain. 'I am sorry. Why did she leave?'

'She'd studied tango when she was young then she met my father and they danced together. Iris had always been independent so after she had me, she struggled to be a mother and wife. She was too caught up in tango and so my dad and I were dropped like hot potatoes. My dad died from a broken heart shortly after.'

'This dying from a broken heart, are you sure?'

'Yes! He did have early onset heart disease but her leaving didn't help matters.' Her tone held an angry edge.

Carlos held up his hand. 'I understand. You were young, this is how you would see it.'

'That's how it was!' Dani jumped from her seat. 'Sorry. It's not your fault.'

Carlos reached for her hand then gently pulled her towards him. He wrapped his arms around her and she leaned against his chest, nestling her nose against his neck. In his arms, she felt cocooned in the pure masculinity of his being. This was a happy place.

They sat in silence and as much as she didn't want to move away, a river of tingles spread up her arm and increased to a point where it hurt. Slowly, she moved back and the cool slapped the places that had been warm.

'I'm not sure I want to find her.'

'Is it because your grandma is angry? Hurt? Disappointed?'

'Yes and no.'

'This is not an answer.'

'Technically, it is. I don't want to upset my grandma any more than I already have and I don't want to find Iris because if she'd wanted me in her life, she would have come looking for me by now.'

'Hmm . . .' Carlos rubbed his thumb and index finger on his chin. 'You have valid reasons but family and relationships are never easy. You need to talk to Iris. If it does not work out, at least you will have tried.' He tilted his head, daring her to disagree.

'I can't do it. Too much time has passed. She has another life. One that hasn't included me for a very long time. We're connected by blood, not relationship.' Visions of the mothers with missing children haunted Dani.

'Society's strength is built on the bonds we establish with our families.'

'Maybe in your eyes, but it's different for me and millions of others around the world,' she said.

'Perhaps the world would be a different place if people liked their family, yes?'

'Maybe.' Dani stared at the wall. Time to change the subject. 'Did Iris really mention Eduardo Canziani and sheet music?'

'We are back to this again? Do you have . . . what is it called? ODC?'

'OCD? Obsessive compulsive disorder?' Carlos nodded and she said, 'No, I don't. Though I do have VPP.'

'What is this?'

'Very persistent personality. It helps in my line of work.' *When I'm actually writing.*

A laugh slid from between his lips. 'Perhaps, but it makes you a little crazy, yes?'

'You calling me crazy?' She shot him a faux glare.

'I would never say this. I understand what the females are like.'

She studied the waves of his dark hair, the warmth of his olive skin, his perfectly symmetrical face and large eyes. 'I have a feeling you know a lot about the fairer sex.'

'I can always learn more.' He leaned in, his lips hovering near hers.

Dani's breathing slowed, her mouth grew dry, and the room turned in a slow, lazy spin. When their lips met, her soul dipped into a pool of ecstasy. She'd never felt this way with anyone else, not even Adam. Carlos's lips pressed hard against hers, and a small laugh echoed inside her head. Adam who?

CHAPTER 17

Present Day - Dani

Once again, Dani woke to white organza curtains billowing in the early morning breeze. Sunlight streamed onto the bed where she lay, her body half covered by a cotton sheet, a man's arm resting lazily across her stomach. Stretching her arms and legs, she sighed and turned on her side to face Carlos.

Since arriving in Argentina, she'd found ways to break the stringent rules she'd set up for her life—no getting involved with interview subjects; no dancing tango; and, just to make it a hat-trick, no contacting Iris. So far she'd broken two rules and was contemplating smashing the third. *Nice work, McKenna.*

What had happened to her since setting foot on Argentine soil? From the moment she left immigration, it was as though she'd come home. The language, the atmosphere, the people, they all combined in a heady mix of familiarity, yet she'd never been to Argentina. Dani had heard about people visiting the motherland of their ancestors and feeling like they'd been there all their life but . . . She shook her head. No. No. *No.*

Carlos opened his eyes, his lips sliding into a cheeky grin. *'Buenos días.'*

'Good morning to you, too.' She felt as satisfied as he looked.

'What is your decision about Iris?'

'How did you know what I was thinking?' First he read her body language, now her mind. She didn't like this. Not one bit.

'I could hear your brain go tick-tick-tick.' He drew circles with his index finger near his temple. 'And Iris has been the main conversation topic, except for when we weren't talking.' He followed it with a wink. 'So what is your decision?'

Dani chewed her lip. 'You better not expect a teary reunion.'

'I promise I will not pack the tissues.' He crossed his heart, face solemn but eyes twinkling.

'I'm on a deadline here. I have to get my stories to my boss—'

'Adam.'

'Yes, him.' It felt weird to hear Carlos say her ex's name. 'I'm not sure we should be wasting precious time trying to find someone who doesn't want to be found. Who's to say she'll talk? And anyway, I'm not that big on interviewing family members.'

'See how it goes. I will come with you and while we are looking for her, I will give you the information you need for your articles on the tango's history. Gualberto has already written the facts about the *bandoneón* to make your life easy.'

'Why didn't he tell me this?'

'Maybe he could see you were occupied with other things.'

'How could he know about . . . ' She waved her hands over them. 'This?'

'I call him The Diviner. Often he sees events before they happen. Let us get ready and we will start our search for the elusive *Gringa*.'

'I thought you two weren't talking with each other.'

'Maybe it is time I rebuilt the bridge. Just like you.'

'So do I have to learn more dance moves before you answer questions for my articles?' Surprisingly, she'd be disappointed if he said no.

Trailing a finger up her bare arm, Carlos said, 'I think you have shown me some moves of your own. Perhaps you have more to demonstrate?'

He pulled her naked body against his and once more, Dani forgot the world outside existed.

~

She traipsed the streets of Recoleta, hoping for inspiration as to Iris's whereabouts. Carlos had left a short while earlier to attend to business and she'd welcomed the chance to go for a walk and process all the recent happenings. Guilt consumed her for going against her grandma's wishes, but the ball was rolling and there was no stopping it now. Anyway, she wasn't so sure she wanted it stopped.

If she looked at all the events leading to this moment, Dani had no doubt she was in the right place at the right time. Who was she to go against what the universe threw at her? She was here for a reason, and whether it was to meet her mother face-to-face or something else, Dani should be open to possibilities. If it included more time with Carlos, she was willing to go with the flow.

It disturbed her a little, though, how easily she'd fallen for him. And even though their relationship had gone a lot further than she'd intended, Carlos should only have been rebound guy. But her stomach did a silly flip whenever she thought about the tall, suave Argentine and, comparing that to the emotional numbness she had when thinking about Adam, it was obvious things had gotten out of hand. Learning tango was less complicated than mastering the ins and outs of romantic relationships, no doubt about it.

Spying an ice-cream shop on the corner, Dani scooted across the road, figuring sugar might kick-start her brain. She bought a cone with her new favorite flavor—*dulce de leche*—and crossed the road to United Nations Square, all the while licking the sweet, caramel-like delight. She took a seat on the park bench, stretched her legs, and gazed at the Floralis Genérica, a giant metal sculpture in the middle of a large pond. She'd read about it having a heat sensitive element that opened and closed the petals according to the sun's proximity, like real flowers. Right now, the metal flower was fully open. Dani checked her watch and sure enough, it was close to midday. In two hours she'd meet Carlos at her hotel room and with luck, he'd have a lead on Iris. And if he didn't, well, Dani was sure they could fill in the time.

The sculpture hypnotized her and when she broke out of the trance, she noticed her T-shirt had turned into a brown, sticky mess; the ice cream had melted and dripped through to her bra. The best thing she could do was go to the hotel to shower and change.

Dani played dodge 'em with the traffic. She skipped up the gutter and kept her eyes straight, trying not to look in the windows of the leather shops selling handbags for minimal pesos. Her bank account had dwindled dramatically and spending money on more bags and shoes, no matter how gorgeous, would deplete funds further. Crossing another street, she gave in and allowed herself an occasional peek at the shops. She got halfway up the block before a familiar figure made her halt, and she peered through the window, shading her eyes with a hand.

'Carlos,' she breathed.

He sat in the corner of the café with two burly men in dark suits, all of them hunched over documents spread across the dark wood table. As if sensing her presence, Carlos looked up and spotted her waving. His expression pinched and he got up and walked out the front door, looking back to check it closed behind him.

'What are you doing here?' It had been a while since he'd used this gruff tone and Dani hadn't missed it one bit.

'Well hello to you.'

'I am busy.'

'I can see. I was walking to the hotel because I got ice cream all over my top—'

'Yes, it is obvious but I do not need the details. Daniela, I have business to attend to.'

'About Iris?'

'No, not about Iris. It's about . . .' he paused, as if searching for words, 'UNESCO business.'

'But I thought it was all over?'

'It is never over. We have to send reports to UNESCO on a regular basis.' She heard his words but he didn't meet her eyes and that said so much more. Apparently, he also sucked at lying. A heavy silence settled around them and he shifted from foot to foot while she fiddled with the strap on her handbag.

'So no news on Iris?' she asked.

'No. And you?' He kept glancing at the men in the coffee shop, who sat watching Dani and Carlos.

'*Nada*,' she said.

'I need to go.' Without a kiss or a smile or even his trademark cheeky wink, Carlos reentered the café and sat with the men, continuing their conversation as if she'd never appeared.

Dumbfounded, Dani tried to collect her thoughts. Talk about Jekyll and Hyde. *Please don't let him be one of those lovers who treats women badly in public but loves them passionately behind closed doors.* Indignation pushed her along the streets to the hotel, where she stormed up the stairs to her room, slammed the door, stripped off, and let the water spikes sting her skin as she muttered a series of expletives in English and Spanish.

She turned off the shower and stared at the taps. Hot. Cold. Just like bloody Carlos. Sure, he was in a business meeting and her arriving unannounced would have surprised him, but surely his reaction held more meaning. Carlos had lied through his teeth then felt guilty about it. At least he had a conscience, unlike Adam, who could look you in the eye and tell you the Earth was flat and you'd believe him.

Adam. Urgh.

Flopping onto the bed and opening her laptop, Dani scanned her emails. Sure enough, Adam had sent yet another missive.

Dani,

Why didn't you reply to my last email? Are you too busy gallivanting in the bars? I need the stories you promised me and I'm surprised you haven't delivered. You've always stuck to your word. What's happening? Email me with an update the minute you get this. I'm making it clear now—I am not happy.

A

. . .

Not happy, eh? Oh well. Dani's lack of emotional response to Adam's email, on a personal and business level, surprised her. This thing with Carlos, whatever the hell it was, had superglued her broken heart together, although cracks had already appeared. But not panicking about getting her stories in on time . . . this was out of character. What was Argentina doing to her?

She needed to get to work.

Closing the email program, Dani opened a page to search the Internet. Biting her lip and rolling her eyes, she stared at the ceiling and racked her brains. The only information she had to go on were memories of her mother and the puff pieces written about Iris. Dani had no idea what her mother was really like, what interests she held, what she ate, drank, watched, read. Casting her mind back to the corkboard in the kitchen of the house she once lived in with her parents, Dani tried to conjure the images stuck on the wall with colored pins: houses, oceans, forests, wineries with mountains as backdrops. All these were pictures her mother had chosen. Every photo was of a place in Argentina.

Dani stared at the empty search box. *Come on, think.* Her fingers moved quickly as she typed *Wineries Argentina.*

The screen came alive with a list of wine regions in the country: San Juan, Río Negro, Córdoba, La Rioja, Catamarca, Salta, Tucumán, Jujuy, Mendoza. Searching the images, they all looked similar until she came across a photo with vineyards stretching as far as the eye could see, snow-capped mountains towering behind. Memories stirred of countless hours staring up at her mother's photo board and dreaming of running away to these exotic places. Jolting back into the present, Dani read the caption on the screen: *Luján de Cuyo, Mendoza Province, Argentina.*

Bingo.

Iris was about to get a nasty shock. Until now, her mother had gotten away with her actions scot-free but her luck had run out. Iris Kennedy had to face her reality.

CHAPTER 18

1953 - Louisa

Louisa arrived at the port with twenty minutes to spare. The stench of rotting seaweed penetrated the salty air but the calm waters lapping against the pier pylons soothed her. The scenario reminded her of when she first arrived in Buenos Aires: She was lost, lonely and desperate to find her place in the world. The exact feelings plaguing her now.

Louisa tiptoed to a dark corner where she was hidden from the dockworkers but close enough to observe people entering the gates. She pulled down the brim of her hat to obscure her eyes, her most distinctive feature and the one all Argentines recognized. She'd done a terrible job with cutting her locks but the black hair dye she'd used looked convincing and a pair of one of Eduardo's many glasses finished off the disguise. Using one of Eduardo's possessions to cover her trail, however, did not feel right.

She sat on the small case packed to the brim with the same clothes she'd arrived with in Argentina. They were simple designs in coarse material, unlike the designer clothes Eduardo had bought her over the years.

Checking the large clock on the wall of the shed, her heart fluttered. Ten minutes until the boat's scheduled departure.

'Come on,' she muttered, staring at the entrance.

A dark figure strode through the gate, stopped, looked about and continued straight ahead. He was tall like Roberto but his shoulders were broader and steps longer. *Héctor.*

Stepping out of the shadows, she approached him. She could barely speak. 'Where's Roberto?'

'He's not coming.'

Inhaling deeply, she asked, 'Why?'

'I did find him.' Héctor paused. 'He's in a state.'

'What do you mean?'

'He can't string a sentence together. I found him three blocks away from his house, in a gutter.'

'What happened?' Guilt ripped through her. She should have gone back to him, made sure he was safe.

Héctor shrugged. 'I do not know.'

'Maybe he had concussion. Perhaps he got confused . . .' Her hands flew up to cover her eyes. 'It's all my fault.'

'No, it's not.' Héctor squeezed her shoulder gently.

Dropping her hands to her side, she looked at him. 'I can't go without Roberto.'

'Louisa, you have to. Roberto's in safe hands. A doctor friend is looking after him at my house and is getting him through the worst part. He'll be well enough to travel shortly.'

'When?'

'Look.' He nodded toward the sky, which was changing into predawn gray. 'It's getting too light and there's no way he's going to make this boat. Tonight, I promise, he'll be on the first sailing after sunset.'

She glanced at the boat. Lights silhouetted a lone captain, who hadn't taken his eyes off her and Héctor.

'You need to go. Find the Hotel Flamenco and do not move until I contact you.'

'I can't.' Her feet were rooted to the ground. How could she be sure Roberto would get on the boat tonight? As soon as the public heard about their affair, and they would, he'd be a victim of their witch hunt. 'I'm not going.'

'I promise you, Louisa, he will meet you in Montevideo tonight. After dark. You need to leave. This is the only way for me to save you both.'

With trembling hands she grabbed the case and held it close to her chest.

Héctor shoved his hands in his pockets and looked away. 'You need to go.'

The boat blew its horn and she dropped her case and threw her arms around her friend, kissing him on the cheek. He embraced her in return, so tight she could barely breathe. Eventually he let go and she grabbed her belongings and spun and hurried away before she changed her mind.

Silently making her way along the gangplank, she tried to convince herself everything would be all right. She trusted Héctor. He'd never let her down and he'd kept Roberto and Louisa's relationship quiet. She had no reason to doubt he would get Roberto on board and into her arms by day's end.

The captain nodded a hello and held out his hand to help her onto the deck. The boat had seen better days, with rust on every surface, a deck that hadn't been scrubbed since the vessel was built and grime on every window. It didn't matter, though. This was her ticket out, and as the boat pulled away from the dock, she held onto the railing, cold wind whipping hair against her face. Pushing the stray curls from her eyes, she watched the red dawn break over Buenos Aires and the streetlights glimmering throughout the city she loved so dearly. She closed her eyes and prayed it wouldn't be long until she could remain in Roberto's arms forever.

It took less than a day for the news of Eduardo Canziani's death to reach Uruguay. Mourners poured onto the streets, their heads hanging low as they carried candles and marched slowly to gather in plazas and parks. When Eduardo's mentor, Carlos Gardel, had died in a plane crash in nineteen thirty-five, riots had spread like wildfire across Latin America. With Canziani's death, however, the crowds were calm in their grief but Louisa had lived in South America long enough to know people's temperament could change in a flash.

She'd spent hours trudging to and from the hotel to the public phone at the *cabina*, battling with the pathetic phone system, trying to contact Héctor. Checking the clock on the bedside table of the hotel, Louisa prepared to make yet another trip down the street. Hopefully, this would be the last time she'd need to; Roberto was due at the port in four hours.

Closing the door behind her, she passed the unmanned reception and she scooted through the doors that led outside. A light evening breeze danced through the streets. It wasn't cool enough to dampen the rising heat of the growing crowds, though. A boy of about fifteen traveling in the opposite direction collided with her.

'Sorry,' she said.

His wide eyes fixed on her, taking in every detail. People surged around them as he stood and stared. Discomfort and panic sent her running into the mob and she rounded a corner, dashing into an alley. Leaning against the wall, she panted, her heart racing.

The place reeked of decaying fish and vegetables, and when she looked around, she found a row of six bins, full to the brim rotting food. Although Louisa dry retched she didn't want to leave the hiding spot as she needed time to calm her frayed nerves. Of course, the boy would stop and stare at a woman with blue eyes. They weren't that common in South America. But it was his flicker of recognition that spooked her. If a teenager could recognize her, then she'd have no hope of hiding her identity in Latin America. If word got out she was in Montevideo and not in Argentina mourning for Eduardo, people would track her down and point the finger. Luckily, no news had come through about love triangles. Not yet, anyway.

Now that she'd had time to process the events of the last day, she wasn't so sure heeding Héctor's advice had been the wisest decision.

Not far from the alley, a slow murmur gathered momentum as people stopped and clustered in small groups, talking among themselves. Some gasped and others placed hands over their open mouths, eyes wide. Louisa emerged from the alley just as a young woman rushed past.

Louisa grabbed the woman's arm. 'What's happening?'

The woman waved a newspaper. 'They know who murdered Eduardo Canziani!'

'Who?' Louisa's voice came out hoarse.

'Eduardo's muse and protégé. This is them, here.' She pointed to the newspaper's front page. The press had used a photo of Louisa and Eduardo taken at a recent concert and someone at the paper had placed an X across Eduardo's face. Next to that was a photo of Roberto. She'd never seen this image before and had no idea how the press had got hold of it.

'Have they found them?' Louisa's hands trembled and she adjusted her hat, using the brim to shield her eyes. Her pulse raced and she licked her lips, trying to diminish the sudden dryness.

'Not yet. They're in hiding, but the police have offered a reward for information.' She let out a low whistle. 'The reward's large enough to support a king for life.'

The woman took off, waving the paper above her head and shouting about the latest development. Louisa's knees threatened to buckle but she managed to get to the hotel, up the stairs and to the safety of her room. Sitting heavily on the bed, she wrapped her arms around her stomach, ill to the core. In theory, Roberto was due to arrive shortly but that hinged on whether Héctor had helped him avoid detection.

She grabbed her clothes and threw them into her bag. Despite the urge to run, she casually walked down the stairs, sauntering past the empty reception and out on to the darkened street. The crowds had subsided slightly and she picked her way through, careful to avoid eye contact. Arriving at the port, she hid in the shadows, almost unable to contain the rising panic in her belly.

After what seemed an eternity, the boat arrived. She stood in a pocket of darkness as the men unloaded cargo but not a single passenger disembarked. Her heart pounding, Louisa watched and prayed she'd see Roberto's long legs carrying his beautiful frame across the docks.

She shifted uncomfortably from foot to foot, dread coursing through her veins and as each minute passed, her hopes crashed like the sea against the rocks. Collapsing in the dark corner, she fought the urge to fall into an inconsolable, hysterical mess. Removing her glasses, she placed her palms on her eyes to stop the tears from breaking free.

Moments later, heavy footsteps stopped near where she sat on the cold, dusty ground. Opening her eyes and sliding on the glasses, she spied boots around the same size as Roberto's. Smiling, she looked up, only to find Héctor gazing down at her.

She gathered her bags and jumped up, looking around the dock. 'Where is he?'

'He's . . . he's not coming.'

'What? Why not?'

'He . . . can't.' Hector looked up and down the dock then placed his hand under her elbow. 'We need to go.'

'But what about Roberto?' It took all her might to not to shout.

'We must go from here. I will tell you everything when the moment is right.' He wrapped his fingers tighter around her skin. 'Come.'

'No!' She yanked her arm from his grip. 'I need to know now!'

'Louisa . . .' Héctor placed his hands on her shoulder. 'You're in danger, you need to get out of here.'

'I am not budging until you tell me were Roberto is.'

Héctor removed his hat, wiped his brow then replaced it again. 'I am sorry.'

'For?' Panic gripped her insides and a dull, low ringing started in her ears.

'The doctor . . . he was surprised at how fast Roberto deteriorated . . .'

'Oh god.' Louisa sunk to her hands and knees, stones poking into her skin. Her lungs constricted, her mind hazy.

Kneeling beside her, Héctor rested his hand on her shoulder. 'He was in and out of consciousness but he didn't suffer pain. The doctor suspects he had a brain hemorrhage.'

'He hit his head on that gutter . . .' Air. She needed air. A slow shake started in her legs and arms. A lump stuck in her throat as she rasped, 'I should have been with him.'

'It wouldn't have made a difference. No one could help.' Héctor brushed a chunk of hair from her tear-stained face.

'We were meant to be together! It wasn't supposed to be like this!' She looked up through blurry eyes, her body aching from the inside out.

'I know, dear Louisa' Héctor held her against his chest as her dam of sadness, fear, and regret exploded in a succession of deep, gut-wrenching sobs.

The bells on the buoys rang in the distance, warning of danger ahead. She prayed that didn't foretell her future.

CHAPTER 19

Present Day - Dani

Dani's slumber was ripped away by someone pummeling on her door. She squinted at the bedside clock and a bright green ten-oh-three p.m. glared at her. Stumbling to the door, she opened it then rubbed her bleary eyes.

Carlos clutched a bunch of wilted daises and a cloud of alcohol hung in the doorway. His hair, shirt, and pants were disheveled and his eyes red.

'I am sorry.' He remained in the hallway, not moving.

She touched his arm and said, 'Come in.'

'No.' He looked at the ground and shook his head.

'Don't be ridiculous. Come in and I'll send for coffee. You look like you could do with a bite to eat as well.'

'No.'

'Carlos, look at me.' She put her finger under his chin and tilted it upward. 'Have a shower, eat and drink something, and I promise, you'll feel better.'

'I am sorry.'

'Tell me you're sorry in here.' She stuck her head out the door.

A few feet away, an elderly couple stared. She grabbed his arm, hauled him in, and shut the door.

He thrust the flowers in her direction. 'For you.'

'Thanks.' She placed the flowers on the table. 'You need a shower.'

Carlos didn't put up a fight as she unbuttoned his top and undid his pants. He stepped out of them with difficulty, leaning against the wall for balance. Even though they'd been naked together, Carlos had taken great pains to conceal his damaged leg, but as she knelt before him, he allowed her to look at his scarring and the large depression in his knee. Normally faint-hearted when it came to injuries, this time Dani didn't recoil. Instead, she ran her fingers gently along the damaged flesh and looked up at him.

'It does not make you sick?' he asked quietly.

'No. It is a part of you.'

'I have never allowed anyone apart from doctors to see it this close.'

'Not even Cecilia?'

He shook his head.

Standing, she gently guided him to the bathroom and he stood in the middle of the room, looking lost. She ran the shower and motioned for him to enter. Dani didn't know what was going on in his head but she couldn't stand seeing this strong-willed man looking so defeated. He'd already apologized and later they'd discuss his behavior from earlier in the day, but right now he needed some TLC.

She grabbed his clothes, put them in the bathroom, then closed the door. Sitting on the bed, she opened the laptop and clicked on Adam's latest email. Hitting Reply, she wrote:

Adam, thank you for your concern, but I am fine. I am not gallivanting, I am working. You'll get your stories and you'll get them with time to spare.

D

. . .

She hit Send. Dani wanted to say more but it could wait until she got to New York. Although the thought of leaving Argentina didn't fill her with excitement like it initially had. These days she felt less like a foreigner and more like an expat. This alone should have set alarm bells ringing, but the winds of change had picked up and if she wasn't careful, this slight breeze would turn into a hurricane.

It concerned her immensely she had failed to finish an article. She felt blocked. Of course, Dani could blame this entirely on the state of the relationships with her mother and grandma, but it went deeper. In a way, this inability to write felt like self-sabotage. But why would she want to destroy the only chance she had to break into features after battling a tsunami of emotions this past fortnight? What was wrong with her?

Opening her notebook, she flicked through the pages, anger propelling her fingers. She stopped at the notes she'd scrawled earlier:

Tango arrived in Marseille, France, in the early 1900s, by way of Argentine sailors dancing with the local women. It slowly made its way to Paris and by 1912, tango had put France under a spell.

At the time, Argentina was enjoying newfound wealth, but it was a case of the rich getting richer and the poor remaining in squalor. The wealthy families of Argentina sent their sons to Europe to study or travel and, as is the tendency of most young men, they strayed into areas and establishments that would horrify their family families.

The well-to-do Argentine men enjoyed the company of women they wouldn't take home to Mother, and as most of the men were excellent tango dancers, they taught the French women moves that wouldn't be acceptable in elite Argentine society. Upper-class Parisians were fascinated by the tango and soon it took over the dance floors as the number one dance.

By 1913, tango had spread across the world. Establishments such as the Waldorf Hotel and Selfridges department store in London adopted Tes Dansants *(high tea with tango dancing) and everyone wanted to be a part of tango.*

Even though small groups still disapproved, tango had a major influence both on and off the dance floor. The corsets and hoop skirts of the era morphed into tulip skirts that opened at the front so women could dance tango more easily. The fashion of wearing a feather that swept horizontally across the face changed to vertical so the accessory didn't hinder women dancing with their tango partner.

A whole industry sprang up and the Parisian fashion houses took advantage of the desire to look and feel what they perceived as an authentic tango dancer. Shoes, stockings, hats, and dresses were marketed as tango attire. One clever fashion designer had an excess of orange material he couldn't sell. When he renamed it 'tango,' he sold all of his stock and had people lining up to order more.

The popularity of tango throughout the world's upper classes saw it filter back to Buenos Aires. This time, Argentina's elite accepted the dance but only in the new, Parisian version, which didn't involve the 'vulgar movements' that originated in the slums of Buenos Aires.

The door to the bathroom clicked open and Carlos stepped out, hair wet, color in his face, and shirt tucked in. 'I am—'

'My amazing powers of deduction tell me you are about to say you're sorry.' She gave him a wink. 'Do you want to share why you're late by eight hours and why you turned up in a state?'

Taking a seat on the bed's edge, Carlos stared at the ground. Eventually, he fixed his eyes on her. 'It is Cecilia.'

Dani's head spun with the possibilities that lay within his words but rather than let her imagination run away with itself, she stilled her mind and asked, 'Did you see her?'

'No.' He shook his head vehemently. 'The men, the ones you saw me with today. They were not from UNESCO.'

'I figured as much. Remember my amazing powers of deduction?' Her lips twitched into a small smile. 'By the way, did you know you suck at lying?'

He nodded. 'The men are detectives.'

'Police or private?'

'Private. I have been looking since she left me months ago.'

'Have they found her?'

'No.'

'Oh.' A pang of sympathy tugged at her. His relationship with his ex still had an effect and he was dealing with it as best he could. Much like how she'd been trying to cope with her feelings for Adam, although her emotional tie with her ex was now one of anger. 'Is this what you needed the money for?'

'What money?'

'Your consulting fee.'

'Yes. All I want to do is find her so I can meet my baby.'

Her stomach hollowed and it took a moment before she could form words in her head, let alone say them. 'You have a baby?'

'Yes.' His glassy eyes locked on hers and a solitary tear slid down his cheek. 'After the accident, we tried to repair our relationship but the media poisoned her.'

'How?'

'They told untruths.'

'Like?' She was wary of pushing too far.

'The media told her stories against me.' He twisted his lips. 'The accident disfigured her face.'

'Is that why she gave up dancing?'

'You must understand, Cecilia believes her looks are what gives her value. After the crash she became a recluse, much like Iris. Then Cecilia moved out one day, leaving a note that said we were finished and she was pregnant and I should not contact her again.'

Irritation flared at Cecilia's cruelty. What kind of woman leaves a note declaring she's pregnant with her lover's child then disappears? Leaning over, she placed her hand on the side of his face. 'I'm so sorry.'

'You do not need to be sorry. I will be all right. The tragedy is my child may never meet me. I feel nothing for her.' His jaw tensed. 'She is a disgrace, but my baby,' he sighed, 'it is for my baby I mourn.'

'How old is the baby?'

'He or she is not born yet. This is why I wish to find Cecilia. I want to be there for the birth of my child.'

'What can I do to help?'

He shrugged and bit his lip. Dani opened her arms and Carlos collapsed into them. She stroked his hair as he lay on her lap, the bond between then strengthened forevermore.

∿

The plane banked to the right and Dani glimpsed the Andes for the first time. Beneath lay vast farmland dotted with patches of arid desert.

'You are looking for the wineries?' Carlos asked.

'Yes,' she said, resting her forehead against the cold window.

'They are in the other direction, not far from Mendoza.' He squeezed her hand. 'I am sure you will find the place you seek.'

She gave a half-hearted smile and stared at the expanse below.

Turning to him, she asked, 'Are you doing okay?'

'Yes, yes, I am fine. Do not worry about me. If the detectives have news they will call. Or if they find nothing, they will also call.' After a restless night, he'd woken with a hangover but in a more positive mood. 'Let's concentrate on this job, yes?'

'Yes.'

From the moment they'd booked the flights that morning, Dani's emotions had run rampant. Ironically, thoughts of her mother invariably resembled some of the moods of tango—sadness, anger, and trepidation—yet when she thought of Carlos, passion, happiness, and fulfilment drowned everything else.

'If we find Iris she might tell you where Cecilia is,' she said.

'Yes, it had crossed my mind.'

'Is this why you're coming with me?' She had to ask.

'No. I am here to offer you support and assist with your articles. I told you I would help, and I will.'

'But if you get the chance to ask Iris about Cecilia you will, right?'

'Yes, I will ask Iris.'

'Fair enough.' The engine slowed and the plane started its descent. Dani's stomach swirled with nerves although she wasn't sure which kind.

'You are not angry?' he asked.

'Why would I be angry? Your child is about to be born and if I were you, I wouldn't leave any stone unturned.'

Carlos smiled for the first time in twenty-four hours. 'You are amazing.'

'No, I'm not. I could never deny a parent the chance to be with their child.' It made sense for her to help Carlos find his baby because until he did, he would remain a broken man. She believed him when he said it was over with Cecilia and her heart ached that he'd had to suffer her cruel actions. There was every chance Iris could help, which meant any thoughts of bailing now were nixed.

The wheels hit the runway with a skid and the plane taxied across the tarmac. As other passengers grabbed their bags and made a dash for the door, Carlos leaned over and cupped his hand under her chin. His dark eyes searched hers, his intimate smile inviting her to lean forward and kiss him.

After a few luscious moments, he pulled away gently and said, 'Our honesty makes us an excellent team.'

This was the perfect moment to tell Carlos the new reason she wanted to find Iris: to ask about the fight she had with Diego Alonso. Iris could have chosen any other tango composer to argue about, so why Eduardo Canziani? She wondered if Iris had discovered a connection. There was only one way to find out.

Once again, guilt swept over her at keeping something from Carlos, especially after what he'd just said. His pleas for her to leave the Canziani case alone echoed in her head and didn't encourage her to make an admission. Carlos collected the bags from the overhead locker and the opportunity to reveal her truth melted away. She hoped their blossoming relationship didn't suffer the same fate.

Dani sipped ice-cold Jerome beer as she sat at an outdoor table in a restaurant on Mendoza's main pedestrian mall, Avenida Sarmiento. Families, couples, friends, and tourists wandered, alone or in clusters, glancing at menus shoved in their faces by eager restaurateurs. Even though it was ten at night, the day's heat clung to her body. The lights of the boutiques shone brightly, enticing shoppers to buy one more item before collapsing and dining under the large, leafy branches of the trees of downtown Mendoza.

'The beer is good, yes?' Since arriving, Carlos's demeanor had lightened.

'Yes, it's excellent.'

'They make this beer in the Andes. It is one of a kind.'

Taking a long sip, Dani let the amber liquid slide down her throat and cool her body from the inside out. They'd arrived in Mendoza late, so they planned to set out early the next day with refreshed bodies and minds. Also, Dani needed more time to process the whole Iris thing. Her emotions needed to catch up, although more time to think about it might be to her detriment.

Her stomach rumbled and just as she was about to comment on her hunger, the waiter opened the door and delivered their meal on a large platter. He efficiently placed the *brasero de mesa* in the center of the table.

'Yum.' She eyed the dish, not entirely sure what lay before her. 'This is a typical Argentine *asado*, right?'

'*Sí*. This is *morcillas*—lack pudding, *mollejas*—sweetbread, and chorizo sausage.' He pointed to each piece proudly.

'Most of this is innards, right?' Surprisingly, she hadn't dry retched which was her usual reaction.

'Yes, yes. And this is *ensalada rusa*, salad of the potatoes.' He heaped a serving of meat on her plate before she had a chance to say she'd just go with the salad. She didn't want to offend an Argentine by not eating one of their national dishes.

'This is *vacío*—steak, and of course, this is chicken.'

'Thanks,' she said, eyeing off the ridiculous amount of food sitting on the table. 'I don't know where to begin.'

'Begin with the *mojellas*, they are delicious.'

Dani looked at the white sweetbread glistening in the streetlight. *You can do this, you've eaten worse. Remember the crickets in Vietnam?* Pasting on a smile, Dani cut into the meat, trying to imagine it was chicken. She slid a small amount on her fork, put it in her mouth, chewed for a moment, and quickly swallowed. The breadcrumbs made it palatable but not enough to warrant tucking into a plateful of the stuff.

She stuck her fork into the potato salad and set to work while Carlos concentrated on devouring his portion. Swigging more beer and emptying the glass, Dani motioned to the waiter for another. He promptly returned, silently placing a large, frosty bottle on the table.

'Daniela, you do not like these things you call innards?'

'No. Sorry.'

'May I?' He motioned to her plate and she nodded, thankful the revolting things would soon disappear. The grease made her stomach turn.

'Do you always eat this much?' she asked.

'*Sí.* Gualberto, he is always laughing and telling me I will get fat.' He patted his six pack and she instantly had an image of running her tongue across his stomach. Her fork clattered noisily onto her plate. Carlos said, 'But this extra weight has not happened yet. If it does, I will eat the lettuce leaves like some of the Argentine women.'

'They don't eat much do they?' Dani glanced at the women seated nearby. They did more talking than eating.

'No. Many do not. It is a shame, because excellent food and wine is the secret to a happy life.'

'Do you think it's so easy?'

'In the reality, no. But it would be nice if this was the case, yes?'

Dani reached for a breadstick and chewed on it, her thoughts meandering. 'Life would be boring if it were easy. How could we build our character if we didn't make mistakes? And how could we appreciate our blessings and happiness if we didn't experience ugliness and sadness?'

'It is like tango, no? A good tango dancer or musician uses every emotion they have lived through to tell the complete story, even if it causes great pain. This is the beauty of tango. This is the beauty of life.' Slapping more food on his plate, he said, 'Unfortunately, my country possesses much sadness. Thousands starve and the rich dine on gold plates. Yes, I understand we are the lucky ones.' He pointed at his plate. 'The people, they get away with murder, so what example does it set for the citizens of Argentina? Look at the Canziani case you are fascinated by. Argentina's greatest legend was murdered and no one has ever been punished for it.'

The breadstick hovered near Dani's mouth as she observed Carlos's passion. His hands flailed about more than usual and a fire burned in his eyes.

'Why does this case get you so agitated?' she asked.

'You cannot understand.'

'You've said this before.' She crossed her arms. 'Try me.'

'No.'

'On the plane you said honesty makes us an excellent team.' She didn't like to use his words against him, but if she wanted to get to the bottom of this, she had to do it. That way, if she understood his point of view, she could decide whether or not she should reveal her desire to speak to her mother about Canziani and Louisa.

'Yes, I did say this.' Carlos pushed the food around the plate with his fork. 'I cannot guarantee you will like what I have to say and I ask you not to take it personally.'

'I can't guarantee anything but I'll try.'

'This is all I ask.' He shifted in his seat and poured them more beer. 'I have a problem with outsiders because every time a foreigner has interfered with the Argentines it has ended in disaster. Look at Louisa Gilchrist and the trouble she caused. If it weren't for her, Eduardo Canziani wouldn't have been murdered.'

'No one can know that for sure. Besides, Canziani chose to have her in his life, right? She was his muse, so she inspired his great works. How can that cause trouble?'

'Louisa Gilchrist had an affair and that was the downfall for Canziani.'

'You truly believe that?' Dani leaned against the back of the chair. 'From what I've read, Louisa had made it abundantly clear to Eduardo their relationship wasn't a romantic one.'

'He loved her.'

'But she didn't love him romantically,' she said. Why was Carlos so against Louisa Gilchrist? It's not like he ever knew her.

'She took his money.'

'No, he gave her food and shelter in return for being his muse. That's how he paid for her services. In a way, it was a business transaction.' Dani prided herself on retaining the information she'd gleaned from reading up on the limited resources available.

A sigh came all the way from Carlos's bootlaces. 'You are not an artist, you do not understand.'

'I understand matters of the heart.'

'Yes, I think you do. But we are getting off the tracks. What I want to say is, foreigners like Louisa Gilchrist have interfered with my people and as a result, we have lost some of our most influential Argentines before their time. The foreigners have gotten away with a lot, including murder.'

'Louisa Gilchrist was considered Argentine royalty so how could she be considered a foreigner? And besides, no one knows who killed Eduardo Canziani.'

'An adopted Argentine is not the same. All the evidence points to her. She left the country the night of the murder.'

'Just because she left doesn't mean she was guilty. If I were her, I would have fled as well. You can't tell me she wouldn't be on top of the suspect list. Roberto Vega and Héctor Sosa also were motivated to kill Canziani.'

'Do you always do so much research?' He replaced his intense frown with a crooked smile.

'It's part of the job, plus I'm naturally inclined. But back to you and your weirdness about this case. Why is it important for an Argentine to solve it?'

'We like to complain about our country's failings but we still love our land, our people, our heritage. If a foreigner solves this cold case it will show the world we are incapable of bringing justice for our dead. Daniela,' he placed his hand on hers, 'you have heard of the atrocities of the seventies, what is called the Dirty War, yes?'

She nodded, remembering the mothers in Plaza de Mayo.

'The way our people treated the citizens is a national disgrace. It is time we looked at our failures and made new successes.'

She nibbled on a breadstick, unable to look Carlos in the eye.

'Who's to say Louisa or Roberto would get a fair trial if they were ever found?'

'They would.' His naïve confidence surprised her.

'You can't tell me that, after all these years, the Argentines wouldn't chuck them in jail and throw away the key. People want someone to blame. This is human nature: guilty before proven innocent.'

'This may have been so in the past, but my people are working hard to change this system.'

She didn't want to get sucked into the whole political thing. Scooping some *chimichurri* onto her plate, Dani dipped the breadstick into it and took a bite. Her taste buds danced with parsley, garlic, and coriander.

'You're familiar with the term kangaroo court, right?' she asked and Carlos nodded. 'So when a national figure is murdered, the people will blame anyone as long as the case can be closed and someone is punished.'

'We need closure.'

'But you can't condemn an innocent person!' Dani suppressed her urge to shout across the table.

'Why do you have this obsession with the case?'

Dani's shrug ended up bigger than she'd planned.

'Hmm.' He frowned and sipped his beer.

She leaned forward and wiped the froth from Carlos's upper lip, his stubble prickling her fingers. He held her hand, their eyes connected, and the world melted away. Sliding her fingers down his palm, she wrapped them around his wrist and pulled him to her.

'Let's go to our room,' she whispered.

Dani held her hand over her eyes to protect them from the glare of the dipping sun. Carlos steered the car left and rolled up the driveway of Bodega Luigi Bosca, a vineyard tucked in Luján de Cuyo's rural sector.

Dani opened the door and slung her bag over her shoulder. 'A snail could have got here faster, you know.'

Carlos held out his hands in a *what can I do about it?* manner. 'I have always been a slow driver yet that didn't stop the . . . never the mind.' A cloud of pain appeared above him.

Dani mentally slapped her forehead. 'Oh, Carlos, I'm sorry. I didn't mean to—'

'It is okay. I have not done the driving much since the . . . the accident. Now even a sloth can beat me.' He gave a lopsided grin.

Wiping the grit from her eyes, she took in the whitewashed Dutch architecture of the homestead.

Carlos squeezed her hand. 'Is this it?'

'No.' The word stuck in her throat. This was the last winery on their list of possibilities. None of the owners or employees she'd already spoken with had seen Iris Kennedy or anyone who looked remotely like her. 'We've wasted so much time.'

'I would not say it is wasted. How would you feel if you had not looked for her?'

She shrugged. 'I didn't think I'd be this disappointed.'

Carlos wrapped an arm around her shoulders, pulled her in and gently kissed her on the forehead.

'Thanks, Carlos, I don't know what I'd do without your help.'

'Bah!' He waved a hand in the air. 'You would do fine but I like that you think you need my help.'

'It appeals to your whole Latino macho thing, doesn't it?' she asked, grinning.

'Maybe. Are you ready to finish for the day?'

She shook her head. 'No, not yet.' She wandered to the other side of the dusty driveway and stared at the Andes towering above, the sky swirling with hues of blue and pink. Carlos remained a short distance away, giving her the space she needed.

Turning, she said, 'The mountains and vineyard are familiar, but the building is all wrong.'

'Daniela, it was a long time ago you saw this picture, yes? Perhaps the vineyard no longer exists or maybe it has been reno- vated. The things, they change.'

'They do, but . . . I can't explain it. It's like an invisible umbilical cord has pulled me to this region and all I have to do is follow it to find her.'

'You do not give up easily, do you?'

'Nope. Come on, we're here, we might as well ask.'

Gravel crunched beneath their shoes as they hurried to the main building and pushed through the double doors. They wandered the rooms and came across concrete 3D murals. The relief work that depicted this history of the settlers that began winemaking in this region entranced her. A plaque explained local artist, Hugo Leytes, had made the murals.

'May I help you?'

Lost in the art, Dani hadn't heard anyone approach. Turning, she found a woman in her twenties wearing a freshly pressed white linen suit and a cobalt blue sash wrapped around her waist.

'Yes, I'm hoping you can.' Dani pulled out the photo Carlos had given her. It was one of the last pictures he'd taken before Iris disappeared. 'Have you seen this woman?'

'*La Gringa Magnifica*?' The woman's eyes widened and she stared at Dani. 'You want to know if she has visited this winery?'

'Yes. Or if you've seen her around Luján de Cuyo. Or Mendoza. Or anywhere, for that matter. I need to find her, it's urgent.'

'Ah, but she is retired, no? No one knows where she is.'

'You're right, but it's important I find her. Perhaps she's changed her hair.' Dani pointed to Iris's long, dark tresses that made her look more Argentine than Anglo-Saxon.

'There is a woman who looks a little like *La Gringa* but with the short hair, *rubia*—blonde. She lives in a small vineyard near Tupungato, an hour south from here.'

'Do you think it could be her?' Dani asked, failing to quell her rising hopes.

'It is the eyes. Look,' she pointed to the photo then studied Dani, 'they are the same as yours.' After a brief pause, she asked, 'You are a relation, yes? You also have the same . . .' She pointed to her nose.

This question was bound to surface but Dani still wasn't sure how to answer.

The woman held up her hand, closed her eyes for a brief moment and said, 'It is not my business. Please, follow me.'

They were led through a series of doors and rooms that grew smaller until they arrived at a tiny office, barely large enough for the desk and chair. Dani and Carlos waited in the hallway while the woman fussed around with a map and pen, frowning and scribbling at the same time. She folded the paper and handed it to Dani with a hopeful smile.

'Maybe this is the woman you seek. She does not have an accent when she speaks the Spanish, she sounds Argentine. I imagine *La Gringa* would have an accent, but who am I to know?' The woman wrapped her hands around Dani's. 'I wish you much luck.'

'Thank you.' Dani bid the young woman farewell and followed Carlos out to the car. Flopping onto the passenger seat, she blew her bangs off her forehead and took a swig from a water bottle.

'What do you think?' she asked.

'I think we should go now. It is not so far.' Carlos started the car and turned to face her.

'But it's getting dark—'

'And you won't sleep if you do not go. I may not have known you long, Daniela, but I understand you cannot relax if something is on your mind.'

'But—'

'But nothing. You are making the excuses. We go.' Carlos clunked the car into reverse, changed to first gear, and left the winery behind as they slowly rolled into an unknown future.

From the moment they left the bodega in Luján de Cuyo, Dani and Carlos fell into silence. Darkness fell and it grew harder to read the road signs and, with the bumpy roads, Dani found it difficult to read the map. In order to get her bearings she turned it around.

'Why do the women do this?' A smirk crossed Carlos's gorgeous lips.

'What? Turn the map around to face the direction we're going?'

He nodded.

'Because it makes total sense. Why don't men stop and ask for directions?'

'It is nonsense, this asking for directions.'

'Why?'

He shrugged.

Dani rolled her eyes then turned her attention to the map. 'Shit.'

'What?'

She looked up, and pointed to a tiny road on the left. 'There! There! Turn!'

Because of their lack of speed Carlos had enough of a chance to negotiate the turnoff without trouble. She cracked open the window and enjoyed the fresh mountain air, smiling as crickets chirped a serenade. The car bumped along, its headlights barely cutting through the darkness.

Dani sensed a change in Carlos's demeanor as he pulled over, stopped the engine and faced her. 'Maybe we should not continue.'

'What? You're the one who said I needed to do this tonight!' Narrowing her eyes, she asked, 'Don't you want to see Iris?'

'Yes. No. I don't know.' His voice conveyed the same confusion she'd been tussling with.

Dani leaned over and gave Carlos a long, sweet kiss. In a low voice she said, 'I'm not sure why the cosmos has thrown us together but here we are.' She smiled, recalling Argentina's fastest racing car driver. 'Come on, start the engine, Fangio, let's do it.'

The gravel road narrowed the higher up the mountain they climbed and by the time they neared the top, the road almost wasn't wide enough for the vehicle. Carlos edged the car along, the wheels slowly turning on the loose stones. Dani was thankful for the darkness so she didn't have to look at the long drop into oblivion should Carlos miscalculate.

A heavy silence surrounded them and Dani felt an unbreakable connection to her companion. His strength bolstered hers to the point where she finally felt confident in dealing with a reunion with Iris.

Carlos rounded another corner and stopped the car. They gazed ahead at the tiny white house with dark trim. Rows of vines surrounded the residence, highlighted by the brilliant moon shining brightly on the pristine peaks towering behind. In the front room of the cottage, a snippet of light shone through the crack in the curtains.

Carlos shifted his position, the leather seat creaking under his weight. 'Is this it?'

Dani stared at the scene before her, waiting for familiarity to strike. Nothing. 'I don't think so. Maybe my memory's distorted.'

His fingers trailed her jawline. 'There is only one way to find out, *sí*?'

Dani nodded, gripped by fear that that woman living here could be Iris but also afraid that she might not be.

Carlos rubbed her shoulder. 'Do you want me to stay in the car?'

'Yes, please. She'd probably have heart failure if we both showed up on her doorstep.' She had to do this alone but it was comforting to know Carlos was only a yelp away.

'I will be here, waiting. You will signal if you need me, yes?'

'Yes.' They embraced, and as much as she wanted to stay in his safe arms, she had to make her move. Pulling away slightly, she gave Carlos a lingering kiss, trying to borrow his energy.

Dani exited the car and traveled the brick path, breathing in the scent of dewy roses. Taking the last step onto the veranda, she froze, unable to raise her hand to knock. Her eyes turned to the heavens and she exhaled slowly before rapping on the door. She waited. Then waited some more.

'I guess no one's home,' she mumbled, still unsure whether disappointment or relief would win out. She turned to step down from the veranda but a shot of determination made her stop. Puffing out her cheeks, she turned and bunched her fingers, knocking hard. Within moments, footsteps fell lightly across a wooden floor.

The door cracked open but a chain prevented it from opening all the way.

'¿*Quién es?*'

An almond-shaped eye peered through the gap. Dani opened her mouth but nothing came out. She'd spent so long working out how to find her mother she hadn't thought about the all-important first line. Perhaps she hadn't really thought it would happen but this dream, or nightmare, had just become a reality.

'It's me,' Dani said in English.

'Who is me?' The words had the distinctive Spanish twang of someone speaking English as a second language. Could Iris have lost her Aussie accent? Or maybe—*oh god, no*—maybe Dani had the wrong person.

'Who is me?' the woman asked again, her tone drenched with annoyance.

'Dani.'

'Dani?'

The door slammed shut, followed by a gasp on the other side. Dani stood on the veranda, unsure what to do. She waited for what seemed an eternity but the door never opened. Her fear of rejection came rushing back as she remembered her grandma's warning: 'If you see Iris, you'll only end up more hurt than you already are.' Dani leaned against the doorframe, emotionally exhausted. She hadn't known how Iris would react but closing the door in her daughter's face had not been on her list of expectations.

Footsteps approached from behind and soon Carlos stood beside her, his brow creased with worry.

'Daniela.' He placed a hand on her shoulder. 'Maybe this is someone else?'

'No, it was her all right.' Anger surged through Dani, spurring her on. 'You know what? She doesn't get to do this. No one gets to desert their daughter and not face the fallout.' Dani banged on the door, her fist hurting with each bash against the wood. 'Open up! I know it's you, Iris Kennedy! I am your daughter! Open up now!'

Silence.

She stopped the bashing and leaned her forehead against the

door. In a softer voice, she said, 'Please, open the door. I've come a long way to see you. Just let me in.'

Dani could sense Iris on the other side, breathing deeply as if trying to stop from hyperventilating. Carlos rubbed Dani's upper back and she turned around, falling into his arms. She rested her head against his strong chest and let his heartbeat soothe her.

'She's not going to talk to us, is she?' she whispered.

'I do not think so.'

A click signaled the door opening and Dani spun to find Iris standing in the doorway, her blue eyes glistening in the moonlight. Without saying a word, Iris turned, motioning for them to follow, and they traveled down a dark passageway toward the rear of the house. The place smelled musty and the plaster on the walls had come away in large patches, exposing rotten beams. They turned a corner and bright light poured from the kitchen. Dani halted her march, needing a moment for her eyes to adjust to the glare. When she focused, she took in shiny blue tiles framing the cement sink, potted herbs lining the windowsill, and a fire burning in a potbelly stove, giving warmth against the cold outside.

Although the kitchen appeared homey, there were no personal effects in sight. No photos of Iris. No posters of productions she'd performed in or choreographed. It was as if Iris wanted to remain anonymous, even in her own home. This lack of evidence meant she could easily pick up and leave at a moment's notice.

Leave.

Again.

Dani squeezed her eyes shut and wondered what the hell she was thinking turning up at Iris's like this. It was too late to bail now and she had to see this through, whatever the outcome.

Iris gestured for Dani and Carlos to take a seat at the battered wooden table then she set about filling the kettle and placing it on the stove. Her expression remained calm but her shaking hands made it difficult to put the teabags in the cups and the bowl of sugar on the table.

'Iris . . .' Carlos started.

With her back to them, she put her hand up to halt conversation. Dani couldn't work out if Iris's behavior was from rudeness or shock. After all, having two people from her past lob on her doorstep at an ungodly hour would freak out most people.

Dani studied the woman who was her biological mother. Her short blonde hair was different from all the photos Dani had seen. Iris had barely aged, her skin still smooth and unblemished, with a beautiful olive hue. Her bare feet showed off shiny hot pink toenails and the mauve shirt she wore overpowered her petite frame. Her black linen pants were too baggy but somehow she pulled off the outfit with ease.

Carlos caught Dani's eye and he held out his hands in a questioning manner. Dani shrugged.

Iris took the milk from the fridge and poured boiling water into the cups, setting them on the table. She took a seat opposite then leveled a gaze on them.

'Now we talk.'

CHAPTER 20

Present Day - Dani

Hot tea sloshed in the mug as Dani desperately tried to hold it still. Her heart beat loudly in her chest, a hollowness grew in her belly. Struggling to remain calm, she tentatively brought the mug to her mouth and let the steam float across her face. She hadn't expected either party to dissolve into tears and hugs and cries of 'I've missed you,' although it might have helped. Iris's aloofness certainly didn't make Dani want to divulge her deepest, heartfelt emotions.

Carlos shifted in his seat. She sensed his unease, not only for her, but also for himself. It couldn't be easy sitting across from the woman who had been like a second mother to him and his ex-fiancée. And now he showed up with Iris's daughter and they were . . . what? Things had gone so fast they hadn't stopped to figure it out.

A hint of patchouli hung in the air and Dani was instantly transported to her early childhood when she would sneak into her mother's room and dab one or two drops on her wrists. At the time it had helped Dani feel closer to her mother but that was before Iris had left. Now the scent caused nothing but torturous memories. Dani vigorously rubbed her nose with the back of her hand.

'Iris, it has been a while. You are looking beautiful as always,' Carlos said, his warm tone attempting to lighten the heavy atmosphere.

Iris blinked and shook her head, as if breaking out of a trance. She lit a cigarette, her gaze moving from Dani to Carlos and back again.

'Tell me, to what do I owe this honor?' She took a long drag and exhaled a thick smoke cloud that acted like a screen between her and the visitors on the other side of the table.

Incredulity swept through Dani. 'That's all you have to say?'

'What did you want to hear?' Iris tapped her cigarette against the edge of the ashtray, an air of defensiveness settling around her. Sure, she'd been caught off guard and was clearly annoyed her peaceful haven had been invaded but that was beside the point. She'd had twenty years to prepare for this and now her day had come.

Carlos squeezed Dani's knee then cleared his throat. 'Iris.'

'Yes?'

'Daniela has come a long way. It has taken much courage to find you. The least you can do is talk with her. She is not a threat. She is your daughter.'

'I am aware that she is my daughter,' Iris snapped.

'Then you should be aware that you should be treating her better than you are.'

Dani was grateful Carlos was on her team. His calmness and strength helped immensely, even though he was probably busting to ask a mountain of questions about Cecilia.

'Believe it or not, I am happy to see you.' Iris directed her comment toward Dani but didn't make eye contact.

'Then act like it!' The dam of years of suppressed anger burst and Dani stood and slammed her fist on the table. Iris flinched as the crockery rattled.

Fury raged through Dani, her shoulders tensed, pain gripped her temples. Carlos placed his hand on hers but she shook it free, angling a finger at Iris. 'You abandon your five-year-old daughter and leave the man you married and you think it's okay to act all nonchalant?'

Iris remained silent, puffing on the damn cigarette, tufts of smoke mixing with the tension to create a thick, insufferable atmosphere.

'For ten years, *ten years*, Iris, I blamed myself for you leaving. Do you know what that does to a kid? Can you even imagine the messed up state I was in?' Iris opened her mouth but Dani shut her down. 'If you had any inkling of the pain you've put us through, you wouldn't have done it. Or maybe you would have. Perhaps being callous is the only thing you know.'

'But I—'

'There are no excuses!' Dani's voice raised an octave. 'Not only did you destroy a little girl's life but you killed the man you promised to love *forever*. My father, *your* husband, died of a broken heart.'

'No one dies of a broken heart.' Iris's low voice faltered ever so slightly. And her eyes reflected . . . what was it? It wasn't the aloofness that Dani had initially encountered. Could it be regret? Sadness? Or was Dani being hopeful Iris was capable of these emotions?

Like lava spewing from a volcano, Dani couldn't stop herself. 'I don't care whether you think it's possible or not, it happened. And you're responsible for it.'

A flicker of hurt creased Iris's perfect complexion. 'That is . . . I . . . he . . .' Her shoulders slumped and she studied her hands resting on her lap. Looking up, Iris's moist eyes met Dani's for the first time. 'I'm sorry.'

'Sorry for what, Iris?' Dani hoped using her mother's first name hurt. 'Are you sorry for the state of the economy of Argentina? Sorry for global warming? Or sorry I came all this way only to be met by a woman who doesn't care about meeting her daughter twenty years after she abandoned her?'

'It's not like that at all, Daniela—'

'Call me Dani.'

'But Carlos calls you—'

'*You* can call me Dani.' Her tone remained even.

Iris looked so small in the chair, as if she'd aged ten years in the last five minutes. A ripple of sympathy ran through Dani but she quickly brushed it away.

Iris sniffled. 'All right, I'll call you whatever you want.'

Not one for losing her cool or using her words to hurt, not even on Adam, the rage swirling within Dani scared her. Had she been so naïve to think she would be the calm, mature adult she'd envisaged upon meeting her mother? Instead she'd resorted to behaving like a five-year-old having a tantrum. Iris's nonchalance, her distance, the lack of feeling had come as a shock. Reality had just slapped Dani hard on the side of the face and it stung like crazy.

Gritting her teeth, Dani said, 'People need licenses for dogs yet anyone can have a kid, whether they're a fit parent or not. You couldn't handle the responsibility, so you ran away the first chance you got.'

Iris stared at the far corner, her brow furrowed, her bottom lip trembling.

Jesus, McKenna, who are you? Sure, she had every right to let Iris know how she really felt, but these cutting words? If there'd been a line to cross, Dani had just leaped over it.

'Daniela,' Carlos stood and gently put his hand under her elbow. 'Please, let us talk.'

'Later.'

'No, Daniela, now.' Carlos's stern look told her there was no point in arguing.

'Fine,' she huffed. Carlos guided her out the kitchen and down the hallway. When they got to the front door, she halted. 'I'm not going to leave. She has more home truths coming her way.'

'You will not get a chance if you do not calm down. Come.' He opened the front door and they stepped out onto the veranda. The late evening air cleared her lungs and cooled the heat radiating from her body.

Leaning against the railing, she crossed her arms. 'What do you want to say?'

'Do not be angry with me, Daniela. I am on your side. This is why I took you away. Iris has done many things wrong, of this I am aware. And you have every right to tell her how you feel, but if you bombard her with all the anger and hate you have spent years cultivating, then we should leave now because you will not succeed in getting your answers from Iris.'

'She deserves what she gets from me.' Dani pursed her lips.

'You are not a spiteful person. Why would you be one now?'

'You seriously have to ask this?' She balled her hands on her hips.

'You are upset, angry, want vengeance perhaps, but you are not a mean person, Daniela McKenna. Deep down in that big heart of yours, I think there is some hope you can mend the broken bridge with your mother.' He arched an eyebrow. 'Will you tell me I am wrong?'

Shit. From the moment Diego and Carlos decided finding Iris was the idea of the century, Dani had allowed herself to be swept along the Tide of Iris. Dani could have reached out for a life raft at any time by saying no but instead she sailed the murky waters and had now landed onshore. She had the answer to Carlos's question but wasn't willing to admit it to herself, let alone anyone else.

'What about you, Carlos? Aren't you angry? Don't you want to yell and scream at her?' *Ooh, nice deflection.*

'Of course I am angry but yelling will not help the matters.' He tucked a lock of hair behind her ear. 'It is good to do the venting, this I understand. But if everyone is yelling then who is listening?'

Dani bit her lip and focused on the line of rosebushes lit by the silvery moon. Carlos did have a point. After all, Iris had also betrayed him. The turbulent emotions churning inside her made it impossible to know what to do. Yes, she'd sought out Iris for myriad reasons, yet now the moment was upon her, Dani didn't know how to deal with it. Anger wasn't working for anybody, especially Dani. Nope. She was better than this. She would hold her head high and show Iris that she'd survived quite well without her, thank you very much.

'All right,' she took a deep breath and moved toward the door. 'I'm calm now. We can go back in.'

Carlos stepped in front and blocked her path. Placing a finger

192

under her chin, his lips met hers and the barbs that had sprung up since seeing Iris disintegrated. She had no idea how he could be so composed. Admiration for this handsome, caring Argentine multiplied tenfold.

'You should go in by yourself. This is between mother and daughter.'

Panic shot through her. 'No! Carlos, I need you in there. Please.'

'This is not my business. I will talk with Iris later.'

It surprised her how much she wanted him with her. 'But what if I lose it with her and she throws us out?'

'I have faith this will not happen.' He kissed her on the forehead. 'Be brave. Be strong. Say what you need to in a way that will ensure you are heard.'

Dani allowed a small smile. 'And I thought Argentines were supposed to be hot headed.'

'I am not your everyday Argentine.'

'That, I know.' Wrapping her arms around Carlos and squeezing him tight, she said, 'Thank you.'

'Go. You will do good.'

He opened the door and she took a deep breath and stepped across the threshold. The door clicked closed as she slowly made her way to the kitchen, splashing and clunking sounds echoing up the hallway. Arriving at the kitchen door, Dani paused and Iris turned around from the sink, her eyes red and glassy.

Iris said, 'I'm sorry about my behavior before. Your arrival shocked me and I just didn't know how to react.'

'Do you think being aloof is going to help matters?' Dani was so confused by the way everything had unfolded she had no idea which direction she wanted to head.

'Of course not.' Iris nodded toward a shoebox sitting on the table. 'I have something for you.'

'I don't need any gifts,' Dani said then instantly regretted the tone. Carlos was in her head, urging her to remain calm.

'It's not a gift, Daniel—Dani. Please, open it.' She dried her hands on a tea towel and moved toward the hallway. 'You may want some time to look through it so I will give you the space.'

'Where are you going?'

'To speak with Carlos but please, do not think I'm leaving because I don't want us to talk. What's in there will show you what I find difficult expressing verbally.' Iris rested her hand on the doorframe. 'When you are ready, come and find me.'

Iris grabbed a woolen jacket off the coat hook and hurried down the hallway. The front door opened and shut and Dani strained to hear Carlos's comforting voice but she heard nothing.

Turning her attention to the shoebox in front of her, Dani checked out the label. It was for a pair of tango shoes. What was Iris playing at? Was she deliberately trying to hurt her daughter? Why would Dani want frigging tango shoes?

'For god's sake.' Ripping off the lid Dani found a pile of envelopes with her old Australian address written in perfect, round letters. Taking out a handful of envelopes, she opened them and flicked through the cards with images of flowers, cartoon rabbits and ducks, balloons, rainbows, and snowmen . . . *Happy eleventh birthday, Daniela. Happy fourteenth. Happy nineteenth birthday, Daniela. Merry Christmas, Daniela. I will always love you. I miss you. I long to see you.*

'What the hell?' Grabbing more, she ripped open the envelopes in quick succession.

Scanning the messages, she read: *I am so sorry. I don't expect you to ever forgive me but know I think of you every day. I wish I could see you. I wish I could turn back time. You will always be in my heart.*

Dani stared at the small pile. Iris couldn't have conjured these up in the last few minutes so they had to be genuine. Why hadn't her mother sent them? If she had sent just one of these cards or a letter explaining why she left, then Dani's life could have been so different. Perhaps she would have tracked Iris down earlier and they could have started repairing the relationship. Or maybe Dani wouldn't have spent all those years blaming herself for something that wasn't her fault. So many different scenarios could have played out if Iris had sent just one bloody card.

'Damn it!'

Grabbing the box she pushed back the chair, the wooden legs

scraping against the floorboards. She marched down the hallway, tucked the shoebox under her arm, and yanked open the front door. Iris and Carlos stood at the edge of the garden. Her mother spoke quietly while Carlos slowly shook his head. The scene didn't appear comfortable but there was no yelling to be had. How could he be so civil in the presence of this woman who made a habit of messing up people's lives?

Stomping down the stairs and crunching across the gravel Dani strode up to the pair. She thrust the shoebox near Iris's face.

'Is this supposed to make me feel better?'

Iris's eyes widened. 'I . . . it . . . they was supposed to show you that I thought of you constantly.'

'But you didn't send them!' She shoved the box at Carlos who took it reluctantly. 'Look! Inside are the years and years of hope that I could have had but Iris didn't send one frigging card. What was the point of writing them if they weren't sent?'

'I was too scared,' Iris said quietly.

'Scared of what?'

'Scared they would be returned.' Iris massaged her temples.

'So what if they were? At least you would have tried.' Dani shook her head. A wave frustration and sorrow rushed up and exploded in hot tears. 'Why didn't you try? Haven't you seen the mothers of the *desaparecidos*? They've spent a lifetime looking for children who are probably dead. Yet here you are, the mother of a living child, and you failed to contact me.'

'Oh, Dani.' Iris put her hand on Dani's arm but she wrenched it away. 'You have no idea how many times I took a card to the post office only to back out at the last minute. Not only was I scared of being rejected, I didn't feel I had the right to barge in and dredge up painful memories. Trying to get back into your life would have upset any balance you had living with your grandma.'

'What kind of balance could I ever have after you left?' Despite her desperation to stop the tears, they continued their watery descent. Her hands shook and she had an overwhelming desire to sit down before she fell under the weight of anguish. Collapsing on the gravel, she tucked her knees under her chin and wrapped her arms around them. Cold traveled up her spine and her entire body shivered.

Carlos passed the shoebox to Iris and wrapped his jacket around Dani. 'We should go inside, yes? The cold, it will not help.'

'Nothing will help,' she mumbled, allowing Carlos to guide her to a standing position. 'We're leaving.'

Carlos folded his arm protectively around Dani as he led her a short distance away from Iris. Leaning in close, he said, 'You have traveled a long distance to get here—physically and emotionally. Think about how you will feel in one week, or one month, or one year from now if you give up this chance. Will you regret it, even though you are full of pain in this moment?'

Bang! Carlos knew exactly where to aim his arrow. At the heart. 'I don't know. I'm just . . . confused and . . . and . . .'

'And maybe asking the questions you've always wanted will help with your confusion.' He cocked an eyebrow and smiled.

'Fine,' she mumbled. 'One more shot but if it goes pear shaped we leave.'

Carlos held her hand as they turned to find Iris blowing her nose in a handkerchief. As soon as she saw them watching she tucked it into her pants pocket and smoothed down her shirt. 'Will you come back inside and talk some more? Please?'

Carlos squeezed Dani's hand and she nodded, leading the way back into the house and Iris's kitchen. Dani sat at the table while Carlos stood behind, his hands resting lightly on her shoulders. Iris sat on the opposite side, her eyes glassy, her nose red.

'I . . .' Dani rested her elbows on the table and placed her head in her hands. If she could just pinpoint the exact need clawing at her then she could express it and move on. Unfortunately, the root of her angst kept shifting—frustration, hurt, hope, anger, loneliness all mingled together until she was left with one large raw gaping wound.

Iris's big blue eyes concentrated on her daughter. 'There are not enough words in the world to express how sorry I am. If I could turn back time, I would.'

'Would you have given up dancing tango?'

'I . . . I loved you and your father with all my heart and I'm not making excuses but there was something way bigger driving me. Please, Dani, know that I accept full responsibility.'

'You haven't answered my question,' Dani said with firmness.

'No, I haven't. The answer is not pretty and I'm not sure if you're ready for it.'

'I'll be the judge of that, thank you.' Dani's words were civil but it felt near impossible to keep her emotions in check. If things blew up, Dani doubted she'd have the strength to try again.

Carlos squeezed her shoulders and said, 'I will take leave now.'

'Stay.' Dani clutched his hand to her shoulder.

'No, you need more time. Iris said earlier I could wait in the front room.' He leaned down and kissed Dani on the cheek. Whispering, he said, 'Believe in your strength, Daniela McKenna.'

Nodding at Iris, Carlos walked behind her to the doorway leading out to the hall. Turning, he placed his hand on his heart and mouthed 'stay strong' to Dani before blowing a kiss. Carlos's uneven footsteps and cane echoed down the hallway.

'He cares for you a lot,' Iris said quietly.

Dani nodded, wishing the tears would dry up. Although maybe it was a good thing that Iris finally saw the impact of her actions.

'There are so many questions I want to ask.' Iris looked down and studied her perfectly manicured hands. 'I'm . . . I just . . . I don't have the right, I know. However, you should have the opportunity to ask all the questions you want. I will answer with one hundred percent honesty, I promise.'

Although Iris had initially put up a wall, she'd started breaking it down piece by piece and shown a willingness to face the onslaught of emotions Dani hurled at her. Perhaps Iris could be trusted to tell the truth. *Only one way to find out, McKenna.*

Sucking in air then exhaling slowly Dani said, 'We'll start with you explaining why you left me.'

CHAPTER 21

1953 - Louisa

Héctor passed Louisa a flask of water as they sat beside the dusty road, vast fields of wheat stretching out before them. The midday sun beat down relentlessly and flies buzzed around Louisa and Héctor as they took shelter under a lone tree, trying to regain some of their depleting energy. Since leaving Montevideo a few days before, they'd traveled back roads by foot or hitched rides to achieve their goal of going as far inland as possible. But with news spreading quickly through the larger cities, it was only a matter of time before the smaller villages found out about the scandal surrounding the death of their beloved tango composer. Héctor and Louisa had to decide about what to do next, and they had to make it soon.

The heat from the sun burnt the skin through her light shirt but she didn't care. Since finding out Roberto had died in such a sad, lonely way, she'd lost the will to go on.

'Drink.' Héctor nodded at the flask in her listless hand.

Louisa bit her lip and shook her head.

'You need to look after yourself.'

'What's the point?' Her vision blurred again, not just from tears but from lack of sustenance.

'The point is that you are a young, intelligent woman with a life-time of wonder ahead of you. My heart is broken for Roberto, also, but we cannot change what is. Do you think Roberto wants to see you suffer like this?'

'I deserve to suffer,' she mumbled, drawing her knees up around her chin. 'If I'd just kept my feelings to myself, resisted Roberto then . . . then . . .' An all too familiar sob filled the air.

'Then what?'

Louisa shrugged, the hollowness in her chest growing. 'I'm going back to Argentina.'

'No! You can't!' Héctor grabbed her arm but she shook it free.

'Why not? I killed them.'

'How can you say that?'

'Roberto died from an injury he received fighting about *me*. And Eduardo wouldn't have been on the streets alone that late if he hadn't been so upset with *me*.' She jabbed her chest with her finger, not caring about the pain. Louisa didn't want to contemplate the possibility that Roberto may have found Eduardo and killed him. He just . . . couldn't have. Straightening her spine, bubbles of certainty brewed within. For the first time since fleeing Argentina, Louisa had a clear vision of what she needed to do. 'I'm going to return and tell the authorities exactly what happened in San Telmo.'

'They'll crucify you. It doesn't matter that you're innocent. Haven't you seen the papers? No matter what you say, you'll be charged with murder, especially as you left Argentina so quickly. They're baying for blood and if you go back it will be yours.'

'I know that but what kind of hell would I endure if I continue to run?' Narrowing her eyes she stared at the bright blue Uruguayan sky, determination rushing through her veins. Standing, she grabbed her bag. 'I'm not changing my mind. I feel responsible for their deaths and I have to make things right.' A hard lump formed in her throat as she adjusted the strap on her shoulder. 'Héctor, thank you for looking out for me and I appreciate everything you've done but you've already put yourself at risk by helping me flee, I couldn't cope with being responsible for your downfall as well. Please, just let me do what I need to. That way you can move on with your life without me complicating it further.'

Héctor cradled his head in his hands. Rocking back and forth, he muttered, as small clouds of dust swirled at his feet.

'Héctor?' She knelt down and squeezed his shoulder.

Looking up, he stared at her with large eyes then he quickly leaned in and placed his dry lips on hers. 'I love you, Louisa.'

Her lips burned, as if they'd been branded. Anger and shock swept through her as she recoiled, unable to fully comprehend what had just transpired. Louisa had always thought Héctor's flirting had a tinge of truth but she'd never known for sure. Now she did and her heart hurt. 'How could you? I'm in mourning for Roberto!'

'I . . . I . . .' Héctor looked to the heavens then locked eyes on her. 'I am so sorry.'

'You should be, Héctor.' Her pulse raced with fury. 'Have I ever given you the impression I've felt the same way about you?'

'You've a good heart and you've always been so kind to me.'

'That doesn't mean I love you like I love . . . loved Roberto.' Why would he do this when she'd just lost the only man she'd ever wanted to be with? 'What were you expecting me to say? I love you as well so I won't turn myself into the authorities? Are you insane?'

'I . . . Jesus.' Héctor hung his head, raking his fingers through his hair, the trademark ponytail in disarray. 'I just thought that if I helped you . . . if you saw I was a good person—'

'Up until now I've held you in high regard but this is reprehensible, Héctor.' She stood. 'I'm leaving.'

Jumping up, he reached for her hands but she balked. 'Where are you going?'

'Argentina, like I said. '

'You can't go!' His shout carried across the fields.

'Nothing you say will change my mind.' She grabbed the flask and took a long drink, trying to soothe her parched throat. 'You were right in questioning me about whether Roberto wants to see me suffer like this. No, he wouldn't and I'm going to rectify this now.'

She took off, determination pushing her forward. *Wants.* Wants? Do you think Roberto *wants* to see you suffer like this? Those were Héctor's exact words. Louisa turned and marched back to Héctor who had his hands shoved in his pockets.

'You've changed your mind?' He beamed.

'You said *wants* before.'

'What?' Fear flashed in Héctor's eyes. 'Oh that? It was just . . . a . . . a mistake. Everyone gets their tenses mixed up.'

'The human mind has an amazing capability of changing everything to past tense when someone dies.'

'A mistake, that's all it was.' Héctor studied the vast wheat fields.

Then the words Héctor had uttered in Roberto's apartment echoed in her ears. *But alas, the love of my life has chosen another. Maybe one day I will steal her out from under your nose.*

'Héctor, what the hell have you done? You need to tell me. Now!'

Héctor remained silent.

'Tell me!' She screamed.

'Roberto's alive.' Héctor closed his eyes as if waiting for an attack.

'What?' The heavy bag dropped on her foot but she barely registered the pain.

'The night you left I went back to collect him from my house and I had every intention of bringing him to Uruguay but . . .'

'But what?' She yelled, unable to contain her rage. 'What the hell did you do?'

'I told him it would be safer for him to leave separately and he should go through northern Argentina then Bolivia.'

'And?' Her heart felt like it was in her throat.

'And I'd gone out to get supplies but when I was returning to my apartment I saw police in my street.'

'No!' She staggered slightly, reaching out for the tree.

'I . . . I didn't stick around long enough to know if they took him in. Call me selfish but I wasn't going near them.' Héctor's eyes darted away from hers.

'So he was arrested? How would they know he was at your place?'

'Maybe they were coming to question me again. Louisa,' his eyes pleaded with hers, 'Perhaps he managed to escape.'

'Why didn't you tell me this before?' Her temples throbbed and she massaged them. 'Why did you lie?'

'I was going to tell you the truth but on the boat to Montevideo I thought it might be better if you thought he'd died. If he was arrested he'd be as good as dead. I remembered how you've always been a good friend and how much I loved you and . . . it was a stupid, opportunistic act.'

'But you kept this up for almost a week! Couldn't you see the pain I was suffering? Did you get a kick out of that?' Stepping forward she put her hands on his chest and gave him an almighty shove. Héctor let her. The release felt good and she pushed him harder. 'How could you?'

'I'm—'

'Sorry? Forget it, Héctor. The only thing you can do for me right now is tell me where he planned to go if he got out of Argentina.'

Holding his hands up in a protective fashion, his eyes earnest, Héctor said, 'All I know is he planned to go north and into Bolivia. I didn't ask where else because I didn't want to know.'

'You're lying!' She shoved him so hard he stumbled back, fighting to regain balance.

'I'm not, I promise you.' His voice shook as if he feared what she might do next. 'You have no reason to believe me but I swear I don't know where he's going. He did say one thing, though.' He took a breath, as if debating whether to tell her.

'What?'

'He mentioned he wanted to take you to the place you two dreamed about.'

Excitement rippled through Louisa and she hauled the bag over her shoulder. Although they were in wheat territory, a faint aroma of cashews filled her nostrils as Roberto's words floated back to her: 'Brazil. That way I wouldn't have to worry about running out of cashew nuts ever again,' he'd said. She pictured the map in her pocket—the one Roberto had drawn their dream house on. If her lover had miraculously escaped, she knew exactly where to find him. Taking a deep breath she faced north.

'What are you doing?' Héctor asked, his face clouded with worry.

'I'm following my heart.'

CHAPTER 22

Present Day - Dani

Iris placed her hands on the kitchen table, taking her time before responding to Dani. 'No matter how many times I rehearsed answering your question about me leaving, it never came out right. Perhaps it was because I didn't think we would actually see each other.'

'Because you didn't want to find me,' Dani said in a low voice.

'I'll be honest, for years I've had conflicted emotions about finding you.' Iris reached for her hand but Dani withdrew it quickly. 'I've replayed us meeting so many times in my head. Especially on the long, sleepless nights when the unforgivable things I've done came back to haunt me.'

'You brought this upon yourself, Iris.' Yes, Dani's comments were pointed but at least she wasn't yelling and, in a strange way, this civil behavior felt much better.

'I know, I know.' Iris reached for the cigarettes and placed one in her mouth. Striking a match, she paused. 'Are you okay with me smoking?'

'No.'

'All right.' Iris blew out the match and put the cigarette back in the packet. Her fingers drummed on the box while Dani impatiently waited for her to continue. Eventually Iris said, '*Entrega.*'

'What has that got to do with anything?'

'You know it?' Iris raised her eyebrows.

'Of course I do. I'm not hanging around with one of the world's leading experts on tango for nothing.' In fact, it was for a whole lot of things but Iris didn't need to know the details.

'When I was seventeen I first discovered tango,' Iris said slowly. 'My friends and I went to a movie theater that was screening old movies and I saw Rudolph Valentino dance tango in the *Four Horsemen of the Apocalypse.* I instantly fell in love with him and the dance and music. Of course, I later discovered his version was more theatrical than traditional but it didn't matter. The music and idea of tango captured me and it took a long time to find someone in Melbourne who taught Argentine tango. When I told my mother, your grandma, that I wanted to learn, she responded like I'd said I was going to dance with the devil.'

'So she hated it even then? I thought it all started after you left us.' Dani tried not to choke on the last sentence.

Iris twisted her lips, pausing before she spoke. 'Your grandma and I had no reason to talk about tango until I decided I wanted learn and that's when I discovered how much she detested it. Stella never explained why and I was too afraid to ask. I didn't want her ruining the one thing that injected a life force into me, especially as it was sucked out when I was a child.'

Dani leaned forward. 'What are you talking about?'

'There are so many things to discuss, Dani, but let's focus on your first question. It's important for you to know how everything transpired.' Iris ran her fingers along the edge of the table and back again. 'So I snuck around for a couple of years, fitting in as many lessons as I could but by the time I was nineteen I'd had enough of the deceit.' She ran her fingers through her hair. 'I told Stella what I'd been doing and I had to endure her wrath but even though I'd complicated our already unstable relationship, I persisted because dancing tango was like breathing. I tried to give up tango a few times to keep the peace but it was impossible. I'd feel like I was dying. Then I met your father.' Iris's eyes clouded over. 'Your father was the kindest, most caring man I'd ever met. Instead of demanding I give it up, like your grandma, he joined me on the dance floor and for a moment in time, it was heaven on earth.' She paused to wipe a stray tear.

Dani bit her lip, unsure if she could cope with hearing the rest. If she walked out now, though, what hope would she ever have of fully understanding her mother's actions? Dani closed her eyes briefly. *I'm asking these questions for you as well, Daddy. Maybe now we'll finally understand.*

'Dad blamed himself from the moment you walked out that door to the day he died. You were the one who broke his heart. You—'

'Yes, I am aware of what you think. Please, Dani, let me finish explaining. I don't expect you to understand, though my hope is one day you will.'

'Keep going, please.' Dani sounded so civil, so unaffected by Iris's words but on the inside, her heart ached and her resolve to remain calm began to dwindle.

'After your father and I had been dancing together for a while, there came a time when everything aligned to culminate in one magical moment—the music, dance, heart, and soul entwining perfectly.'

Memories of her father and mother floating across the dance floor flooded back. Just above a whisper, Dani said, '*Entrega.*'

'Yes.' Iris paused, as if lost in her own memories of dancing with her ex-husband. Giving a small shake of the head, she said, 'Although the word *entrega* doesn't fully represent the true meaning. It has to be experienced.' Looking directly at Dani, Iris said, '*Entrega* became a drug. I hadn't felt anything like it before. So many tango dancers spend a lifetime trying to achieve *entrega* but I'd had it. Once. And I wanted more. I needed more. I craved it day and night. Your father had felt a snippet but he couldn't comprehend the impact *entrega* had on me. I tried to find it again with him but that moment was lost forever, so I looked to other dancers in Australia but *entrega* never happened.'

'You wanted the impossible.' Dani clenched and unclenched her hands.

'You're right, but I couldn't see it at the time. I was caught in a spiral and thought if I cut ties with tango all together I could achieve some sanity. So your father and I gave up tango, much to Stella's relief, and I set about repairing the relationships I'd damaged. It worked for a while then I got pregnant. I thought . . . I . . .' Iris stared at the ceiling as if searching for the right words. 'I thought nurturing a young child would cancel out the need for tango.'

'So you used me as a device? Was I even wanted?' Dani gripped the edge of the table so hard pain her fingers ached.

'Of course you were wanted! One of the happiest moments in my life was the day you were born!' Iris seemed genuinely surprised by Dani's outburst.

What the hell was wrong with Iris? Couldn't she see the pain she was causing by saying these things? But Dani had asked for the truth and whether she liked it or not, Iris appeared determined to give it to her.

Shifting in the chair, Iris said, 'I tried, Dani. I really, really tried to be the best mother possible but as with everything else in my life, apart from tango, I was a miserable failure.'

'A kid is a lifelong commitment, Iris. You're not supposed to give up after five years.' The muscles in Dani's neck tightened and the tell-tale signs of a stress headache emerged.

'You're right, but you had your father. And Stella.'

'But I didn't have a mother!' Dani slammed the table with both hands, the tea in the cup sloshing over the sides. 'Every kid deserves a mother!'

'But I wasn't any good.'

'You could have gotten better with practice!' Dani pulled at the roots of her hair, the action relieving the increasing ache in her head.

'I wanted to. I so desperately wanted to. But I had no idea how to be a mother. Your grandma wasn't exactly the perfect role model.'

Dani's eyes widened. 'You're blaming Stella now? The woman who raised both her daughter and granddaughter?'

'I left you with your father but please know I do not blame Stella for where I was at. I was an adult, I had to figure it out for myself and I'm just trying to give you an understanding of what I was struggling with.'

'It's not all about you, Iris!' *God, had this woman always been this so self-centered?*

'Believe it or not, Dani, I left to help you.'

A tide of fury lapped at Dani's feet, rising quickly. She didn't want to be this angry, screaming person but Iris had the ability to get under her skin and seek out every emotion she normally kept at bay. 'So you're blaming me for pissing off to Argentina and dumping your family?' She stood up, about to leave.

'No! God no!' Iris held her head in her hands then looked up, a stream of tears flowing down her flawless complexion. 'This is no one's fault other than my own. I was a fool, Dani. I spent years chasing the *entrega* dream but now I know I only experienced it because I was with your father.'

'Too little, too late.' Dani shook her head, staring out the kitchen window at the moonlit snowy peaks. Quietly, she asked, 'Was it worth all the pain you caused?'

'I was confused. Everything I did ended up hurting someone even though I had honorable intentions. I thought coming to Argentina would make it easier for everyone.'

'You seriously believed that?'

She rested her elbows on the table. 'I honestly did. I know now I was stupid and what I did was unconscionable. And once I realized that, I didn't know how to come home. I felt like I'd severed any hope.'

Iris's moist eyes looked deeply into Dani's. Her heart skipped a beat and sadness for what could have been flowed through Dani. Up until today she'd convinced herself that Iris had been nothing more than a biological mother. Even the first five years of Dani's life Iris had barely shown the maternal instincts other mothers possessed. Yet now, in the middle of the Andes, remorse emanated from her mother as well as a desire to make things right. Although Dani wasn't so sure she was capable of giving Iris that opportunity.

Iris grabbed the cigarettes and matches. 'I really need a smoke.'

'It's your house.'

Iris smoking was the least of Dani's worries. Her head spun with information overload and, thankfully, her emotions hadn't quite caught up. But when they eventually did, she had no idea what the end result would be. Dani prayed the powerful anger would soon disappear because it had knocked her off-kilter, making her realize how many other emotions she'd suppressed all these years. If she didn't deal with them now she could easily end up as a basket case. Just like Iris. *Please, no.*

Iris lit the cigarette, took a long drag, and waved her hand in front of her, trying to redirect the wafting smoke away from Dani.

'You haven't changed much since you were little. You've just blossomed and are still beautiful, still with those gorgeous blonde curls.' Iris offered a slow smile. 'And the Kennedy eyes and nose.'

Dani shifted in her seat, unsure how to respond. She got the feeling Iris didn't say it to confuse her daughter further but it had that affect anyway. This continual seesawing between emotions kept Dani on knife's edge—crying one minute, gripped with anger the next.

'There's something else you need to know.'

'I'm not sure how much more I can take right now.'

'I'm sorry to dump all this on you in one hit but it's important, I promise.' Leaning forward in a conspiratorial manner, Iris said, 'There was another reason I came to Argentina.'

Dani held her breath. If Iris said it was for a man Dani was marching out the door and never looking back.

Iris waggled her index finger. 'It wasn't for a man.'

Relieved, Dani allowed a small smile. 'You read my mind.'

'I thought that might be the case. When I arrived here I was still mourning the end of my relationship with your father. The last thing I wanted was to get involved with anyone else.'

Dani wanted to ask about Diego but she wasn't ready to deal with that aspect of her mother's life right now. 'So what was the reason?'

Iris concentrated on putting out the cigarette. Eventually, she looked up, her blue eyes now a darker hue. 'You're going to need a very stiff drink.'

CHAPTER 23

Present Day - Dani

Iris shuffled to the cupboard then brought out two crystal glasses and a bottle of Frangelico. She grabbed some Coca-Cola from the fridge, along with ice. Returning to the table, Iris filled the glasses with ice, added the Coke and liquor, and mixed the concoction with a teaspoon. 'Here. It's a local favorite.'

Iris pushed a glass toward Dani, who accepted, thankful to have alcohol to temper the long, emotional day. Taking a sip, she enjoyed the quick buzz, surprised at how hazelnut could blend so well with sickly sweet Coca-Cola. Afraid to ask but overwhelmed by the desire to do so, Dani said, 'I'm ready. Say what you need to.'

Iris bowed her head for a moment as if willing herself to find the strength to continue. Looking up, she locked eyes with Dani. 'You'll need to know some background first, so please bear with me.'

'Okay.' Sipping the drink, Dani was glad she drank alcohol because she sure as hell needed something to get her through this evening.

'So when I was six Stella got a job as a live-in nanny for a wealthy Italian family in Melbourne. Her hours were long but we had a roof over our heads, food in our bellies, and there was an army of staff to look after me when she was busy with the children she was in charge of.'

'Sounds like a decent deal.'

'It was. For a while. Stella was a good mother—'

'Hang on,' Dani said. 'You said she was a terrible role model.'

'Please, Dani, just let me finish. For the first ten years of my life she was a fabulous mother. She worked hard but always found time for me, even though her demanding employer pulled her in many directions. A couple of years after we'd been living there she was sent on a trip to Italy to nanny the kids while the parents lived it up on Lake Como. As I was an employee's kid, I had to stay behind but Stella's good friend Lucy, the housekeeper, looked after me for those few months.' Iris reached for another cigarette, withdrew her hand, then grabbed the packet. 'I'm sorry. Smoking calms me and telling you all this now is dredging up a lot of memories I've suppressed for years.'

'It's okay,' said Dani and, for the first time since arriving at Iris's house, things actually did feel okay. It would take days, weeks, hell, even months, to process everything that she and Iris had spoken about but Dani wasn't so scared anymore. Carlos was right, she could be strong. She could deal with this. Sometimes the anticipation of an event can be way more traumatic than when it actually occurs. Perhaps this would be the case with Iris. *Early days, Dani, early days.*

Striking another match, Iris lit a cigarette, took a long puff then pushed the packet away. 'When Stella returned from Italy she was a shell of her former self. She barely spoke, never made eye contact. She'd lost all affection for me and I was forced to rely on myself. I was ten, goddamn it!' Iris lips pursed around the cigarette as she dragged long and hard. She breathed out a cloud of smoke and her angst floated along with it. 'I was pushed into being independent when I should have had my mother to nurture me through the difficult teenage years.'

'Are you daft?' Dani flung her arms wide. 'Do you realize what you did to me was way worse than what Stella did to you?'

'I . . . oh god.' Iris slid her hands across the table but Dani refused to hold them. 'I'm so, so sorry.'

'I know you are, Iris, but this road is long and littered with potholes.'

'But there's a chance we could repair things, right?' She sat up straight, her eyes hopeful.

'I'm not making any promises. I'll listen to what you have to say and that's the best I can offer for now.' Although Dani had an inkling, deep, deep down that perhaps she and Iris could start a relationship again. What kind of relationship, she had no idea. 'You've given me a history lesson on your life but you still haven't told me your other reason for coming here.'

'Right, right, of course.' Iris smoothed down her peroxide locks. 'So the changes in Stella were drastic after she got back from Europe. Not only did she push me into growing up too fast she'd lock herself in her room for hours on end, sobbing uncontrollably, mumbling in a language I'd never heard before.'

'What language?'

'I didn't know it then but I'm now convinced it was Spanish.' Iris's words echoed in the kitchen. Drips from a tap landed in the empty sink.

'How would she know Spanish if she was working for an Italian family?'

'Exactly.'

'I still don't get what this has to do with Argentina. Why . . .' Dani let the words fall away. Could Iris suspect the same thing she did?

'Why what?' Iris tilted her head to the side.

'It's nothing.'

'It doesn't sound like nothing but you don't have to tell me if you don't want to. There is, however, something you need to see.' Iris got up and opened the door to the cabinet on the far side of the kitchen. She rustled around before pulling out a manila folder. 'As part of your research on tango history did you ever come across Eduardo Canziani?'

Dani remained still. 'How did you know I was . . . Oh. Carlos told you how we met.'

'He did and I'm not surprised you're a journalist. You could write your name by the age of three.' Iris sat heavily on the chair. 'Sorry, these reminiscences no doubt hurt both of us.'

Although Dani agreed she wasn't so sure she didn't want to hear them. Knowing her mother remembered aspects of her daughter's life helped Dani grip the connection they once shared, even if it had been tenuous.

Pushing the folder toward Dani, Iris said, 'So Eduardo Canziani was Argentina's most famous musician and his muse, Louisa—'

'Louisa Gilchrist was suspected of murdering him, along with Roberto Vega, Canziani's protégé.'

'I'm impressed with your knowledge.'

'Research is an important part of my job.' *That I am going to fail at miserably if I don't get my act together.*

Iris motioned for Dani to open the folder. She fished out a stack of newspaper clippings and slowly went through the yellowed papers, some badly creased and tattered around the edges. They were from national and local Argentine newspapers and dated 1954, 1966, 1986, and 1996. All the stories commemorated an anniversary of Eduardo Canziani's death.

Dani looked up. 'Why do you have these?'

'I have this too.' Iris got up and went to the cabinet, returning with an envelope. She took out the contents and unfolded them with great care. The letters were written in Spanish and addressed to *Querida Lunita*.

'What's this?'

'I found these years ago in your grandmother's possessions. I wasn't snooping, I was just helping her out with laundry when she had to go to hospital for a short stay.'

'Did you ask her about them?'

'She told me it was old junk that had been left in a second-hand chest of drawers she'd bought.'

'So why didn't she chuck them?'

'I asked the same question. Here, look at this.' Iris leaned across and pulled out more letters. 'The writer talks about how their life resembles the tango songs of woe that he writes. He talks about leaving Argentina with her and living in their own paradise. He calls her his little moon and goes on about the stars losing their luster when he's not with her. All very romantic but the author never signed the letters. And check this out.' Iris reached for a plastic bag and unfolded the first page of a musical score.

'Luna Tango'? asked Dani. 'So these are copies, right? Where are the originals?'

Iris shrugged. 'When I first found the papers, Stella denied prior knowledge and put them back where I'd found them. I think she was trying to give the impression she didn't care but I didn't buy it. Otherwise she would have gotten rid of them, right? So just in case she decided to do that later, I snuck them out and made copies.'

Dani's heart raced. Missing pieces of the puzzle were joining together and her theory that Iris had information appeared to be correct. Yes, she'd come here with this in mind but she'd also gotten a whole lot more than expected.

Iris leaned back against the chair, her hands resting on the table. 'For years I doubted my sanity because of my obsession with tango. I was a mess and even though my whole world turned upside down when I found those letters and sheet music, for the first time in a long while I felt a ray of hope that I could finally figure out who I really was.' Iris poured more Frangelico into her glass and downed it. 'I begged Stella to tell me the truth about her mysterious stash but she insisted it didn't belong to her. Of course I didn't believe her so I set out to find answers myself.'

'Why didn't you confide in Dad? He would have helped.' Hurt on his behalf weighed heavily on Dani.

Iris shook her head. 'It was too late by then. He'd started out enjoying tango but grew to hate it because I became obsessed with it and it ended up taking time away from him. I also suspect Stella may have had his ear, encouraging him to make me stop dancing. I did try to tell him about Stella's letters and music but he'd already shut me out. By that stage our relationship was so far down the hole we had absolutely no chance of ever rescuing it.' Staring out the window, she said, 'I don't blame him at all. I was a terrible wife and an even worse mother. The guilt and pain of those actions have eaten me up over the years and if I knew then what I know now . . .'

'He wanted nothing more than for you to have stayed with us.' Dani held an even tone, even though anger had started to swell again.

'I know he did but what life would we have had? We fought all the time. I was miserable without tango, he was miserable with it. You were suffering because of our constant bickering—'

'I would have preferred bickering over abandonment.'

Iris looked down and gave a small sniff. Her eyes didn't meet her daughter's but by the way her bottom lip quivered, Dani knew Iris was holding back tears.

Quietly, Iris said, 'I still don't know which choice would have been best. I truly thought I was doing the right thing. Although in hindsight . .' She let out a long sigh. 'Hindsight is not always a good friend, I'm afraid. All I knew was discovering the music and letters made me question my heritage and identity as well as my mother's. I didn't want you to end up like me. Or her. I truly thought going to Argentina would solve my identity crisis and I could get some answers.'

'How?'

'I had no clues but I had determination. The moment I arrived here I set about gathering information on this anonymous person who wrote 'Luna Tango.' When I wasn't researching I was dancing but I got swept into the world of tango so fast my head spun. For the first time in my life, I felt like I truly belonged.'

'You never felt that way in Australia? With me? With Dad?'

Iris hung her head. 'I loved you both with all my heart, but I was dealing with something so powerful that if I didn't face it head on it would eat my soul. I really didn't have a choice.'

'You *always* had a choice!' Dani slapped the table. 'You could have taken me with you!'

'No, no. That could never have happened. What life would you have had?'

'A life with a mother.'

'But no father or grandmother. You were settled. There was no way I could rip you from your roots and drag you to the other side of the world. Besides, the theater is no place for a child to grow up.'

'It was good enough for Carlos. He turned out all right.' Sure, he was prone to mood swings, but that was a result of the accident, not his childhood surrounded by show business.

'Yes,' Iris said, 'Carlos turned out wonderfully, but at the time I didn't want to risk subjecting you to a world I was only beginning to comprehend, in a foreign country where we didn't have any family or friends. Didn't even know the language. You needed stability and I couldn't give you that.'

They'd circled around it more times than a satellite around Earth and Dani needed a break from the subject. Holding the glass near her lips, she eyed her mother over the rim. 'Don't you want to know what it was like for me growing up with Stella?'

Iris raked her fingers through her hair and concentrated on the wooden table. 'I'm not sure I want to know.'

'Why not? In case you left me with someone worse than you?' *Keep calm, Dani.*

Iris flinched like she'd just had a blow to the belly. The good manners Stella had instilled in Dani made her feel like she should regret the last comment but the torn, traumatized five-year-old Dani held back from apologizing.

'It's okay, Dani. Say what you need to.'

Dani didn't know whether to feel relieved her mother could read her mind or worried. 'Just so you know, Stella was loving and caring and supportive. She guided me through some difficult times when I was a teenager but she never lost faith in me. We are a tight knit team.' *Except for when I announced I was going to Argentina.*

'I'm so sorry I wasn't there but I am happy Stella looked after you so well.' Iris's words sounded strangled.

Ice cubes tinkled against the glass as Dani swirled the liquid. 'So did you end up getting answers about the Canziani case?'

'Not until recently,' said Iris.

'What?' Dani clanked the glass down hard on the table. 'It's taken all this time?'

Iris looked to the heavens, as if asking for an answer then fixed her gaze on Dani. 'Your grandma has a much stronger connection to Argentina and tango than I could ever have suspected.'

CHAPTER 24

Present Day - Dani

Dani swallowed slowly, Iris's kitchen closing in on her. 'Why would you think that?'

Getting up, Iris went over to the cabinet and grabbed a large envelope. She pulled out a black-and-white photo with a post-it note stuck on the top. Neatly written in green ink was Stella's current address.

'You have her details?'

'Yes.'

'But she only moved a few months ago.'

'You don't become as rich as me and not find ways to access information. Everything has a price,' said Iris.

Dani lifted the post-it note to reveal the exact same photo she'd seen at Carlos's dance studio the first night they'd met. *Man, that was a lifetime ago.* She stared at the image of Louisa Gilchrist with her soft eyes and warm smile conveying a loving nature. A complete contrast to the scowling Eduardo Canziani seated in front.

'I've seen this before.' Dani pressed down the post-it and handed back the photo.

'Where?'

Dani reached into her bag and pulled out the photocopy. She placed it on the table and raised her eyebrows.

'How did you . . . oh, of course, your tango history research.'

Dani shifted in her chair, once again transfixed on the woman standing behind Eduardo Canziani. Glancing at Iris in real life, Dani was taken back by the similarities between her and Louisa and if she added herself into the mix . . .

Iris said, 'It wasn't until I arrived here that I discovered the Canziani case. There wasn't a lot of information around so it took years to piece together. The more I discovered, the louder the alarm bells rang. It seemed near impossible for Louisa and Stella to be one and the same and I often thought I was chasing some weird fantasy. I gave up a few times but it wasn't until the authorities released the only existing photo of Louisa and Eduardo that the connection became obvious.'

'Since seeing this photo I've wondered if Louisa and Stella could be the same but, like you, it seemed absurd. I started researching the case myself but I had to put it on hold. Well, sort of.' Dani tilted head from side to side, stretching her neck muscles.

'Truth is stranger than fiction, right?' Iris asked.

'It can be. So why has this image only recently surfaced?'

'Because of the public's outrage at the time, photos of Louisa and Roberto Vega were destroyed. People took to the streets and burnt them.'

'That's silly,' said Dani. 'Wouldn't they want to keep a handful so they could identify them when they were arrested?'

'You've seen how passionate Argentines are. At the time of the murder they were infuriated. Many retain that anger. A few years ago, the photos that had been locked away in archives were released in a series of articles in the national newspaper.' Iris stared out the window then returned her attention to Dani. 'What hurts most is I suspect Louisa was pregnant when she fled Argentina.'

'Why?'

'Think about it. I was born not long after Louisa left Argentina. I've never met my father because Stella said he was an Aussie soldier who died before I was born but his name never appeared on my birth certificate.'

Leaning forward, Dani said, 'But the general consensus is Louisa and Roberto left separately then caught up with each other after leaving the country.' Dani expected Iris's determined expression to sag but her mother only clenched her jaw harder.

'My gut tells me that may not be the case. I suspect you have the same intuition that runs in our family.'

Dani readjusted her position on the chair. In a quiet voice, she said, 'You don't know me, Iris.'

'I'm sorry, I was being too familiar. I'm just not sure how I'm supposed to be around you.'

'I have no clues, either.' It felt strange to be in the presence of the woman who had given birth and raised her for five years, yet not have a single idea about how to act around her. 'You are right about the intuition.'

'The gut is never wrong?'

'Well, not never, but it's definitely more right than wrong.'

'It's a good trait to possess.' Iris placed the glass on the table and eyed the bottle.

Dani remained silent, her head spinning with everything she needed to process. She'd spent years only hearing Stella's version about Iris's departure and now it felt strange to finally hear her mother's point of view. Dani got the impression Iris could charm a snake but in this instance, with the reunion with her daughter, she felt Iris's words to be genuine. The judge and the jury needed more time for deliberation before the final decision, though.

'Thank you, Dani.'

'For?'

'For finding me and giving me a chance even though I don't deserve it.'

How to answer this? 'Iris—'

Her mother held up her hand. 'You don't have to say anything. We'll cover the ground as we need to. For now, perhaps we should concentrate on this photo.' She gestured at the image of Louisa and Eduardo. 'I'm not making this all about me, I promise, but if anything comes of this discovery, it will have a major impact on me. And you. Have you ever felt a pull toward tango?'

'No,' she shot out quickly. 'Well, a little.' A little? What about the excitement of learning a new step? Dancing voluntarily in the bathroom? Yeah, and what about the fingernails down the blackboard when hearing the *bandoneón*?

'I'll ask you to consider this. Let's suppose I'm the love child of Louisa and Roberto. The ramifications could be detrimental.'

'Like?'

'I'm famous because I'm a foreigner who can dance the tango like an Argentine. I'm *La Gringa Magnifica*, right? How do you think the media and public would react if they found out at least one of my parents was Argentine? And one or both of them may have murdered this country's greatest composer? I'd be ostracized and my reputation would be ruined. I'd also be branded a liar. You know how the media crucified Carlos, right?'

'Yes.' And she felt guilty about her profession doing such a thing even though she had never been involved.

Pounding the table, Iris spat out, 'This bloody dance is cursed. It messes with your head and makes promises it can't deliver. Look at what happened to Louisa and Roberto. Tango tore them apart. And now you're with someone who was one of Argentina's best dancers and look what happened to him, the poor bugger. Bloody Cecilia.'

'Carlos said you have taken her side.'

'Had, not have.'

'You've changed your mind?'

'Yes.' Iris grabbed another cigarette but Dani covered her mother's hand.

'Maybe you should cut down.'

Iris put down the cigarette and nodded. 'When he needed a friend I wasn't there. God! I'm an awful person!' She covered her face with her hands then slapped them on the table. 'It wasn't until I spoke with him this evening that I discovered it was Cecilia's fault and he'd lied to protect her.'

'That was chivalrous.'

'But stupid.' They said in unison. Despite the tense atmosphere, they both smiled.

Dani felt a whole new level of compassion for Carlos, mixed with confusion. 'I don't get why he hates the media so much when he was the one who lied to them.'

'For years the media had clamored for interviews, unable to get enough of tango's pretty boy. His talent captivated everyone and he could do no wrong.'

'Until the accident.'

'Exactly,' said Iris. 'After his fictitious admission, they turned on him like a pack of rabid dogs and invented all kinds of stories to drive him and Cecilia apart. They crucified him for destroying Argentina's most famous tango couple. What you need to understand is tango runs through the blood of the Argentines, so if anyone dares mess with their beloved tango performers, well . . . It kills me to know he was only protecting the little tramp. Especially after she ran away and he—'

'Found out she was pregnant?' It felt like someone had shoved a wad of cotton wool in her mouth.

'So he's told you.' Iris waited for Dani to confirm with a nod. 'That piece of work Cecilia had Carlos, me, and the whole nation under a spell. She was the golden girl of their generation but she messed it up and destroyed an innocent man's career.' Iris breathed heavily through her nostrils. 'There's something else you need to know.'

'I'm not sure I can handle much more.'

'I wouldn't dump this on you unless I thought it was important.'

'All right.' Why did Dani feel she was going to regret this?

'Carlos told me you'd spoken to Diego. I'm not surprised you've met him. The world of tango is very small.' Iris paused then said, 'I've been worried for a long time that Diego knows I'm looking into the Canziani case. I tried to keep all my research away from him but he was always tracking my moves, trying to control me. I caught him snooping in my desk at our apartment but I didn't have anything written down. At that point it was a bunch of suppositions rattling around my brain.'

'He's not seen any of this?' Dani pointed at the material lying on the table.

'No. But I'd spent so much time trying to gather my own evidence he thought I was having an affair. I told him I was doing research for a book I was writing but he didn't buy it. He's a doom-and-gloom type, always expecting the worst to happen, so it does.'

'Yeah, I'm aware of that sort.' *Adam.* Wow, she hadn't thought about him for a while and looky here, no emotions or self-esteem spiraling into the abyss. *Things are looking up, eh, McKenna?* 'He asked me to give you a letter.' Dani leaned over and scrounged in her handbag.

'Save yourself the trouble. I won't read it. He'll have written a heap of romantic crap. The stupid bastard thinks he can gamble every cent, sleep with any woman he wants, then apologize with a soppy love letter. His gambling is the reason I didn't tell him about the Canziani case.'

'Why?'

'Because of the reward. Five million dollars is a helluva lot of pesos, especially to a destitute music director who threw away the dance company's money on stupid horse races. When did you last see him?'

'Yesterday. He was preparing for a show, then heading to the country for a few days.'

'More than likely he was avoiding a bookie. Unbelievable. He does what he wants because he's a genius and he gets away with it. I also didn't tell him about the Canziani case because I feared he'd find out about my possible heritage.'

Silence fell around them but it was less uncomfortable than before.

Shifting forward, Iris asked, 'Have you said anything to Carlos about Stella possibly being Louisa?'

'Definitely not. He has a stringent view on Argentines sorting out their own messes, including the Canziani case.'

A small smile reached Iris's rosy lips. 'He's always been patriotic. And pigheaded.' She placed her elbows on the table and rested her chin on her hands. 'I'm glad you haven't mentioned anything to him.'

'Why would I? Up until tonight I wasn't entirely sure there was a connection.'

'You shouldn't trust him.'

'That's lovely coming from someone he considered a second mother.' Dani made sure her indignation was obvious.

Irish flinched and took a moment before speaking. 'I am fond of him, still, but we're talking about Argentina's biggest murder mystery here. When it comes to the Canziani case, no one can be trusted. Not even your Carlos.'

'You're wrong about him.' Dani pushed her chair back from the table.

'I'm just saying, the Canziani case tends to bring out the worst in everyone. The Argentines are very protective of their own.'

'It doesn't mean Carlos would turn.'

'Maybe not. Just be careful. Please.' Iris cleared her throat. 'I know I haven't earned the right to tell you what to do, but please watch out for yourself. This damn dance messes with everyone in our family.' Dani opened her mouth, but Iris put up her hand. 'I know, I sound like Stella. It took me too many years to realize her words were true.'

'Why is it so important to know if Stella and Louisa are the same person? If they are, she could be arrested and put on trial. You don't hate her, do you?'

Vehemently shaking her head, Iris said, 'Absolutely not. In fact, the more I learn about Louisa's history, the more I empathize with her.'

Dani closed her eyes briefly, picturing Stella sitting on her red leather reading chair, crocheting the animals that she gives to the children's hospital. She'd done this for as long as Dani could remember. 'There is no way on earth Stella could have killed anyone. No matter how horrible the situation.'

'I agree. Stella and I may have had our differences and she may be more stubborn than a bull, but it's impossible to imagine her ever hurting someone deliberately.' Iris grabbed the cigarette packet and tapped it against the edge of the table. 'What if we're wrong?'

'What if we're right?' asked Dani. 'If we can figure this out who's to say someone else can't?'

'You need to talk to her.'

'I'll try.' Dani held her hand in front of her mouth, covering a yawn.

'It's been a long night. We should get some rest.' Iris stood, packed up the files and placed them in her kitchen cabinet, hiding them behind a collection of perfectly matched china.

Dani got up and straightened her jeans, unsure what to do. She and Iris had spent hours peeling away the top layers of their problems but there were so many more to go.

After riding out waves of emotions, Dani's body ached. Her mind felt numb and she just needed a really good hug. Pursing her lips, she stared at Iris putting away the files. Iris had never shown affection so did Dani want to risk an awkward moment if her mother didn't return the gesture? And was this need for an embrace going to be same if it was given by anyone or did she really, truly want to feel her mother's arms around her?

With her back to Dani, Iris held on to the cabinet, her hands shaking, head lowered.

Dani had her answer.

'Iris.'

Her mother turned around, her eyes moist. 'Oh, Dani.'

They rushed forward, enveloping each other in a long overdue embrace. Tears flowed and as the sun crept from behind the mountains, it signaled a new day and, hopefully, a bright new future.

CHAPTER 25

1953 - Louisa

Clouds of dust flew behind the cart as the horse sped along the narrow potholed road lined with palm trees and tall grass. Louisa gripped the wooden rail, her legs dangling over gravel while she used her shoulder to nudge away a bag of cashew nuts that threatened to push her onto the sharp stones. The stench of horse manure seeped into her every pore and the late afternoon sun seared her skin, the thick layer of dirt offering little protection from its fierce rays. Wrapping her fingers tightly around the wooden rail, Louisa closed her eyes and told herself this ordeal would be worth it in the end.

For three weeks she'd traveled overland through Uruguay and Brazil, mostly using local buses. She'd journeyed across swamplands, mountains, and along Brazil's pristine coast. Countless times she'd wanted to jump off the bus, run across the smooth sand and immerse her weary body in the crystal clear waters of the Atlantic Ocean but she had to continue her journey, because each day that passed meant she had less chance of finding Roberto—if he hadn't been arrested.

As she'd traveled through small and large towns, Louisa had

surreptitiously tried to gather information about whether Roberto had been detained like Héctor had implied. Eduardo's death was now the main topic of conversation in tiny villages and large cities so if there had been any news it would have flashed across the continent like lightning. So far, she'd heard nothing. Perhaps Roberto's supposed arrest was just one more lie that easily rolled off Héctor's tongue.

Rage fueled her steps every time she thought of the man she once trusted like a brother. Héctor's lies had tumbled from his mouth so easily and when he'd admitted his wrongdoing, she couldn't figure out if he held genuine remorse or not. Héctor's actions had been stupid, misguided, and incredibly selfish. It worried her that because she rejected him Héctor might be angry enough to tell authorities of her last known whereabouts. But if he loved her like he said he did then perhaps he would let her be . . . either way, she had to move fast and get to Chapada do Russo as fast as possible.

Sighing heavily, she reflected on how much had changed in a matter of weeks. She'd slid from the upper echelon of Argentine society to hard, rocky ground, now an anonymous pauper. With a bruised ego and heart, she could easily slink into the nearest hole and wither in self-pity, but she owed it to herself, and Roberto, to keep going. Once again, life had spun a suffocating cloud of turmoil and she'd ended up displaced, alone in a foreign country with no one to turn to. At least this time she had finances to keep her going, even if it was money Héctor had given her back in Buenos Aires. Thank goodness she hadn't thrown it at him when they'd had that confrontation.

The cart rounded a corner and the palm trees gave way to open fields dotted with wooden and stucco buildings. The main street of Chapada do Russo was deserted, even though people were due to return from the cashew plantations. With a loud whistle, the driver yanked on the reins and the horse stopped obediently, allowing Louisa to slip off the back of the cart and grab her bag. She dipped her hand inside for some notes and handed them over, smiling her thanks.

'*Lá.*' He quickly stuffed the money in his shirt pocket and pointed at the house across the road. Dark green paint peeled from the walls, revealing rotting wood. The roof had large gaps where terracotta tiles should have been, and the front yard contained nothing but dust.

The driver whistled loudly, shook the reins and offered her a salute as he took off down the main street. Dust flew up her nostrils and she broke into a coughing fit and rubbed her eyes. Arching her back, she massaged her lower spine, thankful this part of the journey was over. Alighting from the bus at the wrong destination miles ago had thrown her into a spin, but as she'd barely slept for three days and was traveling to a town she'd never seen, the mistake had been easy to make. At least she had a knight with a cashew cart to rescue her.

Biting her lip, Louisa pushed back her hair, still not used to the new length and color. Her disguise had worked brilliantly, as the few people she'd met had never questioned her authenticity. Her years of living in Argentina meant she could pull off a flawless accent, so to Brazilians, she was just another traveling Argentine.

Gathering her bag and her courage, Louisa crossed the road, not bothering to look for traffic as she still hadn't detected signs of life. Her low heels crunched along the gravel, creating small dust clouds as she made her way to the red door of the green house. Raising her closed hand, she hesitated, wondering if this was a mistake, but the cart driver had promised her Senhor Santas could help.

Louisa puffed out her cheeks and rapped lightly on the door. Red flecks of paint attached to her knuckles. She waited, rapped again, and waited some more. Nothing. Louisa hung her head, not sure what to do. Despite her lack of Portuguese, she'd managed to get by but now, in the middle of rural Brazil, she really needed someone who spoke fluent Spanish. Senhor Santas had been her only lead, although it looked like her streak of bad luck continued.

'Please. Please be home,' she muttered and rapped on the door so hard pain shot through her knuckles. Behind the door she heard a chair being pushed back along tiles and heavy boots echoing up the hallway. Louisa's heart raced in time with the footsteps. The door swung open and a man with a tuft of bright white hair stared her down.

'*Sim?*' His eyes narrowed and he crossed his arms.

'*Bom dia, Senhor Santas.*' Louisa switched to Spanish. 'Senhor Alves, who drives a cashew cart between villages, suggested I speak with you as I have little knowledge of Portuguese.' She concentrated, ensuring every nuance led him to believe she was a native of Buenos Aires.

He tilted his head to the side and studied her with such intensity she felt he could see right through her.

'Why are you here?'

'I'm looking for my brother. He came to work on the plantations recently but I'm afraid I have some tragic family news and I need to find him.' The lie rolled from her tongue with ease and guilt consumed her.

'His name?' Senhor Santas arched an eyebrow, showing no emotion for her supposed family tragedy.

Even though she'd braced herself for this question, it still scared her. Forcing a gentle smile, Louisa said, 'Adolfo Maldonado.'

'I do not know of him.' Senhor Santas moved back and placed a hand on the edge of the door.

'He may not be using this name.' Her words tumbled out, eager to explain. 'Our family has had much trouble and when my brother left, he was angry with my father. But my father is very ill and now I want to find Adolfo to beg him to return to make amends.'

'It is not right a dying man should go to his grave with disagreement in his heart.'

'Yes, and for that reason, I need to find my brother. I know he doesn't want to be found, which is why he has probably changed his name, but I'm his sister and I know he will listen to my request. Is there any chance you can help? Please?' She used her charm, even though she detested exploiting her femininity.

'No.'

'No?' Her heart sank. The cashew cart driver had promised her Senhor Santas had a kind heart and would assist her.

'No, I do not know of this Adolfo. Please understand, we have a transient population on the ranches and the workers come from all over Latin America. Unless you have a photo, it will be impossible to find him.'

'I'm sorry, I don't have one.' Louisa knew this would be difficult. She didn't possess any photos of Roberto in case someone questioned why she carried an image of Argentina's most wanted man. Chances were Roberto had changed his appearance by growing facial hair, as well as changing his name and, possibly, his nationality. Roberto's talent for listening not only helped with his music, but for mimicking accents. She suppressed a small smile, remembering how he'd regale her with impressions of Chileans from Santiago and Uruguayans from the *campo*.

'Then I can be of no help. I am sorry.' Senhor Santas pushed the door but Louisa forced her foot against the door jamb. Staring directly into her eyes, he said, 'Miss, I am sorry, but I cannot help you. Now please, let me go. I have work to do.'

'Please, just listen to me. He loves the tango.'

'Most immigrants do.' He twisted his mouth as if tasting lemon.

'Yes, I know, but he has a talent. A very special talent.' Saying more could put Roberto in jeopardy but she didn't have a choice. With so many ranches surrounding Russo, it could take days, even weeks to find him—if he'd even made it here. Louisa placed her hand on the pocket that contained the map Roberto had drawn.

'What is his talent?'

'He plays the *bandoneón*.' She doubted Roberto would allow people to discover his genius, even if he was living in one of Brazil's most remote farming regions.

'Many, many immigrants play the *bandoneón*, sing, and dance tango. I'm sorry.' He pushed the door into her foot and her bones ached from the force. With this conversation over, she had no choice other than to withdraw her foot and watch the door click into place.

CHAPTER 26

Present Day - Dani

The midday sun warmed Dani's toes as she wiggled them against the bright green grass in Iris's backyard. Leaning against a stone wall, she sipped chamomile tea and gazed at the vista before her. No wonder her mother enjoyed living here so much, especially after the busyness of Buenos Aires.

'You look like you are at home.'

She glanced up to find Carlos smiling, sunshine framing his muscular physique. He leaned on the wall and grimaced as he eased himself onto the ground.

'We could sit on those chairs.' Dani tilted her head toward a battered wooden picnic setting.

'No. Like you, I prefer to be close to the earth.' He used his cane to tap her toes. 'Did you have a nice talk with Iris last night?'

'It was difficult but we covered a lot of things.'

'Did you expect to solve your problems before breakfast?'

'No. I just . . .' She sighed. 'Maybe I expected too much.'

'If you do not expect anything, you do not get disappointed, no?'

'Maybe.' They fell into a companionable silence, a cool breeze gently blowing their hair.

'Where is Iris now?' he asked.

'In town, getting supplies. She hadn't anticipated guests lobbing on her doorstep.'

Carlos laughed. 'Perhaps not. What do you think? Is she like you remember?'

'I don't ever recall her smoking. And she doesn't trust in anyone.'

'Not even you?'

'Well, she said she does but I think it's only to a point. Probably because of—' Dani shut her mouth so fast her teeth smashed into each other.

'Because of what?'

'It's not important.' Her left eye twitched and she donned her sunglasses. Carlos leaned over and attempted to lift them but she gripped harder.

'Daniela, you are doing the lying thing.' He crossed his arms, disappointment darkening his eyes.

Rats. She should have known better. Wrapping her fingers around his, she said, 'Iris needs my help but she wants me to keep quiet about it for now.'

'You do not trust me?'

'I do, Carlos, but Iris—'

'Does not trust me?' His tone sounded bitter as his fingers gripped hers. 'I thought after our talk last night we had made the amends.'

'And I believe, according to Iris, you have but this is something only I can help her with.' Feeling bad, she said, 'I'm sorry, Carlos.'

His grip loosened and the circulation in her fingers came back in a painful burst. Turning to face her, he stroked her hair and gave the private smile that always made her stomach flip. 'If you do not want to tell me, I will accept this.'

'I want to tell you but we need to sort some things out, then you'll be the first to know.'

'Maybe I could help.'

233

'I wish you could, but . . .' What? Carlos had been caring, supportive, and a gentleman, aside from the odd grumpy moment. Now she understood his history better, she could see why he'd acted the way he had when they'd first met. Why wouldn't he give journalists a hard time? And despite being badly hurt by a woman and the press, both of which Dani was, Carlos had opened up and trusted her.

'Daniela?'

'Please, give me a minute.'

He dropped his hand and leaned back, face turned skywards, soaking up the rays. He could have kicked up a stink but didn't. Iris was wrong. Dani could trust him and she needed his opinion.

'It's the Canziani case.' The words fell on top of each other.

Carlos studied her with unnerving intensity. 'Not again.'

'It's complicated, and I know you don't want foreigners sticking their noses in but I have reason to. Iris has been researching it also.'

'Do you not care what I think?'

'Of course I do! I wouldn't get involved unless it was important.'

'Is the Canziani case the reason you wanted to find Iris? Because you thought she was looking into it also? How could you know?'

'You mentioned they were fighting over Canziani and the missing sheet music and—'

'Are you saying you did not want to find your mother to make happy families? You told me this was the reason. Did you lead me here under the false pretenses?'

'When I first came to Argentina I wanted to find out about Iris but I didn't plan to meet her. I was happy just to get any information I could to help me understand what went through her crazed mind all those years ago.'

'You used me to secretly get information on Iris?' His large eyes held hurt and her mind raced to explain herself better.

'No! It was nothing like that. I needed you for my articles but it was a blessing . . . no, that's the wrong word . . . fortuitous, that you had that connection. Then you and Diego had the idea to track her down for my stories and I went along with it, all the while trying to find a way out. Then I was swamped by the urge to make her suffer once she saw what she'd done to her own daughter, but the discovery of the women of the *desaparacidos* inspired me to reconnect with Iris. . . and I was conflicted and confused. Then I heard about her interest in the Canziani case and . . . well . . . once I started down that road I didn't know how to turn around.' She let the words fall away, unsure how to fix the web she'd just tangled.

Silence enveloped them and a light breeze rustled the trees and grass. Dani waited for what seemed an eternity, unable to meet his eyes.

She reached for his hand but he pulled away. He used the stone wall as support and, with effort, stood. Clasping his cane in one hand, he rubbed his leg with the other and looked down at her. 'I was wrong. You are like all the other journalists. All you want is a story, even at the expense of people's emotions. How am I to believe anything you have told me? Am I right in thinking what we shared was also a lie?' Although he held an even tone and stony expression, his eyes told her she'd hurt him deeply.

'Carlos, I'm sorry. It wasn't like—'

He put up his hand. 'Save your words. I am upset you have ignored my request to leave the Canziani case alone, but it is your dishonesty that has made me angry.'

'Carlos.'

'This is getting too complicated, Daniela. I need space. A lot of space.' He turned and slowly made his way across to the house. Dani stood, mouth open, eyes wide. As much as she wanted to chase him, she had to respect his wishes. Lord knows she needed time to figure out things as well. She hated being branded a liar and it cut deeply because Carlos was right.

A car zoomed into the driveway and Dani hurried to the side of the house and peered around the corner. Iris got out, slammed the driver's door, and kicked the tire. She opened the door again, loaded her arms with grocery bags, and cursed under her breath, blowing the bangs from her eyes as she climbed the veranda steps. The scene unfolded as if Dani was watching a movie. But this was real life. Iris, the mother Dani hadn't wanted to meet, was here. Now. In the flesh. All thanks to Carlos.

Oh god. Carlos.

Bolting to the rear of the house, Dani took the steps two at a time. Dashing through the kitchen then into the living room, she expected to find Carlos brooding in a corner.

'Carlos?' She stuck her head into the dark room in case he was out of her line of sight.

He wasn't there.

'Crap!' Racing up the hallway, Dani wrenched open the door and found Iris standing on the veranda, still clutching the groceries, as she watched Carlos's car exit the driveway and head into the valley.

'Where's he going?' A lump formed in Dani's throat.

'He said he's had enough and is going to Buenos Aires and you and I needed more time alone. What the hell did you say to him?'

'Not the right things, obviously.' She watched the dust settle. Dropping onto the steps, Dani wrapped her arms around her knees and let her head slump forward, hot tears pricking her eyes. Speaking into her sleeve, she said, 'He says I don't trust him.'

'Do you?'

'Yes.'

'Why?'

'He convinced me to track you down.' She looked up to find Iris staring at her.

'So you didn't really want to see me?' Iris placed the grocery bags at her feet. The tub of ice cream rolled out, it's lid ajar.

'I had Stella warning me meeting you would only lead to heartache and . . . It's all very complicated.'

Hurt clouded Iris's eyes. 'Of course.'

'I'm sorry.' Dani stood and placed her hand on the rail.

'It's okay. This road is going to be fraught with ups and downs. We'll figure it out somehow.' Resting against the railing, she said, 'Tango is like chess, you know. The male dancer makes a move and the woman decides which direction she will go. It's a constant nego-tiation with lots of pushing and pulling. Love is the same. You need to go after Carlos. Come on.' Iris rustled in her bag for her keys and hurried to the car, signaling for Dani to follow. Iris shoved the key into the ignition, revved the car, and slammed the vehicle into reverse.

'What about the food?' Dani eyed the sad collection of paper bags on their sides sitting mournfully on the veranda.

'Forget that. Love is food for the soul.'

Iris swung the car into the driveway of Mendoza Airport and sped to the entrance, slamming on the brakes. Propelled forward, Dani closed her eyes, threw out her arms for protection, and waited for her head to smash against the windscreen. It didn't happen. Crashing back against the cracked leather seat, she watched a gaggle of security guards and attendants yell and gesture angrily as Iris leaned over Dani to open the door.

'I'm sorry it took so long. Damn bloody car.'

'Lucky I know how to change tires.' Dani smiled, despite her heavy heart.

'I love that you are so practical.' Iris gave Dani a gentle shove. 'You need to go.'

'You're not coming? What about them?' She nodded toward the security guards.

'I'll stay here and sort them out. Call me after you find him.' Iris handed her a thick card embossed in gold with her phone number and name. 'He'll have cooled by the time he hits Buenos Aires. Typical artist, huh? We get all emotional and storm off when we should stay put and deal with our problems.'

'I guess,' Dani said, doubting she'd ever fully understand those in the arts. She pecked her mother on the cheek, not sure if it was because she was used to this Latin American kissing thing or if it was done as a daughterly gesture. 'Thanks.'

Dani opened the door and moved to step out but Iris grabbed her hand.

'We'll see each other again, won't we?' Iris's voice waivered.

'Of course.' And she meant it. Iris had shown so many sides of herself that Dani never knew existed and she wanted . . . no, she *needed* to know her mother better.

The security staff hadn't let up with the yelling and gesturing, crowding around the dilapidated car.

'Go, Dani. Figure it out with Carlos and I'll talk to you tonight. You've got my number.'

Dani wove between the half-dozen porters and officials and as she hurried through the airport doors she heard Iris using colorful *lunfardo*, the slang spoken by Porteños, the locals of Buenos Aires. Arriving inside the hall, Dani scanned the screens.

Mendoza–Buenos Aires—Departed.

Damn. If they hadn't got the movie-cliché flat tire and Iris's car had been capable of traveling more than forty-five miles an hour, Dani would have made it in time. It killed her that Carlos was somewhere in the heavens, stewing over their argument. She hated that he didn't trust her anymore and she detested giving him reason not to. All she could do was take the next flight, which left in three hours.

Shuffling over to the ticket counter, Dani stood in line to buy her passage, her foot tapping impatiently as she waited for the line to dwindle.

'I'm sorry you didn't make it.'

Dani spun and faced Iris, surprised by her arrival. 'I thought you were going back to your place.'

'I was but all I kept thinking about was you getting on the plane and I had to know if it happened.'

'It didn't.'

'I can see.' Iris placed her hand on Dani's shoulder. 'I'm so sorry.'

'You don't need to be. Carlos and I did the fighting, not you.' She closed her eyes briefly, replaying the argument.

'But I pushed you. I told you not to trust him when you should have.'

'I don't blame him for leaving. I should have listened to my gut and told him the truth.'

'It's the curse of the tango on our family, I'm telling you.'

'Oh for god's sake! I'm so tired of hearing that! You and Stella are as bad as each other.' The line moved and Dani stepped up to the counter, credit card at the ready. 'Next flight to Buenos Aires, please.'

'Make that two and put it on this.' Iris reached around Dani and placed her credit card on the counter.

'What are you doing?' Dani asked.

'Trying to make things right.'

Dani slid the key card into the hotel room lock and the light shone green as the door clicked open. Sighing, she kicked off her shoes and flopped onto the bed, grateful for the air-conditioning and she planned to enjoy it while she could as her time as a guest of Tourism Argentina was just about up. A flicker of guilt ran through her at not having done more work for them by now. Iris shuffled in and sat on the chair, placing her large handbag on the table. She unwrapped her scarf and sunglasses, finally revealing her face. The disguise had worked and no one had hassled her for an autograph during the flight.

'Maybe you should call Stella again,' Iris said.

'I will.' Dani placed her arm over tired eyes.

'Maybe you should call Carlos, also.'

Had her mother always been this pushy? She sat up and looked Iris square in the eyes. 'I appreciate your suggestions but I am a grown woman and can make decisions for myself.'

'Yes, yes, you are.' Hurt flickered across Iris's face.

'Listen, this mother–daughter thing is new to me. There's a lot of stuff going on and we're both under pressure.' Pausing, Dani let a wry smile grace her lips. 'Maybe you should call Diego.'

Iris let out a belly laugh then her expression turned serious. 'No, I don't think so.'

'I don't think you should, either.' At least they agreed on that. Dani tilted her head toward Iris's handbag. 'That's a massive bag for someone so small.'

'Yes, it is.' She patted it like it was a prized poodle. 'It has the files in it.'

'You carry them everywhere you go?'

'Diego was always nosy, so I learnt to carry my most valuable possessions with me whenever I left the house.' She rummaged in her bag, pulled out the manila folders, and motioned for Dani to take them. When Iris pushed the bag from the table, another photo fell out. The picture showed a young girl and a woman on a beach, framed by bright blue sky, lush green grass, pine trees, and pristine sand, their wide smiles captured in a moment of pure bliss.

Dani reached for the photo but Iris grabbed it first.

'Please, can I have a look?' Dani asked.

'It's nothing.' Iris's voice cracked.

'Iris.' Dani held out her hand, palm up, waggling her fingers.

'Fine.' Iris thrust the photo at her daughter, who took it eagerly. 'That's us at Torquay, isn't it?' Memories of happier times spun inside Dani's mind.

'Yes.' Iris studied her perfectly manicured nails.

'You've carried it all these years?'

'I've looked at it every single day. I've wished for a lot in my life but what I've wished for most is for you to be as happy as the day this photo was taken.'

'I could have been.' Dani's voice sounded as small as she felt.

'I know.' Iris hung her head. 'I shouldn't have been selfish but I—'

'Couldn't help it.' Dani got up and headed to the bathroom. 'I'm taking a shower, then I'm going for a walk. You're going to sit tight and not draw attention to yourself, right?'

Iris nodded.

'Good.'

CHAPTER 27

Present Day - Dani

Dani shuffled up the stairs to the hotel room, her legs barely able to hold up her weary body. Her search for Carlos had yielded nothing, not that she knew what she'd say if she did find him. Finishing off a banana, her only sustenance for the day, Dani wrapped the peel in a napkin and shoved it in her bag. The food hardly registered but she had to keep up her strength. She swiped the key card, the door clicked open, and she was met with gut wrenching sobs.

'Iris?'

Her mother sat on the corner of the bed among a sea of white tissues, a hot pink scarf wrapped around her neck. She looked up with bloodshot eyes and a red nose. 'I've done something really, really stupid.'

Taking a seat next to her, a cold fear shot through Dani as she rubbed Iris's back. Deserting a child was a really, really stupid thing to do. What could be worse?

'Diego has the files,' Iris buried her head in her hands.

'What? How did it happen?' Her mother bawled and Dani's patience wore thin but she kept a steady voice, aware an outburst could make Iris clam up.

'Someone told Diego I had returned.'

'I thought your disguise was half decent.'

Iris sniffled. 'I went downstairs to the café.'

'Are you insane?' Seriously, her mother was worse than a three-year-old. 'You told me you'd stay put.'

'I needed a caffeine hit. And I was only going for a minute.'

Dani resisted the urge to roll her eyes. 'How did he steal the files? Did you have your bag with you?'

'No.' Iris wiped her nose with a tissue. 'I left them in the room. I wasn't worried about running into Diego, for God's sake. How was I supposed to know the idiot theater manager would see me and tell him?'

Dani had a hard time keeping annoyance out of her voice. 'So how did he get the files?'

'I had my coffee, left the café, and Diego was in the lobby, all cool, calm, and collected. The bastard grabbed my arm and marched me back to the room.'

'Why didn't you scream? Someone would have come to help you.'

'I didn't want to cause a scene.'

'Don't you remember the fight at the theater?'

'I'm over being the diva. I want a quiet life. I don't want drama anymore.'

'I doubt you'll get your wish any time soon. What happened next?' Dani tried to quash the myriad scenarios that could transpire if those papers got into the wrong hands.

'I brought him up to the room, hoping to calm him down and talk sense into him. But he tried it on with me and—' She put her fingers to the scarf and pulled it away from her neck. Dark red marks the size of a man's fingertips dotted her pale skin.

'He choked you?'

Iris secured the fabric again. 'He tried.'

'Jesus.' As annoyed as Dani was with Iris's carelessness, she felt for her mother after the ordeal she'd just experienced. 'You fought him off, I take it.'

'An elbow in the ribs will do that.' She attempted a feeble smile. 'I'm sorry, Dani, I really am.'

'Did he leave straight away?'

'No. After he got off the floor he saw the papers on the table.'

'They weren't in your bag?'

'No. I'd been sorting through them, trying to see if I'd missed anything.' Iris squirmed on the bed. 'He slammed me into the wall and grabbed the file before I had a chance to stop him. He mumbled something about me regretting crossing him, then he was gone.'

'Oh, shit. Was Stella's address still stuck on the photo?'

'Yes but it was only an address, not her name.' Iris's hand flew to her heart. 'Oh God.'

Dani sat on the bed, tapping her nails against the phone, willing it to answer. 'Come on!'

It rang out and she slammed the phone down and dialed again. It annoyed her that Skype wasn't an option due to the Internet dropping out. Stabbing each digit on the telephone with a pencil she waited while the phone rang out. Again.

'Shit!'

'Dani—'

'Just one more time.' She dialed the number again. As it was evening in Buenos Aires it would be morning in Melbourne so by rights, Stella should be at home. Dani muttered, 'Please, please, please', under her breath.

Click. 'Hello?'

'Grandma!' Dani bounced on the bed with excitement and Iris gripped her arm, beaming from ear to ear.

'Are you calling from New York?'

'No.'

'Then I don't want to talk.'

'Wait! Wait! Don't hang up! Iris wants to talk with you!'

Iris shook her head, eyes wide.

'I definitely don't want to talk. Goodbye.'

'No! Wait! Please!'

'Why?' Irritation sped down the line and slapped Dani across the cheek.

'Are you Louisa Gilchrist?' There. She'd asked it, and all she had to do was wait for the fallout.

Steady breaths came from the other end of the line and Dani pictured Stella pursing her lips and staring at the out-of-date wall calendar on the kitchen cupboard.

'Grandma?'

'I am Stella Kennedy and if you think it's acceptable to ask impertinent questions then you are best suited to your mother's company.'

'I'm sorry you feel that way but if you are Louisa, you need to know someone might come looking for you. It was an accident, but someone has your address and it might be best if you go away for a while.'

'I will do nothing of the sort. This is my home and I will not have a dimwitted stranger harassing me. Dani, I am not impressed with your behavior. Not one bit.'

The phone clicked and a continuous tone signaled a dead connection.

Iris leaned forward, her face flushed. 'What did she say?'

'She hung up on me.' Dani held the hand piece out and stared at it. 'She told me she wasn't going anywhere.'

'Do you think she was bluffing?' Iris grabbed a cigarette and Dani was oh so tempted to ask for one but changed her mind.

'I don't think so, but if she is Louisa, she's spent decades hiding her true identity. Or maybe she is just Stella Kennedy.' Dani stood and threw a pencil and notepad into her handbag then slung it over her shoulder. 'Perhaps we're off the mark and we're harassing our own flesh and blood, just like the Argentines did to Louisa.'

'She is Louisa.' Iris's confidence was convincing.

Dani couldn't help but agree.

～

The second her feet maed contact with the pavement outside the hotel, Dani knew which direction to head. When she'd visited the place earlier, no one was there, but maybe her luck would change. She strode along Lavalle and passed the restaurant La Estancia. Through the window, Dani spied sides of beef cooking on hot coals and chefs dressed as gauchos to entice diners, mostly tourists, to enter the famous Argentine restaurant. As much as her stomach grumbled, Dani pressed on, refusing to give up on her mission.

She marched down Avenida Cordoba and arrived at the beautifully preserved baroque building. Dani placed her hand on the brass handle of the heavy door, hesitating. The first time she'd graced this entrance she'd been determined not to fail at her career and to glean some understanding about her mother's personal life. Dani had planned to get Carlos Escudero on board if it killed her. So much had changed in a short time: She now found herself on an unknown path with Iris and she wasn't as concerned as she should be if her career nosedived before it had even taken off. It was more important to right her wrong and make Carlos understand how sorry she was. She didn't like her chances for a warm welcome but she would try regardless.

Dani dashed up the stairs two at a time, giving the elevator only a cursory glance. Reaching the landing, she ran to the doors and yanked them open, bursting into the dance studio only to find Jorge and his young dance partner half naked and in a tangle of arms and legs. Did all tango partners end up this a different type of dance?

Jorge sat up quickly and the girl did the same, pulling her short skirt down as far as it could go.

'Sorry,' Dani said, not sure who was more embarrassed.

'It is fine.' Jorge's dark eyes were wide.

'Don't worry, I'm not going to tell Carlos.' Relief swept across the young couple's faces. 'Don't you have somewhere better to meet, though?'

'Carlos said he was going away and we don't have money for a room, even by the hour, so we, uh . . .'

Poor Jorge.

'You don't need to explain yourself, although you might want to find a better place for your rendezvous.' Dani raised her eyebrows and gave them a small smile.

'Yes, yes we will.' The couple grabbed their shoes and discarded clothes.

'You haven't seen Carlos?' she asked.

'No. Not for two days.' Jorge hastily shoved his arms in his jacket.

'Do you know where he could be?' Hope clung to her every word. Carlos had refused to answer the twenty-odd messages she'd left him.

'No. Sorry.' They bolted toward the door. Jorge turned around and said, 'I thought you left town with him.'

'I did.'

'So why aren't you with him?'

'Jorge, that is an excellent question.'

Entering the foyer, she climbed the stairs to her room. Water ran in the bathroom so she figured Iris was taking one of her numerous daily showers. Rather than announce her presence, Dani sat on the edge of the bed and reached for her notepad. No matter what was going on with her personal life, she still had to get the articles written for Adam. Her conscience didn't want to let anyone down, even if it was an ex. She just wished this damn writer's block would clear.

After the success of tango in Paris in 1913, it spread to other capitals around the world, such as London, Berlin, and New York. Despite its popularity (or because of), leaders around the world denounced tango as a tool that corrupted the soul.

Cardinal Basillo Pompili, Vicar General of Rome (representing the Pope), issued a pastoral letter to officially declare tango as a perversion of the souls and accused it of single-handedly bringing paganism back into their sanctified world. He warned parents to protect their children and not allow their participa-

tion in tango, for if they didn't do as the church said, the parents would be failing God.

French ecclesiastical authorities and American Catholic priests jumped on the bandwagon, placing pressure on dance halls and closing down community dances held in their own church halls. Church leaders from many religions referenced tango as 'moral turpitude' and a 'disgusting exhibition of wantonly ways.' All except the rabbis.

Rabbi Jacob Nieto said condemning the dance would do more harm than good. He mentioned the Middle Ages, when young Jewish people gathered to dance on a Sunday afternoon while parents and Rabbis watched, and the atmosphere was one of convivial and innocent enjoyment.

He begged for people to use common sense and not condemn the tango because, when danced by cultured persons, it is a thing of beauty. He declared anyone could take a religious ceremony and make it a farce if they were so inclined.

The bathroom door clicked open and Iris walked out. She hadn't bothered tying her robe properly, and Dani caught a glimpse of her mother's body—flat stomach, round hips, and perfect skin—a figure that would make most twenty-year-old women insanely jealous. Iris brushed her hair with nonchalance.

'Can you do up your robe, please?'

Iris's eyes widened with realization then she pulled the robe together and secured it with a tie.

'Thanks,' said Dani.

'I need to tell you something.' Iris sat down on the chair opposite.

'Am I going to like this?'

'I'm not sure.'

Dani put down the pen and paper, readying herself for whatever came. She didn't know her mother that well, but it was enough to realize her life was never dull.

'I had another reason for retiring.'

'Okay.'

'I knew they'd do a TV special about my dancing career because

247

they'd been working on it for a few years, in anticipation of me finally hanging up my tango shoes.' Iris fiddled with the tie on her robe. 'When they last interviewed me, I slipped in a message in case Roberto was watching. Of course, I have no idea whether he's alive or even watches television, but I felt it was worth a try. And because the TV station planned to run it once a week for a month all over Latin America, I thought my chances of reaching him were relatively high. If he's still alive and living on this continent, that is.'

'You're really that famous, huh?'

'Ridiculously so. I'm still not sure why but that's the way life worked out. Anyway,' puffed out her cheeks, 'I knew they would ask me what I planned to do next so I said I was going to hole myself away and write a book.'

'A biography?'

'No, I told them I wanted to try my hand at fiction. I said I was writing a story about a character called Lunita, who was a muse to a famous musician.'

'Like Louisa?'

'Yes. I knew if Roberto saw it, he'd see it as a sign because no one, apart from Roberto and Louisa, knew about that nickname. Well, not until I discovered the letters and told you. And because I look so similar to Stella, I hoped Roberto might get that connection as well, even though he may not know he has a daughter.'

'But you don't know if he's your father.'

'I worked on the assumption he is.' Iris's tone sounded defensive. 'Anyway, it made sense to announce I was writing a book because all celebrities think they can write. I'd already told Diego about my fictitious writing so this TV interview seemed a logical way to get my message across.'

'And?'

'I've heard nothing. The special aired for the first time four weeks ago. Perhaps Roberto is dead.'

The women fell into silence while the tap dripped in the bathroom.

'But you shut yourself off from the world. How could you expect him to contact you?'

'I have a public email address and it doesn't give away my location.'

'What if he doesn't know how to use email?' Her mother's idea was out there, for sure, but if it had worked, it would have been pure brilliance.

'If he wanted to get in contact, he would find a way.'

'You certainly took a long shot. It was risky, also,' said Dani.

'I know, but what else could I do? Every other option had been exhausted and this was my only chance. I didn't want to lose it.'

'I'm sorry it didn't pay off.'

'Yeah, me too.' Iris reached for the pack of cigarettes.

CHAPTER 28

1953 - Louisa

Louisa took a long drink of water from the canteen and wiped the thin film of dust and sweat from her brow. For almost two weeks she'd visited every ranch in the vicinity of Chapada do Russo, accompanying Senhor Alves on his pick-up route. She'd gotten used to sacks of cashew nuts threatening to jostle her from her position on the back of the cart. Her balance had improved dramatically but her luck hadn't.

'Maybe I'm wrong and he's not here,' she mumbled to herself as a wheel of the cart dipped into another pothole. This trip had been a long shot and so far she'd missed every single mark.

They turned left and traveled up a narrow road lined with palm trees. It looked just like any other plantation, with the large, white-washed ranch house, tin sheds for workers to sort nuts and endless fields of cashew plants. The only distinctive feature of this ranch was the fountain, which had an immaculate carving of three angels surrounding a small lamb. They held out their arms, forming a protective circle around the young animal, and water spilled out from holes near their feet.

Tears formed in Louisa's eyes and she wiped them away,

annoyed at the intensity of her emotions. She needed to keep them in check because if she didn't, she would fall apart. Concentrating on the unusual fountain, Louisa took a few deep breaths and braced herself for more disappointment.

The cart stopped and Louisa alighted. Senhor Alves saluted her and strode off to the shed to speak with the foreman and arrange for more bags of cashews to be loaded onto his cart. Louisa climbed the wide wooden steps that led to the front door of the ranch house. She rubbed her hands on her linen pants, then rapped on the door. At least the owner of this establishment had a working knowledge of Spanish so it was easier to straddle the great language divide. Louisa braced herself for making up more lies. Right or wrong, the stories that fell from her lips were for preservation. For herself and Roberto.

No one answered the knock but in the distance she could hear a *bandoneón*. Expecting a recording being played in the shed, she walked down the stairs and across the dusty road to where the men had gathered in a circle. They'd downed their tools and were drinking and eating, fascinated with whatever was happening in front of them.

Louisa stopped a short distance away, hand resting above her heart. Her pulse raced and she held her breath. It couldn't be . . . but Roberto wouldn't be so careless as to show off his skills with the *bandoneón* so soon, would he? Although tango was in his blood and with so many Argentines and Uruguayans desperate for a taste of home . . .

She took a step forward then paused. There was no doubting the player had talent but his performance was just a little off. Louisa's shoulders slumped.

Senhor Alves turned and motioned for her to join the crowd. Even though women on plantations weren't common, the men didn't seem to mind her presence. Standing on tiptoes, she craned to see the musician who played with his head bent forward, his eyes and face obscured by a wide-brimmed hat. Hair brushed the edge of his collar and a short beard covered his face.

Hope shot to the surface. Perhaps Roberto's playing had suffered since the tragedy in Buenos Aires.

Despite wanting to dash forward, Louisa slowly edged her way through the crowd, the men silently moving to the side so she could pass. The man playing the *bandoneón* was hunched over, lost in the moment, his hat hiding his face. His long fingers deftly played the notes, just like Roberto. Passion oozed from his soul, just like Roberto. He finished the song and looked up, smiling at the crowd —he was not Roberto.

Louisa clapped and smiled and did her duty as an appreciative audience member, aware her presence as the only female would be noted. Turning, she smiled her excuses as she rushed through the cluster of hot bodies and broke free. Bolting across the gravel, she crouched behind Senhor Alves's cart.

Clasping her hands over her head, Louisa tried to catch breath. How ridiculous she'd been. She'd allowed hope to cloud her judgment and now she suffered for it.

'I'll find him,' she whispered.

'Will you?'

She jerked her head up to find the *bandoneón* player. Now he stood closer, she could see why her hopefulness had led her to believe he could be Roberto. The width of his shoulders and shape of his jaw were very much like her lover's. Even his nose was similar.

'You speak Spanish?' she asked, standing up and dusting off her trousers.

'Yes, of course. I'm from Uruguay. You are from Argentina?'

'How did you know?' Panic froze her to the spot.

'Your accent.' He gave a lopsided smile that was more friendly than flirtatious. 'I hear you are looking for your brother.'

'Yes.'

'He plays the *bandoneón* also?'

'Yes,' she said, still not sure if it was the smartest thing to have revealed when searching for Roberto. But she'd been desperate, just like now, and anything that could lead her to him was worth the risk. 'Have you seen him?'

'No.' He shook his head. 'There are many of us that play our music. It's in our blood, yes?'

'Like breathing.'

'Exactly. I am a relief worker, so I know many, many people. This is why I am talking with you now. I wanted to let you know that if your brother was in or around Chapada do Russo, I would know.'

'Thank you.' Her throat tightened as she fought back the emotions that wanted to spill out in an ear-piercing scream.

'If you wish to leave your address, I can contact you if your brother arrives. You need to return to Argentina to your ailing father, yes?'

She closed her eyes for a moment, gathering her lies like a bunch of daisies. 'I would like to return but I'm afraid I must stay here. I need to find my brother.'

'But your father is dying, yes?' She sensed distrust in his tone.

'Yes.'

'Surely you would prefer to spend time with your father instead of riding in the back of a cashew wagon. No one understands why you remain here. Forget your brother. If he wanted to be found, he would have been.'

Louisa nodded. Of course Roberto would be covering his tracks, just like she'd done. Surely the world would know if he'd been arrested so why hadn't he made it here? Had she been completely wrong to assume he would? But the cashew nuts . . . the map . . . their dream . . .

As much as she wanted to stay, the small community was watching her every move and if she remained too long, it would raise more suspicion. Like the *bandoneón* player said, they all thought she should return to Argentina to be with her dying father. Her time in Chapada do Russo was nearing an end and because she'd lived the lie so well, she couldn't undo it.

Louisa sat on the veranda of the boarding house staring at the deserted main street of Chapada do Russo. She sipped the ice-cold water the landlady had given her but it made her nausea worse. She'd grown quite fond of the place and the tight-knit community as the people had assisted her without expecting payment in return. And they had happily taken up her quest to find her fictitious brother like they were looking for their own flesh and blood. Guilt burrowed into her soul at having led these generous people into believing a string of lies but she hadn't a choice. Is this what her life was to become? A facade she'd have to keep track of so she didn't falter and reveal her true identity?

Taking another sip and forcing the liquid down, Louisa tried not to think about the nausea. It had grown worse over the past few days and she'd gone off food completely. She couldn't understand why, especially since she had access to an endless supply of fruit and the boarding house owner cooked wonderfully fresh food. Perhaps she'd caught a stomach bug.

The wire door to the boarding house creaked open and the senhora brought out a tray of sliced lemon. She motioned for Louisa to suck on it. She did so, not perturbed by the bitterness of the fruit. The senhora smiled, happy Louisa did as she was told, and she bustled back inside the house, the screen door slamming behind her.

Normally Louisa had a cast-iron constitution and the food she'd been eating in Brazil hadn't been that different to what she'd had in Argentina. If anything, it was fresher, so why . . .

Putting the glass on the table beside her, Louisa placed her hands on her stomach. She'd been so busy trying to build a new identity and find Roberto she hadn't paid attention to her monthly cycle. Now that she thought about it, she was overdue by weeks.

Burying her head in her hands, hot tears slid down her cheeks. Of course something like this would happen. Why not? Everything else had fallen apart, and now she was to be a single mother? Staring at the worn floorboards, Louisa sat back and gave in to the shock. The sun dipped behind the horizon and the cicadas scurried out of their burrows to create their evening orchestra.

Taking a deep breath, Louisa assessed the situation. She had to move on from Chapada do Russo because once she started showing, the locals would question why she wasn't with family. But if she left and Roberto turned up, she'd have no way of knowing; her lie meant she couldn't leave a forwarding address. And Héctor had double-crossed her, so she couldn't ask him to receive any notifications even if he had gone back to Argentina, of which she wasn't sure.

Once again, Louisa would have to leave a place involuntarily and move on to somewhere new where she didn't know anyone. But where could she go? If she remained in Latin America, she ran the risk of being found out. She needed to go far, far away. Somewhere tango was barely known and she could assume a new identity. Perhaps a place where people spoke English. Wherever she chose, she had to get there soon, before she was too far along in her pregnancy and couldn't travel.

Running her hand across her belly, she focused on the life force inside. Out of all the challenges she'd had to face, this would be one of her toughest.

The full moon hung above, bathing the veranda in soft light. Louisa looked up, closed her eyes and said, 'Dear baby, even though you may never know your father, please know I loved him with all my heart. You were made with the love of the stars and the moon and your father's love will always protect us, no matter where he is.'

CHAPTER 29

Present Day - Dani

The doorman didn't blink twice when Dani hurried through the rotating doors and into the opulent foyer on Avenida Paraná in the barrio of Olivos. She hadn't expected Gualberto to answer his phone so early in the morning, let alone agree to meet her at such an ungodly hour, yet here she was, about to enter this famous musician's apartment.

Dani eyed the art nouveau elevator with the elaborate ironwork. Beautiful as it was, she wasn't going near. Instead, she climbed the twelve flights of stairs to the penthouse suite, wishing she would get over herself and take a damn elevator. Arriving on the landing, Dani caught her breath and let the burning in her legs subside while she admired the formidable double doors of Gualberto's apartment. Carved into the wood was an intricate pattern of raised swirls painted with gold. *Impressive.*

She raised her hand to knock but the door flew open before she had a chance.

'Dani!' Gualberto stepped forward and folded her into his arms. She leaned into him and gulped back sobs but the harder she tried to hold it in, the stronger the tears pushed until they rushed out in a heavy stream. Pulling away, he said, 'Come in, come in.'

She followed him into the entrance that was larger than her apartment in New York. Crystals from the chandelier twinkled against each other in the warm breeze drifting through the open doors that led out onto a terrace.

'You look terrible.' Gualberto held her hand.

'Thanks,' she said and followed him into his living room. The large maroon sofa looked like it would swallow her up should she sit on it, so she did. Her body basked in the excessive stuffing and the velour's softness as her aches disappeared. She ran her hand gently across the furniture's curves. 'This is amazing.'

'Thank you.'

'Where is your wife?' Dani studied a photo sitting on the table beside her. The woman had large, dark eyes, a heart-shaped face, and delicate nose and lips. 'She's beautiful.'

'Yes, she is. She is sleeping now.'

'I'm sorry to call on you at this hour. Maybe I should go.' She went to stand but couldn't find the strength to push herself up.

'No, no. Mariela is fine, she doesn't mind if I have the visitors at strange hours.'

'Not even women?'

'She is used to me entertaining the women. Usually musicians and singers and dancers.'

'I'm impressed with your wife's attitude. Doesn't she ever get jealous?'

'No. She has no reason to.' Gualberto disappeared for a moment and returned with two large glasses of ice and juice. He took a seat on the Edwardian chair opposite, handed her the drink, and she took it, grateful for something cold in her hands. Dani rubbed the glass across her forehead then took a sip, enjoying the freshly squeezed oranges.

Sipping his own drink, Gualberto said, 'I am sorry, but I have not seen or heard from Carlos. Him leaving has affected you immensely, yes?'

'How did you—'

'I can see it in your face, Dani. Have you looked in the mirror? Your skin is paler than an albino and there are bags under your eyes that are as red as tomatoes.'

'No wonder your wife doesn't mind you entertaining women if this is you being charming.'

He smiled, took another sip and waved a finger at her. 'I have not seen Carlos since you two left for Mendoza. I thought he was with you until you called. While I waited for you to arrive, I contacted some people but not one person has seen him.'

'At this hour?'

'Many are returning home from dancing.'

'Right, of course. He wasn't at the dance studio or his apartment, either.' She paused before asking, 'You didn't seem surprised when I told you Iris is my mother.'

'Why would I be? At first I didn't think there were any similarities but the more I got to know you I could see the resemblance.'

'I'll tell you the unabridged version of our story one day.' A sigh escaped her lips and she stared at the half-melted ice cubes.

'We will find him, Dani. So, how may I help?'

She hoped her words didn't trip over each other as she spoke. 'I need to understand Diego's connections. I want to know who he owes money to—'

'You need to speak to Pablo Mendez. He is a benefactor who takes struggling musicians and turns them into superstars. Diego is his pet project. Mendez is financing Diego's latest masterpiece, although I have heard the money may not be where it should be. Mendez is angry and is threatening to close the show before it opens but he doesn't want to because he has been promoting this as the biggest tango event in history. Mendez is relying on the world's most influential critics and performers to see this show, but without money—'

'It'll flop. Why can't Mendez get someone else to do the show?'

'Because Diego is the drawing card. Before *La Gringa* retired, she would have been the number one attraction and Mendez could have done the show without Diego.'

'But that's not going to happen, right?'

If Mendez hassled for the return of his money then Diego would do anything to get his hands on some cash. And if he already suspected Iris had clues about the Canziani case, he'd want to get enough evidence so he could swagger down the street clutching a fat reward check.

Shit.

~

Dani left Gualberto's by taxi just after seven and she'd jumped out a few blocks shy of the hotel, anxious to stretch her legs. Taking a sharp left, she ambled through Recoleta Park where shadows barely concealed the plethora of couples pawing each other on benches even though it was barely breakfast time. The more she pretended the lovers didn't exist, the more obvious they became. Putting her head down, she scooted across the grass and almost ran head first into a couple canoodling.

'Get a bloody room,' she muttered.

They didn't appear fazed by her grumpiness and they carried on whispering sweet nothings into each other's ear and giggling like the world was one big love fest. Taking off again, Dani chastised herself for being so cranky. Just because she couldn't hold on to a relationship didn't mean others couldn't bask in the joy of love. Buenos Aires, the Paris of the Americas, certainly lived up to its name with the overabundance of canoodlers on every street corner. When she'd first arrived and was trying to get over Adam, she hadn't paid much attention to the fornicating couples, but after a glimpse of happiness with Carlos, seeing these lovers added salt to an already deep wound. It pained her to think of Carlos out there, angry as hell and bitterly disappointed with her. She felt the same way about herself.

In theory, it should have been easy for Dani to give up on Carlos and walk away but he'd tapped into emotions she hadn't known existed. And she needed his support if she was to have any hope of bandaging her family's wounds.

Dani's phone beeped with an incoming message. Dreading it

was Adam, she ignored it and quickened her pace. The shops were barricaded with metal shutters and the streets remained quiet, a stark contrast to the frantic activity that would take over in a couple of hours. Curiosity got the better of her and she stopped to look at the message.

Dani, your grandma wants you to call her urgently. Don't panic, she's fine. She just wants to talk. Hope that makes sense. Ness xoxo

If Stella had gone to the effort of getting her young neighbor, Vanessa, to text Dani, then something had to be up. Especially since it was late evening in Australia. Breaking into a run, she rounded the corner, dashed into the hotel foyer and up the stairs, reaching her floor in record time. Shoving her key card in the door, Dani burst into the room and found Iris lying on her bed, wearing glasses, and leisurely reading a Regency romance novel.

'You read romance?'

'It's my guilty pleasure, okay?'

'Fair enough.' Throwing her bag on the bed, she said, 'Stella wants to talk with me.'

'Really?' Iris removed her glasses and sat up. 'Why wouldn't she call your mobile phone?'

Flopping on the chair, Dani reached for the phone then put it down. 'You know Stella, doesn't like to spend money if it can be saved.' Dani exhaled with a puff and sent her bangs flying. 'I don't know what to say to her.'

'She's the one who wants to talk. Let her start the conversation.'

Dialing the number, Dani waited while the phone rang half-a-dozen times before it clicked.

'Hello?'

'Grandma! It's Dani.'

'I know it's you. Who else calls me at this hour?'

'Oh, sorry.'

'Never mind. I take it you received my message?'

'Yes.'

'That Vanessa, such a reliable young lass. It's nice to see people of your generation looking after the elderly.'

The barbed comment stung. Of course she looked after her grandma, it just wasn't in the way Stella wanted.

'Ness said you had something you wanted to talk about?'

Iris moved off the bed, stood next to Dani, and leaned in close. Iris's nosiness should have annoyed her but instead she gained comfort knowing her mother was nearby to help deal with whatever Stella had to say.

Silence.

'Grandma, whatever it is you want to say, I'm listening.'

Stella breathed heavily through her nostrils. 'I'm sorry.'

The words spun around Dani's head. Wow. If the conversation started like this, what else did Stella have to say? 'What are you sorry for, Grandma?'

'I'm sorry I gave you grief about Argentina and your new career. Of course you are capable of being a features journalist. I was just scared.'

Dani looked at Iris with wide eyes, trying to convey her surprise. 'Thank you, Grandma.'

'But that's not why I want to talk to you.' She sounded ominous.

Dani's stomach flipped then flopped.

'I received a letter today.' She cleared her throat. 'I need you to go to Brazil.'

'What? Why do you want me to go to Brazil?' Dani repeated the words to keep Iris updated. Her mother shot a questioning look.

'I need you to find someone for me.' Stella was quiet for so long Dani wondered if she'd walked away from the phone.

'Grandma?'

Another pause, then Stella said, 'You were right.'

'About what?' Dani frowned.

'I am Louisa Gilchrist.'

Words escaped Dani as she tried to comprehend the gravity of her grandma's admission.

'Dani?'

'I . . . uh . . . You're really Louisa Gilchrist?'

Iris stepped back, hand to mouth. 'Oh my god!' she mouthed and grabbed Dani's arm.

Shaking herself free, Dani asked, 'Who do you want me to find?'

'Roberto. He's alive.'

'Roberto's alive?' Dani moved to the side to avoid Iris grasping her again.

'I have no idea how you worked out my secret but that's not important right now. I need you to find my Roberto.'

'Where?' Dani asked, still not able to comprehend what her grandma had said.

'Brazil. I stayed there until I was forced to move on but my Roberto made it, he really did. You're very close to where he is.' A paper rustled in the background. 'My Roberto, my sweet Roberto, sent me a letter.'

'How could he possibly know you're Louisa?'

'I have no idea but he's a smart cookie. Something must have given him a clue.'

Dani didn't mention Iris's effort with the TV special but she wondered if it was somehow connected.

'I'm trusting you with this, Dani.'

'I know. Thank you.' And she meant it. Although Stella had been prone to bouts of prickliness with her granddaughter over the years, Dani always knew her grandma loved her. She'd attended every school concert, exhibition, sports match, and had her giggly teenage friends over for sleepovers. Basically, Stella did everything Iris hadn't.

'I know it's him. It couldn't be anyone else. The letter was in Spanish and addressed to *Lunita* and made reference to things only we could know about. He was very careful, though, so anyone else who read the letter wouldn't have a clue what it meant.'

Dani found it difficult to find words that conveyed her surprise— about what, she wasn't sure. She'd suspected Stella could be Louisa but hadn't fully believed it. After all, how could her kind and caring grandma ever be involved in such a scandal?

Iris waved her arms, trying to get Dani to repeat what Stella had said. Dani frowned and turned her back to her mother.

'I need you to go to Roberto and tell him about me. It needs to be done in person. We've spent a lifetime apart when we should have been together.' Stella sounded like a lump had formed in her throat.

Dani's heart went out to the woman whose heart had been broken for decades. What kind of suffering had she endured, keeping her past hidden?

'Will you come here to see him?' Dani asked, worried not only about her traveling such a long way, but also about the authorities that have never given up looking for Louisa Gilchrist. And that was without throwing Diego stealing Iris's information into the mix . . .

'I want to see him more than anything but you're so close. You can go there, tell him about me, then we can work out a way to be reunited.' Stella sighed. 'I spent a lifetime wishing for this but it's come when I'm old and decrepit and have one foot in the grave.'

'Don't be ridiculous, Grandma. You can run rings around sixty-year-olds.' Dani's eye twitched.

'Thank you, Dani. You're lying but I appreciate your sentiment.'

'I'm sorry things turned out the way they did. You've been through so much.' Now the truth was out Dani still couldn't comprehend Stella leading any kind of life that Louisa had.

'Don't worry about me. Now's the time to get things moving,' she said, returning to a matter-of-fact tone. 'Will you do it?'

'Of course I will. Where does he live?'

'In Chapada do Russo in northern Brazil. It's a small town, at least how I remember it. The name of the ranch is Sonho. It means dream. Rather romantic, isn't it?' Stella sounded like a lovesick schoolgirl. 'That's the only information I have.'

'It should be enough. I'll keep you updated.'

'Thank you, Dani. I don't know what I'd do without you.'

She gulped down the lump of empathy lodged in her throat. 'I feel the same way, Grandma.'

Stella hung up and Dani stared at the receiver. 'Holy crap,' she finally said. 'We were right.'

Iris collapsed onto the edge of the bed, her mouth open. 'I thought we were but—'

'Wow,' they said in unison.

A rap at the door halted further conversation. Dani hurried over and peeked through the peephole.

Her heart stopped then raced.

She spun around and pressed her back against the door, closing her eyes and praying she could hold it together. She didn't like her chances.

'Daniela,' the deep voice said from the other side of the wood, 'I can see your shadow under the door, yes?'

Crap.

'Daniela, open the door. I do not like standing in the hallways.' After a moment, he said, 'Please.'

His dark, silky voice melted her resolve.

'Daniela?'

'Open up, Dani!' her mother hissed.

'All right!' she yelled, not sure to whom she addressed her outburst.

Dani unlocked the door. Carlos wore the same shirt as the last time she'd seen him but now it was a crumpled mess. Dark rings had formed under his eyes and his trousers hung loose.

'I'm so sorry, Carlos, I—'

He held up his hand. 'It is I who is sorry.'

Iris cleared her throat, got off the bed and grabbed her handbag. 'I'm heading out for . . . something.' She opened the door and turned to face Dani and Carlos. 'Play nice, kids.'

The door clicked closed and Carlos reached for Dani's hand. His cold, sweaty fingers wrapped around hers as he squeezed them gently. 'Sometimes I do the flying off the handles. I should have stayed to talk things through, yes?'

'And I should have been honest with you from the beginning.' Dani studied his lovely lips, hoping she'd have a chance to kiss them again. She'd missed him immensely but it wasn't until now, with his nearness tormenting her, that she truly realized how much she needed him in her life.

'I must sit. My knee, it is sore.' He leaned heavily on the cane and made his way over to the chair in front of the desk.

'Can I get you some ice?'

Shaking his head, he sat awkwardly. She had nowhere to sit other than the bed and that was well out of hugging distance to Carlos. Collapsing heavily on the mattress, her shoulders slumped. Yes, they'd apologized to each other but the road ahead would be a long one. If it hadn't come to a dead end, that is.

'I . . .' They both said.

'The lady first,' said Carlos, nodding in her direction, his dark eyes serious.

'Okay.' Sucking in a deep breath, she let it out slowly. 'I'm sorry I didn't tell you the other reason I wanted to find Iris but I didn't want to disappoint you. You seemed happy to think I wanted to find my mother and rebuild our relationship.'

'If you do not want this then why is she here with you? Because she will let you interview her? Is that not strange?'

Oh shit. The articles.

'It has nothing to do with interviewing her. This is all very complicated and I'll explain the best I can.' God, Carlos felt so far away sitting on that stupid chair. If they were physically closer it would help her say what she needed to. But if she went over to him, what would he do? Unfortunately, she didn't have the nerve to find out. *Patience, McKenna.* 'After I met Iris and we spent that night talking, I heard a different side to the story behind her leaving.'

'And?'

'And I don't forgive what Iris did to my dad or me and I will never really understand her actions, but her remorse is real. I don't ever expect us to have a strong relationship but she's my mother. I refuse to be the person who turns her back on her own flesh and blood.' Pulling her shoulders back, she said, 'You got under my skin, Carlos, with your talk of family and how important it is. I came to Argentina thinking I could zip in, gather information, then zip out. I guess that's not the case.'

'I am glad you listened to me but I did not expect you to have such difficult relationships. It is good to have everything in the open spaces, yes?'

'There's one more thing.' *Now or never, McKenna.*

'Will I like this?'

'I'm not sure.' Of course she was bloody sure but it had to be said. Staring at the ceiling, she willed her mouth and brain to connect properly. Fixing her gaze on him, she said, 'First, you have to promise me you will keep this secret.'

'I will do the promise,' he said, licking his finger and crossing his heart.

'Louisa Gilchrist is my grandmother.' Done. No going back. Was that her conscience giving a round of applause?

Carlos barely blinked. His chest rose and fell in a steady rhythm and the damn tap kept dripping in the bathroom.

'I did not expect this.' Carlos shifted in his seat and rubbed his knee. His large eyes held some hurt when he asked, 'You have known this all along?'

'No, but through serendipity, the universe, God, Google, or whatever, my grandma has now 'fessed up.'

'What about Roberto Vega?' He leaned forward.

'He's alive and has just contacted her.'

Carlos blinked. 'Pardon?'

'She got a letter today and it contained stuff only Roberto could know. She's convinced it's him and she regrets living her life without him and—'

'Please, give me a moment.' He rubbed his temples, his brows furrowed. 'I am with the confusion, also the shock.'

'I know it's a lot to take in.'

'I do not know what to think.'

'I understand, Carlos.' Boy, did she understand. 'There's one more thing.'

He nodded slowly; as if he wasn't sure he could take in much more.

'My grandma wants me to go to rural Brazil but my Portuguese is crap.'

'*Eu falo o português,*' he said, tapping her foot with his cane. 'I speak the Portuguese.'

'Really? Will you come with me?'

'I will think about it.' He closed his eyes and rested his hand on his cane. When he opened his eyes he revealed the sparkle Dani had missed so much. '*Sí*.'

CHAPTER 30

1954 - Louisa

The ship shuddered as it cut speed in readiness to enter Port Phillip Bay. Louisa gripped the railing, the pounding in her head increasing as the ship inched closer to dry land. Finally, after months of tedious travel, she would arrive at her destination—Australia, a country so far removed from tango that she could keep her turbulent past hidden.

Trees she couldn't name lined the rocky shore as waves pounded against jagged rocks. The sun's heat, similar to what she'd experienced in Brazil, dredged up memories of her fruitless search for Roberto as she closed her eyes and placed a hand on her belly. The baby kicked and she smiled, reminding her she'd made the right choice.

Inhaling the fresh salty air, she was thankful for another chance to get things right. The Australian government had opened their arms to immigrants and the timing couldn't have been better, although she wasn't sure how long the arms would remain open if they found out her real identity. But how could they? Louisa had covered her trail and she'd found someone willing and able to change the name on her British passport even though it had cost a quarter of the money she possessed. It hadn't been difficult coming up with a new identity: Stella was an adaptation from the Spanish word *estrella*, meaning star. And because the stars twinkled next to the moon, the dear, cherished moon she and Roberto loved so much, the name fit perfectly.

A small smile tweaked at the corner of her lips as memories of Roberto rushed back. Even now, months later, she could smell his sandalwood scent, feel his warm, smooth skin against hers and his dark, thick hair curling around her fingers. Her elbow rested against the sheet of music for 'Luna Tango' folded up in her pocket. She'd clung to the hope she could return what was rightfully his and the music score would be reunited, just like she and Roberto, but fate had other plans.

Louisa tried to stem the bitterness churning within. Roberto never had the chance to learn about his impending fatherhood. But she'd experienced enough in her short life to know the world was rarely fair. Gently rubbing her belly, Louisa allowed her love for Roberto to cocoon their unborn child and she prayed she had enough strength and love to equal two parents.

'Miss, you need to get ready,' a young sailor said as he rushed by, repeating the same words to the hundreds of passengers crowding the decks. People craned their necks and pushed each other for a better view of the land where they would start new lives.

Louisa gathered her battered suitcase and adjusted the large purse that hung from her shoulder. As she joined the throng edging down the gangplank and onto the pier, suitcases and bodies bashed against each other in the rush to leave, and the stench of sweat assailed her delicate nostrils. Since becoming pregnant, she'd developed an affliction in which most odors left her nauseous. Swallowing hard, Louisa allowed herself to be carried with the mob, using her spare arm as protection over the precious being in her belly.

When she'd left England all those years ago, she'd never expected life to turn out as it had in Argentina. Never could she have imagined falling so deeply in love with a country and a man, and finding a family in Eduardo Canziani. A dull thud of pain reverberated in her chest, remembering once again that Eduardo had died with anger in his heart as a result of her selfish behavior. Perhaps she should have stayed in Argentina and dealt with the consequences like she'd planned to do before Hector's revelation.

The baby kicked against her abdomen, a harsh reminder that she'd done the right thing. If life had turned out differently, this baby could have been a tango dancer or musician but that could never happen now. As soon as her feet landed on Australian soil, Louisa had to forget tango. Forget Argentina. Mourning for what could have been would not change a thing. All it would do was cause stress to herself and the baby. Roberto's precious, beautiful, baby.

'Lines! Form lines!' yelled a tall, thin man in a faded gray suit. 'Women and children there! Men here! Elderly over there!' he barked and the large group broke apart, hurrying to join the appropriate queue.

Louisa shuffled forward, happy no one paid attention to the lone pregnant woman in the ill-fitting floral dress. She kept her head down and concentrated on her scuffed leather shoes, a pose she'd adopted since leaving Uruguay. Gone was the confident sway of hips and head held high from when she was one of Argentina's elite. This slower walk, hunched shoulders, and shyness helped convince people she was a woman who didn't have much in the world. A statement very close to the truth.

Men in dark blue suits sat behind makeshift tables set along the pier. The recent arrivals edged forward and the officials seemed unperturbed by the wall of humanity approaching them.

Even now, on the verge of entering yet another new country she hoped to call home, Louisa questioned her ability to start a new life. Meeting Eduardo had been fortunate but encountering another person willing to help her now was nigh impossible. She had no idea what the future held but she couldn't give up, not now that she carried Roberto's baby. They both deserved a chance to thrive in this new world, no matter what challenges lay ahead.

The administrator waved her forward. She took a moment to steady herself, barely able to breathe, then stepped toward him. Sweat pooled in her lower back as she passed her papers to the official. His bushy eyebrows created a veranda as he frowned and studied her documents and the passenger list. Louisa didn't move, her mouth dry and skin wet with perspiration. She desperately wanted to wipe away the moist beads on her forehead but didn't dare in case the official detected something was wrong.

'Your husband?' he asked, looking at her large belly.

'He passed away. Farm accident.' Her dry lips made it almost impossible to speak, even though she'd rehearsed this story for weeks.

'No other family?'

'No. My parents died in the London bombings and my only family was an uncle and aunty in Brazil. I moved there just after war broke out.' She still hadn't got used to hearing her voice in English after so many years speaking Spanish. During the voyage she'd practiced speaking her mother tongue and had worked on ironing out the language irregularities she'd developed.

'Why aren't you with your relatives now, given your condition?' The official tilted his head to the side, his tone more concerned than authoritative.

'They have passed, too.' Louisa bowed her head, recalling the sadness of losing her parents and hoping to pass this off in place of her fictitious Brazilian family.

'Why Australia?'

'My baby and I need to start fresh in a land with opportunity. Brazil holds too many sad memories for us.'

'Hmm . . .' He returned to studying the paperwork. 'How far along are you?'

'Six months.' She gripped the sides of her flimsy skirt.

He gathered her papers and stood. 'One moment.'

The official strode off into the crowd of disheveled immigrants who parted like the Red Sea. As soon as he'd cut through, the crowd reformed and the heat and stench of jostling, unwashed bodies overwhelmed her. She looked around, desperate for somewhere to sit but there was nothing. Her breathing grew shallow and bright lights exploded in front of her eyes as she reached out for something, or someone, to help her stay balanced. Her fingers found a solid object and she gripped on for dear life.

'Hey lady, watch it!' A deep voice shouted and her support was tugged away.

'She's going to faint! Grab her!' a woman's thick Irish accent pierced through the crowd. The woman tried to hold her but Louisa crashed to the ground, landing heavily on her stomach. A sharp pain stabbed her abdomen and she clutched her belly.

'No! My baby! My baby!' she moaned, and writhed as the agony spread across her stomach and to her lower back.

'Get a doctor! Now!' Panic laced the Irish woman's tone as she stroked Louisa's forehead.

'Move! She needs room!' shouted a man, less gruff than the one who had rejected her desperate grab. With outstretched arms, the Australian soldier pushed the crowd apart and knelt down and patted her hand. 'Don't worry, love. We'll look after you.'

His eyes traveled from hers to the young woman with thick red hair.

'She's a friend of yours?'

'No,' said the Irish woman. 'She's alone.'

'Alone?' He turned to Louisa and forced a smile although deep concern clouded his blue eyes. This stranger's presence calmed her slightly, and she tried to sit up. 'Stay still, darlin'. You're not alone now.'

Louisa nodded and closed her eyes. Pain came in waves as voices in various languages ricocheted around her. She lay on the hot ground with stones digging into her flesh and shivered despite the midday sun burning her pale skin.

Louisa went to speak but a scream escaped when another pain stabbed her abdomen and a warm, sticky wetness oozed between her legs.

'No!'

CHAPTER 31

Present Day - Dani

Stifling heat surrounded Dani as she moved out from behind the bushes at the side of the highway. Carlos waited for her in the car they'd hired in Fortaleza, his arm resting casually on the back of her seat, a smirk gracing his lips.

'Better?'

'Yes. Too much coffee, methinks.'

'Do not mind, it is nature, yes?'

'Hmm.' Oh, but she minded very much, especially as her relationship with Carlos was still on rocky ground. Since they'd met up again in Buenos Aires there hadn't been any hand holding or kissing, not even an accidental shoulder graze on the airplane. Peeing behind a bush didn't add to the romance factor, either.

Dani got in and clicked the seatbelt in place. Carlos turned the car onto the road and drove so slowly she could have walked backward faster. She desperately wanted to kick him out of the driver's seat so she could slam down the accelerator and do her own impression of Argentine race car driver Juan Fangio but she refrained, figuring her being pushy wouldn't improve matters with Carlos.

Leaving the pristine beaches behind, they traveled inland and into the rural highlands. Dani stared out the window, trying to appreciate the beauty of the palm trees and clear blue sky. She still couldn't comprehend her grandma's past or the fact that Dani was on the way to meet the only man who had captured Stella's heart. It was disappointing that it took until their twilight years to find each other. Life could be so cruel sometimes.

'Two more hours and we should arrive, yes?' Carlos's smooth voice intruded on her downhearted state.

'Why did you volunteer to come on this trip?' she asked then wished she could take it back.

'You needed a person who speaks Portuguese, yes?'

'And?'

'Iris does not speak Portuguese. It is best if she stays in Buenos Aires and deals with Diego. You need to know if he has done anything with the information he stole, yes?' When Dani filled in Carlos on the flight to Brazil, he'd been horrified by what he'd done to Iris. Diego was lucky Carlos was on his way to another country and out of punching-in-the-nose range.

'I worry about Iris's safety,' said Dani.

'Iris is resourceful, she will be fine.'

Knowing she had a captive, albeit possibly reluctant, audience, Dani said, 'I'm a little confused, because you've been telling me you wanted someone, anyone, to be held responsible for Canziani's death. Now my grandma's landed in your lap as one of two suspects. And—' She cut herself off, too scared to finish the sentence.

Carlos's gripped the steering wheel so hard his knuckles turned white. 'You want to know what I will do with this information?' he asked in an even tone.

'Yes.' She hated questioning his intentions but in her excitement and haste upon hearing Stella's confession, Dani hadn't thought about the consequences of telling Carlos. All she'd cared about was being honest. But now she wished she'd been more careful, although it was a little like shutting the gate after the llamas had escaped.

'If you say she didn't do it, then I must take this into my account, yes?'

'My grandma may have been many things but a murderer she is not.' Dani drew her lips together.

'And Roberto?'

'I have no idea but I can't believe Stella would ever be in a relationship with a man capable of killing someone.'

'People do many things we don't expect. Life is unpredictable. People are unpredictable. Tango—'

'Is unpredictable. You do like your life and tango references, don't you?' She shifted in her seat and faced him. There was a fluttering in her belly as she took in his tanned skin, dark hair and perfectly straight nose. *Stupid bloody laws of attraction.*

'Daniela, maybe now you know your heritage, you might believe me when I refer to this life and tango business. The beauty of the tango is that it is unpredictable. There are no two dances the same, just like there are no two lives the same. Different dance partners, music, dance halls . . . they all combine to make the tango experience unique for every person. And it all starts with the tiniest dance step. One little move can change the entire direction of the dance and create an experience we never imagined. Just like life. Ah!' He raised his finger in the air. 'Your raw talent, I was right! Look at your genes!'

'Fat lot of good that's done. And anyway, we don't know if Roberto is my grandfather.'

'You do not know for sure?'

'Nope. My head was spinning with everything Stella had told me and I completely forgot to ask. How stupid is that? One of the most important questions in my life and I failed to ask it. So much for being a journalist.'

He smiled for a millisecond. 'You can ask when you call her, yes? Or you could ask Roberto.'

'Ask him if he slept with my grandma?'

'Surely a woman of words like you can find a more delicate way of asking this but you do not need to make the decision now. If Roberto is your grandfather you can embrace your true heritage and it will help you understand who you are.'

'I am who I am because I am me. Like you said, *my* experiences shape *my* life. My steps. My choices. My dances. It has nothing to do with who I'm related to.'

'It is your heritage. You, my dear Daniela, are showing a sense of family even if you cannot see it. You are looking after your own, which is what we do for family. I now understand why you lied. I am not happy about it but I appreciate your actions. You were, and are, protecting your family, yes?'

'I am, aren't I?' Surprised by his observation, Dani turned her attention to the farmlands outside the window and mulled over Carlos's words. For the first time in her life, Dani felt part of a family bigger than just her and Stella, even though it was more fractured than the leg she'd broken skateboarding when she was twelve.

'So is this the reason you wanted to help?'

'Yes.' His smile melted the ice wall between them.

The car's air-conditioning blew Dani's hair across her face and she clawed at her hair, trying to keep it from slapping her. The uneasy silence filled the car as her mind zapped with countless questions. What if she'd been upfront with Carlos in the beginning? What if her grandma had met up with Roberto in Brazil all those years ago? What if Stella had told Iris the truth when she'd first wanted to learn tango? Would that have stopped Iris from going to Argentina in search of who she was?

Catching a glimpse of herself in the rear mirror, she recoiled. Even though the air conditioner was on she was still hot. The heat had frizzed her hair and the eyeliner had run and pooled in the bags under her eyes. Rubbing her face, she turned to face Carlos. Man, even in the heat he looked cool and oh so handsome. 'I have a question.'

'Shall we stop so you can learn a dance step first?' A mischievous glint shone in his eyes.

'You can't be serious.' Dani wiped the sweat from her brow.

'I will let it pass today. Please, ask your question.'

'Is another reason you're helping me because Argentine blood might be running through my veins?' This revelation could explain why it felt like returning home when she first arrived in Buenos Aires.

'You ask this because of my feelings about foreigners and the Canziani case?'

'Yes.' She bit her lip.

'This is a very good question. You are lucky we are not doing the questions for dance steps because I would make you learn some-thing very difficult.' Sniffing, he said, 'It does help, yes. You may think my patriotism is extreme but maybe one day you will understand.'

'Maybe.'

Silence overtook them again. Carlos concentrated on the road while Dani focused on his hands gripping the steering wheel. It had been so long since he'd caressed her. Ran his fingers through her hair. Stroked her face. Touched her breasts.

A small sigh escaped her lips.

'You wish to say something?' Carlos glanced at her then returned his attention to the road ahead.

'I . . .' How to express these thoughts? 'I don't know what *we* are.'

'You and me?' Carlos pulled on to the side of the road and gravel crunched underneath the tires. 'I do not know how to answer this question.'

'Because you don't know?'

He stared out at the palm trees surrounding them. Shifting his gaze to her, he said, 'Just like the relationship with your family, ours is complicated also.'

'Not so complicated that we can't work things out, right?' A ball of panic lodged in her chest.

Carlos tapped his finger on the dashboard. Each second dragged by as worry gripped Dani's muscles, pulling them taut.

'I just do not know. I am sorry, Dani.'

'Then why did you come back?' Her voice sounded loud in the small rental car.

'I was worried about you and I wanted to apologize.'

'And?' She leaned forward, holding her breath.

'And that is all. I am sorry if this makes you upset but you are a good person, Daniela McKenna, you deserve to know the truth and not be led along the path of a garden.'

Pausing, she let his words play back a few times in her head. 'I still don't understand.'

'We need time to figure out the things between us but your grandma and Roberto do not have the same luxury, yes? We should go.' Looking over his shoulder at the empty road, Carlos pulled out and they continued their journey through the Brazilian farmlands.

They didn't look at each other and the silence drove Dani insane. She wanted to end the torment but how? It felt like everything had been said, for now, and they both needed to stew in their own thoughts.

After twenty long minutes they arrived at Rancho do Sonho. Carlos turned off the main road and they drove up a long road that led to a whitewashed house with a veranda and bright red shutters and doors. A fountain out front featured a stone carving of three angels surrounding a small lamb. The outstretched arms of the angels formed a protective circle around the young animal and water spilled from the holes near their feet.

Dani and Carlos got out of the car and shut the doors. He placed a hand on her shoulder, no doubt to show his support but instead it only increased her tension. She wanted to shrug off his hand but doing so could give the wrong signal.

The house looked deserted so they made their way over and into the sprawling tin shed that was hotter than the midday sun, the scent of cashews and damp soil filling the air. A group of workers in various states of dishevelment gathered at large tables, sorting nuts by size and throwing them in canvas sacks. They joked as they worked, the lines on their faces deepening as they laughed. Each had sun-stained skin that probably made them look older than their years.

One man, more ancient than the rest, coughed and spluttered into a handkerchief. Even though he was at the back of the shed, his wheeze was audible. He caught Dani staring and offered a friendly smile. Her heart went out to him.

Ignoring their problems for a moment, she nudged Carlos so hard he almost lost balance. 'It's him.'

'Where?'

'There!' She pointed at the old man, unable to break her stare.

Forcing her arm down, Carlos said, 'What makes you say this?'

'A feeling.' Now, more than ever, she hoped her intuition was spot on.

'I do not know about trusting this feeling business but I will go ask just for you.'

'No. I need to do this,' she said.

'But—'

'I need to embrace my heritage, right?'

He gave her a lopsided smile. 'I cannot argue with my own argument.'

'Wish me luck.' Dani puffed out her cheeks and took a tentative step forward. As she moved through the shed, the men gave cursory glances but none were so rude as to stare at her outright. The old man continued sorting, oblivious to the fact that his life was about to change.

Drawing up beside him, she studied the cracked skin on his fingers as he deftly sorted the nuts. Glancing up, he smiled then continued with his work. Dani leaned in close so no one could hear and in Spanish she said, 'You're Roberto Vega, aren't you?'

'*Não, não. Eu só falo português*' he said, concentrating on the nuts.

'I know who you are and you speak more than Portuguese,' she continued in Spanish. Her heart raced with her daring assumption, the pull toward this man impossible to ignore.

He broke the shells with power, the veins around his temple throbbing.

'You sent Louisa Gilchrist a letter.' Dani swallowed, praying she had the right person. 'You called her Lunita. I'm her granddaughter and she sent me to find you.'

The hammer fell out of his hand and clattered against the table.

Looking up at her with tearful eyes, he said, 'I am him. I am the Roberto Vega you are looking for.'

CHAPTER 32

Present Day - Dani

Dani clutched the edge of the table, trying to regain her balance. She didn't know whether to jump for joy or break down in tears.

'You really are?' She rasped.

'Yes,' he said in Spanish. He took off his hat, revealing a large bald spot. Looking around at the other men hard at work smashing the shells, he whispered, 'We cannot talk here. Go to your car. I will meet you there soon.'

Leaving him behind, Dani moved quietly among the workers, and crossed the gravel parking lot, barely able to contain her excitement. Carlos leaned against the vehicle, his eyes not leaving hers. When she drew close, Carlos stepped forward and folded her into his arms. Dani leaned against his strong chest, her body shaking as the tears ran freely down her face and were soaked up by Carlos's collar.

'You found him?' He whispered.

'Yes.' She drew back and wiped her eyes. 'I told you I had a feeling.'

A slow smile graced Carlos's lips. 'And I had a feeling your sense of family was much stronger than you thought, yes?'

'You're right.' She loved the feel of his arms around her—the security, the affection, the . . . Her shoulders slumped. *Don't read into things, McKenna.*

The sound of someone shuffling across the gravel took their attention away from each other. Roberto drew close, but stopped to catch breath. Taking out a handkerchief he coughed into it, his chest rattling. Roberto tucked his handkerchief into his pocket, then eyed Carlos. Reluctantly breaking his embrace, Dani stepped away.

'This is Carlos Escudero. He's my . . .' What? What was he now? 'Don't worry, you can trust him.'

'I am aware of Carlos Escudero. You have entertained me for many hours when I watched you on DVD and television. You are a great credit to tango.'

'And I believe you are very talented,' Carlos said, a slight tinge of red creeping up his neck. Dani couldn't work out whether it was Carlos being humble or if he was struggling in the presence of the man who may have murdered one of tango's greatest legends.

'I am Roberto Vega, but people know me as Cristian Villa.' His accent confused her as he sounded more Uruguayan than Argentine.

'How did you find Louisa?' Dani asked.

He looked at the vast cashew fields then turned to her. 'Your mother is Iris Kennedy, yes?'

Dani nodded.

'I may not have much but I do own a television. I saw a TV special and she talked about a book with a character called Lunita.'

'You saw that? Why didn't you contact Iris?'

'Because the presenter mentioned the name of Iris's mother and I thought it best to find my Louisa first, just to make sure I had the right woman.'

'Well, you most definitely do, but how on earth did you track her down in Australia?'

'I spent much of my savings on a private detective but in the end it wasn't too difficult or risky because I was looking for Stella

Kennedy not Louisa Gilchrist.' He narrowed his eyes and tilted his head. 'Do you know you look like your grandmother?' He sighed then his lips sprang into a cheeky smile. 'A grandmother. Ha! Are we that old?'

'You don't have family?'

'No. I never married. Never wanted to. Not unless I could wed my Louisa.' He quickly drew out the handkerchief and coughed into it.

'She never married, either.'

Stuffing the handkerchief back in his pocket, he shifted from foot to foot, his large eyes fixed on hers. 'So if she didn't marry then is Iris my . . .?'

'I haven't asked Stella. Perhaps this is a question you should ask.'

'Then you could be my granddaughter?' His dark eyes studied her with intensity. 'This is hard to believe. Five minutes ago I had no one.'

'I understand your surprise.' She felt as overwhelmed as he appeared. 'How long have you been here?'

'Many, many years, I am afraid. Unfortunately, it took me too long to arrive in Chapada do Russo. There were complications leaving Buenos Aires then when I finally got out I headed north to the Argentine border with Bolivia. The plan was to travel across Brazil to Chapada as I was convinced my Louisa would be here, waiting for me. But the floods were bad that year. So, so bad. I was delayed in crossing the border for almost two months. When I finally arrived, there was no sign of my girl.' Blinking, he asked, 'Please, what is your name?'

His politeness endeared him to her even more.

'My name is Dani.'

'Short for Daniela?' She nodded and he said, 'Such a beautiful name.'

'This is what I say,' said Carlos. He raised an eyebrow and she rolled her eyes in reply.

'You prefer Dani, yes?'

'Yes.'

They fell silent as the chatter of workers and scattering nuts filled the air.

'So what now?' she asked.

'I must finish my work for the day.' Roberto cocked his head toward the shed. 'Please, tell me where you are and I will meet you after eight o'clock.'

Dani scribbled her phone number on the pensión's business card and handed it to Roberto. He saluted, turned, and shuffled into the sweltering heat of the shed.

'What if he doesn't come find us? What if he disappears?' she asked, wishing logic would overpower her emotions instead of letting them churn into a blinding panic.

'Why would he contact your grandma and tell you he is Roberto Vega then not show?'

'Who's to say he won't change it again?'

'Why?' asked Carlos.

'I don't know! Maybe he sent the letter not thinking he'd get a reply and now I've shown up and he's too overwhelmed.'

'You think this is so?'

Dani shrugged.

'We go and wait at the pensión, yes? There is nothing we can do here. We must respect his wishes.'

Reluctantly, Dani got in the car and Carlos climbed in next to her. He reversed slower than a granny then pointed the car in the direction of a tree-lined driveway. Dani glanced at Roberto, who watched them leave while the other workers sorted nuts around him. His expression didn't relay a single emotion.

She turned to face Carlos. 'I hope he shows.'

Pacing the pensión's small veranda, Dani flung her arms about and muttered obscenities while Carlos sat in a padded chair, infuriating her with his calm demeanor. Darkness surrounded them, bringing a welcome relief from the sun's heat but a heightened anxiousness at Roberto's nonappearance.

'It's ten o'clock. He's not coming ,' she said.

'He is South American, yes? Clocks are an inconvenience for us. He will come when he is ready.' Carlos took a long sip from his can of pop.

Dani flopped onto a chair and kicked out her feet. 'Maybe we should go and find him.'

'Daniela, chasing a man will only end in your tears.'

'But—'

'Oh no.' He held up a hand. 'You scare me when you start sentences with this word.'

'Why?'

'Because it means you have more questions than people can answer.'

'I'm a journalist,' she said, but it didn't sit right, as she hadn't finished a single article.

'I am aware of your profession, Daniela.'

'Yet you're still talking to me.' She smiled and nudged his foot with hers.

Carlos drew his brows together, an air of seriousness descending upon him. 'Maybe we should pass time working on your articles. You must have at least one finished. I would like to read it.'

Dani bit her bottom lip.

'You have done nothing?'

'I've been working! See?' She reached into the bag beside the chair and wielded her notebook. Flipping it open, she thrust the pages at him.

Whenever I hear tango music, I conjure up visions of dapper men in sharp suits, hats tilted to the side, wooing women in fishnet stockings and low-cut dresses that cling to sensuous curves. The couple sways to the music, a soulful bandoneón *dictating their every move. Most onlookers focus on the dancers, barely giving the orchestra a second glance. But if you can take your eyes off the tango dancers and concentrate on the* bandoneón *player, you'll notice the passion that pours from his soul into the instrument. There is an undying love and connection between the player and his* bandoneón, *not unlike tango dancers and their partners. Unfortunately,* the bandoneón *is under threat of extinction and without it, tango music as we know it will change forever.*

Today there are only two bandoneón repair shops in the world, both in Buenos Aires. Originally made in Germany in the nineteenth century, the bandonion *(as it was called in Germany) was used for religious music in churches. In the 1850s, the German and Italian sailors and emigrants brought the instrument to the shores of Argentina. They incorporated the* bandoneón *into a new music and dance that started in Buenos Aires. We now know it as the tango.*

Thousands of instruments were sent to Argentina from Germany, but production stopped when the manufacturer closed down during World War II. These days, only a handful of the original instruments remain. There are no spare parts and their legacy relies heavily on the craftspeople continuing a century-old tradition.

Even though to the untrained eye the bandoneón *may look like it's related to the accordion, it comes from a completely different family. The* bandoneón *is part of the concertina family and doesn't have the piano-like keys found on an accordion. Instead, a* bandoneón *has buttons on both sides of the instrument and has two-voice notes—when a button is pressed, two notes play at the same time. There are over seventy buttons on the* bandoneón, *giving the instrument a wide range and adding a richness and depth to the music that is recognized worldwide as an integral part of tango.*

With the resurgence of tango over the last decade, musicians and collectors have bought up the remaining bandoneóns *and pay up to US$7,000 per piece. The Argentine government recently passed a law that prohibits anyone other than an Argentine musician on tour from taking an original* bandoneón *out of the country.*

Argentina has produced new versions of bandoneóns, *but according to tango aficionados, the sound is less authentic and doesn't have the soul of the originals. One of the reasons they are lacking the original sound is because the wood of German-made* bandoneóns *was aged for ten to fifteen years before being made into an instrument.*

With the originals dying out, the sound of tango will change. The love and care the instruments have received over the years are not enough to keep them alive forever. Even with the proper care, it is expected the originals may only last for another fifty years. Let's hope someone can find an answer to this problem and prevent the loss of something that is as Argentine as the tango.

'And I'll add in a whole lot about Gualberto,' she said, feeling defensive as well as hypocritical since she couldn't stand the instrument but had written as though she loved it.

'All you are doing are notes, notes, notes, yes? When will you finish the articles?'

With an indignant thrust of the hand she grabbed the book and shoved it back in her bag. Carlos had a nasty habit of hitting the wrong button at the right time.

'Writer's block. Heard of it?' she asked.

'This really happens?' He laughed, then stopped when he saw her scowl.

'It's not funny. My entire career depends on it and I can't find a way to finish!'

'You do not love the dance,' Carlos said matter-of-factly.

'Of course I don't love it. Why would I? All it's done is cause grief in my family. Look at what it did to Stella. To Louisa and Roberto. To my mother and father. To my mother and me. . . How can I find inspiration in a dance that doesn't love me?'

'You are trying too hard.'

'Too hard to hate it? That comes easy.'

If her words hurt, he didn't show it. 'Daniela, stand up.'

'I'm not doing any more lessons.'

'Stand up.'

She shook her head and crossed her arms like a petulant child. 'I'm the break in the link, okay? The tango gene has skipped me and I have no problems with that whatsoever.'

Carlos stared at her, his lips taut. 'You are full of words, Daniela McKenna. Just words.'

'I'm obviously not because I can't write a flipping article!'

'Up, please.' He arched his eyebrows, indicating he would tolerate no further argument.

Realizing this was a battle already lost, she stood and shifted the chair back a few inches. 'I will do as you ask but I don't have to like it.'

'That is okay. I have no problems with that whatsoever.' He did a cruddy job of mimicking her Australian accent.

Dani stifled a giggle and stood straight. 'Dazzle me.'

'You talk too much, this is your problem.'

'I do not! What about the way you—'

Carlos's frown stopped her.

'You do not listen to what is within. All this blah, blah, blah, you do, it is not good for anything. For success you need to be quiet here and here.' He pointed to his head then mouth. 'If you allow peace in those places, you will listen to this.' Carlos put his hand over his heart. 'This beating, loving device will guide you in the direction you need. What does yours say?'

Carlos lifted her hand and placed it over her heart. It beat a million miles an hour under his touch so she closed her eyes, willing the frantic pace to slow. She tried to still her busy mind. The same mind that kept yelling, 'Jump him!' Concentrating on her heart, she listened but got nothing. She went to move her hand but Carlos held it firmly in place.

'Do not give up so easily.'

Dani tried again. This time, warmth spread deep within her chest. Tango music filled her ears and her mind played images of her mother dancing, her grandma as a young woman in Buenos Aires, and a pair of violet tango shoes—the pair she'd tried on in the shop.

Dani gasped and ripped her hand away. Opening her eyes, she took a step back.

'What's wrong? You are shaking.'

'I—'

'Good evening.'

Carlos and Dani turned to find Roberto struggling up the stairs of the veranda. He gripped the balustrade with one hand and carried a *bandoneón* case in the other. Roberto paused with each step, allowing his lungs to fill with air, his wheezing worse than earlier in the day.

'Please, do not let me interrupt.' He made it to the veranda and Dani rushed to him, ushering him to a chair. Roberto sat down, placed his case beside him, and smiled his thanks. 'You two make a lovely couple.'

'We are not together. We are just friends,' Carlos said quickly.

Cut by his words, Dani stared into the darkness. Had he already made up his mind?

'I am surprised you are not a couple. There is a connection between you two. Interesting . . .' She turned to find Roberto coughing into a speckled handkerchief.

'I'll get you some water,' said Dani, anxious to find a moment of solitude as worry for Roberto's health edged in on her. Entering the pensión, she grabbed a glass and filled it with water from the tap. Hanging her head, she breathed deeply a few times, trying to steady her nerves.

'You are all right, Dani?' Roberto leaned against the doorframe. She stepped forward and placed her hand under his elbow. 'Please, you need to sit.'

'I have spent too much time sitting in my life. It is very hard to play the *bandoneón* standing up, yes?' When he laughed his eyes sparkled with youthful cheekiness, briefly covering the dullness of an elderly man.

'So you've been playing all these years?'

'I stopped just after I left Argentina but when I established my new persona as a Uruguayan—'

'That's why you have that accent! I couldn't work it out, now I understand.'

'I've always been good at mimicking. It comes with being a good listener, which makes me a good musician.' He slid her a wink, not giving the slightest hint of arrogance.

'I heard you were the best.'

He shrugged. 'Maybe but that life disappeared the day I lost Louisa. It took me a long time before I could play again but when I did, I realized it was the only way I could feel close to her. And the moon,' he sighed, 'The moon always brought her back into my heart.'

'Lunita,' Dani said.

'Yes. My little moon. Ever since I wrote a song for my *lunita*, I have dreamt of romancing her with a serenade at midnight. I would have given anything to see her beautiful face highlighted by the light of the full moon.' He gazed into the distance, his mind no doubt conjuring up memories smoothed by time and life experience. He shook his head and blinked. 'But that is the past. It is dreams of a young man who is now old. Tell me, what scared you just then? The fear in your eyes was deep.'

'It wasn't fear, it was . . .' What was it? The music and images were so real. She felt every movement as her mother danced. She felt as if she were her grandmother, walking through the streets of nineteen-fifties Buenos Aires. She felt the soft violet shoes on her feet. She felt . . . a connection to tango. 'I don't know what it was.' *Liar, liar, pants on fire.*

'Perhaps I can help.'

'How?'

He took her hand and led her back to the veranda. Carlos sat in the chair, rubbing his leg. The moment he saw her, he removed his hand.

'Stand here.' Roberto went to his case and opened it. Glimpsing the battered *bandoneón*, she craned her neck for a better view. Just looking at the instrument sent chills of distaste up her spine. He moved tattered papers out of the way then pulled out his phone. Dani glanced at Carlos, who raised his eyebrows, just as surprised as she.

Roberto fiddled with the phone, wheezing and coughing as he did so. A moment later he let out a triumphant 'Ah!' and handed it to Carlos. 'When I say play, do so.' Roberto moved to her side. 'We dance.'

'Thank you but I'm really not in the mood.'

'You will feel better. I promise.' He held her hands in the tango pose. 'I want you to trust me.'

Even though her mind doubted he could change her state, she forced herself to let things unfold in the way they were meant to. Roberto nodded at Carlos, who pressed play. Once more Dani's ears filled with the whining *bandoneón* but no fingernails on a blackboard were present. The climb and fall of the notes had a hypnotic effect and she closed her eyes, wary this had been her downfall before.

She sensed Roberto move and she leaned to the left, taking a tentative step. The thin skin on his hands meant his bones jutted out and even though he was frail, a deep energy surrounded him and embraced her. Violins and the piano joined the *bandoneón*, and although the accompaniments sounded amateur, the music seeped into her soul. The fear that had gripped her melted away, leaving an air of tranquility, a willingness to let go, a desire to be in the moment. Roberto guided her across the veranda and Dani trusted him without question.

A stone caught under her foot and she stumbled, eyes wide. Carlos jumped up and grabbed her just before she hit the ground face first. Twisting in his arms, she faced him. Concern clouded his handsome features, although it was soon replaced by a smile as he helped her into a standing position. She moved away, his nearness disconcerting.

'I'm sorry, Roberto,' she said, taking a seat on the rail of the veranda far, far away from Carlos. Roberto sat also, his fragility appearing once again. His breathing became shallow and she asked, 'Are you okay?'

'Yes,' he wheezed. 'I am good.'

'You don't look so great.' She got up and passed him more water.

He took a long drink, his hand shaking slightly. 'Why do you resist?'

'What? The tango? Like I've told Carlos before, I don't have my mother's talent.'

'It is there, I feel it. You must stop burying your abilities within your worries.' He took another sip. 'Did you like the music?'

'It was beautiful.' Even the *bandoneón*, for a nice change. 'Who was that?'

The wrinkles around Roberto's eyes deepened when he grinned. 'It is me with some friends from the plantation.'

'What?' Carlos and Dani caught each other's eyes. He had to be her grandfather, otherwise why would every other *bandoneón* player make her cringe while he sent her on a magical musical journey?

'It is a good machine, no? I like technology very much.' He reached for the phone next to Carlos. 'I have almost every tune I have written on here.'

'Don't you worry about people discovering who you are?' she asked.

Roberto shook his head. 'I never recorded when I was Eduardo's protégé so no one can compare my playing. To everyone here,' he swept his arms over the sleeping town of Chapada do Russo, 'I am a Uruguayan who never took advantage of my talent.'

'It's sad the world never heard you play,' said Carlos.

Shrugging, Roberto smiled. 'It is okay. The men at the plantation appreciate my efforts. I am too old to dwell on past regrets. However, there is one song I have never recorded.'

She leaned forward. 'Really?'

'It was a song I wrote for your grandma. I called it 'Luna Tango'.'

CHAPTER 33

Present Day - Dani

The sharp trill of Dani's phone pierced the night. She reached into her bag and pulled it out, almost dropping it on the veranda.

'Yes?'

'Have you found him?' asked Iris.

'Yes and—'

'Good. I've got some news.' She sucked in hard, no doubt taking a long drag on her cigarette. 'I've had confirmation Diego's gone to the police with the information.'

'Shit.'

'The Argentine authorities are investigating his claim.'

'What?'

'I'm not surprised. After all, this is the biggest lead they've ever had.'

'Shit.'

'Dani, cursing doesn't help.'

'Sorry.' She felt like a teenager. So this was what it felt like to have a mother? 'The Argentine authorities are notoriously slow, right? And even if they did urgently contact the Australian Federal Police, who's to say the file won't gather dust in Australia? Or maybe they'll jump on it because they have a good lead. Either way, we need to be careful.'

'I'm worried but I haven't hit the panic button yet. I've called Stella but she's not answering.'

'Crap,' said Dani.

'Your mouth, Dani—'

'Sorry! We'll return tomorrow, okay?'

'Will Roberto be with you?' Dani could hear the hope in her mother's voice. She hadn't thought that far ahead.

'I don't know. If he is, you'll have to call him Cristian Villa. He's been going by that name for years. Call me if you get hold of Stella otherwise I'll see you in BA.'

'Goodbye, Dani.'

'Iris?'

'Yes.'

'Thank you for looking out for Stella.'

'It's my pleasure. I'm beginning to understand why she did what she did. Perhaps one day, she and I will be able to sit down and work through our issues. Lord knows we have plenty but let's deal with our immediate concerns first. I'll check in again soon.'

The phone went dead and Dani pocketed the phone and faced the men. Carlos stood and took her shaking hands, his warm, soft skin instantly comforting her.

Roberto took a moment then said, 'I must return to Argentina. I must speak with the authorities. I need to tell them who I am.'

'But don't you want to meet with Stella, I mean, Louisa? Why can't you meet here, in Brazil? Then you don't have to worry about police or—'

'It is time, Dani. I have spent too long on the run and I cannot entertain the possibility the authorities could arrest my Louisa.'

They sat in silence, accompanied by a symphony of cicadas. Question upon question raced through her mind but she didn't know where to start.

Clearing his throat, Roberto said, 'It will be problematic for me to prove who I am as I have spent many, many years pretending to be someone else.'

A simple DNA test would solve the problem of establishing Roberto as Iris's father, if that was the case, but that lead to a whole other set of challenges. Stella hadn't put Roberto's name on Iris's birth certificate and if authorities discovered this . . . Dani dreaded to think what Pandora's Box this would open. 'Roberto, you going to Argentine authorities and handing yourself in is gallant but it will only be of use if you were the one who killed Eduardo.'

Roberto raised an eyebrow. 'Do you think Louisa did it?'

'No! Of course not!' How could the woman who spent her days crocheting for sick kids kill a man? Nope. No way. No how.

'Please, sit.' He nodded toward the chair. She did so and crossed her legs then uncrossed them. 'Now is the time for you to learn the truth.'

Dani and Carlos exchanged hopeful glances.

'How much do you know?' Roberto asked.

'I read the witness accounts. They believed the alibi Héctor Sosa gave them. He said he was with his mistress the entire night and she backed it up.'

Roberto took a sip of water and set it down. His eyes closed for a moment, as if gathering strength. 'Canziani hit me and I fell unconscious. A doctor helped and I woke in my apartment with Louisa doing the fussing.' His dry lips curved into a small smile. 'Then I fell asleep. When I stirred again she wasn't there and I knew she had gone to see Canziani to speak her mind. She was a feisty girl. She is like this now, yes?'

'Most definitely.'

'I am happy. This is one of her best qualities.'

'It's served her well,' said Dani.

'It's hereditary.' Carlos winked at her and heat rushed across her cheeks.

'When I left my apartment to find Louisa, I met him near my place.'

'Canziani?'

'Yes. He had a bloody eye and his collarbone was damaged. Lots of blood. So much blood. He'd come looking for me because he thought I had sent Héctor Sosa after him.'

'Had you?' Dani asked.

He tsked. 'No, of course not. You must know that Louisa and I were friends because we took solace in each other over Canziani's moods. Then we fell in love.' He stared out into the darkness. Shaking his head, he smiled. 'Sorry, I got lost.'

'That's okay,' she said, patting his hand. 'Take your time.'

Roberto squared his shoulders. 'When Canziani saw me again that same night after we had fought in San Telmo, he was furious about me taking Louisa from him. I demanded he give back my *bandoneón* and the sheet music.' Roberto's breathing grew shallow. 'He had a gun.'

Dani gasped. She took in the words but their gravity had yet to register.

'Eduardo, he rarely fought with his fists preferring to use words to hurt. Although this night he felt the need for a weapon. He said my career was dead so I might as well be, too.'

'What happened?' asked Carlos, his eyes wide.

'I asked him to calm down but he aimed the gun at my chest. He said if Louisa wouldn't be with him then she could not have my heart and he would blow it to pieces.' He pulled out his handkerchief and wiped his brow. She glanced at the red stains and looked away. Her heart beat so loudly she was afraid it would drown his words.

'I put my head down and I ran at him. I knocked him over and he hit his head on the gutter.' He grimaced. 'The sound, it was horrible. It stunned him but then I saw the gun on the ground next to him.'

'What did you do?' Dani and Carlos asked simultaneously.

'I grabbed it and pointed it at him. He pulled a knife from his jacket, got up and ran at me. He cut my arm and I . . .' He covered his brow with a trembling hand.

Dani knelt in front of him. She placed her hand in his. 'It must have been torture keeping this inside for so many years.'

'I am fine. You need to know this.' A wheeze rattled his chest.

Her heart went out to Roberto. As she held his hand, she sensed the years of pent-up anger, hurt, and heartbreak within.

'I pointed the gun at his leg and asked him to stop. He did not listen. He would not listen.' His hand shook in hers. 'I kept the gun aimed at his leg but he ran at me and tripped. He fell, and . . . and the bullet went in his stomach.' Doubling over, he quietly wept. Dani rubbed her hand up and down his spine, his clothes doing a pathetic job of disguising his bony frame.

Roberto straightened, determination flashing in his eyes. 'The sheet music went everywhere. And the blood, it was on my hands, the road . . . he was dying. I heard people running toward us so I knew he would get help. I panicked. I picked up the gun, my *bandoneón*, and music, and ran. I must have run fast because no one came forward to say they'd seen me.'

Breathless, Dani asked, 'Where did you go?'

'I tried to find my Louisa. I went to the house of Canziani. I planned to go through the back garden but Héctor Sosa was in the alley. I told him what happened.' He hung his head. 'He told me to go back to his house and hide. He said would make arrangements for me and Louisa to get out of the country.'

'And?' she asked, her heart breaking as the story unfolded.

'I did as he asked but when I got there I passed out. It was the concussion, I am sure. By the time I woke up Héctor and a doctor were there but it had been many, many hours since I was conscious. Things had heated up and he had to get Louisa out so he did and had returned to get me when I could travel.' Pulling the collar up around his neck, Roberto said, 'Sosa left to gather a couple of things but before he returned the police were knocking on his door and I . . . . I . . . had to escape. I had no choice. If I didn't leave then they would have arrested me.'

'Do you think Héctor turned you in?' Surely Roberto had asked this question himself.

'I like to think no but . . . desperate people do desperate things.' Tilting his head to the side, Roberto's sad eyes looked into Dani's. 'Héctor loved her. I can see that now. Why did I not know that back then?'

Roberto's revelation about events on that night stunned Dani. This man held answers to a mystery Argentina had struggled to solve for decades. If she were a true journalist, she'd jump on this story but she couldn't. Dani wanted to protect Roberto, not expose him.

Finding it difficult to imagine Stella breaking hearts all over Latin America, Dani asked, 'So Louisa had three men in love with her?'

'I guess she did and I can understand why. My Louisa had a heart of gold and a soul of beauty.' Roberto frowned, as if a disturbing image from his past had intruded on his pleasant reminiscing. 'I lost everything that night. Louisa, my career, my mentor . . .'

'What did you do with the gun?' asked Carlos and Dani shot him a 'Should you be asking this now?' look.

Roberto didn't seem perturbed by Carlos's question. 'I pulled the gun apart and put different pieces in trash around the city.' He shifted in his seat and rested his clenched fist against his heart.

'Are you okay?' she asked and patted his hand. 'Do you need to rest?'

'Yes.' His hacking cough returned with force. 'And no.' His eyes traveled from Dani to Carlos. 'It is obvious I am sick, yes? In truth, I am not long for this world. I have cancer.'

'But people survive that all the time!'

'I am old. It is okay, Dani.' He coughed again. 'The cancer, it has spread from my lungs into other parts of my body. The doctors said this would happen.'

Dani moved closer to Carlos, who grabbed her hand and squeezed it tight.

'I have had a good life. Not the one I planned but I have done the best with what transpired.' Dani's lips quivered and Roberto placed his hand under her chin. 'Please, do not be sad. I am going to finish my life the way I started: with honesty. Too many times I have succumbed to telling lies to protect myself. I am done with this. Truth is now my guide.' Satisfaction pushed his lips into a smile. He broke into a coughing fit and she rubbed his shoulders.

'You've told us the truth, isn't that enough?'

'No, I am afraid it is not. I do not expect you to understand but I cannot continue living this lie.'

'What about Louisa? As soon as we get hold of her she can come here. She can be with you, just like you've both wanted.' Dani tried to keep the desperation out of her tone but couldn't. If she had to get down on her knees and beg, she would.

Roberto shook his head. 'I am sorry, Dani, but I've made up my mind. Believe me, I want nothing more than to see my Louisa and spend my last days with her but I cannot, out of good conscience, have her under threat. It is my fault she is implicated and I will do everything in my power to ensure she is struck off the list as a suspect. Time is not an extravagance I possess. I wish I did, but I do not.'

'But doctors are always wrong! My friend was told she had six months to live and that was three years ago. Miracles happen all the time!'

'I am sorry but this is not so in my case. The cancer is everywhere. I can barely breathe. I have no energy. I am very, very sick and there is no chance for recovery. Please, accept this is my fate and allow me my final wish: to ensure my Louisa is safe.'

'But it could take ages for the authorities to—'

'This is my point. By the time they realize who I am I will be dead and cannot protect her. They will arrest her and she will suffer. I am doing what is right. Please understand.'

'I can't.'

'I do not expect you to. No one can appreciate this unless they have lived a lie for many decades. No one should die with a secret as large as mine. It must be set free and I must endure the consequences.'

'What about us? What if I'm your granddaughter?'

'You are, I am sure of this.'

'Where does that leave us? We spend one day together then you disappear behind bars? Is that what you want? To destroy our family?' A heavy hand pressed on her shoulder and she turned to face Carlos.

'Daniela, please, respect Roberto's wishes.'

'How can I?' Her voice raised an octave. 'All my life I've wanted a grandfather and now I may have one, he's ripped away?' She bit her lip and her eyes welled with tears. 'Life's bloody unfair.'

'That it is.' Roberto patted her hand. 'We will talk in the morning. Yes?'

She nodded and said, 'Please, take my bed.'

She guided him to the small room and he settled quickly, his snores punctuated by a crackly cough. Closing the door behind her, Dani stared down the dark hallway, her mind a mess of conflicting thoughts. Either way, she was about to lose a grandparent.

Dani stared out the plane window. Cotton wool clouds floated below, framed by a bright blue sky stretching across the horizon. She glanced over at Roberto, who sat in the aisle seat, sleeping fitfully, his skin grayer than when they'd met the day before.

'He is tired, yes?' Carlos asked, his arm accidently bumping hers as he swirled ice and water in a plastic cup.

'Yes. I worry about him,' she whispered.

'He might be frail in body but he is strong in the mind, like his granddaughter.'

'*If* I'm his granddaughter.'

'Your grandmother can let you know when you speak with her, yes?'

Dani nodded, concerned neither she nor Iris nor Ness, Stella's neighbor, had been able to get hold of her.

'At least he's arriving in Argentina using his Uruguayan name,' she said.

'You think you can still change his mind?'

'I can't believe he killed someone, even if it was by accident. Look at him!' She leaned over to study his sleeping form. He looked angelic.

'Maybe he did the murder, not the manslaughter.'

'You don't believe him?' she asked, hurt by his cynicism. 'Perhaps he'll take a lie detector test and prove me right. Watch this space.' Carlos shrugged and his nonchalance sent a ripple of annoy-ance through her. 'I still don't understand why he couldn't just stay in Brazil and meet Stella there. Then they wouldn't have to worry about any of this Canziani business.'

'Even though you may have Argentine blood running through your veins, you still do not understand.'

She narrowed her eyes. 'Yes, I do.'

'A little, yes, but not all. We love with passion, we fight with passion, we uphold justice with passion. Your man Roberto is doing what any self-respecting Argentine would do—he is following his heart to protect the one he loves.'

'He's done that for decades.'

'But now she is threatened.'

'Only if the authorities get off their fat arses. He could be handing himself over for no reason. Like I said, they could meet in Brazil and—'

'And what? They spend a few days together then he dies and with him goes the only chance of your grandma clearing her name? He is right to come to Argentina. When he does pass, he can do so knowing he has integrity intact and that is the most important for an Argentine.'

It hadn't mattered how much she'd pleaded, Roberto had been determined to get to Argentina. She now saw why he and Stella were such a good match as they were as stubborn as each other.

The flight attendant arrived and handed them each a small bottle of wine, a plastic cup, and pretzels. They busied themselves opening, pouring, and eating while the cabin filled with their uneasiness.

'Why did you lie to protect Cecilia?' Dani asked, instantly regretting breaking the silence with this question. 'Chivalry should only go so far.'

'If you must know, Cecilia was strong when she tangoed but frail off the dance floor. She could never have coped with the anger from the Argentines and the media if they knew she caused an accident out of stupidity. And you know what they did to me.'

'Yes, and on behalf of my profession, I apologize.'

'Thank you, but it is not necessary. I did what any man would do. I protected the person I loved, but it was for nothing.' Carlos lifted the cup and studied the ice. Putting it down, he said, 'I love tango but it is so complicated in the way it affects people.'

'Are you going to say it's cursed like my grandma and Iris?' Dani asked.

'A curse, no, but it gets under the skin, changes people.'

'I know, I've seen the result.' Collecting her thoughts, she said, 'Tango creates a range of emotions and experiences, right? Like life? So if there is hardship in tango there is also joy. A *lot* of joy. Take me for example. I hated tango because it took my mother away. Well, she let it. The thing is, though, tango also brought me to her. I'm still angry with Iris, I don't know if I can ever forgive her, but I'm willing to give it a shot because you helped me appreciate tango and in doing so, I've gained a better understanding about relationships and life in general.' She placed her hand on his but his muscles tensed. Dani removed her hand and grabbed the drink in front of her, taking a long gulp. *Bloody Carlos, what is his problem?* Facing him and staring him down, she asked, 'Are you acting weird because I might be related to someone who killed Eduardo Canziani? Does that mess with your Argentine sensibilities?'

'Things change, Daniela. I can see the remorse in Roberto's eyes. He's carried this burden for many years. Jail is nothing compared to what he has already suffered.'

'Then what is your problem?'

'Daniela, there are many problems but none are your fault. I am sorry. I was hoping the things would settle but I cannot see things changing any time in the near future.'

'You didn't have a problem when you were in my bed. And you didn't have a problem dragging me along and letting me fall in love with you. But now you're happy to dump me mid-flight?'

He rubbed his forehead. When he looked at her again, his eyes were full of sadness. 'You are in love with me?'

'Yes!' She wanted to punch him in the arm. Hard. 'You don't feel the same way?'

'Yes.' His voice sounded small.

'So why are you breaking this off?'

He paused for a moment, then said, 'Please, respect my wishes. Know I will help you with Roberto and Stella but once this is finished, we will part for good.'

'I think you've helped enough, thank you.' She placed her drink on the tray, crossed her arms and stared out the window.

'I'm sorry,' he said quietly.

Hot tears pricked her eyes but she refused to give in to them. She clenched her jaw, every muscle in her body tense. What a sucker she'd been. She'd gotten carried away with the romance of Argentina. And she'd let Carlos Escudero dance into her life and into her heart. *Dani McKenna, you're nothing but a sentimental fool.*

Carlos put down his drink and checked his phone yet again, the same thing he'd been doing since the early morning.

'You can't receive messages up here.' Dani took a sip of wine.

'I am aware of this, Daniela.' He stared at the phone.

'Are you waiting for something?'

'I have already received it.' Tucking the phone in his jacket, he faced her and said, 'I am now a father.'

'What?' Red wine flew up her nose and burnt her nostrils.

'I should have told you earlier but you were upset about Roberto and we—'

'Carlos! This is a significant moment in your life. Did the detectives find Cecilia?' He nodded and picked up his cup to down the last of the wine but it was empty. She offered him hers. 'Are you okay?'

He shook his head and swirled the alcohol in the plastic cup, the contents spilling red liquid onto the tray. 'Emilio Juan is his name.'

'Where are they?'

Carlos stared out the window. 'The detectives found them in Bahía Blanca. They are both healthy. Emilio is one week old.'

This revelation could explain a lot about his recent behavior. If she'd known about Cecilia and his baby, she would have backed off and not pushed him. It hurt that he hadn't shared the news with her earlier, but then again, they hadn't exactly been sailing calm waters since Mendoza.

'I'm glad you found out about your boy but I'm sorry it's such a difficult situation. Will you go straight away to meet him?'

'Cecilia, she has people around her who will not let me near my son.'

'He's your child as well, for god's sake! Surely there is a way around this?'

He lifted his shoulders then let them fall. She bit her lip, a turmoil of emotions crashing inside. The drone of the plane's engines punctuated the uncomfortable silence that surrounded them. Flicking through the inflight magazine, Dani desperately wanted to find the right words to console Carlos. Saying she was sorry for his troubles just didn't cut it. His newborn was his number one priority now so she needed to wait and talk with him later about his decision to break it off. Maybe they still had a chance. Carlos clutched the armrests as he stared out the window, his brows drawn together. Judging by the vibe she received, that chance appeared to be very, very slight.

The plane dropped slightly and an announcement came over the PA, advising the passengers of their imminent descent.

How apropos.

CHAPTER 34

Present Day - Dani

Dani hit redial on her phone. She paced the hotel room while Roberto slept fitfully, the flight from Brazil having exhausted him. Carlos sat by the bed, gently sponging Roberto's sweaty brow, his caring actions breaking her heart. Why did she have to fall for a man whose life was more complicated than a *telenovela*?

Turning her attention to the telephone again, she gritted her teeth. 'Come on, come on!'

'Hello?'

'Stella! Where have you been?'

Carlos looked up, his lips kicking into a smile. Roberto stirred for a moment but fell back asleep.

'I've been at the doctor getting a medical clearance to fly. I also had to sit for two days in offices to get my passport and my visa for Brazil.'

'We're in Argentina.'

'Why haven't you left? You promised me, Dani!'

'It's a long story and I don't have time to explain right now but we found Roberto in Brazil, just where you said he would be.

Grandma, listen, please. Roberto's really unwell.' Dani squeezed her eyes tight.

Stella breathed out slowly. 'How unwell?'

'He's dying, Grandma. He has lung cancer that's spread and he doesn't have much time left.'

'But why Argentina? They'll find him and arrest him! I can't return there, I'm a wanted woman!'

Dani had barely processed events in her own mind so she could only imagine how hard it was for Stella. All Dani could do was keep her cool and not let Stella hear her pain and angst.

'Grandma, the authorities could be on your doorstep at any minute.' She hated being the bearer of bad news and she was just about to make it worse. 'Roberto wanted to turn himself in before they tried to extradite you.'

'But he didn't do it!' Panic laced her voice.

'He did, Grandma.' Dani allowed the words to sink in.

'No. Not my Roberto. There is no—'

'Grandma, it was in self-defense. I've seen his remorse and know him enough to believe he didn't do it on purpose. His . . .' She took a breath. 'His dying wishes are for your name to be cleared and the truth to be known.' Sobs flew down the line and pierced Dani's heart. Sensing there wouldn't be a perfect time for her next question, she pressed on. 'I'm sorry but I have to ask a question for Iris and Roberto.'

Blowing her nose, Stella sniffled. 'Yes, of course they're father and daughter. Look at the way she dances. It's Roberto's tango blood that flows through those veins.'

Relief swept over Dani at finally having the answer they'd hoped for.

'I'm coming to Argentina.' Her grandma's tone told Dani not to argue, but she was sure as hell going to try.

'You can't. You just said you're a wanted woman.'

'Well, I'm wanted as Louisa Gilchrist, aren't I? Why didn't I think of that earlier? Louisa Gilchrist doesn't exist. Hasn't for decades. I am an Australian called Stella Kennedy.'

'Yes, but—'

'Then problem solved. I'm coming over. You tell Roberto to hang on and I will be on the next flight. No one is going to keep me from him. Not even the Argentine police.'

'But—'

'I will be on the next flight.'

The hotel room looked much like the one she'd stayed in before. Dani liked the familiarity, as it was her one constant from all the twists and turns that had taken place over the past few weeks. Roberto sat on the bed wheezing, his back against the wall. Carlos paced the floor and Dani looked everywhere but at him. Each time she caught his eye, her heart ached and she wanted to curl into a ball of self-pity.

A staccato of snorts filled the room and Dani rushed over to Roberto, placing her hand on his forehead.

'He's burning up,' she turned to Carlos who came over and knelt next to her. His nearness tugging at her already frayed nerves. 'He needs medical help.'

'We should ring for someone.' Carlos stood, pulled his phone out of his back pocket then put it back when Roberto's eyelids flew open.

'No,' Roberto croaked, his eyes wide.

'You're awake!' Dani leaned in close, struggling to keep her voice steady. 'I spoke with Louisa. She's coming to see you.'

'She cannot . . . too dangerous.'

'I can't stop her and besides, she's under threat in Australia if authorities come looking for her.'

'You must stop her.'

'It's too late. She's already boarded the plane and is on her way.' Stella's neighbor Ness had sent Dani a text confirming Stella's departure, having been told Dani had organized a surprise holiday for her grandma. Innocent Ness bought it, bless her. Rinsing a cloth in the bathroom sink and squeezing the excess water, Dani dabbed Roberto's forehead. 'Don't you want to see her?'

Roberto nodded slowly, his eyes moist. 'More than anything.'

'You have waited decades to be with her, why give up now?'

He used his elbows to hoist himself up but was too weak. Collapsing on the pillow, he said, 'There is great risk. Her name is not cleared.'

'According to her passport she is Stella Kennedy, Australian citizen. She hasn't kept her identity hidden for all these years because she's stupid. Trust her, Roberto. Trust that you two will finally be together.' Although her words sounded positive, fear gripped her inside. Dani was petrified of Stella being caught but she couldn't deny this beautiful pair the chance to finally reunite, even if their time was borrowed.

'I must confess to authorities. If she arrives and they discover . . .' Roberto broke into a coughing fit and Dani passed him a glass of water.

A solid rap on the door announced Iris's arrival and Dani jumped up and exited the room, ushering her mother a small way down the hall.

'You've dyed your hair again,' Dani said.

'Yes.' Iris fluffed her black tresses. 'It's still short but I like it better this way. Everyone's heard I'm in town, so no point in hiding my identity, huh? Plus blondes don't have more fun.'

'Have you seen Diego?'

'No, he's gone into hiding. I swear to God, if I ever see him again—'

'He's here,' said Dani.

Iris's eyebrows shot up and panic raced across her face.

'No, not Diego. Roberto,' said Dani.

Iris stared at her hands as she took deep breaths. 'What's he like?'

'Why don't you meet him and find out?'

'Dani, I don't think I can,' she said, backing away.

'Please, come and meet him.' Dani placed her hand firmly underneath her mother's elbow. 'Just be aware he's frail, okay?'

Iris bit her lip and nodded, her eyes glassy. Dani gently steered her mother into the hotel room and as they entered, Roberto made to get up but his arms couldn't hold him and he collapsed against the wall.

Kneeling in front of Roberto, Iris took his hands in hers. Dani leaned against the wall by the bathroom, sensing Carlos watching her, but she refused to look at him, the hurt from their last conversation still raw. Since landing in Argentina their conversations were with measured words and tones with no discussion of personal topics. She'd expected him to jump off the plane and head to Bahía Blanca to fight to see his son. Yet, after making half-a-dozen secretive calls, he'd remained in Buenos Aires.

'So you are Roberto.' Iris patted his weathered hand.

'Yes.' His voice had turned as fragile as his body.

'It's nice to meet you,' she said softly.

Dani studied the pair and marveled at how alike they seemed. Even though Iris and Stella looked the same, the way Roberto and Iris tilted their heads and blinked rapidly every so often added up to one very big thing: They were most definitely father and daughter, no DNA test required.

'She is his daughter,' Carlos whispered in her ear.

Dani jumped, unaware he'd snuck up beside her. 'That's exactly what I was thinking.'

Roberto coughed into his handkerchief and Dani noticed new speckles of blood on the material. He saw her look and shoved the handkerchief under the sheets. Then he gasped and reached for his throat. What little color he had in his skin and lips disappeared.

'He's choking! Get an ambulance!' Dani shouted at Carlos, who already had the phone in his hand. He spoke rapidly while she worked with Iris to help calm Roberto. The coughing turned to vomiting blood and the women were quickly sprayed by the sticky substance.

Carlos raced out the door and into the corridor, returning with paramedics minutes later. They rushed to Roberto, who had stopped coughing but was now gray, his breathing shallow. The two young ambulance men worked on him, taking his pulse, listening to his chest and hooking him up to an IV drip.

'I'll go with him.' Something in Iris's tone told Dani not to argue.

'We'll follow.' She looked at Carlos, who hadn't moved since the paramedics had arrived.

They wheeled an unconscious Roberto out of the room with Iris following, struggling to keep up in her heels.

Dani grabbed her phone, threw it in her handbag, and slung the bag over her shoulder. Carlos grabbed his jacket and Roberto's *bandoneón* case and ushered her to the door.

'Oh Jesus.' Dani stopped and slapped her hand on her mouth. 'Stella's flight left a couple of hours ago. She won't be here until tomorrow.'

The heavy traffic meant it took Dani and Carlos an hour to reach the hospital. Dani's phone had died. Carlos had left his behind at the hotel in their mad dash to leave, although he'd grabbed Roberto's *bandoneón* case. She had no idea why and didn't feel like questioning him. The moment they arrived, they raced across the black-and-white–checked linoleum to the reception desk. Panting, Dani asked for directions. The nurse pointed at the elevator and Dani halted.

'Come.' Carlos held out his hand.

She shook her head. 'No. The stairs are fine.'

'But—'

'Stairs, Carlos.' She dashed up the six flights. Her lungs screamed for air and her leg muscles burned but she pushed on. Arriving at the sixth floor, she hurried to another nurse's station, Carlos following dutifully.

The nurse looked at them over her glasses. 'Who do you wish to see?'

'Cristian Villa,' said Dani, praying Iris had enough sense to admit him under his false name.

The nurse peered at the screen. 'Ah, yes. The doctor says no visitors. You may wait over there.' She pointed to a sad, cracked leather sofa down the hallway.

'Thanks.'

Iris trotted around the corner and burst into tears as soon as she saw Dani. Placing her arm around her mother's shoulder, Dani guided her to the sofa.

'It was horrible. He regained consciousness in the ambulance then flat-lined. When he came to again, he begged the paramedic to call the police as he had something to confess.'

'What?'

'The paramedic didn't do it, of course. He was too busy trying to keep him alive.'

'Do you think the hospital has contacted the police?'

'I don't know.' Mascara had pooled under Iris's eyes. 'I told them he had dementia and often had delusions he was other people.'

Dani leaned forward. 'Did the paramedic believe it?'

'I have no idea.' Iris sniffed.

'Look, even if the paramedic did as was asked, who's to say the cops will come straight away?' asked Dani. 'I'm sure they've had their fair share of people confessing to all sorts of stuff on their deathbed even if it isn't true.'

Except Dani knew Roberto's story was one hundred percent true.

Iris sobbed for three hours after Dani confirmed Roberto was her father. Carlos stayed by their side, a pillar of silent strength as they'd sat on the sofa, waiting for an update that hadn't come. She'd suggested to Carlos that he was free to leave and find his child, but once more, he'd shook his head and pursed his lips. Finally, Carlos had taken a heartbroken Iris to the hotel to convince her to get some rest, as she wasn't doing anyone in the hospital, including herself, any favors. Dani had promised to keep them updated with the smallest news but so far, she'd received nothing other than a sore butt from sitting in the one place.

Dani couldn't get used to Stella being Louisa, even if only in her head, and she worried about her grandma coping with the stress of arriving in Argentina after so many years. It was little comfort to know Stella had suffered many traumatic experiences yet had made it through with her sanity intact.

The corridor remained eerily quiet, unlike the busy hospitals she'd been in before. Every so often a nurse would walk by and Dani felt like an exhibit in a museum. A doctor entered Roberto's room and exited ten minutes later then made his way over to Dani, sitting beside her, the sofa creaking under his weight.

'You are Dani McKenna?'

'Yes.' A lump formed at the back of her throat.

'Your grandfather would like to see you.'

'Really?' She stood, hardly believing her ears.

'You must understand, he is very ill. You can only stay for a few minutes. He must remain calm.'

'I'll do as you ask, I promise.'

Following the doctor, Dani's excitement quickly turned to apprehension. What condition would he be in? It took a few moments for her eyes to adjust to the dark. Roberto lay silent, his complexion as gray as the sky outside. Tiptoeing over, Dani sat on the chair next to the bed and held his limp hand.

'I'm here, Roberto,' she whispered. He squeezed her fingers gently and while that act deepened their connection, her heart plummeted. She placed her head on his shoulder. 'I'm sorry things turned out the way they have.'

'Child, it is the will of God.' His raspy voice made her sit up with a start.

'Louisa will be here tomorrow.'

He nodded and tears formed in his dark eyes. His chest rattled as he breathed.

'She's confirmed Iris is your daughter.'

Caressing her chin with shaky fingers, he said, 'And that makes you my granddaughter. This is very good news.'

'We could have had a lifetime together.'

'Do not let sadness . . . contaminate the time we have left. We *have* met . . . and you will always be . . . in my heart. You are a good girl . . . you love your family.'

'It hasn't always been that way.'

'No matter.' He shook his head. 'The past is the past.' A bout of coughing shook his body and he sat up. Passing him a clean tissue, he coughed into it and she tried to spot the blood. There was none. She sent thanks to the powers that be.

'I need you to promise me something.' Roberto sipped from the straw in the glass she handed him.

'Anything.'

'Open my *bandoneón* case . . . take out the sheet music.'

She reached over and clicked open the lock, grateful Carlos had grabbed it when they'd left the hotel. The *bandoneón* lay in its velour bed, looking like it had gone through as much trauma as Roberto. Her fingers searched until the familiar rustle of paper told her she'd found it. Pulling out the tattered yellowed pages, she handed them to Roberto.

'This is the highlight of my life's work.' He held out the sheet music so she could read the title written on the top of each page.

'"Luna Tango",' she said.

'I feel better now.' His ashen complexion didn't reflect his words. 'I am going to check out of here but I will need your help.'

'But you're sick!'

'I am dying, this is a fact, but I have no intention of perishing within these walls, God willing.' Roberto's pauses for air when talking had disappeared but she wasn't sure for how long. Perhaps knowing Stella was on the way was enough to give him strength. 'I want you to film my confession and I will write it also. We will do this today.'

'But—'

'The documents are only a precaution. Just in case my body wins over my mind. You are to hold on to my confession until I see my Louisa, but if I pass before she arrives, you are to take it to the authorities. Do not deny a dying man his wishes.'

She smiled, in awe of his strength and determination. 'Are you laying a guilt trip on me?'

'Is this not what a grandparent does?' He raised his eyebrows and winked. 'I need you to enlist the help of your friend Carlos and his musician friends.'

'I'm not so sure Carlos will be of much help.'

'He will do as you ask,' he said with confidence.

'Are you going to—'

'Yes. But if I don't make it, tell my Louisa that every night I looked at the moon and thought of her.' He coughed again, this fit lasting longer than the previous one. Dani offered him water but he waved it away. 'My Louisa's soul is entwined with mine. Although we weren't physically together, I never left her side. I never will, even when I'm no longer in this world.'

'But you're still here.'

'For now.' He showed no fear, only regret. 'Just remember these words in case . . .' He lifted his shoulders in a small shrug.

'I wish I knew you better. I think we would have been excellent friends.'

'Yes, we would.' His lips twitched into a small smile. 'Take care of her.'

Dani nodded, finding it difficult to give words of comfort. She tried to erase any possibility of Roberto not lasting until Stella . . . Louisa arrived. She didn't even want to imagine that someone at passport control could realize she was Louisa Gilchrist and not Stella Kennedy. Impossible. How could they?

'Dear girl, if I have learnt anything about life, it is this: Do not give up on love, no matter how hard it gets. All the external 'life' things.' He waved his hand weakly. 'Forget them. Love is what feeds our soul, and without it, we wither and die. We must stop fighting our past because if we do not, we waste our present. Go to your Carlos.'

'But we're just friends, plus he has his own stuff going on.'

'I may be old and sick but I am not blind. There is a connection between you two that is as wonderful as the most perfect tango.'

'He thinks our relationship is too complicated because of all the external life things going on.'

'Nonsense! The most beautiful tango is full of difficulty and tears. This is what makes it special, just like love. Do not let him walk away. Go see him then return for me.'

CHAPTER 35

Present Day - Dani

Once more Dani climbed the staircase to Carlos's dance studio. In a short time, she'd gone from complete stranger to lover, to who-knows-what with Carlos. He'd called her just after Roberto had given her strict instructions to sort things out with Carlos for once and for all. It was as though he'd received a cosmic kick in the bum. She'd pleaded with Roberto to let her remain by his side, but he had refused, telling her he needed rest and he would do better if he knew she was heeding his advice about Carlos.

Her hand hovered over the handle for a moment before she pushed open the wooden door and stepped into a deserted dance studio. She'd worked herself into a state about seeing him and he wasn't even here.

'Carlos?' She stuck her head through his office door, only to find the desk light on but no Carlos. Frustrated, she turned to wait on the sofa but slammed into him standing directly behind her. 'Shit!'

'Sorry.' He grasped her arm to steady her.

'You scared the crap out of me! Why'd you sneak up?'

'I went to get us these,' he pointed to two coffee cups on the side table next to the sofa, 'and when I returned you were here. I didn't want to say anything because I'd much rather be doing this.'

He drew her near, his lips so lusciously close. His eyes searched hers, love, tenderness, and caring shining brightly from within. The moment their lips connected, Dani's stomach lurched and confusion, tension, hurt, and hope twisted around each other, surging through her body with force. The moment he pulled away, the painful emotions she'd battled for so long dissipated and all that remained was pure love.

'Wow,' she breathed.

'*Sí*. Wow.' His eyes crinkled as he took her hand.

Still reeling from the energy they'd created, Dani said, 'I thought you wanted us over.'

'I was overwhelmed by my emotions and my head said I should leave because I needed to concentrate on my problems.' He frowned, searching for words. 'I had to have the time alone to get my head straight, yes? You make me confused, happy, frustrated, joyful. It all combines to make me crazy when I'm with you and depressed when I am not.'

'I'm a tad familiar with these feelings.'

Carlos wrapped her in his arms, her head resting against his strong chest, his heart beating quickly. This is where she was happiest but the questions she'd been struggling with since their flight from Brazil kept nagging her. Drawing a breath, she looked up at him and asked, 'Why are you refusing to go to Bahía Blanca?'

'If you know Cecilia, and it is probably good that you do not, you will find she is an unreasonable person whose stubbornness runs deeper than the Earth's rivers. The detectives did find her and Emilio, but the moment she realized she'd been discovered, she disappeared again. Once more, the detectives found her but she is even more angry with me for sending people to invade her space. If I arrived on her doorstep, I would only seal my fate and not ever see Emilio. Instead, Gualberto has gone to see her, as he is the only person she will listen to.'

'I can understand that.' How many times had Gualberto talked Dani through trying moments with Carlos?

'Still, I do not know how it will eventuate. Gualberto tried to reason with Cecilia after the accident but he failed. I do not hold much hope but it is the only hope I have.'

'You could get lawyers involved.'

Carlos's face creased like he'd been punched in the gut. 'The lawyers are nothing but parasites.'

'Like journalists.' Dani smiled.

'Maybe not all lawyers are parasites.' He stroked her arm. 'Gualberto will talk to her about the importance of family and I hope this will appeal to her softer side. She is not all bad, just very confused.'

'We've all experienced moments of confusion, huh?'

'I am sorry for my behavior.' He appeared genuinely remorseful.

'You did what you felt was right at the time.' She kissed him lightly on the lips. 'You drive me nuts, you know.'

'And you me.' He squeezed her fingers. 'So what now for us?'

She sighed. 'I have no idea.'

'We will find a way.'

Surprisingly, she didn't feel jealousy toward Cecilia for giving birth to Carlos's son. A few months—hell, even a few weeks—ago, Dani would have been weird about being with a man who had just had a child with another woman, even if the relationship had disintegrated.

But Carlos wasn't Adam.

'I will make sure I have a strong relationship with my son. Family bonds are the lifeblood of our souls.'

'Yes, they are.' She closed her eyes, basking in his warmth. 'Yes, they most definitely are.'

Dear Adam,

Sorry for the delay. Attached are your stories, which will make Tourism Argentina tango for joy. I've also attached my letter of resignation and I am canceling my return ticket to New York. I sincerely wish the best for you and hope you're happy with your choices. It's taken me a while to decide what's best for me, but I've finally figured it out and that means some monumental changes.

You'll also find attached an extra piece that sums up my experience in Argentina. Do with it what you will, but I hope you share it with our readers because we all need some music in our lives.

Best wishes,

Dani

Opening the article one more time, Dani quickly scanned what she hoped would be her *pièce de résistance.*

When I first traveled to Argentina, I intended to write about the history of tango and unearth the reasons why this dance has a hold on so many across the world. What I discovered was that you do not choose tango, it chooses you.

Fighting the pull of tango will only result in melancholy—tango's favorite theme—so there is no other option than to surrender to the allure of the music. You have no choice but to allow your body to engage in a dance that rips apart every emotion, only to hold you in an embrace of ecstasy and pain that is pleasurable and terrifying at the same time.

Like everyone, I have stories buried within the depths of my soul. Tango reaches in, yanks them out, and twists and turns every hurt, every joy, into something unrecognizable and leaves one gasping for air.

Tango gives permission to share emotions with a stranger, to discuss one's innermost feelings without uttering a single word. This private conversation between dance partners travels through touch and movement and conveys an array of emotions—happiness, sadness, frustration, fear, love, heartbreak—and when the dance is over, the dancers walk away from each other, having shared intimate details and trusting the other with that knowledge.

I have yet to understand why tango has this effect on people. Ballet, the Viennese waltz, flamenco and salsa encourage dancers to express their feelings but none can compare to tango. The music, history, and freedom of expression combine in a heady mix of desire, but it isn't sexual, as is commonly thought by outsiders. Sexual attraction can hinder a dance between partners as it blocks out nearly all the other emotions that are needed to dance the tango effectively.

I arrived in Argentina a tango skeptic and I am now a believer. As a dear friend once said to me, 'tango, like love, is complicated,' and it shouldn't be any other way.

She hit Send and let out a long breath. Dani was happy she hadn't gone into the whys and wherefores of her decision and at last, the Adam saga had been kicked to the curb. It felt damn good.

While waiting for her grandma to arrive, she'd taken vigil beside Roberto's bed and while he slept, she'd finished her articles, the writer's block having crumbled to a pile of dust. During Roberto's waking moments, he recounted more details of the story after he fled Buenos Aires and she suspected Louisa would be open to revealing her story as well. Her faith in writing renewed, Dani could tell the story of her grandparents and show Argentines, and the rest of the world, that Roberto wasn't a murderer, he was just a man who loved deeply and had to fight for his life.

Dani checked her cell again, making sure she still had Roberto's confessional video and an electronic copy of the signed document in her private email. To allay her paranoia, she got up and rattled the handle of the hotel's room safe where the original confession was signed. Hopefully she'd never have to use the video or document but at least they were covered should authorities swoop in.

Louisa's flight had been delayed because of a medical emergency with another passenger so it gave Dani a few more hours to get everything done. She worried about Roberto's fragile state and what the extra time waiting would do to him but since leaving hospital, her grandfather's health had made a slight improvement. She imagined this had a lot to do with the prospect of seeing his love and that seemed to put a spring in his slow, shuffling step.

A knock sounded at the door and Dani adjusted the straps on her violet dance shoes. She jumped up, smoothed her turquoise silk dress, and rushed to the door, opening it with a flourish.

'Hi!' It was nice to smile freely again.

'Wow.' Iris beamed. 'You look beautiful.'

'Thank you.' Dani grabbed her clutch and glanced at her suitcase where jeans, T-shirt, and runners were buried deep.

Iris fished in her handbag, pulled out a small leather pouch and handed it over.

'What's this?' The soft, inviting leather cooled Dani's fingers.

'It's a present. I wore it in my first ever performance as a professional tango dancer.'

'Really?' Dani gently opened the pouch and unraveled a violet and turquoise scarf. She held it against her dress and shoes. 'It matches.'

'Perhaps our connection is deeper than we thought.' Panic flashed in Iris's eyes as though she'd overstepped the mark.

'Maybe it is.' Dani patted Iris on the arm. 'Thank you.'

'No, Dani, thank you. I've done many horrid things and I'm so ashamed . . . I don't expect you to ever understand why I did what I did, I just . . . just . . . thank you.'

'We've got a long road to travel. Are you up for it?' Dani asked, still unsure about their future.

'I'm willing to do the work. Look.' She pushed up the sleeve of her dress to reveal a nicotine patch.

'You're serious about this?'

'I'm serious about changing many things in my life—for the better. Here.' Iris placed the scarf around Dani's neck and twisted it in a way only a woman with natural style could. 'We should get going.'

Dani slid her arm through Iris's and they closed the door and headed for the stairs.

'Hang on.' Dani stopped and narrowed her eyes at the wrought ironwork and rickety mechanics of the elevator. 'Let's go in here.'

'What? You told me you hated elevator.'

'Maybe I should make some changes, too.'

'You used to love them as a kid. On rainy days we'd go into the city and ride them for hours on end.' Iris looked off into the distance, smiling. 'Nothing made you happier and your giggles always brought me joy.'

All the pieces finally clicked together. 'After you left I avoided the things I loved doing with you. The beach, elevators . . . do you remember the last time we were in one?'

Iris shook her head.

'We'd picked up Dad from work and you two started fighting in the elevator then we got to the bottom and you stormed out, leaving Dad and I alone. A short while later you left for Argentina.'

'Oh, Dani . . .'

'It's okay. I'm working through it all. Jeez, a psychologist would have a field day with our family, huh? C'mon. Let's do it.' She pressed the button and the elevator clunked into action. Panic clung to Dani and when the elevator arrived, her mother threw her a wary look. Dani wrenched open the iron doors and stepped inside. Her mother followed and with a shaky finger, Dani pressed the ground floor button.

Iris squeezed her hand and whispered, 'You can do this. *We* can do this.'

With a shudder, the elevator descended at a slow rate and Dani took a deep breath as her stomach rose to the heavens. This was the exact feeling she'd experienced as a child, ripples of excitement speeding through her body. They stopped on the ground floor and although her legs remained shaky, Dani was proud of the hurdle she'd just jumped. 'Hey, thanks.'

'My pleasure,' said Iris as they walked across the foyer and out the front door. 'Is everything in place?'

'Yep, we're just missing one piece so we better go get that now.'

Arrivals at Ezeiza International Airport bustled with young kids running into grandparents' arms, returning honeymooners smooching, businessmen and women barking into phones, and backpackers studying guidebooks. Every time Dani spotted an airport policeman her heart raced and the tension in her shoulders increased. Even though she'd declined Carlos's offer to go with her, she wished her sentinel was here, but he needed to be with Roberto.

'Where is she?' Dani balanced on her tiptoes, every nerve tingling. 'Her flight arrived an hour ago.'

Iris stood still, blinking as if caught in head lights. She hadn't said a word since the taxi had deposited them at the airport.

The sliding doors opened to reveal an elderly woman, white hair coiffed to perfection, a string of pearls around her neck and sporting a tailored light blue jacket and skirt. Her almond-shaped eyes searched the crowds behind the barriers. The moment her grand-mother's gaze fell upon her, Dani felt the world lift from her shoulders.

Dodging the barrier, she ran to Louisa and threw her arms around her. The familiar scent of fresh roses took Dani back to when she was a young child snuggling up to the warm, soft body of her grandma. 'I'm so happy to see you!'

'I am happy to see you, too, my darling girl.' Louisa's voice shook and Dani couldn't decide if it was from fatigue or nerves. Probably both. Her grandma adjusted her glasses as her gaze took in Dani's appearance. 'Why are you in a dress and your hair and makeup like that?'

'Do you like it?' Dani gave a little twirl to show the flow of the soft fabric. 'Argentina's affected me in lots of ways, Grandma.' She didn't mention the planned surprise because she had no idea if Carlos and Roberto could pull it off.

Louisa's eyes darted around the airport then rested on Iris, who stood thirty feet away, her hands hanging by her sides, surrepti-tiously watching her daughter and mother.

Louisa grabbed Dani's arm, alarm flashing in her eyes. 'You brought Iris?'

'She wanted to come, Grandma. I couldn't say no, could I?' Had Dani done the wrong thing?

'Well, we had to see each other at some stage.' Louisa patted her granddaughter's hand and breathed in deeply as she slowly walked over to Iris, who appeared to be cemented to the airport floor. Iris studied her feet, her back slightly hunched while Louisa took a painstakingly long time to travel the short distance. When they finally came face-to-face, they stared at each other, as if waiting for the other one to speak first. Dani looked on, praying this wouldn't end in a noisy scene that brought too much attention to her grandma. Louisa started the conversation, her eyes earnest as she talked and Iris bit her bottom lip. When Louisa reached out to touch Iris, who shook her head vehemently and stepped back, Dani rushed over.

'I thought I was doing the right thing,' Louisa said, her expression one of angst. 'That trip to Italy gave me the only possibility of getting in contact with Roberto, should he be alive. When I found out his Aunt Elda had died, then all was lost.'

'It wasn't lost, you had me!' Tears streamed from Iris's eyes.

'I was so caught up in grief I thought that if I could teach you not to rely on anyone, not even me, then you wouldn't suffer heartache like I did.'

'I needed a mother and you shut me out!' Iris tightened her jaw and crossed her arms, turning away from Louisa.

Iris was experiencing feelings that Dani had endured and she didn't know whether to be angry or empathetic. This cycle of mothers causing angst and pain with their children had to stop and Dani was going to ensure it never happened again. Ever.

Louisa reached for Iris's hand and this time she didn't back away.

'Iris, I desperately wanted to shower you with the love of two parents. I longed to hold you tight and create precious memories for you and me but I had the threat of being found out and if I was ever arrested I . . . I just didn't want you to be so close to me you wouldn't cope if I was gone. My parents mollycoddled me and when the war broke out I was completely unprepared for what transpired. It was only dumb luck that I landed on my feet, and I didn't want you to suffer the same fate as me. If you knew how to be independent then I didn't need to worry.'

'You were trying to save me?' Iris blew her nose into her handkerchief.

'Yes.'

A text beeped on her cell and Dani checked the message from Carlos.

Ready.

Placing her hand on Louisa's shoulder, Dani said, 'Roberto's checked out of the hospital and he's waiting.'

'Silly old fool,' Louisa said as she adjusted her necklace and gently fluffed her perfect coif. 'What does he think he's doing?'

'What his heart desires, Grandma.'

CHAPTER 36

Present Day - Dani

Darkness had fallen over Buenos Aires, the city lights creating a haze in the warm evening. The minutes dragged on like hours as the women traveled by taxi to their destination. They drove past beautiful architecture that towered above and even though Dani could have been in any large city in the world, Buenos Aires distinguished itself from the others. Tango flowed through the veins of the people, including Dani's, and her connection to the city had changed her life in so many ways.

Dani glanced at Iris and Louisa who sat in silence, holding hands. Iris stared out the window and Louisa concentrated on the road ahead. She had no idea what the future held for the relationship between them but at least a dialogue had opened and it didn't look like the doors would slam shut anytime soon.

Resting her head against the seat, Dani closed her eyes, the pressure of the forthcoming moment weighing on her. Her grandfather, Carlos, and Gualberto had worked hard to create a memorable setting for the reunion but no one knew for sure how it would go. After so many decades apart, how would her grandparents react? Would they break down in tears? Not know what to say to each other? Be bitterly disappointed the person they thought they loved was now entirely different? How would her grandma deal with the heartbreak when she saw for herself how ill Roberto was? And would Roberto find the strength to follow through on his plan?

The taxi halted at the entrance to the park in Belgrano where Louisa and Roberto once sought comfort in each other's arms. As the three women climbed out of the taxi and stepped onto the footpath, Louisa stared at the entrance, her feet not moving.

'It's been so long.' Louisa brought a shaking hand to push back a stray curl. Staring at the wall of trees, a private smile graced her freshly painted pink lips. Louisa stepped forward with Dani and Iris on either side.

'Grandma, close your eyes, please.'

'Why?'

Dani cocked an eyebrow and her grandma did as requested rather than kick up a stink like she normally would. A moment later Carlos emerged from the shadows, his dark hair slicked back in the fashionable style of the nineteen fifties. His immaculately pressed tuxedo fitted in all the right places, while his white shirt gleamed in the moonlight, his smile capturing her heart.

'Wow,' Dani and Carlos said in unison.

'Wow what? Can I open my eyes?' Louisa frowned.

'Not yet, Grandma!'

Dani held out her hands in a questioning manner and Carlos put his finger to his lips then pointed at the trees. A moment later Gualberto and Roberto appeared, both decked out in tuxes. Gualberto had his hand under Roberto's elbow, gently guiding him over to where the women stood, Louisa still with her eyes closed.

When Roberto drew near, he stopped, his mouth open, eyes wide. His chin trembled before tears ran down his face as he placed his hand on his heart, studying every inch of Louisa. Smoothing down his suit, he slowly made his way over to the woman he'd loved his entire adult life.

'*Mi lunita*,' Roberto whispered.

Louisa's eyelids flew open and she gasped, holding her hand over her mouth. Reaching out for him, her fingers wrapped around his as they laid eyes on each other after decades apart. Tears glistened on their cheeks, the lines in their faces maps of the turbulent times they'd suffered while pining for the other and as the moonlight shone on the couple, the agony of their separation and those unbearable years dissipated into the night sky.

Roberto and Louisa embraced tentatively at first, but as their bodies remembered each other, they held on tighter, as if afraid of letting go. The moment their lips met, her grandma's lackluster skin glowed and Roberto's back straightened. His chest still rose and fell as he struggled for breath, but the reunion would not be marred by his rapidly declining health.

Cupping his hand under her chin, Roberto studied Louisa. 'My darling *Lunita*, you are as beautiful as ever. The sparkle in your eyes is just as I remember.'

Louisa giggled like a teenager and nestled in closer. 'And you are just as handsome as the day we met.'

'Come, I have a surprise.' They broke their embrace and Roberto placed his arm around Louisa as they slowly moved into the depths of the park, like they had done so many, many years before.

A lump lodged in Dani's throat, her heart breaking for the decades her grandparents had wasted pining for each other and how the time they had together now was so cruelly short.

Carlos slid his hand in Dani's and leaned in close, his warm breath grazing her skin. 'Perhaps young love never dies.'

'Maybe it doesn't. After all they've been through, they deserve this moment.'

'Then we will make sure they get it, yes?' Carlos and Dani strolled into the park proper, Iris and Gualberto walking quietly behind. The quartet stood at the base of the bandstand.

Louisa and Roberto made their way to the bench where they had once hidden from a turbulent world, hoping their love would be enough. They eased onto the wooden seat, their bodies close, their hands entwined.

Looking up at the stars shining above the leafy canopy, Louisa said with wistfulness, 'This is where it all started.'

'But it has not ended. We will make the time we have count.'

Roberto waved in the direction of the bandstand and a second later the stage lit up, hundreds of fairy lights twinkling in the gentle breeze.

'Oh . . . it's . . . it's beautiful.' Louisa turned to Roberto and kissed him gently on the lips.

He wrapped an arm around her, pulling her close as he stroked her hair. 'That is only the beginning, *mi lunita.*'

Roberto waved toward the bandstand again, five men in suits appeared out of the darkness. They carried instruments and set them up on the stage: two violinists, a double bass player, and a musician with an electric piano and super-long extension cord. Gualberto, who had arrived back from Bahía Blanca with news that Cecilia would allow Carlos to see his son, disappeared behind the bandstand and returned with Roberto's *bandoneón* case and took it up on the stage.

'Please excuse me.' Roberto went to stand but his legs failed. Rushing over, Dani helped him up, his frail body shaking. Louisa stood and held onto Roberto, her strength a stark contrast to Roberto's fragility. Her grandma blinked rapidly but couldn't hold back the tears.

Worried, Dani said, 'If it's too hard—'

'Nonsense,' Roberto wheezed. 'I have waited too long for this. It will happen.' He motioned for Carlos's assistance and was helped up the stairs. Carlos gently ushered him to a padded stool and when Roberto's eyes met Louisa's, his gray skin flushed pink.

Leaning into her grandma, Dani whispered, 'You should be next to your man.'

Louisa nodded and Dani held out her hand, leading Louisa to the top of the gazebo. Their light footsteps echoed underneath the roof as they slowly walked across the stage. Louisa bent over and moved the vacant stool closer to Roberto then placed a weathered hand over his. They looked longingly into each other's eyes, decades of unspoken conversations, love, and companionship flying between them. Roberto's eyes caught the sparkle from the fairy lights as he gazed at his love and squeezed her hand.

'Do you remember I had written a song for you but never got to play it?'

"Luna Tango'?' Louisa asked, her cheeks rosy.

'*Sí, mí amor*, I have lived every day in the hope you would hear our song.'

'Then you need this.' Louisa reached into her handbag and tentatively offered the folded paper to him.

He raised his eyebrows then frowned as he unfolded the paper with shaking hands. When he smoothed out the sheet, he placed his hand over his heart. 'You've had it all these years? I thought it was lost when Eduardo and I—'

'It's never been lost, *amor*. I found it after he stormed off and I've kept it close to me ever since. I've hoped my entire life you would one day hold this and reunite it with the rest of the score and look,' she glanced at his shaking hands, 'now you can.'

Roberto's eyes brightened as he studied the paper, a long, slow smile appearing on his lips. 'I'd rewritten the first page from memory because I'd never forgotten these notes. They were composed for you. But I can't tell you how happy I am to see the original.' Roberto patted Louisa's knee then held her in a loving embrace. 'You and the music are worth the wait.'

'And so are you.'

Roberto coughed and doubled over, gasping for air. Louisa's eyes widened as Dani grabbed a bottle of water. She rubbed his back and he took a few sips as his coughing fit subsided. Surreptitiously wiping his mouth with his handkerchief, he gave Dani a warning look. It hurt to see him so unwell but she understood his need to keep the full severity of his illness away from Louisa as much as he could.

Roberto took a shuddery breath, reached for the *bandoneón*, and balanced it on his knees as he caught Gualberto's attention and gave him a wink. Roberto closed his eyes, straightened his back, and coughed again, but not for long. He sat up straight, determination flashing across his handsome features. Letting go of Louisa's hand, albeit reluctantly, Roberto checked his watch.

'It is time,' he rasped.

'Time?' asked Louisa.

'Time for your midnight serenade.'

Roberto placed his fingers on the buttons of the *bandoneón* and played the first melancholic notes. They floated along the cool breeze and caused goose bumps to sprout on Dani's skin, giving her a sense of witnessing history in the making. Gone was the scratching of nails against the blackboard and in its place was the beauty of an instrument and song that embraced a love that had never been forgotten.

Gualberto signaled the pianist, double bass player, and violinist to join in as Louisa swayed gently to the music, no doubt lost in a world of what could have been. Iris rose from the bench, wearing a sad smile as she leaned against the rail on the gazebo stage, close to her mother. Louisa smiled with teary eyes, and patted her daughter on the hand, the tenuous connection between the women strengthening.

Every nuance of the light and dark notes flowed through Dani's body and as the music twinkled like bright stars in the inky sky, she turned to find Carlos staring at her. Dani's fingertips and toes tingled with excitement. For almost sixty years, most of the music score had remained trapped in a *bandoneón* case, waiting for one more sheet to complete it and now it had been set free, celebrating a love that spanned decades.

'Please, allow me.' Carlos hung his cane on the banister and motioned toward the dance floor. He reached for her hand, then stared at her violet dance shoes.

Answering his unasked question, she said, 'I will do them justice, I promise.' She glanced at his leg. 'Are you okay to dance?'

'I believe so, yes.' He moved to rub it but stopped. 'Sometimes we need to work through the pain to experience the ecstasy, yes?'

'Are you talking about your leg or love?'

'The choice is yours.' Carlos leaned forwards and placed his lips on hers. Lost in the enticing warmth of the kiss, she closed her eyes and when she opened them again, he gently led her to the dance floor. The music swirled around them and her body melded with his, their movements in perfect alignment. She followed his lead, allowing her legs to move in long, swift lines over, around, and between his feet. The pointers Iris had given her helped immensely, but there was something more. A passion and certainty coursed through Dani, each movement feeling like a natural extension of her soul.

Dani had expected Carlos to move stiffly because of his injury but his body was one of strength and grace. Her fingers zapped with energy, enjoying the power between them. Something in the back of her mind whispered *entrega*—tango's Holy Grail.

'Dani . . .' he breathed.

'Call me Daniela. It's a perfectly good name, I should use it.'

He smiled and they spun around the floor, their dance steps quickening as the music built to a crescendo. She wrapped her leg around his, her center of balance the steadiest it had ever been in her life.

His muscles tensed and she anticipated his next move before he nudged her leg away. She flicked her leg behind, the ball of her foot landing on the ground, light as a feather. The music flowed through her body and she followed Carlos's movements with ease, changing direction and shifting her weight as he guided her across the dance floor.

A moment later, Carlos let go and stepped back, shaking his head.

'What is it?' She moved forward but he backed away.

'The intensity, it is killing me.' His voice shook and his dark eyes held fear.

'It won't.' She placed her finger under his chin.

The musicians kept playing, lost in their own magic. Roberto pressed the notes and squeezed the *bandoneón* like his life depended on it. Louisa studied Roberto's every move, her eyes holding admiration and affection.

Leaning forward, Dani's lips met Carlos's and her body flooded with love. He caressed her waist as she stood on tiptoe and whispered in his ear, 'If you open your heart to tango then you'll discover that truth and love that will cure everything.'

'Does it really? Look at the trauma we've all suffered.'

'What about Roberto and Louisa?' She cocked her head in their direction. Louisa shuffled closer to Roberto, sadness clouding her features one moment, then morphing into pure joy as his music entranced her.

'He's dying. No one knows how long he has and he still intends to turn himself in tomorrow,' Carlos said.

'Just wait until my grandma gets in his ear.'

'It is his wish to confess.'

'Wishes don't always come true, and if she can't change his mind, we can't do a thing about it. But right now he's embracing the moment for all it's worth and he's letting his heart dictate his actions. He's not hiding any more. No one should. All this crap about tango being cursed and causing grief and people losing loved ones . . . it's not the fault of tango. It's us stupid humans who allow our heads to rule our hearts when we should embrace the passion burning within, whether we're Argentine or not. Imagine how beautiful the world would be if everyone listened to their own inner tango.'

Dani gazed at the velvety sky peppered with a powder spray of stars. The full moon hung high, its milky light shining on all who bathed in its beauty. Roberto's midnight serenade floated through the air as Carlos placed his arms around her body and drew her close.

He offered a crooked smile, his dark eyes sparkling under the fairy lights swaying in the small breeze.

'Perhaps tango, like love, is not so complicated.'

ABOUT THE AUTHOR

Alli Sinclair weaves untold stories inspired by real-life women whose courage and defiance challenge society's expectations. Alli's award-winning and bestselling novels capture her passion for storytelling, born from a lifetime of travel, including working as a mountaineering guide in South America.

In addition to writing, Alli teaches workshops and runs the Writer's at Sea retreat, where sun and sea spark creativity. Her passion for powerful female-led stories extends beyond the page and onto the screen where she works as a film and TV producer and screenwriter.

www.allisinclair.com

FIND OUT MORE

To be the first to find out about:

- new releases
- events and appearances
- writer's tips and workshops
- special deals on titles
- competitions

please sign up for my VIP newsletter HERE

you can also follow me on SUBSTACK

And if you've enjoyed what you've just read, please consider leaving a review as they help other readers like you discover my books.
Thank you!

A READING GROUP GUIDE

Discussion questions for *Luna Tango*

1. When Dani first arrives in Argentina she has no intention of finding her mother but as Dani's journey progresses, she changes her mind. How much influence do you believe Carlos had on her decision?

2. Stella kept her true identity a secret for decades. Do you think she was right in doing so or should she have been up front when Iris first started dancing tango and was confused as to why it had such a tight hold on her? Do you think Iris would have still gone to Argentina?

3. Iris leaving her husband and five-year-old Dani had a major influence on all their lives. How do you feel about Iris leaving her family to pursue tango? Do you think it had an effect on Iris's husband's health like Dani believes? And how different do you think Dani's life would have been had Iris ditched her dream and stayed with her husband and daughter?

4. How did you feel about Louisa wanting to stay and help Eduardo through his illness even though she was madly in love with Roberto? Do you think there was a lot of guilt attached to her staying because of what happened to her grandfather?

5. Do you think Louisa was right to flee Argentina? Why or why not?

6. *Entrega* is spoken about by the characters—when everything comes together so perfectly and a special magic takes over. Have you ever experienced moments of personal *entrega* where the stars have aligned for you? If so, can you give an example and what led up to that moment?

7. What did you think about the relationship between Dani and Carlos? Is it possible for people from different cultures to have a successful relationship? How do you think the differences can strengthen or weaken their bond?

8. Stella and Iris often talk about tango being a curse on their family. Do you believe this is the case? Do you think it was genetics or a series of decisions that shaped their futures and relationship with tango?

9. Do you believe a love can be so strong it can live through the decades, even if the person isn't with their lover, like it did with Louisa and Roberto? Can you give any real life examples?

ACKNOWLEDGMENTS

It takes a village to raise a child and the same can be said about writing a book. *Luna Tango* couldn't have happened without the support of many people and I am forever grateful to each and every one of them.

It's wonderful to have village friends who think I am very normal when I talk to myself or to the characters in my head. Thank you to writing buddies: Dave Sinclair, Di Curran, Heidi Noroozy, Juliet Madison, Kathryn Ledson, Louise Ousby, Natalie Hatch, Rachael Johns, Supriya Savkoor, T.M. Clark, and Tess Woods for brainstorming and cracking the whip when needed.

To my Girly Whirlies—Misty Simon, Danita Cahill, Barrie Summy, Maureen McGowan, and our beloved Flo Moyer. Who knew a group of writers meeting online ten years ago would lead to such wonderful friendships?

Every writer needs a muse and mine is called Larry. Thanks Larry for getting in my ear on the days when I'd rather stick hot pokers in my eyes than write. Apparently nagging does work.

Mil gracias Carolina Lagos and Cesar Taboada for making sure my Spanish translations were spot on. Carolina, there may be a big pond separating us but you're always close in my heart.

Thanks so much Sean A. McGee for providing such beautiful tango music to listen to while I wrote and thank you to Pam and Richard Jarvis of Southern Cross Tango for helping me better understand the nuances of tango.

Gracias, gracias, gracias, to the tango dancers, musicians, singers, and historians all over the world who inspire and entertain and ensure tango will live forever. The world is much richer for your dedication and passion.

A whole world of thank you to my extended family and non-writing friends who don't mind when I'm a little distracted with my characters and plotting. This journey is so much sweeter with you beside me. Special thanks to Mum, Dave, and my beloved Dad (missing you always) for encouraging me to follow my dreams.

Massive hugs and love and thanks to my amazing partner Garry and our gorgeous kids Bec and Nick. Sharing this journey with you is extra special. Love you loads.

And a special thank you to you, dear reader, for choosing to immerse yourself in *Luna Tango*. May the experience leave a smile on your lips and a song in your heart.